CATACLYSM

CATACLYSM

TIM WASHBURN

PINNACLE BOOKS
Kensington Publishing Corp.
www.kensingtonbooks.com

PINNACLE BOOKS are published by

Kensington Publishing Corp.
119 West 40th Street
New York, NY 10018

All Kensington titles, imprints, and distributed lines are available at special quantity discounts for bulk purchases for sales promotions, premiums, fund-raising, educational, or institutional use.

Special book excerpts or customized printings can also be created to fit specific needs. For details, write or phone the office of the Kensington sales manager: Kensington Publishing Corp., 119 West 40th Street, New York, NY 10018, attn: Sales Department; phone 1-800-221-2647.

This book is a work of fiction. Names, characters, businesses, organizations, places, events, and incidents either are the product of the author's imagination or are used fictitiously. Any resemblance to actual persons, living or dead, events, or locales is entirely coincidental.

PINNACLE BOOKS and the Pinnacle logo are Reg. U.S. Pat. & TM Off.

ISBN-13: 978-0-7860-3655-4
ISBN-10: 0-7860-3655-9

First printing: November 2016

10 9 8 7 6 5 4 3 2 1

Printed in the United States of America

First electronic edition: November 2016

ISBN-13: 978-0-7860-3656-1
ISBN-10: 0-7860-3656-7

To
Kelsey, Nickolas, and Karley

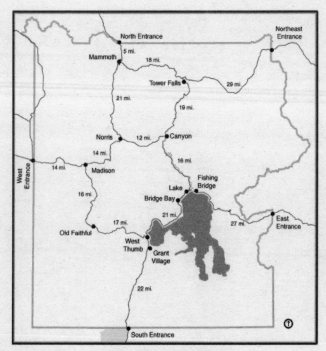

Yellowstone National Park

DAY 1

CHAPTER 1

Jessica Mayfield takes a moment to survey the crowd, smiling at how odd it is to see people sitting ass to elbow in a 180-degree arc with nothing but a barren mound of chalky dirt in front of them. She marvels at the diversity of the people as some chat animatedly with those next to them while others sit, their gaze riveted. But the reason for the gathering becomes apparent when Old Faithful geysers up from mother earth. Oohs and aahs accompany the whir and click of too many cameras to count, many Christmas gifts that had escaped their boxes only for a trip to the nation's oldest national park. Jess watches the amazement on her children's faces as the geyser shoots the steamy water nearly 150 feet into the sky.

After several moments the water retreats back underground, and Jess turns her gaze to the distance. The sage-covered hills and pristine forests of lodgepole pine provide a backdrop for the transparent pools of water whose steamy tendrils drift toward the azure sky.

But, as a geologist, Jess knows Yellowstone's lush vegetation and the clear mountain streams are obscuring a scarred landscape. Scarred not only from glacial movement over centuries, but scarred more deeply by three earth-altering eruptions from one of the largest supervolcanoes on the planet.

As Jess scans the crowd again, she wonders how many of the tourists know about the seething, simmering cauldron of fire lurking beneath their feet. Responsible for the park's most unusual features—the geysers, fumaroles, mud pots, and hot springs—the caldera volcano is three times the size of Manhattan Island and stretches for miles in every direction.

Jess is startled back into the present when a deep rumble cracks across the landscape and the earth underfoot gyrates like a wobbly plate balanced on a stick.

"What was that, Mommy?" nine-year-old Madison asks, craning her neck to look up at her mother.

"I think that was an earthquake, honey," Jess replies. She turns to her husband, who is seated on the other side of their two children. "Matt, maybe we should head for another section of the park for today."

"Why? Yellowstone has small earthquakes all the time."

"That didn't feel small to me." Jess says.

"C'mon, Jess, it's one small earthquake. Besides, Tucker's meeting us for lunch at the inn."

"Has he texted back?" Jess asks. Half Cherokee, with deep bronze–colored skin and dark, cascading hair that brushes across her shoulders with each turn of her head, Jess is tall and willowy. With dark, deep-set eyes, she has the high forehead and broad nose of her ancestors.

"Not yet, but cell service here sucks." Matt, a banker by trade, likes to think of himself as an amateur scientist. A big-boned, broad-shouldered man, Matt has red hair and sapphire-colored eyes. He and Jess are as different, complexionwise, as any two people can be. Matt leans in to speak to Maddie. "Hey, I know something you don't know." He glances at his wife and receives an eye-roll for his efforts.

Maddie overexaggerates a sigh. "What, Dad?" Maddie received a larger portion of her father's genes. She has curly, strawberry red hair, and across her face and shoulders there's a splash of freckles that darken during the summer months.

"Did you know that we're sitting on top of a volcano right this minute?"

Madison's gaze sweeps across the landscape. "I don't see a volcano. I think you're just—"

A louder rumble sounds, followed by a more violent tremor. This one elicits a few shouts of nervous surprise.

"Probably just an aftershock," Matt mumbles. "Anyway, there is a volcano here but it's not like normal volcanoes that look like mountains."

"How could it be a volcano then?"

"It's called a *caldera*. The last time the volcano erupted most of the land collapsed back into the magma chamber."

Maddie arches her barely visible eyebrows. "Is it going to erupt again?"

"Oh sure, someday." Matt chuckles. "But the volcano hasn't erupted in . . . oh . . . about 640,000 years. I think we'll be safe awhile longer."

Jess leans over to whisper in her husband's ear. "I really think we should return to the lodge."

"Why?" He waves his arm in a wide arc. "Look, no one else seems to be alarmed."

Jessica looks around. A group of Japanese students is huddled in a clump while a park ranger snaps a picture. On the left, two small children, both red-faced from too much sun, wrap their arms around each other while Mom clicks away. No one seems to be panicking. But something is gnawing at Jess's gut. She turns and begins whispering again. "Well, I'm concerned. The last tremor was significantly stronger. And it wasn't an aftershock."

Matt leans away, rubbing his ear to dry the moisture from his wife's breath. "C'mon, Jess, this place is lousy with earthquakes."

Jessica grabs his shirt and pulls him closer. "Maybe so, but do you want to be sitting next to a lake of boiling water if there's a larger quake?"

"Dad, can we go now?" Maddie asks.

Jessica stands and grabs for her daughter's hand. "That's a good idea, Maddie girl."

"Mom, I'm still taking pictures," Mason says, never taking his eye away from the viewfinder of his camera, a recent birthday present. Mason, twelve, is the polar opposite of his sister. He has his mother's bronze coloring and dark hair, which he prefers to wear longer than his father would like.

"We'll go as soon as Mason is through," Matt says.

Maddie crosses her arms and sighs. "How many pictures of this stupid thing does he need? Besides, it's not even doing anything. And I thought we were meeting up with Uncle Tucker."

Matt rests a hand on his daughter's shoulder only to have her shrug it off. "Honey, this is a family trip. Besides, Uncle Tucker won't be here until lunch."

Maddie's would-be tantrum is short-lived when another ground tremor forces her to uncross her arms to reach for her mother's hand.

"Matt, that was no small earthquake." Jessica snags Mason's arm. "C'mon, we're going back to the inn right now."

Mason groans, but relents, letting the camera dangle from the strap around his neck. Matt drapes an arm across Jess's shoulders as they walk toward the Old Faithful Inn. He leans in to whisper in her ear. "I guess the only tremors we're used to are when the bed's rocking."

Jess shrugs from under his arm, pointing toward the visitor center. "If there's nothing to worry about, why are there a dozen park rangers headed this way?" Jess stops, plants her feet, and turns to her husband. "I really think we should leave the park altogether."

"C'mon, honey, we've only been here a couple of days. I'm telling you, there's nothing to worry about."

Maddie latches on to her father's hand. "Daddy, I'm scared."

CHAPTER 2

Dr. Tucker Mayfield, the chief scientist at Yellow-stone, glances at the clock and cringes. He had promised lunch with his brother's family, but that was before the current earthquake swarm threw a wrench into his plans. Tucker is tall and husky like his brother, and they share the same eye color, blue, but that's where the similarity ends. Tucker's hair is dark and, while Matt's skin often burns with sun exposure, Tucker's darkens to a deep tan during the summer months. With a Ph.D. in geology, he's one of the youngest people ever to hold the position of scientist-in-charge.

Tucker clicks on his computer mouse to refresh the webicorder display for the seismometer located at Old Faithful. Although earthquake swarms are a fairly common occurrence at the park, what he sees on the monitor ratchets up his concern. The earthquakes are increasing in intensity, pegging the high threes on the magnitude scale. And when you're sitting on one of the largest volcanoes on earth, any seismic activity is a concern.

Tucker pushes out of his chair and heads down the hall to the Spatial Analysis Center. It's not as grand as it sounds, simply a room with a half a dozen computers and the same number of people working on them. He rolls a vacant chair over to Rachael Rollins's work-space and takes a seat. After completing her doctoral dissertation on the park's unique water systems, Rachael is Yellowstone's hydrology expert. "Any changes in the hydrothermal systems?" Tucker asks.

"I've been checking. Temps are all within norms, and I haven't had any reports of unusual activity. But if the seismic activity continues to ramp up, I wouldn't be surprised to see some anomalies. Are you worried about the caldera?"

"Worried? No. Let's just say I'm a little concerned. The GPS units at Old Faithful and Yellowstone Lake are indicating some pretty rapid ground deformation."

Rachael scrolls to the Global Positioning System's website and logs in. "Two inches of upward deforma-tion around the east side of the lake." She glances at the timestamps on the data. "Over a three-hour pe-riod?"

"Yes. Now check the data for Old Faithful."

Scooting her computer mouse around the pad, Rachael clicks on the geyser's GPS data feed. "Almost three inches. And during the same three-hour period." She turns to face Tucker. "That much uplift is signifi-cant."

"I know, and that data is nearly two hours old. I've requested more frequent data dumps from the GPS units.

Might take them a half a day to reconfigure the system."

Rachael crosses her arms and leans back in her chair, staring at the deformation numbers. A product of a biracial marriage, she has latte-colored skin and sports a head of tightly curled black hair that bounces with each movement. There's a splash of darker freckles across her nose and cheeks, but it's her eyes, colored a Caribbean Sea green, that grab your immediate attention. At five-eight, she's long and lean. "What do you think is causing the deformation?"

"I don't think there's any doubt the magma chamber is responsible. But it could simply be gas expansion."

"Maybe . . . but could magma be moving toward the surface?" Rachael asks as she leans forward and clicks back to the seismic feeds on her computer.

"For our sake—"

"Tucker, a larger quake just rocked the Old Faithful area."

Tucker leans forward for a closer look. "Jesus, that's substantially larger than any of the others. What do you think for magnitude?"

"Upper fours. The strongest we've seen in months." She turns to face Tucker. "Okay, mark me down as officially concerned. If these earthquakes continue to increase in scale, we're in for a very long day."

CHAPTER 3

University Seismic Observation Lab, Salt Lake City, Utah

On the first floor of the university's geology build-ing, undergrad student Josh Tolbert, running on coffee and Red Bull, is cramming for today's exam in structural geology and tectonics. His right leg jack-hammers up and down as he reads through his notes again while occasionally glancing up at the eight large video screens displaying real-time seismic data for Yellowstone.

As Josh struggles to remember which of the conti-nental plates are convergent and which are divergent, the computer monitors in the lab chirp in unison. "What in the hell is that?" he mutters. His gaze sweeps the empty room in search of a professor before he re-members that today is Tuesday, staff meeting day. He clicks through the seismometers, and the large, squig-gly lines grow larger near the center of the park. When the seismometer located at Old Faithful pops onto the screen he shouts, "Oh shit," and jumps up from his chair, hurrying out of the lab. Like Wile E. Coyote, his feet scramble for traction on the polished linoleum flooring as he rushes toward the conference room down the hall. His right hand skims the concrete wall for balance, sending announcements and lecture programs raining onto the floor. He pounds down the door lever and barges into the conference room, wheezing. "Dr. Snider, I . . . need you . . . in the observation room."

"What is it, Josh?" Dr. Snider asks in his patented patient-professor's voice.

"Sir"—he pauses to take a breath—"there are earthquakes occurring at Yellowstone."

"That's not terribly unusual, Josh, but thanks for notifying us." Dr. Snider turns back to the group. "As I was saying—"

"Professor, I really think you should take a look."

As if acceding to the wishes of a petulant child, Dr. Snider says, "Okay, Josh, I'll have a look." He turns back to those parked around the wooden table. "Let's adjourn, folks. I think we've accomplished what we needed to accomplish for the week." He turns and clamps a hand on Josh's shoulder. "Let's go see what's got you all riled up, young man." With a Ph.D. in geophysics, Dr. Eric Snider is head of the university's seismology program, which includes oversight of the seismometers at Yellowstone.

There is a total lack of urgency as Dr. Snider ambles along the hallway. "You staying here for grad school, Josh?"

Josh, working hard to slow his pace while his brain screams *Run*, doesn't respond. Instead, he glances at his mentor, saying, "Professor, I think we should hurry."

"You young people are always in a hurry. What has you so worried, Josh?"

"Lots of things. Yellowstone is a very unstable area.

What happens if these earthquakes trigger a volcanic eruption?"

"You need to worry about finding yourself a nice young girl," Snider says, chuckling. But the chuckles die in his throat when he and Josh turn into the lab and Snider sees the data on the screens. His treasured Montblanc pen slips from his grasp, clinking to the linoleum floor. "Josh, run back down the hall and tell everyone to hustle in here."

Josh's gaze sweeps across the video displays. "The earthquakes are swarming and getting stronger, aren't they?"

"Josh, hustle up now. We've got a lot of work to do."

Josh stifles the *I told you so* that lingers on the tip of his tongue and rushes through the door for another race down the hall, his heart hammering faster than hummingbird wings, and not just from the physical exertion.

(Editor's Note: All interviews were conducted by Casey Cartwright as she traveled between survivor camps located throughout the southeastern United States while working on her master's thesis.)

Camp 2—Clearwater, Florida

Interview: Paul from Provo, UT—geology grad student

"The tension and excitement in the seismology lab were palpable. And the tension really ratcheted up when the seismograms indicated the earthquakes were intensifying. Dr. Snider was running around like a wild man. Then we started getting information from the GPS units located at the park. I think everyone knew then that something big was going to happen. It's one of those moments that occur once in a lifetime, like where you were on 9/11 or when JFK was shot. I'll remember being in that room for the rest of my life."

CHAPTER 4

**U.S. Geological Survey Yellowstone Volcano Observatory,
Menlo Park, California**

Dr. Jeremy Lyndsey, chief scientist for the Yellowstone Volcano Observatory, curses under his breath as he wipes at the residue that his breakfast burrito burped onto his freshly laundered shirt. In the middle of his efforts, his office phone buzzes. Frustrated, he tosses the remainder of the burrito into the garbage and grabs the phone.

Before he can even say hello, Dr. Eric Snider says, "Yellowstone is experiencing an intense earthquake swarm."

"Good morning to you, too, Eric. What magnitudes are you seeing?"

"The last one was a little over 4.2. And that follows several quakes in the high threes."

Lyndsey wiggles the mouse to wake his computer, then logs into the seismic feeds. "They're nearly unrelenting, aren't they?"

"Yes, but that's not what concerns me. Look at the rapid increase in magnitude."

"Earthquakes in the low fours are fairly uncommon, but not unheard of for the park," he mumbles into the phone while scrolling through the webicorder displays. "It doesn't appear any of the tremors have exceeded previous levels."

"Yet," Snider says. "Pull up the GPS data. We have increasing uplift out by the lake over the past couple of hours. Some as much as two inches. When's the last time you've seen ground deformation numbers like that?"

"Been a while. But again, not unheard of. Is there any unusual hydrothermal activity?" Lyndsey asks.

"Don't know. Tucker is next on my list of calls."

"Can you have some of your grad students plot the seismic waves to see if there have been any obvious changes in the magma chamber?"

"They're already feeding the data into the main-frame, but it's going to be a slow process. I'm not sure what that's going to tell us, anyway. We know the levels fluctuate somewhat because of the gaseous nature of the magma."

"It might tell us whether the amount of magma is on the increase," Lyndsey says. "Any uplift on the other GPS sensors?"

"Some, but not as significant as the area around Yellowstone Lake. But two inches uplift . . . damn."

"What?"

"Another quake. The needles are bouncing like a rubber ball. This one's the largest of the morning."

"Where and how large?" Lyndsey asks as he clicks between seismometers.

"Old Faithful. Won't know until we run the data, but my guess is in the high fours or low fives."

"Damn," Lyndsey whispers. "Okay, Eric, I need an update every few minutes, either by text or e-mail. I need to makes some phone calls."

"Do you think this activity warrants a discussion about a possible evacuation of the park?" Snider asks.

"We're a long way from even contemplating a park evacuation. The damn thing hasn't erupted in 640,000 years. I think we have a few days to further study the situation."

Chapter 5

Forty miles east of Yellowstone's eastern boundary, Kenny Huff focuses all of his attention on an array of computer screens inside the control room of his wireline truck. A large, burly man with thick arms and broad shoulders, Kenny is a thirty-year veteran of the oil patch, who went from tool pusher to owner of his own business. Huff Wireline Services rig number one, out of one, is parked in a mud puddle near the Christmas tree atop a recently drilled oil well. A large spool of wire mounted at the back of the truck feeds line into the valve stack—an amalgam of wheels, valves, and pressure gauges that stands over ten feet tall with horizontal branches jutting out in every direction. The stack looks like a scarecrow assembled by a mad plumber. But its purpose is critical to control the enormous pressures inside the drill hole that extends ten thousand feet into the earth. Of all the valves and gauges, the production wing valve is the one that controls the flow of oil and natural gas to the production facilities.

But only if they can get the well to flow.

And that's Kenny's job. His eyes dart from one computer monitor to another as the perforation gun sinks closer to the target area.

"Almost there?" Hank Caldwell, the oil company's geologist, asks after an impatient sigh. A short, thin man with rectangular glasses perched atop his aquiline nose, Hank is more at home in his office back at headquarters than out in the oil fields. But as a field geologist, he is required to sit on a well during any scheduled activity.

"Another four feet," Kenny says as his pudgy fingers nudge the joystick controller forward before bringing the joystick to a dead stop. "On target."

Hank compares the depth on the screen to the well log folded out across the desk. "Perf the damn thing. We should have been frackin' last week."

"Fire in the hole," Kenny says as he toggles a red switch.

There is no discernable difference on the surface, but deep in the drill hole a series of shaped charges explodes through the well casing and into the surrounding rock. The perforations will allow the hydraulic fracturing fluids, injected under extreme pressure, a path into the rock formations. If all goes according to plan, the fractured rock will release its hold on the oil and gas that has been in the ground for millions of years.

Kenny swivels his chair around. "Any other zones you want to hit?"

"That's about the only pay zone we've got. But I have another well for you to shoot this afternoon."

"Roger that. Where?"

Hank gives him the location of the next well and

folds up the well log. He pushes out of the chair and eases his cell phone from his pocket. "Now, will you kindly get your wire out of my drill hole so I can get back to work?"

"Hell, Hank, you don't know what work is." Kenny nods toward the cell phone in Hank's hand. "The only thing you work is that phone, and maybe your wife once a month."

"Hell, I wish it was once a month."

Both men laugh as Kenny pulls on the joystick to reel in the line. "Hey, Hank, you ever work offshore?"

"No, I like my feet planted on the terra firma. Why?"

Kenny swivels around, a broad grin wrinkling his weathered face. "You know what the offshore guys call the night before they go off shift?"

"No idea."

"Pussmas Eve."

Hank laughs and reaches for the door handle. "Yeah, Pussmas Eve is closer to Christmas Eve around my house. It only happens once a year. You be out of here before lunch?"

"Should be. When's the fracking crew coming in?"

"They're going to start setting up around one."

"We'll be gone before then. I'll see you this afternoon."

Hank waves a hand in the air as he exits the control room. As his feet touch down, the ground wobbles underfoot, and Hank grabs the door handle to keep from falling. The big truck sways from side to side and after ten to fifteen seconds the motion stops. But Hank's brain continues to spin with fiery images of death and destruction caused by a well blowout. He yanks open the door to see an ashen-faced Kenny still at the controls.

"What the hell was that?" Hank shouts.

Kenny scans the gauges and monitors. "Well pressure's fine. Must have been an earthquake."

Camp 48—Marietta, Georgia

Interview: Eric from Early, TX—oil field tool pusher

"Yeah, we was working up that way. Trying to complete a well just outside Cody. I've tromped through a bunch of oil patches in my time and I can guar-an-tee you, drilling work ain't got nothing to do with earthquakes. All these gotdamn tree huggers yelling about frackin' and drillin' drive me batshit crazy. How the hell they think their heaters work when they get home and click 'em on? Or when they want to take a hot damn shower? Natural gas, that's how. And it don't just pour out of the gotdamn ground. Anyway . . . that's kinda off subject. Yeah, we was already in the truck headed home when it all started."

CHAPTER 6

Lower Geyser Basin

There is no sense of panic among the park guests as the rangers herd them away from Old Faithful. Matt slows his progress as one of the rangers nears. "Sir, are you evacuating the entire park?"

Jess reaches her hand out to slow the children so she can listen in.

"No, just this area around the geysers. They might get a little cranky and erratic during these earthquake swarms."

Jess steps away from the children and lowers her voice when she confronts the ranger. "The earthquakes are increasing in intensity."

"I wouldn't know anything about that, ma'am. What I can tell you is, the park is frequently rattled by small quakes. I don't think there's anything to worry about. You guys staying here in the park?"

"We're staying at the inn," Jess says, "but I don't share your lack of concern. "You do know we're standing on top of one of the largest volcanoes on earth."

"Yes, ma'am, but I also know there wasn't a human alive to see it the last time she popped off."

"All the more reason to be worried," Jess says before turning and stalking away.

The Old Faithful Inn is the largest log structure in the world, and by the time the Mayfields navigate through the narrow corridors toward their room, everyone is tired and hungry, after having skipped breakfast.

"Let's rest in the room for a while before we head back out," Jess says. "Dad's trying to get in touch with Uncle Tucker to see about lunch. That sound okay?"

Neither child replies, and the door to their room swings open. Both Maddie and Mason immediately grab their iPads and collapse on the sofa. Jess waits for Matt to glance in her direction, then nods toward the balcony beyond the sliding glass door. They step outside and she slides the door closed.

"Are we having balcony sex?" Matt whispers.

"Sure. Where the kids can watch, along with all those people milling around below us. I'm worried, Matt."

"Honey, you heard the ranger. They experience quakes all the time."

"Have you ever done any reading about this volcano?"

"Not really, no. I read something about it while planning our trip, but nothing in depth."

Jess snuggles up next to Matt and lowers her voice. "The Yellowstone Caldera is a supervolcano. The volcanoes in the Hawaiian Islands are called *mountain builders* because their lava drifts down the mountainside, building ever higher over time. A supervolcano is a mountain eraser. They erupt with such force that the surrounding land collapses into the magma chamber. Yellowstone's magma chamber is almost eighteen miles wide and nearly fifty-five miles long and extends underground for miles. There will be no bubbling of lava where spectators can snap pictures as the molten rock meanders across the landscape."

Jess pauses to glance in on the children before continuing. "A Yellowstone eruption will be devastating for the entire planet."

"I remember hearing about the Mount St. Helens eruption when I was a kid, but I didn't think there was much to it, other than a fairly large ash cloud."

Jess pinches her thumb and forefinger together to form a tiny circle. "This is the Mount St. Helens eruption." She releases her fingers and spreads her arms out wide. "This would be the size of a Yellowstone eruption. It would be a thousand times larger than the eruption of St. Helens. Some scientists have speculated that an eruption here would be like a thousand Hiroshima-sized bombs detonating every second."

"Okay, I'm spooked. Are you thinking one of these earthquakes could trigger an eruption?"

"If it's large enough, sure. But earthquakes aren't the only thing that could trigger an eruption."

"What else?" Matt asks.

"That's just it, Matt: No one knows for sure what triggers an eruption. Could be pressure or a sudden ejection of magma into the chamber. But a large earthquake has a higher probability for triggering an eruption."

"So you're saying this thing could erupt any moment?" Matt asks.

Jess taps her foot in frustration. "No, what I'm saying is that no one can accurately predict the precise timing of an eruption. It's all guesswork. But I damn sure don't want to be standing here if it does. If these earthquakes continue to increase in intensity we need to pack up and get the hell out of here."

Matt and Jess lean against the rail of the balcony in silence, each consumed by thoughts of their own version of Armageddon. A squeal of laughter from a group of children playing below the balcony does little to lighten the mood. After a few moments of silence, Jess sighs and reaches for the door. She pastes a smile on her face and slides the door open. "Are we having fun, kiddos?"

CHAPTER 7

Back in his office, Tucker hangs up the phone and runs a hand through his hair. Most of those working at the Center for Resources have a science background and are accustomed to dealing with facts supported by reams of data, but they aren't immune to fear. And the just-completed discussion with Jeremy Lyndsey elicited the first real hints of fear for Tucker. He stands to his full height of six feet two and paces the confines of his small office while his mind spins. *Could a stronger quake really cause a volcanic eruption? Not just any possible eruption, but the largest volcanic eruption in the history of mankind? But the park experiences earthquakes all the time. Are these any different?*

Tucker walks toward the window and glances out at the distant peaks of the Gallatin Range. *It's an overreaction. No way the caldera is going to erupt. But what if?*

As if answering his question, the photographs and degrees hanging on the wall jitter and jump as another tremor rumbles. Either the earthquakes are getting stronger or the epicenters are moving farther north. Mammoth Hot Springs is the northern gateway for the park and a good fifty miles from the center of the park, where most of the earthquakes are occurring.

Tucker returns to his desk and sags into his chair. Although the air conditioner is cranked to high, a bead of perspiration pops on his forehead. He wipes away the sweat and reaches for the phone. Park Superintendent Ralph Barlow answers on the second ring.

"Sir, all of us at Yellowstone Volcano Observatory are somewhat concerned about the increase in earthquake activity."

"I just felt one, I think. Where is the epicenter?"

"Most of the activity is centered around the Old Faithful area and the Yellowstone Lake region. Our main concern is the rising intensity of the quakes."

"Where are they on the scale?"

"The last one was just over 4.2 in magnitude at a depth of two miles, centered under Yellowstone Lake."

A hiss of air sounds from the other end of the connection. "Jeez, that's a damn unstable area, Tucker. Any thoughts about what's causing this latest round?"

"Nothing definitive. There is some concern that there might have been a subsurface injection of magma into the main chamber."

"Meaning what?" Barlow asks. His voice lowers a couple of octaves before asking, "You're not suggesting a volcanic eruption is imminent, are you?"

"I don't think anyone believes the caldera is on the verge of eruption. But there is an elevated level of concern. With your permission, I'd like to call in most of the off-duty rangers and have them fan out through the park around the geyser basins and the mud pot areas."

"Why those areas specifically?"

"Mainly to see if there are any significant changes in the hydrothermal systems. A change in intensity of the geysers or the creation of new mud pot areas could indicate an increase in magma activity," Tucker says. "In addition, the GPS sensors in that section of the park suggest an upward moving deformation and the borehole tiltmeters on the east side of the lake suggest a general upward tilt."

"Meaning magma could be rising toward the surface?"

A brief period of silence fills the line before Tucker answers. "Maybe."

"Jesus Christ, we're at the peak of the summer season. We have thousands of park visitors scattered all across the damn park. And the safety of every one of those visitors is my responsibility."

"I understand, Ralph. These could simply be anomalies."

"Or not. I need answers, Tucker."

"We're working on it. If you'll authorize the overtime, I'll have the off-duty rangers on site within the hour."

"Screw the budget. Do it. And get the on-duty rangers working in that direction. I want frequent updates and I want answers."

"I'm going to head down that way for a look at the area. I'll be on the sat phone if you need me." Tucker hangs up and reaches into a desk drawer to retrieve his satellite phone. He checks the battery level and grabs the charger, just in case. After putting on his National Park Service hat, he works his way down the hall and sticks his head into the analysis center. "I'm heading down to the Old Faithful area. I'm on the sat phone if you need me."

Before he can duck out, Rachael Rollins asks for a private word. Tucker nods her toward the hall, and Rachael joins him there.

She leans against the wall and crosses her arms. "I'm not sure now is a good time to leave, Tucker. There's too much going on."

Tucker waves the sat phone. "I'm only a phone call away. I need to see what's going on with my own eyes."

"I'm going with you. I know these hydrothermal systems better than you do. If there are any changes, I'll spot them a lot quicker than you will."

"No, Rach, I need you here to keep an eye on the data feeds."

Rachael uncrosses her arms and pushes away from the wall. "Bullshit. I can't do anything here, sitting on my ass."

Tucker sighs. "I'd really prefer you stay here. Things could get dangerous."

Rachael reaches out and grabs Tucker's arm. "Whether I'm here or there won't matter if the caldera blows. The entire park will be toast."

Camp 27—Meridian, Mississippi

Interview: Denise from Duluth, MN—former seasonal park employee

"Summer before last was the last time I worked up there. Finally finished my degree and got a real job. We knew about the volcano, but it's not like we spent every minute of the day worrying about it. With all the budget cuts, the park was usually short staffed, so we were so busy we didn't have time to think about anything but doing our jobs. In the evenings, we'd sometimes surf the web and laugh about all the Internet rumors that an eruption was imminent. Then you'd see video of running animals some yahoo posted insisting it was a sign of impending disaster. I bet a majority of the park guests didn't have a clue they were walking around on top of an active volcano. We just didn't think about it much. I still had friends that were working up there."

CHAPTER 8

Mallard Lake, Yellowstone National Park

Park Ranger Walt Stringer coasts the four-wheeler up to the western shore of Mallard Lake and kills the engine. Small by lake standards, Mallard would have been called a pond back in his home state of Texas. Walt climbs off the four-wheeler and takes a moment to stretch his back. After riding across rough terrain and steering around downed trees most of the morning, it takes a moment for him to get his legs moving again. With heavily muscled shoulders stacked on his tall frame, Walt is the quintessential mountain man, minus the long hair and shaggy beard. His arms and face are bronzed from his time outdoors and his once-dark hair is shot through with gray. He puts on his ranger hat, snags the two-way radio from the cradle mounted on the handlebar of his ATV, and strides toward the tree line. He works his way toward a patch of bright fabric, a tent tucked into a thicket of pine trees.

"Ranger approaching," Walt shouts from a good distance away. A veteran of the first Gulf War, his search for solace led him to the National Park Service and Yellowstone, where news from the outside can be as limited as one chooses. With no television and no radio, Walt doesn't have to listen to the nightly reports about drone strikes, dead soldiers, or unrest in the Middle East. Now there are just wide-open skies and buffalo roaming across the prairie.

That and the occasional unpleasant encounter with park guests.

With firearms no longer outlawed in the park, Walt is cautious about approaching campsites. But it's not just weapons he's worried about. He's learned from experience to not venture too close to a campsite unannounced. He's been cussed at, cussed out, and has walked up on some truly bizarre situations, including a family of nudists who moved nonchalantly around the campsite in their birthday suits.

The nylon walls of the tent flutter and the long zipper at the front slides open to reveal a bushy-headed man. "What the hell do you want?"

"And fuck you, too," Walt mutters as he steps closer. He spots the leftovers from last night's dinner scattered around a small propane stove.

"Sir, you do realize you're in bear country, don't you?" he says, coming to a stop about six feet away.

"Yeah, so what?" the man says, making no attempt to step out from the tent.

"All this food laying around will draw a bear to your campsite faster than bees to honey."

"We ain't seen no bears. You here to bust my ass about a messy camp?"

Walt keeps his hands loose, the right one hovering near the butt of his service weapon, a Sig Sauer P229. Loaded with 165 grain .40 caliber hollow points. The ammunition is powerful enough to stop a bear and absolutely lethal for anything on two feet. "Sir, would you mind stepping out of the tent?"

"Look, Lone Ranger, we're just camping out here. Communing with nature."

"Sir, I'll ask again. Please step out from the tent."

The man shoots Walt an angry glare before stepping out. He's outfitted in dingy gym shorts and an old ratty T-shirt that reveals a set of skinny arms with more ink than a case of Bic pens.

"Who else is in there?" Stringer asks.

"Just my girlfriend. Jeez, here we are out in the goddamn wilderness and Ranger Ricky shows up swinging his dick around." He turns toward the tent. "Janice, get your ass out here."

A rail-thin, mousy-haired woman slithers through the tent opening and takes a spot behind her boyfriend. She sneers at Walt, displaying a black hole of rotted teeth.

Walt's jaw muscles clench, release, then clench again. "Kind of late to be sleeping, isn't it?"

"I don't remember asking for a wake-up call. But, now that we're up"—the man crosses his arm over his midsection and bows—"what can we do for you, Ranger Boy?"

Walt relaxes his body, but his hand doesn't stray too far from his weapon. "Can I see your camp permit, please?"

"I know you're itchin' to pull your gun, Mr. Ranger Man. You got that look, you know. Probably the most exciting part of your day is hassling us campers."

Walt takes two long strides, stopping only inches from the man. "You'd be a waste of a good bullet. Now, I'll ask again, where's your permit?"

"It's . . . it's in my wallet," the man stammers.

"Let's have a look at it."

The man snakes his hand into his grubby shorts and pulls out a paper-thin wallet that nearly slips from his now-trembling hands. He removes a crumpled piece of paper and hands it over.

Walt studies the proffered paperwork. "So you're here for two more nights?"

"Yeah."

He hands the permit back and offers the couple a smile. "I hope you enjoy your stay. Remember, no campfires. It's dry as a tinderbox out here." As Walt walks back to the ATV, the radio squawks.

"Walt Stringer, what's your twenty?"

He unclips the radio from his belt. "I'm down at Mallard Lake."

"We need you at the Lower Geyser area."

"What's up, Brenda?"

A brief pause before she answers. "I'd rather not say over the radio."

Stringer stares at the radio in his hand then punches the transmit button. "Oookaay. So what do you need me to do?"

"Another ranger will brief you when you get there."

A small tingle of dread creeps down his spine. He can't recall another instance during his twenty-year career where radio communications were cloaked in secrecy.

"Ten-four. I'm on my way." He slaps the radio into its cradle and fires up the four-wheeler. Contrails of sand and grit swirl up from the tires as he gooses the throttle, racing across the rugged terrain. His mind clicks through possible complications, conjuring up one possible horror show after another, with no thoughts whatsoever about the possibility of the greatest horror show of all.

CHAPTER 9

University Seismic Observation Lab

The seismology lab is a beehive of activity. Scientists are studying the data while others are in constant contact with other colleagues, their phones pinched between shoulder and ear. Dr. Eric Snider scurries from his office, his head on a swivel, searching for anyone not otherwise engaged. He spots his prey in an instant. "Josh!" he shouts across the room.

Josh Tolbert, startled by the booming voice, jumps to his feet and hurries over. "Yes, sir?"

Snider hands over a Post-it note scribbled with a series of phone numbers. "These are some of our contacts at NASA. I need you to get on the horn and find out whether Terra or Aqua are anywhere in the vicinity."

"Terra and who, sir?"

"Terra and Aqua are two satellites with thermal infrared capabilities. I need thermal images of Yellowstone and I need it yesterday."

"Can't I just get online and find the images?" Josh asks.

"There may not be any. We're not a frequent stop for them. But I damn sure need them now. See how long it'll be until we can get some new images."

"I'm on it," Josh says, hurrying toward the nearest phone.

Snider threads his way through the obstacle course of hastily assembled tables and sidles up next to Emily West, a postdoctoral fellow studying plate tectonics and seismicity. "Are these quakes occurring in all the usual places or in more unique locations?"

West glances up from her cluttered workspace. "A little of both. Most are confined to the caldera, but one interesting aspect is that the seismic activity originated on the east side of the park."

Snider arches his brows. "That's unusual. There's not much in the way of faults to the east." Snider pauses to think for a moment before saying, "Emily, will you pull up a topographic map of Wyoming?"

With a few clicks of the mouse a topo map pops onto the screen. "There's nothing east of the park that would stimulate seismic activity."

West taps the screen around Cody with the tip of her pen. "I know they're punching a bunch of new gas wells in the Bighorn Basin." She moves the tip of the pen farther south. "And the Green River Basin is littered with more new gas wells than you could count."

Snider stares at the screen. "You think the drilling has triggered this new round of seismic activity?"

"Not necessarily the drilling. But I know they're fracking a majority of the wells. And where there's fracking there'll be a slew of injection wells to dispose of the wastewater."

"Son of a bitch."

"Regardless of what triggered the seismic activity, it's now our problem." She tosses her pen onto the desk and arches her back against the chair. "The area around Lake Yellowstone is bustling with tremors. The intensity has leveled off somewhat, but the quakes are becoming more superficial."

"How deep was the last one?"

"A little less than a mile."

"Magnitude?"

West leans forward and clicks on the seismometer for the West Thumb area of the lake. "Judging from data, I'd guess it's in the neighborhood of four-point-three."

"Plate activity?"

West curls a strand of her dark, curly hair around her finger. "Maybe some of it. But I believe the seismicity we're seeing now is magma related."

"Couldn't it also be a large influx of water into the area?"

"Maybe. Hell, Eric, it could be a bunch of different things, but my gut tells me the earthquakes are magma related."

"Is the magma rising toward the surface?"

"If it is, the ground deformation monitors will provide the answers."

Snider pats her on the shoulder. "Keep me posted."

Before Snider can slip away, Emily stops him with a tug on his shirtsleeve. She glances around the room, then stands up and steps in close. "Do you really think there's a chance the caldera will erupt?"

"I don't know, Emily. The one question buzzing around my brain is, after 640,000 years, why now?"

Camp 133—Millington, Tennessee

Interview: Brad from Boulder, CO— pharmaceutical sales

"Want to know something funny? I went on a hiking trip up around Mount Rainier right after my senior year of high school in May of 1980. Know what else happened during that time frame? No? Mount St. Helens erupted. Crazy, huh? Am I like a magnet for volcanic activity?"

CHAPTER 10

Tucker steers the old pickup toward the entrance of the Old Faithful Inn and parks. Both of the truck's doors, shot through with rust, squeal in protest as he and Rachael exit. They both take a moment to survey the area around the geyser. Midmorning in June and the area is as desolate as a day in the dead of winter with six feet of snow on the ground. A group of park rangers are standing at the entrance to the walkway, turning away tourists. Tucker offers a wave and ducks into the lobby, Rachael following closely behind.

Stepping into the lobby of the Old Faithful Inn is like traveling back through time. One of the largest log structures in the world, the lobby of the inn soars nearly one hundred feet overhead. A framework of lacquered pine logs supports the gabled ceiling, creating a wide-open space framed by balcónies on three levels. The anchoring element is a massive four-sided fireplace, sixteen feet square, with a chimney eighty-five feet high. The five hundred tons of rock were quarried on site, back when the only tools were man and beast. The midmorning sun streams through the high windows, casting long shadows across the wide-plank pine flooring. Tucker pauses to allow his eyes to adjust before scanning the lobby. The lobby is clogged with people, but no sign of his family. He steps toward the registration desk and removes his hat.

"Tucker!" an attractive female shouts as she travels the length of the counter toward him.

"Hey, April."

At five-five, with a willowy frame honed by daily hiking, April Todd's dirty blond hair is pulled up in a tight ponytail. Large silver earrings dangle from her ears, winking in the morning light. A small emerald-colored stud protrudes from the crease of her left nostril, and her fingers are devoid of jewelry with the exception of a silver band encircling her right thumb. The beginning of a tattoo is visible at the cuff of her short-sleeve shirt. This is her third summer working at the park and probably the last, since she recently completed her master's program. She latches on to one of Tucker's hands.

Rachael, with a look of disdain on her face, leans against the counter.

Tucker tries to slip his hand free, but April won't let go. "April, Rachael, you've both met, correct?"

The two women barely acknowledge each other, leaving Tucker to wonder about what's going on between them. He decides it's not his problem and leans in, lowering his voice. "How strong have the earthquakes been down here?"

"Enough to scare the hell out of me." April glances

around to make sure none of the park patrons are within hearing distance. "I swear it sounded as if the roof was going to cave in."

"Larger than what we've previously experienced?"

"Absolutely. I'm surprised the fireplace is still standing. That's how strong they were."

Tucker turns to glance at the tall column of stone, then turns back. "That fireplace has been standing for over a hundred years. I don't think it's going to suddenly topple over."

"You weren't here when the ground was rocking and rolling. It felt like walking through a fun house at the state fair." April leans in closer. "You don't think the earthquakes could trigger an eruption, do you?"

"Not impossible, but also not very likely."

Rachael uncrosses her arms and leans in to join the conversation. "I hope you're keeping those fears to yourself. The absolutely last thing we need right now is a bunch of hysterical tourists." She glances at Tucker. "Can we get on with business?"

April shoots Rachael a nasty scowl. "For your information, I haven't mentioned anything about an eruption. But these people aren't idiots. They know something strange is going on."

Rachael leans in farther, her forehead nearly touching April's. "All they know is the park is experiencing earthquake activity. Something that frequently—"

"April, I'm looking for Matt and Jessica Mayfield." Tucker reels his hands back and steps away from the counter.

April offers Rachael a sneer before stepping over to one of the computers. "Any relation?"

"Brother and his wife."

"They're here. Or at least they've checked in. Want me to ring the room for you?"

"Please."

April hands the handset across the counter and punches in the digits. But before Tucker gets the phone to his ear, the ground shakes violently and screams sound throughout the lobby. A heavy thud sends tremors up his legs. Tucker drops the handset and whirls around. The upper third of one side of the massive fireplace has crashed to the ground.

"Everyone, stay back," Tucker shouts as he and Rachael hurry over. The wood floor is splintered, and an older gentleman is pinned down, his legs buried under the rubble. Tucker kneels as he yanks the radio from his belt. "We have a situation at Old Faithful Inn. I need immediate medical assistance. All available rangers are requested on scene."

"My legs. I can't feel my legs," the man on the ground screams.

Tucker surveys the scene. Removing the boulders, even if he could, might well cause more damage. He puts a hand on the man's shoulder. "Sir, help is on the way. Can you tell me your name?"

"My legs. I can't . . . feel my legs." The man is gasping for air and his face is a mask of agony.

Tucker looks helplessly at Rachael. She kneels next to the man and grabs one of his hands. "Do you have family with you?"

Before he can answer, an older, heavyset woman barges through the gathered crowd. "Sam!" she shouts as she lumbers closer to the scene.

Tucker holds up a hand. "Please stop there, ma'am. This area is unsafe."

"But that's my husband." The woman breaks into sobs.

Tucker glances back toward April and nods toward the distraught woman. April walks around the counter and puts an arm around the woman.

The man is on the verge of hyperventilating. "Sam, I need you to take a couple of deep breaths. Can you do that for me?"

Sam slows his breathing and Rachael squeezes his hand. "You're doing good, Sam. Just hang on a little longer."

Sam looks up at Tucker. "Can you get me out of here?"

Tucker leans sideways for a closer look. Most of Sam's legs are hidden from view, but an ever-widening pool of blood is visible between the gaps. "Sam, we really need to wait for medical personnel before trying to move you."

"My legs. Oh God, it hurts so damn bad. Can't you just pull the rocks off?"

Sam is pale and his entire body is shivering hard enough to make his teeth chatter. Tucker glances at Rachael and she mouths the word *shock*. Tucker nods and reissues his radio plea for medical assistance.

The front doors open, spreading a shaft of light across the scene. Two rangers hurry in and Tucker waves them closer. "You need to keep those people back. The rest of the chimney could come crashing down at any time." He pauses to glance up at the soaring atrium held together by a fretwork of logs. "We should consider evacuating the entire lobby. If a couple of those logs have been jarred loose, the whole roof could collapse."

The two rangers tilt their heads up, and the ranger on the right dry swallows and nods. "You may be right." He turns to the group of tourists, which has suddenly swelled in size. "Folks, you need to vacate the lobby premises. Either return to your room or kindly step outside."

The two rangers begin dispersing the crowd, enduring more than a few grumbles and complaints. Another shaft of light shoots across the interior. Tucker glances up to see two people heading in his direction, but because of the backlighting he can't tell who they are until they draw closer. He breathes a sigh of relief as he stands to meet with Ron Engel and Patty Craft from the Old Faithful medical clinic. "Ron, his legs are in bad shape."

"Patty, grab some surgical tubing from the bag," Ron says. "We need to get some tourniquets on his legs."

As Patty kneels next to Sam and begins digging through her bag, Ron takes Tucker by the elbow and leads him a short distance away. "Tucker, I'm merely a physician's assistant, but I do know enough that if that man doesn't get to a level-one trauma center soon, he will lose both legs and possibly his life. Can you call for a medical helicopter?"

Tucker makes the radio call. "Where's the closest trauma center?"

"Salt Lake City. I'll do my best to stabilize him, but time is the enemy."

Rachael stands to give Patty more room to work.

Tucker steps over and hands her the satellite phone. "I know this is a terrible situation, but will you call the seismology lab? We need data."

Rachael nods and brushes a tear from the corner of her eye as she moves over to a quiet corner of the lobby to make the call.

Tucker spends a few moments conferring with the rangers before checking the status of the helicopter via radio. Life Flight is still fifteen minutes out. Tucker's hoping they'll find a live patient when they finally do arrive. He works his way over to Rachael, who's still on the phone. He mouths the words *How large?*

Rachael holds up a hand with all five fingers splayed.

"Epicenter?"

Rachael covers the phone's microphone. "Close to Mallard Lake."

"Ask about ground deformation."

Rachael nods and forwards the question on. Tucker watches as her forehead wrinkles with concern.

She pulls the phone away from her ear. "Mallard Dome is up six inches since this morning. But, it's worse over at the Sour Creek area. The GPS units indicate an uplift of over a foot over the last twenty-four hours."

Tucker kicks at a piece of loose stone that had ended up on this side of the lobby. "That's not good."

CHAPTER 11

Old Faithful Inn

"Hello . . . Hello?" Jessica hangs up the phone, bewildered.

Matt steps in from the balcony. "Who was on the phone?"

"No one. But I heard noises—"

There's a series of popping sounds as the building shakes violently. A water bottle wobbles toward the edge of the dresser and drops to the floor. The floor undulates like a slimming machine at a health fair. Jess reaches for the wall and Matt braces himself in the doorway. In seconds, the shaking stops, and Jess turns to her husband. "That's not a small earthquake. That was the largest of the morning. We should really consider leaving the park."

"Let's wait until we talk to Tucker. He'll have a better idea of what's going on."

"I know what's going on. The earthquakes are getting stronger and"—she pauses and turns to check on the children before lowering her voice and moving closer to her husband—"with longer durations. We need to find Tucker right now. We can't wait and hope he receives a text."

"How?"

"Let's go out to the lobby. Maybe we can ask a ranger to radio him." She looks back into the living room where both children are still clicking and swiping away on their iPads. "I'd like to get the kids away from their tablets. Knowing your son, he's probably surfing the web about supervolcanoes. The last thing we need is for him to start telling Maddie all about it."

Matt pushes off the wall. "Good point."

Jess pauses, tucking a stray strand of hair behind her ear. "Maybe we should go ahead and pack our bags."

"Let's talk to Tuck first. No sense getting the kids all worked up if it turns out to be nothing."

"This is well beyond nothing, Matt." Jessica brushes past and enters the sitting area of the king suite Matt booked. "Kids, let's head to the lobby to find Uncle Tucker."

Maddie tosses her iPad onto the sofa and jumps to her feet. "Maybe Uncle Tucker can take us to see the bears."

"What makes you think the bears will be out this time of day?" Mason asks as he closes the Smart Cover of his iPad.

Maddie scrunches her forehead. "There're bears out all the time. I saw the pictures in *National Geographic*."

Mason scoffs as he stands up. "Just because you saw the pictures in a magazine doesn't mean the bears will be out now."

Maddie turns to face her brother, her hands fisted on her hips. "Uncle Tucker will know."

Jess sighs and pulls the heavy door open. "Quit arguing and let's go."

Maddie sticks her tongue out before stomping out into the hall. The Mayfield family winds through the dimly lit, log-lined corridor toward the lobby. The heavy timbers create a rustic atmosphere that feels heavy, confining. There are no windows and the only illumination is provided by an array of single bulbs staggered along the wall. Underfoot, the carpet is worn with a noticeable furrow down the center from years of foot traffic. After several turns, they arrive at the lobby, where park rangers are herding people away from the center of the room.

"Look, Dad," Mason says, pointing toward the chimney. "I bet the earthquakes caused that."

Matt tiptoes up to see over the crowd and spots a familiar face. He turns to his wife. "I see Tucker, but it looks like they're trying to evacuate the lobby area. I'll grab him and bring him back this way." Matt nudges his way through the crowd, but as he breaks into the clear a park ranger grabs him by the arm.

"I'm sorry, sir, but we're evacuating the lobby."

Matt yanks his arm from the ranger's grasp. "I'm trying to find someone."

The man steps into Matt's personal space. "You'll have to go around. As you can see, we have a medical emergency."

Tucker glances over at the commotion, and Matt waves. Tucker heads over, a grim expression on his face. The two brothers hug.

"How badly injured is that man?" Matt asks.

"Bad. Chopper's on its way." Tucker leans around

to peer behind his brother. "Where're Jess and the kids?"

"On the other side of the lobby."

Tucker takes Matt by the elbow and leads him away from the crowd. "Listen, Matt, you and Jess should probably pack up the kids and get out of the park. Or, at the very least, head up toward my office in Mammoth."

"Jess has been bugging me to leave but I told her we'd talk to you first. What do you think is going on?"

Tucker lowers his voice. "The earthquakes are getting stronger, and I have some very real concerns about what might happen."

Camp 39—Ozark, Alabama

Interview: Carl from Clovis, NM—small business owner

"As the morning went on, the earthquakes felt like they were getting stronger. My wife and I were celebrating our first vacation in years. We'd left our two kids with their grandparents, and were hoping to make it kind of our second honeymoon, being the first one wasn't much—a night or two in Vegas. When you own a small business, time off is hard to come by. Anyway, back to your original question, yes we were staying at the Old Faithful Inn. Our second day there, and really hadn't had a chance to test the bedsprings, if you know what I mean. We were aware of the volcano, but who'd have ever thought? After what happened in the lobby, we decided it was time to get the hell out of Dodge. You could tell panic was setting in."

CHAPTER 12

Yellowstone Lake, Yellowstone National Park

Jimmy Pickett tugs down the brim of his John Deere hat as he gooses the throttle of the 15-horse Evinrude outboard motor, propelling his small twelve-foot boat across the glassy waters of Yellowstone Lake. A gaunt, tall man, Jimmy's three years into his retirement after selling all of his dairy cows. His life vest is buckled up tight. His only swimming experience was wading through the small pools along the creek running through the old family farm.

Yesterday, he had bagged a couple of eight-pound lake trout off the banks of Stevenson Island, and he's eager to return to his honey hole. The lake trout are a nuisance fish that the National Park Service is begging anglers to remove from the lake. Jimmy aims to oblige them during his one-week stay with his wife, Maryjean, who's still racked out in their travel trailer, watching *Ellen*.

The serene surface of the lake belies what lies beneath. What Jimmy doesn't know is that the lake bottom is riddled with hydrothermal vents, previous volcanic flows, and an inflated plain that rises nearly a hundred feet near his favorite fishing spot. The bulge, resting atop the magma chamber only two miles below, has increased in size over the past week. A fact unknown to scientists, because the last lake bottom mapping was three years ago.

Jimmy kills the engine and coasts closer to his spot, using the stealth approach to keep from scaring the fish. He trails his hand through the water and is surprised at how warm it is. That's usually a bad sign for trout, which prefer their water icy cold. He scans the area to make sure this is the spot he was fishing yesterday and decides it is. Maybe the water's colder below the surface, he thinks, as he grabs up his fishing pole. He uncoils the line from his bought-for-the-trip, state-of-the-art spinning reel and threads the line through the eyelets of the ultralight rod, also new. The new rig set him back about five hundred bucks, a fact Maryjean is not privy to.

Jimmy carefully rummages through his tackle box and selects a shiny spinner bait and, per park regulations, snips off one of the three hooks with a pair of pliers. He flattens the barbs of the other two hooks and ties the spinner onto his line. Yesterday's lure, the one responsible for the big hogs, is somewhere underwater, snagged on a tree limb. This one is a close approximation, but Jimmy's kicking himself for not stopping at the bait shop for an exact replica.

After snapping over the bail, he flicks his wrist and shoots the lure out into the clear water. He gives it a minute to sink, then slowly reels it in. No bites. He moves ten degrees right and flicks it out again, this time giving little jerks as he reels. Nary a nibble. Jimmy fires up the Evinrude and steers the boat to the other side of the island closer to shore and Bridge Bay, where the Yellowstone River empties into the lake.

He kills the engine and casts out his line. Even before he starts reeling, he gets a hit on the line. "Hot damn," he shouts as he lurches to his feet, yanking on the pole to set the hook and nearly capsizing the small boat in the process. With slow determination he reels in his fish. When the catch is within range, Jimmy is bending over to grab his net when a hydrothermal explosion rips through the water. The small boat is tossed around as Jimmy grabs for the side of the boat, launching his $500 fishing rig into the deep.

Another explosion of water rushes up from below, shooting the boat twenty feet into the air. Jimmy screams as the boat flips upside down, hurling him into the cauldron of superhot liquid. His screams are swallowed as the returning water sucks him beneath the surface. He kicks and claws upward as the hot water blisters his skin. Aided by the life vest, Jimmy pops to the surface, shrieking in agony. His vision blurry and his eyes feeling like hot coals burning through his skull, he swivels his head, bellowing for help. He spots the faint outline of the island shore and begins dog-paddling that way, his body inflamed with pain. Crying tears of agony, Jimmy pulls himself ashore as his vision spirals into darkness.

Camp 201—Sumter, South Carolina

Interview: Maryjean from Manhattan, KS— retired homemaker

"I lost my Jimmy up there. He was fishing the lake when all that mess started. Now I don't know where his body is. Everything happened real quick. One of the rangers told me what happened, and not long after that, it all started to happen. I know Jimmy would be mad that I left the trailer, but I'd never driven the pickup with the trailer hooked up. I didn't even . . . get a . . . chance to say . . . good-bye to him . . ." (Note: Maryjean was unable to continue the interview but did say she was evacuated from the Casper area.)

CHAPTER 13

**Yellowstone park headquarters,
Mammoth Hot Springs, Wyoming**

Park Superintendent Ralph Barlow snatches up the phone after the first ring and listens to the voice on the other end, the color draining from his face. "Christ, get everyone off the lake right damn now. And push those on the shoreline farther away. I don't want a park guest within a half a mile of there."

He listens for another moment, then asks, "Is the man still alive?" He waits for the answer. "Get the man stabilized and hustle him over to the Old Faithful area. We've got a chopper on the ground picking up another guest who was injured. I'll call the rangers and have them hold the chopper."

Barlow slams the phone down and grinds his forehead into the palm of his hand. What was a pleasant morning is now turning into an ever-widening series of catastrophes. He takes a sip of tepid coffee and spits it back into the cup before reaching for the phone again. He dials a number and stands, stretching the phone cord toward the window. At fifty-seven, Barlow is a lean, compact man, his body honed by daily hikes across the rugged terrain. His hairline has retreated to the back third of his skull, and he's thought many times about shaving the rest off, but hasn't yet. Serving as a ranger in Yellowstone during his twenties, he'd always hoped to one day be the head guy—the man in charge. *Be careful what you wish for*, he thinks as he stares out the window at the ragged face of Clagett Butte, part of the Gallatin Range, which looms large in the foreground. After several rings, the phone is answered on the other end.

Before the man can even say hello, Barlow says, "Jeremy, you're the scientist-in-charge of the Yellowstone Volcano Observatory. What the hell is going on? Do I need to start herding guests toward the exits?"

Doctor Jeremy Lyndsey sighs, sending a rush of air down the line. "Good morning to you, too, Ralph. What's got you so worked up?"

"I've got two severely wounded park guests, that's what. One was injured as the result of the last earthquake, and the second is suffering from second-degree burns over most of his body. The man was enjoying a peaceful morning of fishing on Yellowstone Lake until a hydrothermal explosion blew him out of the water."

"This is the first I've heard about a hydrothermal explosion. How long ago?"

"Within the last few minutes. About the time of the last big earthquake."

"Listen, Ralph, you need to evacuate everyone away from the lake—"

"Already done."

"Good. Where was this guy fishing?"

"Around Stevenson Island."

"There are known fissures in the lake bottom around that area. This could actually be good news."

"Good news? I've got a man with burns over most of his body."

"Yes, that part is tragic. But the hydrothermal explosion could have released some of the pressure on the magma chamber."

Superintendent Barlow walks back to his desk and sags into his chair. "Enough to alleviate the fear of a volcanic eruption?"

There's a long pause on Lyndsey's end. Finally, he answers, "I don't know. I guess it depends on whether the earthquakes continue to increase in intensity. Tucker and I have been in contact most of the morning. The thing is, Ralph, predicting if or when a volcano erupts isn't exact science. We know there are precursor events such as an increase in seismic activity, but that's been going on at the park for years."

Barlow growls. "There's a lot you don't know to be the scientist-in-charge. Especially since you're ensconced in your office out there in California. I'm here on the ground with tens of thousands of people scattered throughout the park. What I need are some concrete answers."

"Ralph, the situation is fluid. We don't have any certain answers. But, I believe the chances of the caldera erupting are slim."

"Slim enough that you want to fly out here today for a park visit?"

CHAPTER 14

Another round of groans courses across the room as Josh Tolbert sits at a desk, the phone pinched between his shoulder and chin, awaiting a response from NASA. He glances at the video screen that displays a series of colored lines, a different color for every fifteen-minute segment, and sees a large flare of red from the recent quake. The red smudge is larger than anything else on the screen and looks more like a toddler's angry scribbling than the results of a scientific instrument. Josh scans to the top of the screen and winces. The reporting station is a borehole seismometer located at the western edge of Yellowstone Lake. With over thirty seismometers located in and around Yellowstone there are red squiggles on all eight video displays.

Frustrated, he doodles an erupting volcano on a scrap of paper until, finally, a voice sounds on the line. After explaining the situation and waiting for the reply, he shouts, "You could have told me that twenty minutes ago." Josh slams the phone down and stands.

The lab is hot and stuffy with the body heat from too many overstimulated scientists. Josh wipes the sweat from his brow as he weaves his way through the crowd, stopping next to Dr. Snider.

"Professor, I finally got through to someone at NASA."

"About time, Josh. What did they say?"

"Bad news. Terra will make another pass"—he glances at the digital watch on his wrist—"around 18:45. But they're in the midst of doing a software upgrade on the ASTER system."

Snider sighs. "And the good news just keeps coming. When is the update supposed to be completed?"

"Overnight. They think they'll be able to shoot some thermal images of the caldera tomorrow morning."

Snider rakes his hand across his face. "Let's just hope we're around tomorrow to see them."

Josh's eyes widen with surprise. "Why . . . why wouldn't we be here?"

"If these earthquakes continue to increase in intensity, who knows what might happen?"

An ember ignites in Josh's gut. "Do you really think the volcano could erupt?"

Snider places a hand on Josh's shoulder. "We're a long way from worrying about a volcanic eruption."

"Would there be other signs of an impending eruption? Or just more earthquakes?"

"We don't know for sure. Hell, the thing could spontaneously erupt if there's an infusion of magma. That's why I want some thermal images of the park. If you'll excuse me, Josh, I need to makes some more calls."

As Professor Snider steps away, Josh pulls out his cell phone and sits. He punches the first speed dial. "C'mon, answer," he mutters as his leg jackhammers up and down. Josh mutters a string of curse words when the call goes to voice mail. "Dad, you guys need to pack up and get outta there." The ember in his gut flares because his dad, mom, and little sister are in the middle of a two-week vacation at the nation's oldest national park.

Camp 39—Ozark, Alabama

Interview: Andy from Albuquerque, NM—banker

"My wife and I made a pact to take our two children to all of the national parks within driving distance during our vacations. Last year we went to the Grand Canyon and had a fabulous time. This year we vacillated between Yellowstone and the Oklahoma City National Memorial. Unfortunately, we picked the wrong park at exactly the wrong time. We were planning to go earlier in June, but I couldn't get away from the bank. But I guess that's all water under the bridge now. We were camping up around the lake at Grant Village. We could have weathered the earthquakes, but when the hydrothermal explosion at the lake happened, I knew it was time to go. And we didn't waste much time getting out of there. We left the tent and all of our supplies and piled into the car. I knew all about the volcano, but I never thought in a million years . . ."

CHAPTER 15

Old Faithful Inn

With the makeshift tourniquets still in place, Tucker lends a hand with the gurney carrying Sam. Cinched tight to a backboard, Sam moans with each step. Guests hold the doors open as Tucker and the others maneuver Sam through the narrow opening. The emergency helicopter sits in the parking lot, the blades spinning overhead. With grunts of exertion, they load Sam into the helicopter.

One of the other rangers steps up to the cabin and shouts above the noise, "Hold the chopper. We have another patient on the way. He's in critical condition."

Tucker takes the ranger by the elbow and steers him away from the rotor wash. "What happened?"

"Some sort of thermal explosion at the lake."

"How large was the explosion?"

"Don't know. They just radioed to hold the helicopter. You've been here longer than me, Tucker. You ever heard of hydrothermal explosions at the lake?"

Tucker gives an emphatic shake of his head. "We've

had some around the geyser area, but never anything in the middle of the lake."

The ranger's face creases with concern. "What's it all mean?"

"Nothing good." Tucker steps away from the man as Rachael approaches. "Rach, you hear about the hydrothermal explosion over at Yellowstone Lake?"

"Yes, and the borehole seismometer on the north end of the lake recorded a massive spike. You want to go over there?"

"Not yet. I think we need to take a close look at the geyser area, but let me talk to my family for a moment." Tucker approaches Matt and Jess, who are huddled with their children under the covered porch of the inn. He nods toward a brightly painted stagecoach that offers guests rides around the park, and they join him there.

"How come the helicopter's not taking off?" Matt asks.

"They're waiting for one more injured person." He turns to face Jessica and tamps down the sudden images that course through his brain. "Jess, as a geologist, what's your take on—" He glances down at his niece and nephew, who are taking it all in. "Hey, kids, why don't you hop into this outdated limousine. Find out what travel used to be like."

Maddie and Mason climb aboard and Tucker leads Matt and Jess toward the rear. "Jess, there was a hydrothermal explosion in the middle of Yellowstone Lake just a little while ago." He stares into the distance for a moment before continuing. "I hope like hell that these aren't precursor events."

"To what? An eruption?" Jessica asks.

"I think you're both overreacting," Matt says. "Yellowstone endured over three thousand earthquakes last year alone."

Tucker leans in closer. "And I was here for every damn one of them, Matt. Believe me, these are different. I'd like to hear your wife's opinion." The statement is harsher than he intended and his cheeks pink up as he looks down at his boots.

Jessica gnaws her bottom lip for a moment before saying, "Tuck, I'm an oil field geologist, not a volcanologist. But I do think the possibility of some type of further pressure release is possible. The hydrothermal explosion could have done the trick, but there's no way to know for sure. Maybe Matt is correct in assuming it's business as usual. What are your sensors telling you?"

"Plenty, but there's a hundred different ways to interpret the data. These earthquakes are occurring in some unusual places, which would indicate magma movement. But none of us really believe there's enough melt for an eruption."

Jess pushes away from the wheel and steps in closer. "What are the percentages?"

Tucker removes his hat and mops his brow. "Maybe fifteen to twenty percent melt."

"With fifty percent being the magic number?"

"What magic number?" Matt asks.

Tucker turns to his brother. "Most scientists believe a volcano won't erupt unless fifty percent of the magma is viscous."

"And how do you know how much melt is down there?"

"That's the problem—we don't," Tucker says. "We can make projections by timing the seismic waves, but—"

All three reach for the side of the stagecoach as the ground whipsaws beneath their feet. The coach springs squeal as the cab sways from side to side and Maddie and Mason scream. But their cries are drowned out when Old Faithful emits an otherworldly hiss before exploding skyward. All three turn to look and see the geyser growing in size, eating through the surrounding earth and shooting debris hundreds of feet into the air. Rocks rain down as Jessica and Matt help the children out of the coach. Rachael hurries over to join them, and they race toward the safety of the Old Faithful Inn.

As they reach the covered porch, one of the outer support columns collapses, sending a section of the three-story roof onto the pavement. An outpouring storm of dust and debris shoots through the crowd like shrapnel. Tucker feels a prick of pain on his right leg, but ignores it as he scoops up Maddie and hugs her close. Park guests stampede toward the lobby, and within seconds the crowd is wedged so tightly the doors won't open.

Tucker reaches for Mason's hand and shouts, "Follow me." They hurry around the side of the building. Tucker glances back to see his brother limping, a dark stain spreading across his pant leg. Tucker hands Maddie off to Jessica, who has a rivulet of her own blood running down her cheek.

Tucker hurries back to his brother and places Matt's arm over his shoulder. "Mason, can you help your dad on the other side?"

Mason, with tears streaming down his face, shoulders up under Matt's other arm. Together, they half drag, half carry him along the side of the building.

"Where are we going?" Jess shouts.

"To the employee entrance," Rachael shouts.

Tucker tries to mentally calculate how much time has elapsed. The geyser usually blows for only a few minutes, but it's now pushing the upper ranges of historical eruptions.

Rachael leads them to a nondescript door marked EMPLOYEES ONLY and keys in the four-digit code. After she tugs the door open, they duck inside to an area behind the check-in counter. The once-evacuated lobby area is now jammed with people and there's heavy pounding on the glass entry doors. April hurries over as Rachael swings open the door to the manager's office.

"What's going on, Tucker?" April's voice is tight with fear.

Tucker loosens his grip on Matt, and Jess leads him into the office. "Part of the roof collapsed over the porch. Probably a dozen injured. Get on the radio and tell them we need immediate medical assistance."

April whirls around and hurries toward the radio as Tucker turns into the office. A sudden burning in his right leg forces Tucker to slow. "Rach, there should be a first aid kit in one of those cabinets."

Rachael walks over to the cabinets and begins flinging open doors.

"Jess, help me lay Matt on the floor. We need to get a look at his wounds." Rachael returns, carrying a large black bag with a red cross embossed on the front. She kneels and unzips the case.

Jessica cradles Matt's head in her lap while still

holding Maddie's hand. Mason is pushed back against the wall, his chin resting on his knees. Tucker removes a pair of scissors and begins cutting away the jeans encasing his brother's leg. Within seconds, his hands are coated in blood. He finds a large tear near the inseam just below the knee, and carefully shears past Matt's thigh. As he peels back the material, Rachael gasps.

A deep laceration runs down Matt's calf, from kneecap to ankle. Rachael rips open packages of gauze and douses them with alcohol before handing them to Tucker. He looks up at his brother. "Mattie, this is going to hurt." He places the dampened gauze onto the wound and clamps down with both hands.

Matt's leg jerks as he swallows a scream.

"I need to keep pressure on this for a few minutes. Your leg is going to need stitches."

With his jaw clinched tight Matt can only nod.

"Rachael, will you hand Jess some gauze?"

Rachael rips open more gauze, douses on the alcohol, and passes it across.

"Jess, you have some facial lacerations that need to be cleaned up. Kids, you guys have any boo-boos?"

Mason and Maddie shake their heads.

"Probably wouldn't hurt to check them, Jess," Tucker says.

Jess stands to check on the children.

Rachael puts a hand on his back and leans in. "Tucker, you have a piece of wood protruding from your thigh."

"Can you pull it out?"

"What if it makes the wound bleed more?"

"Pull it out and wrap it as best as you can." He feels a tugging sensation, then warmth, as blood trickles down his leg. He lifts one edge of Matt's bandage for a peek as a hot poker lights up his thigh. "Fuuuu . . ." he groans through gritted teeth.

"Need to clean the wound," Rachael says.

"Couldn't you have warned me first?"

"Almost done." Rachael grabs the scissors from the floor and cuts a bigger hole in Tucker's uniform pants before placing clean gauze over the wound. She wraps his thigh with an elastic bandage. "All done." She leans forward again and whispers into Tucker's ear. "Are we safe inside?"

Tucker looks up at the log ceiling overhead. "The roof is used to carrying a heavy snow load but who knows with all this ground movement? Might be best to make our way outside."

CHAPTER 16

Walt Stringer arrives at the Old Faithful area just as a corner of the porch roof at the inn crashes to the ground. He gooses the throttle of the four-wheeler and shoots across the parking lot. A helicopter, with blades spinning, sits at the edge of the lot. He parks the ATV and hops off, hurrying toward the scene of disaster.

Several people are lying on the ground, covered with varying amounts of debris. "What happened?"

"Big earthquake. Can you help triage the patients?" Patty asks.

Walt nods and starts working his way through the scene. He had received some basic medical training in the military, but he's a long way from being a brain surgeon. The first person he approaches is an older woman with a compound fracture to her left leg. The injury is gruesome, with one of her bones piercing the side of her calf. Blood is already beginning to puddle on the ground. Walt carefully lifts the debris off her leg before yanking his belt off and kneeling down beside her. "Ma'am, your leg is broken. I'm going to wrap my belt around your leg to slow the bleeding. We'll get you out of here as fast as we can."

The woman grimaces and nods.

Walt wraps the belt around her leg and cinches it tight, tying a makeshift knot to keep it in place. "I can't leave the tourniquet on long without fear of doing irreversible damage, but I need to check on the other guests. I'll be back as soon as I can."

Walt stands and hurries to the next injured person, this one a teenage male with a portion of log lying across his midsection. The young man is moaning, and a collection of tiny pink bubbles is forming around his lips. *Shit.* Walt kneels down and tells him to hold on before standing to shout for help. Patty rushes over.

Walt lowers his voice. "This boy needs a chest tube, stat. A rib must have punctured one or both of his lungs."

"I've never done a chest tube before."

"Find someone who can. If he doesn't get one in the next minute or so, he's going to die."

Patty turns and screams: "Ron!"

Ron stands from treating another patient and hurries over.

"This patient needs a chest tube," Patty says.

Ron mutters a string of curse words. "I've only done a chest tube once and that was several years ago."

Ron kneels down next to the young man. His eyes are open, but there's no sense awareness.

Walt squats down next to him. "If you've done it once you can do it again."

Walt glances up to see more rangers running toward the scene, and he waves one over. "Radio that chopper to stand by." The ranger grabs for his radio. Walt turns back to see Ron's hands shaking violently. "Ron, take a deep breath. You can do this."

Ron gulps in a lungful of air. "I don't have the right equipment for a chest tube."

Walt searches through the medical supplies and pulls out an IV kit. "We'll make this work." He rips open the package while Ron remains frozen. In his calmest voice, Walt says, "Ron, cut off his shirt and swab his chest."

Ron starts working. He cuts off the T-shirt, then opens a bottle of Betadine and saturates a handful of gauze before wiping it across the patient's chest, the harsh chemical smell enveloping them.

Walt holds up the IV needle. "You think this is long enough?"

Ron looks at the needle and shakes his head. "Maybe if we attach some tubing to the needle I could push the IV catheter further into his chest cavity. We just need another couple of inches."

"Good thinking." Walt pulls on a pair of sterile gloves. "Why don't you make the incision while I rig this up."

Ron rips open a scalpel and pauses. "I don't know if I can do this."

"We don't have any choice, Ron. Just count the ribs and make the incision."

Ron pulls on a glove and counts down to the fourth rib. He takes a deep breath and slices through the skin. Using his finger, he bluntly dissects the incision until his finger breaks into the chest cavity. "I'm in."

Walt hands over the makeshift chest tube and Ron pushes the needle and tubing into the opening, securing it to the patient's chest with tape. Dark red blood begins to drip from the other end of the tube. "We need something to keep him from sucking more air into his chest cavity."

Walt rips open another package and pulls the plunger back on a 15-cc syringe before screwing it onto one of the ports. "That'll work for now, but we need to get him on that chopper. There's also a lady over there with a compound fracture, and she needs to be airlifted." Walt gets to his feet and shouts for more rangers to come help.

Having depleted the supply of gurneys, the rangers load the injured onto roof decking and carry them to the helicopter. With five injured, plus the pilot and flight nurse, the helicopter is overloaded. The pilot takes off his headset and shouts, "I thought we were waiting for a burn victim."

Walt moves away from the rotor wash and grabs his radio. He returns moments later. "The guy didn't make it. Can you get airborne with all the added weight?"

"You bet your ass I can."

Walt slams the door shut as the pilot claps on his headset and grabs the controls. After a painfully slow few seconds, the skids lift from the surface and the helicopter gains forward momentum, making a sweeping left turn over the geyser.

Walt watches the chopper depart. As the helicopter drifts closer toward the geyser, a tingle of dread shoots down his spine. He furiously waves his arms to get the pilot's attention, but the pilot is busy at the controls and doesn't notice Walt. In the next instant Walt's fears are realized when Old Faithful erupts. The plume of water slams into the bottom of the chopper, tilting it sideways. Walt can see the pilot struggling for control, but the helicopter continues to lose altitude until the rotating blades slam into the earth, blasting shrapnel in all directions. With the engine screaming, the helicopter slams into the ground. Walt grabs for his radio as he breaks into a run. Before he's made it ten yards, a massive explosion erupts, sending a blistering heat wave radiating in all directions. A wall of shrapnel follows the blast and Walt shields his face with his hands as the racing debris tugs at his uniform. He moves closer, hoping to find survivors, but knowing in the back of his mind that the possibilities are grim. Walt's shirt begins to smoke as he pushes forward. Black smoke and red-hot flames shoot skyward as the odor of burning plastic and roasting flesh assaults him.

CHAPTER 17

Old Faithful Area

Tucker hears the urgent radio pleas. "Jess, keep pressure on Matt's leg." He pushes to his feet and limps through the outside door, where the searing heat sucks the breath from his lungs. It takes him a moment to process what his eyes see. The scene looks like something from a disaster movie, with a giant fireball shooting toward the sky and Old Faithful gushing water at an unprecedented rate.

Rachael pushes through the door behind him. "What happened?"

"The helicopter must have crashed."

"How many people were onboard?"

"No idea." Tucker and Rachael hurry across the loop trail and spot another ranger just ahead, trying to get closer to the scene. The heat from the jet-fueled fire is suffocating, and water from Old Faithful rains down like liquid fire. Tucker pushes up closer and grabs the back of the ranger's shirt, pulling him away from the scene. He shouts above the noise, "There's nothing you can do."

The man turns with a wild look in his eyes. Tucker grimaces at the burned face of his old friend and long-time park ranger, Walt Stringer. Tucker grabs him by the hand and pulls him away. "Walt, they're gone." Walt allows Tucker to lead him to the other side of the trail. Ron hurries over and begins fumbling through his medical kit as Tucker helps Walt to the ground. "What happened, Walt?"

"The geyser knocked them out of the sky. They couldn't have been more than a hundred feet in the air."

Tucker squats down beside him. "But the geyser went off only moments before. Usually there's a time lag of an hour or so before she goes off again."

Walt nods toward the geyser. "I don't know what to tell you, Doc."

Ron hands across a handful of pills and a bottle of water. Walt feeds the pills into his mouth and chases them down with large gulp of water.

"Ron, how many people were onboard the helicopter?" Tucker asks.

Ron pauses before answering. "Seven."

Tucker winces as he stares at the burning wreckage.

"Walt, you have second-degree burns over most of your face," Ron says. "Let me see your hands."

Walt holds up his hands and Ron inspects them. "You have some burning but not as severe as your face. We need to get that shirt off of you to see if you have any burns on your torso."

Tucker helps Ron peel off Walt's shirt. His skin is as red as if he'd spent all day outside with his shirt off. "You have some first-degree burning. It's going to hurt for a while and may even blister, but you'll live."

"Unlike those on the chopper," Walt mutters.

"It was a tragic accident, Walt," Tucker says. "Nothing you could have done about it."

Walt hangs his head. "I could have waved the pilot away from the area."

Ron breaks the seal on a tube of ointment and gently applies it to Walt's face. "It all happened too quickly. Tucker's right. It was a tragic accident."

Walt swivels his head to look at Tucker. "What's really going on, Tucker? I've been a ranger here for a long time and I've never seen things this bad."

Camp 43—Valdosta, Georgia

Interview: Mark from Marshalltown, IA—farmer

"We were headed south toward Old Faithful and came over a ridge to see a big fireball. We didn't know what the hell was going on. I told Arlene to check the radio but we didn't hear nothing about what was going on. We slowed down as we went past, but you couldn't tell anything because of the smoke. I did see one mighty peculiar thing, but it was only later that I figured out what it was, after we heard what happened. Looked like a giant sword sticking out of the ground. Had to have been one of those helicopter blades. Damnedest thing I ever seen. We got down by the lake about the time one of them big earthquakes hit. I told Arlene we was leaving and, by God, we took off."

CHAPTER 18

University Seismic Observation Lab

"**P**lease keep the noise down," Eric Snider shouts over the babel. The room grows quiet as he paces to the center of the room. "Josh, can we get the latest GPS data on one of the screens?"

Josh hurries to the audio-video room and logs onto the computer. He pulls up the UNAVCO Plate Boundary Observatory site, home to over eleven hundred Global Positioning System stations, including those in Yellowstone National Park. He punches up the feed and pushes out of the chair, returning to the conference room as a series of loud gasps echo across the room.

"Josh, are these the current numbers?" Snider asks, his voice full of disbelief.

"Kind of. The last data dump from the GPS units was an hour ago." Josh glances up at the screen to see ground deformation numbers well beyond historic standards.

Snider wipes the sudden burst of perspiration from his forehead. "The time lag is killing us. Josh, call and see if they can provide us real-time GPS data."

Josh retreats to make the call.

"Okay, people, we have an earthquake above five magnitude and uplift nearing a foot at both the Mallard Lake Dome and the Norris area," Snider says. "I want data and I want it now. We need to know exactly what's going on at the park."

A surge of shouted voices erupts as Snider pulls his cell phone from a pocket.

He scrolls to the favorites' list and punches the call button. The call is answered on the second ring. "Ralph, we're experiencing some rather unusual anomalies."

Superintendent Barlow pauses before responding, but when he does, his voice is laced with anger. "Not anomalies, Eric. This is a clusterfuck. I've got seven dead in a helicopter crash and half of the Old Faithful Inn lying on the ground. You need to get with Tucker and Jeremy to develop a plan. This is something beyond the usual earthquakes. I've got thousands of visitors scattered across more than two million acres. And every single one of them will be dead if that volcano erupts."

"I tried to call Tu—"

"Call his sat phone. Or contact him through telepathy. I don't care. But I want a plan of action within the hour." The phone clicks off on the other end.

Snider sighs and begins scrolling through his contacts for Tucker's satellite phone. He glances up to see Josh hovering nearby. "What is it, Josh?"

"They're not sure they can reprogram the GPS units, sir, but they're going to try."

"How difficult can it be? Jesus, can't we have one thing go our way?" Snider pulls the glasses from his face and rubs the bridge of his nose for a moment. "Thanks, Josh. Let me know when you find out."

Josh lingers. "Sir, can . . . I mean . . . why . . . can't they just issue an evacuation order for the entire park?"

"They could, but it could be a nightmare with only five roads leading out of the park. Add in panic and you'd have a recipe for disaster."

"Maybe they could evacuate the park in sections. That could work, couldn't it?"

Snider waves his cell phone in the air. "Listen, Josh, I've got several more calls to make."

Josh looks down at his shoes.

Snider sighs. "Why are you so concerned about what's happening at Yellowstone?"

Josh looks up with tears shimmering in his eyes. "My mom, dad, and little sister are over there some-where. I haven't been able to reach them."

"Christ. You know where they're staying?"

Josh shakes his head and thumbs away a tear. "They're camping. They could be anywhere."

"They would have needed camp permits. Maybe you can track them down that way."

Josh perks up and palms the tears from his cheeks. "That's a good idea. If I can find out where they are, I could go up and find them." Josh turns to leave, but stops when Professor Snider calls his name. He turns back. "Yes, sir?"

"Sooner, rather than later, Josh."

CHAPTER 19

Midway Geyser Basin, Yellowstone National Park

Nicknamed "Hell's Half Acre" by Rudyard Kipling in 1889, the Midway Geyser Basin looks as if it belongs on another planet, as steamy contrails drift skyward from the multitude of kaleidoscope-colored pools of water. The basin is home to the Grand Prismatic Spring, one of the largest hot springs in the world. Tourists wind their way through the area atop a narrow wooden walkway for an up-close look at some of Mother Nature's most unique artwork.

Among the tourists are honeymooners Seth and Harper Spaulding, who elected not to fly to the Caribbean for a week of sun and fun. Instead, the couple opted for a back-to-nature honeymoon and chose Yellowstone because of flight prices into Salt Lake City. Arm in arm, they sidestep an older, hand-holding couple who are advancing arthritically along the boardwalk. Harper leans in and whispers, "Aren't they cute. Think that'll be us in fifty years?"

Seth grins and gives her a quick kiss. "I hope we'll

be able to move a little faster, but yes, I signed on for life. You're stuck with me."

Harper graces him with a smile and hugs him tighter as they stroll toward the larger pool. A family with two small children in tow passes them, and they both watch their retreat.

"Are we going to bring our kids here someday?" Harper asks.

"Yep, all seven of them."

Harper playfully slaps his arm. "I think seven is a little over the limit. I'd settle for three, though. Girls, boys, or a mix, it doesn't matter to me."

Seth reaches down and gives her butt a squeeze. "Want to go practice?"

"You have a dirty mind, Seth Spaulding. There'll be plenty of time for that later."

The couple arrives at the edge of the spring—or as close as the walkway allows. The surrounding area more closely resembles a Martian landscape, only with water. The ground surrounding the large pool is barren of vegetation and the rim of the pool is an amalgam of orangey-rusty-colored earth with orange trails radiating out in all directions like the rays of the sun. The hot spring itself is a prism of colors, with a deep blue center that melds with green and yellow to form rings around the outer rim.

Harper pulls out her cell phone. "Let's take a selfie with the pool in the background." They two-step a tight circle and paste on big smiles. Harper extends her arm out and snaps a photo. "We can tell our children we went to Mars for our honeymoon."

Seth looks up at the horizon. "Wonder why all those trees are dead?"

Harper tucks her phone back into her shorts. "I don't know. Maybe the ground is too hot for them."

"This place is eerie as hell. I bet that spring is a hundred feet deep." He turns to look at his wife. "You know where the heat comes from?"

Harper takes her husband's hand. "I guess from underground."

"Sort of. Right now, we're standing on one of the largest volcanoes on the planet."

Harper sweeps her gaze from one side of the horizon to the other. "Where?"

"It's called a *caldera volcano*. After the last eruption the ground sank into the crater."

"You're teasing me."

"Google it. It's all over the Internet. It's supposedly due to erupt at any time."

"Well, I hope it waits until we leave. And how do they even know the volcano is active?"

Seth points at the steam rising from the surface of the pool. "They say an eruption of this volcano could produce a worldwide volcanic winter."

Harper shudders and tugs on his arm. "C'mon. Let's work our way back toward the car."

Seth laughs. "Don't tell me you're suddenly worried about an eruption."

Harper laughs and pinches him on the arm. "No, I'm not afraid. I mean, what are the chances?" The couple strolls back toward the parking lot. "It would make a hell of a honeymoon story for the kids, though." They both laugh and Harper leans in to kiss Seth.

With so many feet plodding along the boardwalk, Seth and Harper are unaware of the ground vibration occurring all around them. Until they come to a stop. "What's that?" Harper asks, a furrow of concern creasing her brow.

"I don't know. The whole area is shaking." The tremors increase in intensity and a dull, constant thrum begins to sound. Seth grabs Harper's hand. "Run!"

They're still two hundred yards from the car when the ground beneath their feet explodes upward. Hot water rushes skyward and the boardwalk collapses like falling dominoes. People scramble in all directions, but their attempts prove futile. The screams of horror and cries of anguish are soon drowned out by the rush of scalding water. Seth and Harper have time for a partial "I love—" before the wall of water washes them into one of the simmering cauldrons of multicolored water.

Camp 46—Columbus, Georgia

Interview: Joycelyn from Junction City, KS—high school teacher

"Seth was the oldest of our three children . . . and the first . . . to get married. The ceremony . . . the ceremony was . . . was . . . so beautiful. He and Harper were perfect for each other. They dated for two years . . . You know they say opposites attract? Well, those two were cut from the same cloth. Both loved being outside. Harper's apartment . . . was filled with . . . all types of plants. They were going to come back . . . to . . . to their perfect jobs. Oh God, it's so awful. As a parent . . . you have nightmares about . . . something . . . happening. It took them . . . two . . . days to notify us.

They traced the registration from their rental car. And it . . . lingers . . . you know. There's just no . . . I guess . . . closure. Harper and my baby boy . . . are . . . are gone and we didn't even get to have . . . a . . . funeral. Now they're . . . buried . . . under . . . all . . . all of that . . ."

CHAPTER 20

Old Faithful Inn

Tucker, Walt, and Rachael walk back toward the Old Faithful Inn. A few of the less severely wounded are sitting in the shade of a large pine tree, receiving medical treatment. Medical personnel from all over the park rushed to the scene, and several tourists with medical training are pitching in to help out. Tucker stops to tell Ron about his brother needing stitches, then moves on. The parking lot is brimming with tourists, some watching on in horror as the helicopter continues to burn. To their credit, mass hysteria hasn't settled in—yet. Walt's face is a blistered mess but the pain pills appear to be working. As they make their way around the collapsed roof, Tucker's satellite phone chirps. He answers and waves Rachael closer before putting the phone on speaker.

Superintendent Barlow's voice is subdued. "Tucker, we have fifteen confirmed dead and several others with severe injuries. Mostly burns. There was a hydrothermal explosion at the Midway Geyser area."

Tucker hangs his head. "Jesus, Ralph. We have seven confirmed dead here and a dozen or so injured. The helicopter crashed on takeoff."

Silence fills the connection before Barlow says, "What the hell happened?"

"The helicopter was struggling to gain altitude and drifted out over the geyser area. Walt thinks they weren't more than a hundred feet into the air when Old Faithful erupted."

"Jesus. You know how many deaths we've had at the park since I took over as superintendent? Not very damn many. And now we have twenty-two dead, with several others just barely hanging on—all over a span of a couple of hours." Barlow blows out a heavy breath. "I need some answers, Tucker. I'm not going to sit on my thumbs hoping the worst doesn't happen. I'm leaning strongly toward issuing an evacuation order."

Rachael speaks up. "Won't that just create more panic? We could be creating a situation well beyond our control."

"I'm open to suggestions, Rachael, but we need to act now. Tucker, are we facing an imminent eruption?"

"Unknown, Ralph. All of these events could be a way to relieve pressure on the magma chamber. Or they could be a precursor to a much wider event. The rapid uplift at Mallard and Sour Creek domes is a major source of concern. But again, we've seen uplift at those locations before."

Barlow growls, then says, "So basically, Tucker, we don't have a fucking clue what's going on?"

"There's just no way to predict if the caldera is going to erupt. Let me get with Eric and Jeremy to see if we can get a better handle on what's happening."

"You've got an hour, Tucker. I'm going to contact the highway patrol in all three states in hopes that we can have an orderly evacuation. It will take some time to get all of it set up. But I'm not going to have any more deaths on my watch."

"I understand, Ralph. I'll call you back within the hour." Tucker disconnects the call and turns to Rachael. "You're the hydrology expert. You think these hydrothermal explosions could be acting as relief valves?"

Rachael gnaws on her bottom lip as she stares into the distance. "I just don't know, Tucker." She turns to look at him. "As far as I know, there hasn't been an explosion around the Midway Geyser Basin since the Excelsior Geyser erupted in the mid-1980s. But with this eruption and the one at the lake earlier, plus the erratic activity of Old Faithful, I think we would be naive to think all this is normal. That said, I have a really hard time believing the caldera is on the verge of eruption."

Tucker remains silent as he turns and starts walking. Rachael falls in line with him. He hands her the sat phone. "See if you can get Eric and Jeremy on a conference call. I'm going to check on my brother."

Tucker enters through the employee entrance and ducks into the office. Ron is working on Matt's leg while Jess sits huddled against the wall, Mason and Maddie huddled on either side of her. Tucker summons Jessica with a nod. She stands, and he leads her toward the far corner of the office.

"The helicopter crashed, killing everyone aboard."

Jess's hands go to her mouth.

"There's more. A hydrothermal explosion at the Midway Geyser area killed fifteen people, with many more injured."

"Oh God, Tucker. Is all of this the result of the earthquakes?"

Tucker shrugs. "I don't think so. I'm scared, Jess. Scared of what could happen. As soon as Ron is finished with Matt, I want you to load up everyone and get the hell out of the park. Don't even bother getting your luggage from the room. I'll pick it up and throw it in the back of my pickup. Just get in the car and start driving. Don't stop until you're at least a hundred and fifty miles away."

Jess puts a hand on his chest. "We're not leaving without you. I left once . . ."

Tucker's face flushes with anger as he grasps Jess by the elbow. When he speaks, his voice is low, urgent. "You will leave. Do you want your children incinerated by a pyroclastic flow traveling at hurricane speeds? A pyroclastic flow so hot that it will boil the water from a human body and vaporize everything in its path? Getting the hell out is the only option."

Jess's cheeks turn crimson. "And how do you think they'll feel knowing their uncle could have chosen to come with us and didn't?"

Tucker releases her arm. "I'm not sacrificing myself. There are things I need to take care of. Please, Jess. Please, just load up and go."

CHAPTER 21

51.3 miles east of the park boundary, near Cody, Wyoming

Air hisses as Eldon Harjo takes his foot off the brake pedal of his eighteen-wheeler. Attached to his tractor truck is a muddy tanker trailer with 8,500 gallons of fracking fluid sloshing around with each jerk of the truck. Eldon is next up in a line of six tanker rigs waiting to dispose of the chemicals and briny water from a gas well near his home at the Wind River Indian Reservation. The reservation, covering nearly 3,500 square miles, is home to the Eastern Shoshone and Northern Arapaho Native American tribes. Eldon falls into the first category, with a heavy brow, high, well-defined cheekbones, and a long broad nose with a slight hook at the end. His dark hair is shot through with gray and hangs well below his shoulders.

The driver in front eases away from the disposal well, and Eldon slips the clutch, moving his truck into position. He climbs from the cab and spots Quincy, a Cajun redneck who recently migrated up from Louisiana, headed his way.

"What's up, Chief?"

"Fucker," Eldon mutters as he drags the four-inch hose off the trailer and clamps it to the out-feed line. He attaches the other end of the hose to the wellhead, where the slurry is injected deep underground at pressures reaching 14,000 PSI. The contents of the tanker include: briny water; sand or ceramics, which are proppants used to keep the fractured rock from closing up; and a mix of acids and other chemicals, such as friction reducers, biocides, scale inhibitors, gelling agents, or gel breakers. All of it a chemical soup used to force the shale to release the oil and natural gas that the rock's been clinging to for millions of years.

Eldon clamps down the last connection and turns to find Quincy leaning against the trailer, a lit cigarette dangling from the corner of his bearded mouth. Quincy exhales a stream of smoke as he speaks. "Hey, Chief, you ever wonder what all this is doing to the land beneath the rez?"

"My name's not Chief, you coon ass. What's it to you, anyway?"

Quincy barks out a hacking laugh. "Okay, El . . . don, you got me there. But you ain't never wondered what all this shit is doing to mother earth? I thought all you Injuns were land lovers. Like, it's all sacred ground or some shit."

"Jobs are scarce and I've got a family to feed." Eldon turns away and walks toward the pump shed, but then stops and turns back. Quincy had hit a nerve. "I don't like it. But at least it's not as bad as what you Cajuns did to the Gulf Coast. Fuckin' oil spewing into the ocean for weeks on end." Eldon turns to resume his journey, his mind spinning, again, about the possible side effects of all the drilling going on around the reservation.

Quincy shouts after him, "It's only a matter of time, Chief, until somethin' up here gets fucked up. You wait and see."

Eldon shoots Quincy the finger and ducks into the shed. He powers on the massive pump that injects the wastewater deep underground, and exits. As he approaches his rig, the ground begins to shift beneath his feet. The tremor races up his legs, forcing Eldon to grab for the side of the trailer. In moments the tremor passes and Eldon turns to look back at the pump shed, wondering if that might be the cause for the earthquake. "Just a coincidence," he mutters as he double-checks the connections.

Quincy tosses his cigarette butt to the ground and squashes it with a muddy boot. "What'd I tell you, Chief? Only a matter of time." Quincy laughs as he turns and makes his way back to his truck.

Eldon watches Quincy's departure as a seed of concern forms in the pit of his stomach.

CHAPTER 22

University Seismic Observation Lab

Josh taps on the doorframe and steps into the office. "Professor Snider, I finally got in touch with a ranger station. My parents and sister are camped in the Grant Village area. They still won't answer their cell phones, so if it's okay with you, I'm going to drive up there."

Snider takes off his glasses and rubs the bridge of his nose. "It may not be safe, Josh. Did you ask if they could relay a message to your parents?"

"I did. But I think the rangers have their hands full. The lady on the phone sounded harried."

Snider replaces his glasses and leans forward in his chair. "It's a real shitstorm up there right now. They've suffered considerable earthquake damage and several people were killed in a hydrothermal explosion."

Josh sags against the wall. "Anything happen in the Grant Village area?"

"No. At least not yet, but it's not out of the realm of possibilities. If you're going, you need to leave now. Drive straight through. Get in and out. You should have time." He opens a desk drawer, removes a phone, and slides it across the desk. "Take this satellite phone. I want you to call me every hour or so to give me an update or if you see anything unusual. You're going to be another set of eyes on the ground."

Josh picks up the phone and slides it into his pocket. "What kind of car do you drive?"

"An ancient Civic. Why?"

Snider digs through his pocket and pulls out a set of keys and hands them to Josh. "Take my pickup. It's four-wheel drive. Things could get dicey up there."

Josh pockets the keys. "I'll take good care of it."

"I don't care about the truck. Take care of yourself."

Josh says good-bye and leaves the office. With a growing sense of trepidation, Snider watches Josh retreat down the hall. The phone rings and he glances at the caller ID before snatching up the handset. "Tucker, what the hell is going on up there?"

"Eric, this is Rachael. Tucker will be back in a sec. Can you conference in Jeremy?"

Snider, owner of three degrees, two of them advanced, stares at the phone console with a bewildered expression on his face. "I'm not sure I know how to do that."

Rachael sighs. "Go find a student to set it up for us."

"Okay. Be back in a sec."

Snider returns with a student, who spends less than ten seconds setting up the conference call. In the interim, Tucker rejoined Rachael, and now the three leaders of the Yellowstone Volcano Observatory are interlinked—Dr. Eric Snider, chief seismologist, Dr. Jeremy Lyndsey, scientist-in-charge of YVO, and Dr. Tucker Mayfield, scientist-in-charge on park grounds.

"Gentlemen, I've been on the ground here at Old Faithful most of the morning," Tucker says. "Things are escalating quickly—multiple hydrothermal explosions and earthquakes of increasing intensity. I'm proposing we raise the aviation volcanic threat level to orange and upgrade ground conditions to a watch."

Lyndsey responds first. "Tucker, do you really believe an eruption is imminent?"

"Superintendent Barlow is giving us an hour to figure that out. He wants to issue a parkwide evacuation order. Eric, what's the latest data suggesting?"

Snider picks up a rubber band and stretches it across his fingers. "Nothing good. The GPS units are showing ground deformation at unseen rates. There's considerable uplift at the two domes and general uplift all along Lake Yellowstone as well as the Norris area. The seismometers are in nearly constant flux and the borehole tiltmeters and strainmeters indicate a pattern of extreme unrest. I'm trying to get NASA to shoot some thermal images but they're in the middle of a software update."

"Any indications of a harmonic tremor?" Lyndsey asks.

Snider shoots the rubber band across the room before wiggling his computer mouse to wake the screen. "The surface instruments are so susceptible to wind that I'm not sure we'd ever spot a harmonic tremor. I've got eyes watching all of the borehole seismometers, but no indication yet."

"I don't think we should be banking on a harmonic tremor becoming our canary in the coal mine," Tucker says. "I think there's a good portion of magma already moving toward the surface, and that's causing all the seismic activity. Rachael agrees. She believes magma movement may be pushing the surface water upward, creating these hydrothermal explosions."

"Okay, Tucker. I'm on board with raising the aviating threat level to orange. It'll take a while for the change to work through the system. But I'm not sure a parkwide evacuation is warranted."

"Says the man sitting six hundred miles away," Tucker says with a tinge of heat in his voice. "Ralph will be the one to make that call, and right now he's leaning toward an evacuation. And, frankly, I can't disagree with him. I'm here on the ground and I'm telling you something's off. Too many unexplained events."

"But what if we're wrong?" Lyndsey asks.

"Better that than the alternative," Tucker says.

Camp 5—Panama City, Florida

Interview: Mary from Menlo Park, CA—staff geologist, USGS

"It *was* a helpless feeling being so far removed the park. But we were so busy studying the data that we didn't really have time to discuss it. We were in constant communication with the seismology lab and with geologists on the ground in Yellowstone. We were burning up the phone lines, trying to gather all the information we could. Although thoughts of what might occur were in the back of our minds, we were on the cusp of witnessing something no human had ever witnessed. All the data indicated extreme unrest, but no one thought . . . you know . . . but sometimes Mother Nature has a mind of her own."

CHAPTER 23

Downsized when the major airline he worked for went belly-up, Captain Neil Lockhart takes a half-hearted glance at the preflight checklist while he sips his third cup of coffee of the morning. Once having flown triple-7s into exotic locations such as Bangkok, Tokyo, and Paris, Captain Lockhart is now flying thirty-year-old 737s into less glamorous places such as El Paso and Newark.

He tosses the checklist onto the co-captain's seat and leans back in his too-small seat. Six months from the mandatory retirement age of sixty-five, Neil Lockhart is carrying forty extra pounds, evidenced by his heavy jowls and protruding belly. With a ruddy complexion and a scalp encircled by a single band of hair, he has a brusque manner that's sometimes mistaken for rudeness.

The aircraft dips as someone steps aboard, and he turns to see his copilot entering the flight deck. Victoria Delgado, one of the first Hispanic females to graduate from the Air Force's combat flight school, snatches up the preflight checklist and steps over the communication console to slide into her seat. Her skin is the color of raw sienna and she has a head full of dark hair cut in an asymmetrical bob. She tosses her hat onto the dash and wiggles in her seat to get comfortable. "So another tour of Kansas City and Scranton?"

"That's the plan. A visit to some of America's finest cities."

"God, I hope they don't put us up in another do-drop-inn for the night."

"Yeah, maybe they'll upgrade us to a Motel 6."

Delgado smiles. "I can't believe I left the Air Force for such a glamorous job."

Lockhart drains the rest of his coffee and looks around for somewhere to put the empty cup. "Why did you punch out?"

"I was never going to make colonel. Too many captains pushing up the ladder. Plus my husband and I got tired of moving every couple of years. I put in fifteen and we relocated to Seattle." She picks up the flight log and makes an entry. "How long before we push back?"

"Thirty minutes or so. Should be a smooth flight. Weather looks good."

Delgado closes the book. "What are you going to do, Neil, when you hang up your flight jacket?"

"Hell if I know. We have a couple of grandkids that live out near Jackson Hole. Might just sell everything we own and move to the mountains."

"I'm envious. But, I've got a long way to go. Sure is a beautiful area. We've driven over to Yellowstone a couple of times over the years. The scenery is spectacular. Speaking of which"—Delgado removes her smartphone and clicks on the Internet browser—"I always check the volcano threat level before taking off."

Lockhart chuckles. "We'd see St. Helens from here."

"I'm not too worried about Mount St. Helens." She navigates to the U.S. Geological Survey's hazards web page and clicks on the volcano alerts. "Everything's green except for portions of Hawaii."

Lockhart's chuckle turns to a laugh. "Which one you worried about? The alleged Yellowstone super-volcano?"

Delgado glances up from the screen. "Nothing alleged about it. That's one big mother. Plus, it's right in our flight path."

Lockhart waves a hand of dismissal and laughs again. "I think we're safe for today."

CHAPTER 24

Old Faithful Inn

After the conference call, Tucker slips the phone into his pocket.

"You're not going to call Ralph?" Rachael asks.

Tucker shakes his head. "Not yet. We still have some time before his deadline."

Rachael grabs Tucker by the elbow and pulls him to a stop. "Every minute we delay puts more lives at risk."

"Damn it, Rachael, I know that." He takes a deep breath and releases it. "I don't know what to do. You're the one who suggested an evacuation could be a disaster. What if we evacuate and nothing happens? We'd be crucified for putting the tourists further at risk when there's only a slim chance for an eruption. The damn thing hasn't erupted in 640,000 years, and now it's going to happen on our watch?"

Rachael steps forward and places a hand on Tucker's chest. "I'm not your enemy, Tucker. And I certainly don't have all the answers. But what's occurred this morning isn't *normal* behavior for the park. Do we want to risk thousands of lives while pondering statistical improbabilities?"

Tucker eases her hand off his chest. "You're right. When word spreads about the change in aviation threat levels, the entire country will be in a panic. But if Ralph issues an evacuation order, there's no putting the genie back into the bottle. Pandemonium might ensue."

Rachael rakes her fingers through her curls. "Better pandemonium than annihilation."

Dejected by the lack of alternatives, Tucker places a call to Barlow. After a brief discussion, he disconnects the call and turns to Rachael. "He wants us to return to Mammoth. He's reaching out to the governor as we speak. The evacuation order will go out shortly, and he wants us there to help implement the plan."

"Lot of good that will do. Although we don't have any other options, the plan will probably last all of about thirty seconds. Do you want me to measure gas readings around the geysers before we leave?"

"Yeah, we need all the data we can get. I'm going to check on my brother's progress and give them a heads-up."

Rachael returns to the pickup to retrieve the gear while Tucker walks toward the inn. Smoke from the dying fire at the crash site drifts along the faint breeze, bringing with it noxious fumes of melted plastic. With a portion of the porch roof collapsed and the lobby sealed off by rangers, a large group of people are milling around the parking lot. Huddled mostly into familial groups, they murmur among themselves.

When Tucker turns the corner near the employee entrance he's accosted by an irate older man. Dressed in jeans and an old T-shirt with suspenders stretched over his enormous gut, the man pushes into Tucker's space.

"Just what in the hell is going on around here? We're standing out here in the heat and nobody's telling us a damn thing."

Tucker takes a deep breath and immediately regrets it when his sinuses are swamped by the stench of foul body odor. "Sir, we're trying to work through the situation."

"What situation?" The man stabs Tucker in the chest with a stubby finger as he enunciates each word.

Tucker takes a step back, and the accumulation of the morning's events crashes down on him. "Touch me again, sir, and I'll break your fucking finger." Tucker takes a moment to regain his composure as the man shuffles back a couple of steps. "Tell you what, sir, why don't you return to your room and begin packing your things."

"Why? We're here for three more days."

Tucker's mind fumbles for an acceptable answer. He makes do with: "Well then, enjoy the rest of your stay." Tucker attempts to step by the man.

The man reaches a finger out again but quickly pulls it back. "What do you know that you're not telling us?"

"I know I have work to do. If you'll excuse me." Tucker sidesteps the man and hustles toward the employee entrance as the man continues to shout questions after him. He pulls up short when he spots Walt Stringer sitting on one of the log benches. Walt's face is fire hydrant red and it's hard to tell where one blister ends and another begins. Tucker takes a seat next to him.

"You hanging in there, Walt?"

"I'm a lot better off than those folks that were in the chopper."

Tucker pauses for a moment and then glances around before lowering his voice. "Listen, Ralph is going to issue an evacuation order shortly. You might want to work your way north and help out at the campgrounds around Indian Creek. It'd get you closer to a park exit."

Walt leans back and tilts his head up to look at the cobalt-colored sky and spends a moment or two watching the enormous cottony clouds drifting along the current. "You know, Tucker, I feel like I've been rowing with one oar since cancer took Janet two years ago." Walt blows out a deep breath and turns to face his friend. "I expect there'll be plenty of people here needing my help. How long before the caldera blows?"

"Minutes . . . hours . . . days . . . Hell, I can't say with certainty that it's even going to erupt. But my gut tells me otherwise."

Walt extends his hand. "Whatever happens, happens, Tucker. Thanks for the heads-up."

Tucker grasps Walt's hand. "Take care of yourself, Walt."

Walt nods and releases the handshake. "Back at ya."

Tucker stands and squeezes Walt's shoulder. "Beers are on me when all this is over."

"Sounds like a plan, Doc."

April is still manning the counter when Tucker enters the building. He pulls her aside. The color drains from her face as he explains about the impending evacuation.

"What about the guests? How are we going to close all the accounts for payment? How are we going to evacuate those that flew into Jackson Hole? How are we . . . oh God . . . what am I going to do? Where am I going to—"

"Take a deep breath, April." Tucker takes her by the hand. "These are all things we need to figure out."

"Is there time? Is the volcano really going to blow?"

Tucker gives her hand a squeeze. "I need you to be calm. Can you do that?"

She withdraws her hand and twists the ring around her thumb a half a dozen times before nodding.

"You can come with Rachael and me. We're heading back to Mammoth in a few minutes."

"What about my job? Who's going to look after the guests?"

"Have Jenny cover for you. She'll need to wait for her husband before she can leave."

"Is Mammoth safe?"

He hesitates, trying to strike the right balance for his answer. "No, I don't believe it will be. But we'll be able to head north from there. Up into Montana and hopefully into Canada."

"But Mammoth is over fifty miles away."

"Everything within a sixty-mile radius could very well be vaporized by pyroclastic flows. I'm going to talk to my family. Gather what you want to take with you. We won't have time to go back to your cabin."

Tucker turns and ducks into the private office. Matt is sitting in a chair, his lower leg wrapped with bandages. Tucker waves Jess forward and they huddle around Matt's chair while Tucker tells them of the upcoming evacuation order.

"We're not leaving without you, little brother," Matt says.

"You don't have a choice, Matt. You need to be on the road right now."

Jess rests a hand on Tucker's shoulder. "I agree with your brother. There's no way we could go home to face your parents knowing we left you here. Not going to happen."

Tucker stifles the scream he wants to unleash and sighs. "Then head north up to my office at Mammoth. We'll leave from there. But I want you to go straight to your car and start driving."

"What about our stuff?" Matt asks.

"Is there anything in your room you can't replace?"

Matt thinks for a moment. "Just the kids' iPads and my computer."

"Grab them, then go." Tucker gives Matt and Jess a hug and walks over to the children to do the same. He kneels down to give Maddie a hug.

"Uncle Tucker, are we going to see the bears now?" Maddie asks.

"No, but we might later. Right now you're going to head up to my office with your mom and dad. Okay?"

"Are there bears up there?"

"Yep, big growly bears." Tucker hugs Maddie again and stands, ruffling Mason's hair on his way out.

Rachael bursts through the door, her face pinched with concern. She steps up close to Tucker and lowers her voice. "The gas readings are off the chart. Both carbon dioxide and radon are well past established norms. The amount of helium-4 being released is staggering. And that's gas from way deep in the earth. I don't have the instruments to measure the sulfur dioxide levels but the sulfur odor around the geyser area is suffocating."

"You think magma is rising?"

"Yes, and I believe the amount of gas still in the magma chamber could produce an explosion larger—"

The ground underfoot begins to oscillate and shake, and they reach for the wall. A loud crash sounds as the flooring of the Old Faithful Inn bucks and tremors. They turn and hurry into the lobby, where they see the last of stones from the massive fireplace cascading down. The pile of boulders reaches nearly halfway to the ceiling as the accumulated dust of 110 years hovers, obscuring most of the lobby.

"Thank God we evacuated the lobby," Rachael says.

Tucker ignores her remark as he tries to peer through the dust toward the geyser basin. What he sees makes his blood run cold. Jets of scorching water are shooting skyward from too many locations to count.

Rachael follows his line of sight and gasps. "There aren't that many hydrothermal vents."

"There are now. That evacuation order needs to go out right damn now."

CHAPTER 25

Presidential Chief of Staff Ethan Granger meets up with the President near the entrance to the Situation Room and hands her a slip of paper. "Latest poll numbers on gay marriage. Looks like the public is coming around to our side."

As a gay man in a committed relationship with an attorney at a prestigious Washington firm, Ethan tries to walk a fine line on the issue, without being overbearing.

President Saundra Drummond looks over the numbers. "As well they should. It's about damn time we stopped this nonsense. We need to put this issue behind us and move forward on more pressing matters." The President hands back the paper and steps into the Situation Room. The group of military men, adorned with enough ribbons and stars to decorate a Fourth of July parade, stand, along with a handful of people in civilian dress, including Defense Secretary Lauren Petit.

"Madam President," they mutter in unison.

President Drummond pulls out one of the dark,

high-back leather chairs. "Sit, please." Those present return to their seats as President Drummond sits. "Any reason we couldn't have done this in the Oval?" At sixty-two, Saundra Drummond could be mistaken for just another grandmother if she was seen strolling through a city park. But that was before she was elected as the first female president of the most powerful country in the world. With coiffed gray hair and a life-time of living clinging a little too heavily to her medium-sized frame, she's been described as *frumpy* by some members of the press corps. Outward appear-ances aside, Saundra Drummond graduated first in her class at Yale Law and has the reputation as one of the brightest intellects ever elected to Congress.

"Yes, ma'am. We wanted to videoconference in one of our commanders," the chairman of the Joint Chiefs, General Jose Cardenas, answers. A fourth-generation Hispanic whose ancestors emigrated from central Mex-ico, Jose Cardenas is a small, compact man with dark hair, intelligent eyes, and a hot temper. "And we'd very much like to keep this situation close to the vest."

"What exactly is *the* situation, General?"

"The possible eruption of the Yellowstone Caldera."

"You're kidding, right?"

"No, ma'am." General Cardenas nods toward the large screen on the front wall. "On the video screen is General Bruce Truelove, commander of the Air Force's Global Strike Command at Barksdale."

"Good morning," President Drummond says. "Thank you for joining us.

General Cardenas nods toward one of his staffers who passes papers around the table. "Madam President, an eruption of the Yellowstone Caldera would be devastating on many levels, but this morning we're focusing on national security. If you'll look at the first page of the briefing notes, you'll see a map with the precise locations of our four hundred fifty Minuteman III intercontinental ballistic missiles. As you can see, the missile batteries are spread over a four-state area: Montana, North Dakota, Wyoming, and a small portion of northern Colorado." General Cardenas pauses to allow everyone time to absorb the material. "Now, if you'll flip to the next page."

A series of gasps erupts around the table.

"My God," the President mutters.

General Cardenas continues. "This map displays potential ash—"

"Wait, General," President Drummond says, holding up a hand. "If this thing erupts, I'm going to have a hell of a lot more on my plate than a bunch of missiles." She grabs a pen and begins to furiously scribble on a yellow legal pad. When she's finished she rips out the page and hands it to Granger. "I want these people in my office, and I want them there now."

Ethan nods, takes the paper, and slips out of the room as President Drummond turns back to the table. "Cut to the chase, General Cardenas."

"An eruption could severely hamper our ability to launch those four hundred fifty nuclear warheads."

President Drummond pushes to her feet. "General, the brightest minds in the military are in this room and on that screen," she says, pointing toward the front of the room. "Come up with a plan. There's a hell of a lot more to this than a bunch of missiles that have been in the ground for over forty years."

Secretary of Defense Lauren Petit bristles at her disdain. "President Drummond, these missiles are a very important part of our nuclear arsenal. We can't just close up shop."

"I'm not suggesting that, Lauren. What I want is a plan. I don't need to sit here and hold your hand while you argue over viable alternatives."

A National Security Agency aide enters, temporarily ending the standoff. She walks forward and hands a slip of paper to President Drummond, who reads through it before glancing up. "Yellowstone National Park is being evacuated."

CHAPTER 26

The radio screwed to the ceiling of the truck cab squawks. Eldon Harjo reaches over to lower the volume of the FM radio, and Merle Haggard fades away as the dispatcher says, "Eldon, what's your twenty?"

Eldon Harjo snatches up the grimy handset. "Just finished dumping a load. Why?"

"I need you to pick up a load of water and take it out to the Cundiff well site. They're gearing up to frack."

Eldon's gut clenches. "They're going to frack another one?"

The dispatcher, and wife to the trucking company owner, Sueann, barks out a hacking laugh. "Ain't it great? I've got enough orders to last till Christmas. Gotta make hay while the makin's good."

Eldon shifts to a higher gear and gooses the gas pedal before keying his mic. "Sueann, you ever wonder what all this stuff is doing to the land?"

"Hell, no. I just carry them big oil company checks to the bank. Don't you be gettin' all Injun on me, Eldon. Get the water and get it out there."

Eldon sighs, thinking about all the bills stacked up on his kitchen counter. "Ten-four. I'm on my way." He snaps the handset back into the cradle as his gut continues to churn. A few minutes later he pulls into the water filling station and climbs from the truck. He hooks up the hoses and begins to fill the tanker with 8,000 gallons of fresh water. Two more trucks turn into the lot and pull up behind his rig—just the beginning of the procession to haul more than 4 million gallons of water to the well site.

Eldon stretches out his tight back as the water streams into the tanker at 800 gallons per minute. After a little more than ten minutes, he unclamps the hose and climbs back into the cab. Before he can put the truck in gear another earthquake hits, swaying the cab in a slight left-to-right motion. He mutters more curses and eases off the clutch. With the added weight of 66,000 pounds, he starts in low and is already into sixth gear when he pulls back onto the road.

After driving several miles, Eldon shifts down and turns off onto a dusty stretch of road lined on both sides by cattle pastures. The wind is up and the tall grass sways, dancing to the ebb and flow of the breeze. In the distance toward the west, the sagebrush-littered foothills of the Rattlesnake Mountains stand proud in the midmorning sun. Eldon feels a stirring of nostalgia that moistens his eyes. This is the land of his ancestors—home to the Shoshone for centuries. He ponders, again, the destruction caused by less than seventy years of drilling activity.

He snaps on his left blinker and turns onto another dirt track that leads to the drilling pad. He pulls up behind another water truck and parks. "Best thing that could happen to this earth is for that volcano to blow," he mutters as he climbs from the cab.

Eldon walks toward the crowded space around the wellhead. A dozen pump trucks are backed into a circle, and a massive tangle of piping snakes toward the Christmas tree, where fracking fluid will be forced into the well at pressures beyond 10,000 PSI. Farther out sit dozens of trailers, sand trucks, chemical pumpers, and tank batteries—all necessary components for hydraulic well fracturing.

Eldon turns away and heads toward the stingy shade produced by one of the trucks, well away from all the noise. He squats down on his haunches and shakes a cigarette loose from a crumpled pack before tucking it into the corner of his mouth. Another water hauler walks over, and Eldon offers him a smoke. He pulls a lighter from his pocket and lights both. "When they going to start?"

"Pretty quick, I think," the man says as smoke curls from his nostrils. He cocks his head to one side. "Eldon, you hear that?"

Eldon cups a hand around his ear as his eyebrows arch with surprise. "Sounds like a siren."

Camp 4—Pensacola, Florida

Interview: Bud from Billings, MT—oil rig operator

"We weren't at the park, but I've been there a bunch of times. We were working a rig out in the Powder River Basin. We were in the process of fracking a horizontal well when the home office called. We were told to evacuate the area. Hell, we left millions of dollars in equipment on the pad. But I'm glad we left when we did, I'll tell you that. I tried to get back to Billings but couldn't. I made it to Riverton, where I stayed until the National Guard evacuated us. But if we'd have stayed much longer, there's no way we would have gotten out. I don't know how many oil field hands didn't make it out in time, but I bet there's a bunch."

CHAPTER 27

Tucker rolls down the truck window and floats his hand in the breeze, and the atmosphere in the pickup remains somewhere between frosty and ice cold. April drew the short straw, sitting in the middle, while Rachael rides shotgun. They are ten miles south of Mammoth Hot Springs when the sirens go off. Tucker twists on the radio and the annoying tone from the Emergency Alert System blasts through the speakers, followed by an ear-shattering hiss of static.

"The National Park Service has issued an evacuation order for Yellowstone National Park. All park guests are advised to assemble their belongings and begin an orderly evacuation of the park. Park Service rangers will be available in all camp areas to provide evacuation information. Repeating . . . The National Park Service . . ."

Tucker turns off the radio. "Damn, I hope we beat the onslaught." With the windows down, the pungent, piney scent from the lodgepole pines is heavy in the air.

Rachael tugs a strand of hair from her mouth. "We're only ten miles away. How bad could it be?"

Tucker shrugs and mashes the gas pedal a little closer to the floor, going much faster on the narrow road than the posted speed limit of 45 miles per hour. As they wind around one of the many curves along Grand Loop Road, all three scream as Tucker locks his legs on the brakes. Tires squeal and white smoke billows from beneath the truck as he steers off the road to avoid a herd of bison crossing the road, racing toward the west.

Tucker throws the truck into park and takes a deep breath.

"Think they sense something?" April asks.

"I wouldn't be surprised," Tucker says. "They're pretty attuned to their surroundings."

"Remember all the birds that flew away before that tsunami hit Thailand?" April asks.

"I don't want to think about it," Tucker says, dropping the truck into gear. After the last of the calves cross, he steers the pickup back onto the tarmac and keeps his speed closer to the legal limit. After another couple of miles, they crest a hill to see mayhem laid out before them. The entrance to Indian Creek campground is a tangle of vehicles, with a travel trailer lying sideways across Grand Loop Road. Angry tourists are arguing and jabbing fingers at one another while horns blare in a dozen vehicles trying to get onto the main road.

Tucker eases off the gas and hits the brake, bringing the pickup to a slow crawl. "We're screwed."

"Well, just as I predicted, the plan lasted all of a few seconds," Rachael says in an I-told-you-so voice.

Tucker shoots her an angry glance. "So we shouldn't have issued an evacuation order?"

Rachael throws up her hands. "Maybe we should have done it by sections."

"Oh, so some of the tourists were supposed to just lounge around at their campsites while other sections of the park are evacuating? That would never work. Once word of the evacuation hit, it's every man for himself."

April watches the exchange as if watching a tennis match. "I think it's a little late for this debate."

"How are we going to get through that mess?" Rachael asks.

"We're not going to stop and help them?" April asks.

"No," both Tucker and Rachael say in unison.

Tucker reaches down to flip on the four-wheel drive. "There's a fire trail up ahead if we can get through the brush. We'll have to go all the way around Indian Creek, but it's our only option." Tucker cranks the wheel over and eases down the road bank. They bounce over a couple of deadfall trees as he steers around and through the thick brush. He glances in the rearview mirror to see a string of vehicles following. "We have company."

Both women turn to look behind them.

"They won't have a prayer of making it if they don't have four-wheel drive." No sooner is the statement out of his mouth when one of the cars hits high center on one of the deadfall trees. "What makes that guy think he can drive a car through here?"

"They're desperate, Tucker," Rachael says. "Desperate people do desperate things."

"Well, that desperation could well cost them their lives."

"We have to stop and help them, Tucker," April says. "We can't just leave them stuck."

Tucker slows to steer around an outcropping of rock. "We don't have time to stop and help everyone, April. Our job is to monitor the caldera."

"But if those people can't get unstuck they won't stand a chance."

Rachael gives April an angry scowl. "We'll be happy to stop and let you out if you're so determined to help."

"Screw you, Rachael. How long could it take? A few minutes?"

Rachael grabs the door handle. "Seriously, Tucker, stop and I'll let her out."

April balls her fists. "Why are you always such a bitch, Rachael? How about a little human compassion? Do you know what that—"

"Enough!" Tucker shouts. "We're not stopping. End of story." He hits a clearing and mashes on the gas pedal.

"Besides, it really doesn't matter," Rachael says. "Whether stuck on a tree or stuck in traffic, it's all moot if the caldera erupts."

CHAPTER 28

Seattle-Tacoma International Airport

Captain Neil Lockhart and Co-captain Victoria Delgado fire up the engines of the 737 as the tug pushes them away from the terminal. Lockhart toggles the radio to tell the ground crew of the good engine start and waits for the tug operator to disconnect both the tug and the ground headset. He reaches down to the radio panel and dials in a frequency "Sea-Tac ground control, Affordable Air Flight 2136 is ready for taxi."

"Immediate standby, AA 2136. Repeat, standby, please."

"Roger," Lockhart says, and turns to his copilot. "Have we ever been issued an immediate standby for taxi?"

Delgado shrugs. "Not that I can recall."

Lockhart crosses his beefy arms and stares out the windscreen. His wait is not long.

"SeaTac ground control to all aircraft. The Yellowstone Volcano Observatory has increased the aircraft volcanic activity alert to orange."

The two pilots turn to each other in surprise.

SeaTac ground control continues: "The threat level was increased due to escalating unrest at the caldera. Please adjust your flight plans accordingly. SeaTac flight control will provide updates as the situation warrants. I repeat, the volcanic activity alert is now level orange."

"That's smack in the middle of our flight path," Delgado says.

Lockhart calls up their flight plan on the flight management computer. "We'll just steer around that area when we get closer. Hell, the threat level could remain at orange for weeks on end."

"I'd feel better if we skirted the entire area."

"And end up with another late flight? No, thank you. I've been reamed out enough over departure and arrival times. We'll just keep our eyes open when we get there."

Delgado shoots him an angry glare. "Damn it, Neil, why don't we just divert around the area?"

Lockhart laughs. "What are the odds the damn thing's going to erupt? A million to one? A billion to one? We'll be in and out of that area in a few short minutes. The odds for an eruption during that narrow time frame is probably closer to a trillion to one. I like my odds." He turns away from her when the radio clicks.

"SeaTac ground control to AA Flight 2136. You are cleared to taxi."

"Roger, SeaTac ground control. AA 2136 is taxiing." Lockhart eases the two throttles forward and releases his feet from the brakes. "Ease up, Tory." Lockhart begins to sing. "Everything's goin' to be all right, all right . . ."

Delgado shoots him the finger, and he laughs as he

steers the jet down the centerline of the taxiway. They make two right turns, and as they reach the runway, he gooses the throttles to max thrust. "Everything's goin' to be all right," he sings as the jet gains speed. When their airspeed indicator reaches 140 knots, he pulls back on the wheel and the nose of the jet lifts toward the sky. "Yeah, everything's all right . . ."

Camp 46—Columbus, Georgia

Interview: William from Winfield, KS—chemical engineer

"We've been to Yellowstone a couple of times. Both of our children are outdoorsy types who enjoy scouting. We flew into Salt Lake City, rented a car, and purchased a cheap tent and a couple of budget sleeping bags. Usually we'll camp for three or four days and then move into the Old Faithful Inn for the last couple of days. My wife tolerates the outdoors but she has about a three-day limit. But all hell broke loose and we left early. Took us twelve hours to get back to Salt Lake City. We were boarding the plane when we got pulled off. They grounded all flights out of Salt Lake. The days at the airport were miserable, but I'll tell you, I'm glad that plane didn't take off."

CHAPTER 29

The Oval Office

President Drummond ducks through the study and enters the Oval through the back door and discovers a standing-room-only crowd. The murmur of voices ends abruptly. "This is not going to work," she says, turning to her chief of staff. "Ethan, shoo everyone into the Cabinet Room."

After making a quick pit stop in her private restroom, President Drummond enters the Cabinet Room. A large oval mahogany table is positioned in the middle of the room, surrounded by twenty tan leather chairs accented with nail-head trim. She navigates toward her chair, the tallest of the twenty, and sits. Tacked to the back of the chair is a small brass plate with her title along with the date of her inauguration. A few of the seats at the table remain unoccupied, awaiting their rightful owners as more people stream into the room, choosing seats in the extra chairs lining the perimeter of the room. She turns to Ethan, who's sitting to her immediate left. "Where's Ag, Commerce, Treasury and Interior?"

"The secretary of agriculture is on the way but tied up in traffic, and both the SECCOM and the SEC-TREAS are traveling out of the country. Interior Secretary Fitch happens to be on the ground in Wyoming, not far from Yellowstone."

"Set them up on conference calls. We're going to need all hands on deck."

Ethan nods and waves over a White House aide. He whispers his instructions and the aide quickly departs to set up the calls.

President Drummond swivels her gaze around the table and shrugs. "I don't even know where to begin. Who's the volcano expert?"

A bald, thin man stands meekly from his chair. "Madam President, I'm Hayden Fulton, an assistant secretary of the interior with direct oversight of the National Park Service."

President Drummond waves to one of the vacant chairs. "That buys you a seat at the table, Mr. Fulton. Please come sit."

The man moves toward the table, then stops. "Ma'am, accompanying me is Assistant Secretary Claire Espinoza. Her department includes the U.S. Geological Survey, which encompasses the five volcano observatories."

"Oh, that buys Ms. Espinoza a *prime* seat at the table."

An attractive Hispanic female stands and approaches the table. A little over five-six, she has long black hair and skin the color of raw teakwood. She places a large binder on the table and pulls out a chair. The sunlight streaming through the four pairs of French doors leading to the Rose Garden paint long shadows across the table.

Once everyone is resituated, President Drummond

turns to her new guests. "I wish we had time for introductions, but we don't. You know who I am, but I'd like a couple of sentences about your backgrounds for my own reference. Ms. Espinoza?"

"Madam President, I have a Ph.D. in geochemistry with an emphasis on crustal deformation. I have spent fifteen years with the USGS studying both fault-related and volcanic-related ground deformation all over the country, including Yellowstone."

"Thank you, Dr. Espinoza. You're not leaving my sight for as long as this crisis continues. Is that amenable to you?"

Espinoza nods. "Yes, ma'am. But I didn't bring anything with me."

"Make a list. The Secret Service will round up whatever you need. What I know about volcanoes wouldn't fill a thimble." President Drummond turns to the other new guest at the table. "Mr. Fulton?"

"Yes, ma'am. I have a Ph.D. in fish and wildlife biology. I served at various levels throughout the National Park Service, including both at Yosemite and Yellowstone until Secretary Babcock asked me to move up to assistant secretary."

"Thank you, Dr. Fulton. I want you hanging close, too. Now, tell us what's going on right now at Yellowstone."

"With your permission, ma'am, we'd like to conference in Dr. Jeremy Lyndsey, the scientist-in-charge at the Yellowstone Volcano Observatory."

President Drummond leans forward in her chair. "Dr. Fulton, I don't care if you conference in Jesus Christ, but whoever it is, I need answers and I need them yesterday."

CHAPTER 30

Yellowstone park headquarters

Park Superintendent Barlow pushes wearily out of his chair and heads down the hall of the headquarters building, barking orders. Before now, the most serious things he's had to deal with since taking over the job have been the past earthquakes and an occasional bear raid on a campsite.

"Ralph," his secretary, Melanie, shouts down the hall. "The governor is on line one."

Barlow sighs, steps over to the closest phone, and snatches up the handset. "Governor, I'm ass deep in more problems than I can handle."

"Do you think we should evacuate the entire state?" Governor Abe Cullen asks.

"Hell, we can't even get the park evacuated. Traffic is at a standstill at every road crossing and about half the guests at the hotels and cabins have no transportation. Can you send the National Guard our way to help transport people?"

"I don't know, Ralph. If we evacuate the state, they're going to be needed everywhere."

Barlow pinches the bridge of his nose and looks up at the ceiling. "Abe, I've got over thirty thousand people in the park. And every damn one of them is facing certain death if the caldera erupts. Those residents outside the park have a chance of surviving an eruption if they can get underground."

"Ralph, a majority of the guard's equipment is here in Cheyenne. Even if I could mobilize some units, you're looking at eight to twelve hours for them to reach the park. I could request help from the Montana National Guard, but they're still several hours away if they depart out of Helena. How much time do we have?"

"I don't know. Hell, I don't think anyone knows. Our chief geologist, Tucker Mayfield, thinks an eruption could occur at any time."

"What other options do you have?"

"I'm trying to get some buses rolling this way, but the companies are balking. They're worried about future litigation when they might well be out of business forever."

"Have your secretary e-mail me the information. I'll work on getting you some buses. I'll also deploy some National Guard troops your way, but it might be a day or two before they get up there. In the meantime, keep me updated on what's happening up there."

"I will, Abe." Barlow replaces the handset and returns to his office, where he studies a large park map pinned to the wall. The map details the wildly varied topography as well as all the hiking trails, fire roads, and access roads through and around the park. He becomes more dejected the more he studies it. Although the landscape makes for a beautiful setting, it's hell to get around. Other than the main paved roads bisecting the park, other options of escape are nonexistent. There are too many creeks and rivers and too many impassible mountains.

The radio at the corner of his desk squelches. "Tucker to Ralph. You on the radio?"

Ralph picks up the radio. "Go, Tucker."

"Switch over to channel two-three," Tucker says.

Ralph looks over the radio controls. "Tucker, I don't see—" He stops in midsentence as his brain clicks into gear. With only six radio channels available, two-three could only be on thing—five. He turns the dial. "Tucker, you on this channel?"

"Ten-four. I didn't know if you'd figure out my code, but I didn't want to talk over an open channel."

"Where are you and why all the spy craft?"

"We're on a fire road trying to skirt around Indian Creek. At this rate, it might be a while before we get back to Mammoth. I just received an alarming call from one of the rangers. He was scouting around an area between Norris and Canyon Village when he stumbled upon a large ground fracture. He seems to think it's relatively recent."

"How recent?" Barlow asks.

"Within the last couple of days. He told me it wasn't there the last time he was up that way a week ago."

"How large?"

"Thirty to forty feet long and a couple of feet wide. No idea how deep it is. He says he can't see the bottom," Tucker says.

"What do you think it is?"

"I don't know his exact coordinates but the rim of the caldera runs right through that area."

"Meaning what?"

"Could be a potential vent opening."

"A vent for what?" Ralph asks.

"A vent that could be hundreds of feet—or only a few feet—from the magma chamber."

"I thought most of the activity has been centered around the Lower Geyser area."

"Ralph, the caldera covers over twelve hundred square miles. An eruption, or many eruptions, could happen anywhere within that span. And where the eruption originates is meaningless."

Camp 16—Biloxi, Mississippi

Interview: Fred from Fort Collins, CO—retired

"Hell, I always said I'd rather die than go to an old folks' home, but that's looking pretty good from where I'm sitting now. People every damn where you turn. Yes, I was at Yellowstone. About my damn luck, too. Took my little travel trailer up there for a little R and R. Don't know why, either. Place is packed in the summertime. Nancy had been ragging my ass to take her somewhere. Told her you could see the same damn landscape by looking out the windows. A mountain's a mountain, right? But no, we had to go somewhere. We arrived about the time the shit hit the fan."

CHAPTER 31

Assistant Secretary of the Interior Hayden Fulton squirms in his chair. "Madam President, before we begin the teleconference, I'd like to update you on what has already occurred. I've just received word that there have already been numerous deaths within the park this morning. A medical helicopter crashed on takeoff, killing all seven passengers aboard, and a hydrothermal explosion around the Grand Prismatic Spring area killed fifteen and severely injured forty more."

President Drummond's eyes widen. "Were these events volcano related?"

"We believe they are, ma'am. Dr. Jeremy Lyndsey will hopefully provide more answers."

Espinoza leans in and speaks into one of the triangular-shaped speakers scattered around the table's surface. "Jeremy, you are on speaker in the White House Cabinet Room with President Drummond in attendance."

"Good morning, Madam President." The sound from the speaker is clear, but there are hints of nervousness in Jeremy's voice.

President Drummond leans forward in her chair. "I've had better mornings, Dr. Lyndsey. I'll get straight to the point—is the Yellowstone volcano on the verge of eruption?"

There's a brief pause on the other end. "I know this is not the answer you want to hear, Madam President, but we just don't know. Something is going on with the caldera. As Dr. Fulton told you, there have been several hydrothermal explosions this morning and recent gas readings suggest the magma may be moving toward the surface. We believe an eruption might occur."

The President drums her fingers on the table. "Why all this supposition, Dr. Lyndsey? Are you telling me with all the technology available today we can't predict a volcanic eruption?"

"All we have to rely on is the data from the various instruments arrayed around the park. We can study the known trigger events such as earthquakes, ground deformation, or a change in the hydrothermal systems, but what we can't do is predict exactly when, or even if, the caldera will erupt."

President Drummond sags against her chair. "Give me a percentage, Dr. Lyndsey."

"There's a hundred percent chance the caldera will erupt. But it could be today, next week, or ten thousand years from now. I'm not trying to be snide, ma'am, but the caldera is always restless. This morning's unusual activity might be enough to relieve some of the stresses present, but they could just as well be precursors to a much larger event."

The President pushes out of her chair and stiffens her arms against the table. "Dr. Lyndsey, I need concrete answers. The people of this country are relying on me to make the difficult decisions, but I can't do that based on conjecture or guesswork."

Claire Espinoza steps into the fray. "Madam President, we can't provide concrete answers. We've ordered an evacuation of the park on the presumption of an eruption."

President Drummond throws her hands in the air. "Okay, we've established an eruption might happen, for whatever that's worth. What are the consequences if it does?"

The question is met with silence. "That bad, huh? Dr. Lyndsey, enlighten us, please."

"It will be a catastrophic event." The sounds of typing on keyboard can be heard over the speaker. "I'm e-mailing Claire, I mean Dr. Espinoza, a copy of a computer simulation we ran recently on ash fall estimates." A whoosh of a sent e-mail sounds. "Dr. Espinoza, it should be in your in-box."

President Drummond sits. "Dr. Lyndsey, we'll get to your ash fall estimates, but walk me through what else could happen."

"I think most of us are old enough to remember the Mount St. Helens eruption back in 1980. That eruption ejected a little more than one half of a cubic mile of material. An eruption at Yellowstone will be a thousand times larger. We estimate there could be as much as 250 cubic miles of magma, which translates to nearly three and a half trillion tons of ash. The pyroclastic flows, moving at hurricane speeds, will spread in every direction for many miles, incinerating everything in their path. Ash, and a mix of acids, will be thrust into the stratosphere, where it will drift around the world for years, dropping global temperatures by as much as ten degrees. Here at home, the ash could well wipe out a good portion of the Midwest for many years."

President Drummond leans forward. "Dr. Lyndsey, is ash that much different than, say, a heavy snowfall?"

"Volcanic ash is much, much different. It's very dense and contains pulverized rock, minerals, and volcanic glass that will collapse roofs and structures throughout the central portion of the country. The ash is also hard and very abrasive and doesn't dissolve in water. Rivers, ponds, and city reservoirs will be contaminated, and the ash will clog most of the water-pumping systems. But one of its most devastating aspects is that volcanic ash conducts electricity when wet. Power grids across large portions of the country will be crippled. Madam President, volcanic ash is nasty stuff, and I haven't even broached the effects ash will have on agriculture, air travel, or the other chemical compounds associated with an eruption that will wreck havoc on our planet."

President Drummond leans back, stunned. After a moment of silence, she asks, "You mentioned agriculture, Dr. Lyndsey. What effects will an eruption have on that?"

"You would have to speak with someone in Agriculture for specifics. But, this time of the year, most crops are in the ground, with the exception of the winter wheat. Ash is very acidic, and, with as little as three inches on the ground, the soil will be sterilized, killing any crops planted and preventing future replanting for some time. If you'll look over the ash fall estimates I sent Dr. Espinoza, you will see that the Midwest area, the largest crop producers in the country, will be buried under large quantities of volcanic ash. The computer simulation suggested ash as deep as forty inches over most of the Midwest. Under those conditions, the land will be unfarmable for many generations. That area of the country produces most all of our wheat, corn, soybeans, and other grains. In addition, livestock will die by the millions, further reducing food supply, and"— Dr. Lyndsey pauses for a moment, then lowers his voice—"people will die by the tens of thousands in the immediate aftermath of an eruption. Not only from the ash, but from famine and disease. And the damage won't be confined only to the United States. As I mentioned previously, a Yellowstone eruption could drop the global temperatures enough to eliminate growing seasons all across the planet. If that occurs, we'd be looking at death tolls in the millions, perhaps the tens of millions."

CHAPTER 32

Old Faithful Inn

Park Ranger Walt Stringer removes his hat and carefully blots the sweat from his blistered face. The Old Faithful Inn area is now what his old army sergeant used to call a clusterfuck. He's been cussed out, cussed at, belittled, and berated since the sirens sounded. His patience is running thin and any desire to help the park guests is now leaching away. He slips away from the crowd and hunkers beneath the shade of a young pine tree for a brief respite.

The guests with vehicles sit idling in a long line, waiting for an overturned RV to be cleared from the bottleneck at the entrance to the inn. What they don't know is that the RV is not getting cleared anytime soon. People are fighting mad. Horns blare and curses are exchanged, and it sounds more like a gang fight than a national park.

Not to mention the panic for those guests left stranded with no means of transportation. Not everyone drives to Yellowstone. A large number of people fly into Jackson or some other nearby airport and take a shuttle to their accommodations. But with the heavy outflow of traffic, none of the shuttles are making any headway into the park. Inside, the stranded are taking out their frustrations on the workers behind the registration desk, hurling verbal abuse that rains down like body blows. Walt tried to put an end to it but, short of shooting someone, it's a losing battle. Hence, his trip outside.

A larger group of stranded people are milling around outside, growing angrier as the tension and uncertainty mounts. Unfounded rumors run through the group like a bad case of the runs, and several people are weeping uncontrollably. Walt glances up to see a group of angry tourists striding toward him. He sighs and pushes to his feet.

"How are we getting out of here?" an older, overweight woman asks.

Walt waves to the line of cars. "It doesn't look like anyone's leaving at the moment. But the staff is trying to organize a convoy of buses to transport those guests without transportation."

The woman points angrily at the bottleneck. "How the hell are buses supposed to get through that?"

Walt shuffles backward a couple of steps. "Ma'am, we're doing the best we can under the circumstances."

"Well, that's not good enough. What if that volcano blows while we're still here?"

The events of the morning have sapped all of Walt's goodwill. "Well, ma'am, that'll be one thing you won't need to worry about. If the caldera erupts, me, you, and everyone else around here will be vaporized."

The woman claps both pudgy hands over her mouth.

"Now, if you'll excuse me, I'll go on about my business." Walt sidesteps the woman, but before he can take more than two steps, the ground lurches beneath his feet. The lurch transitions to a violent shaking and, within seconds, what remains of the inn's covered porch splinters and crashes to the ground.

Another loud crack splits the air and the center portion of the parking lot heaves upward, overturning a line of occupied cars. Walt grabs on to a tree for support as the screams from those in the cars reaches a crescendo. Within seconds, the screams are drowned out by a sudden torrent of water that erupts at a spot between the loop trail and the inn. Rocks and debris are launched hundreds of feet into the air, and the roar of water is as loud as a jet engine. The rubble begins to fall, pelting people and vehicles in a hailstorm of debris.

Walt covers his head with his hands and races for shelter at the side of the building. Rocks the size of bowling balls crash to the ground around him. Something slams into Walt's head and he staggers, nearly falling, before regaining his balance. He makes the side of the building as a warm rivulet of liquid slides beneath his collar and drifts down his back. He probes the area gently and his hand comes away bloody. After walking his fingers through his hair, he discovers a large knot and what feels like a deep laceration. A slight concussion, maybe, but with no loss of consciousness he's not overly concerned. And he's less concerned about the cut, knowing scalp lacerations are notorious for bleeding profusely. He rips off a portion of his torn sleeve and wraps it around his head. Up next to the building, the noise level diminishes to dull roar, allowing him to hear the radio.

"Repeating . . . Tucker Mayfield to Walt Stringer. Over."

Walt slips the radio from his belt and puts the handset close to his mouth. "Tucker, this is Walt. We just experienced the strongest earthquake I've ever felt."

"Stronger than the others this morning?"

"Ten-four. Much stronger. And a geyser opened up between the loop trail and the inn, shooting rocks as big as cars into the air. It's a real mess down here, Doc."

His statement is met with silence. He clicks the radio. "Tucker, you still there?"

"Yes, I'm here. Walt, it could be only a matter of time before we have some type of eruption. Are you injured?"

"Just a few cuts and bruises. How much time?"

"Don't know, but you need to get the hell of there."

"Can't. Too many people still here."

"You can. And I need you to. My brother and his family are somewhere on the road to Mammoth." Tucker pauses and the radio goes silent. Then, "Walt, I'm asking as a friend. Will you find my family and bring them north? I know what I'm asking is a tall task but you're the only one I trust to see it through. Plus you know this park like the back of your—"

"Tucker, the friendship goes both ways. I'll find your family and bring them north with me." Walt takes a moment to survey the devastation around him. "If you're a praying man, Tucker, you might put in a good word or two for us, just in case."

Camp 132—Millington, Tennessee

Interview: Lucy from Lubbock, TX—retail sales

"Orderly? No, I wouldn't use that word to describe the evacuation process. The poor rangers were doing the best they could, but there wasn't like a plan or anything. Which really seems odd, looking back on it. I mean, if one of the largest volcanoes on Earth is sitting under a good portion of the park, someone must have put some thought into a plan. Or maybe they had one and it went out the window when the panic set in. Who knows? Ever been to Yellowstone? Well, let me tell you, there are no superhighways through the park. Most are these windy two-lane roads with steep drop-offs. Even on a good day there's a pucker factor to it. And this was as far from a good day as you could get.

CHAPTER 33

Dr. Eric Snider stares at his computer screen as the webicorder displays a live stream from the seismometer located at Old Faithful. The squiggly peaks are much larger than any he's ever witnessed at Yellowstone. He grabs the telephone and punches in a number. The call is answered just as it begins to ring. "Emily, do you have a depth on this quake?" Emily is Emily West, the postdoctoral fellow in plate tectonics.

The sounds of hurried fingers on a keyboard, then, "It's shallow, Eric. Just a little over two kilometers."

"Shit. Any preliminary magnitude numbers?"

"High fives, maybe low sixes. Think it's magma movement?"

"I'd bet on it. Any signs of a harmonic tremor?"

"No. But I have some more distressing news."

"What could be more distressing than the possible eruption of one of the world's largest volcanoes?"

"How about the eruption of multiple volcanoes?"

Snider sits up straight. "Why? What the hell are you talking about?"

"Both the California and Cascades volcano observatories are reporting earthquake swarms. And, like Yellowstone, the earthquakes are increasing in intensity."

"Are you suggesting an eruption at Yellowstone could trigger eruptions in those areas?"

"Maybe. Stay with me for a minute. The magma under Yellowstone extends as far west as a hundred miles. Sixteen million years ago, the hot spot now under Yellowstone was located on the Oregon-Nevada border. The southwest movement of the North American Plate has skimmed over the hot spot, putting it at the current location. Some scientists theorize that the breakup of the Juan de Fuca Plate has created a cross-linked magma system that links Yellowstone's magma with the Pacific Northwest."

"But if that were true, wouldn't an eruption at Yellowstone alleviate the pressure, reducing the risks for eruption at those other locations?"

"Maybe. But an eruption at the park would be so violent that it might trigger other eruptions. The entire northwestern quadrant of the country is riddled with faults. It's not a stretch to believe that the activity happening at Yellowstone is somehow related to the earthquake swarms now occurring in Oregon and Washington. If you remember back to 2002, a large earthquake in Alaska triggered seismic activity at Yellowstone. And that's over two thousand miles away."

"Damn," Snider mutters. "You're talking Shasta, the Three Sisters, Rainier, Hood, and a dozen other volcanoes."

"Yep, it could create whole bevy of hell-on-earth

scenarios. But we're not there yet. How's the evacuation going?"

"About what you'd expect."

"Uncontrolled chaos?"

"You got it. I'm just hoping there's time to get it done. But it's not going to get any easier. The governors of Idaho, Wyoming, and Montana are in the process of deciding an evacuation radius for their states."

Emily clears her throat. "Are we safe here, Eric?"

"We'll be safe from any pyroclastic flows, but Salt Lake City will be buried in ash. And if your theory about the Cascades proves true, there won't be any safe places west of the Mississippi River. Yellowstone by itself will be a world changer, and I can't even imagine the scenarios if any of the other volcanoes erupt. Have you shared your theory with anyone else?"

"I just sent an e-mail to one of my mentors, Claire Espinoza. She's now one of the assistant secretaries over at the Interior Department."

"If you have her cell phone number, you should text her a heads-up about the e-mail. Anything we can do to mitigate the damage needs to start right now."

"Good idea—I'll do that. I'll keep you updated on what's happening in the Casca— Eric, are you looking at the GPS feeds?"

Snider scrambles to bring up the GPS feeds on his computer screen. "Damn. Is this data correct?"

"Yes, look at the timestamps. That's nearly two feet of uplift at Norris in the last two hours."

"And that's very near the epicenter of the big quake back in 1975." Snider takes a deep breath. "Emily, we might be close to witnessing an event no human has ever seen."

CHAPTER 34

Near the Gardiner River, Yellowstone National Park

Tucker eases the truck along the bank of the Gardiner River, looking for a place to cross. A little ways farther on, he finds what might be a promising location and puts the pickup in park. All three occupants pile out to stretch their legs.

"I need to find a tree or I'm going to pop," April says before turning and walking toward a nearby clump of lodgepole pine.

Rachael and Tucker climb down the riverbank in search of the shallowest section of water. Rachael nods toward the direction of April's retreat. "You and her have something going on?"

"April? Nah, just friends. I might ask the same question of you. You two have some sort of disagreement?"

"No. Well, maybe a little spat last summer. She's a little too blond for me. If you ask me, I think she's looking for more than friendship."

"I don't remember asking you," Tucker says with a tinge of anger in his words. "Nevertheless, she'll need to look elsewhere. Besides, who put you in charge of my social life?" Tucker walks toward a shallow portion of the river where the bison have carved a path down to the water.

Rachael follows. "That's the problem, Tucker, you don't have a social life. You live like a hermit. Hell, we've worked together for years and we've never been out for a beer."

Tucker whirls around. "We're facing a natural disaster of unimaginable scale and you want to talk about my love life?"

"I like to think I'm a fairly attractive person. And I've dropped plenty of hints over the years. Is it the color of my skin, Tucker?"

Tucker kicks a dirt clod into the river. "I think we can cross here. Might be a little dicey, but I think it's doable."

"You didn't answer my question."

Tucker sighs. "No, it has nothing to do with the color of your skin. My father is the biggest bigot that ever existed and I vowed to live my life differently. Your skin color, or anyone's skin color for that matter, doesn't make a damn bit of difference to me."

"So what is it, Tucker? Why live the way you do?"

Tucker's cheeks turn crimson. "I don't think that's any of your damn business." Tucker turns for the truck. "We need to go."

Rachael grabs his arm. "Is it something to do with your sister-in-law?"

Tucker turns, steps closer, and lowers his voice. "I said it's none of your damn business."

Rachael takes a step back. "It's something. There's an underlying tenseness when you two are together."

Rachael brushes past, walking toward the pickup. "But as you made clear, it's none of my business. It's your life."

"You're damn right it is," Tucker shouts after her. Tucker inhales a deep breath as he watches Rachael retreat. He releases the inhaled breath and takes a hard kick at a gopher mound, before starting for the truck.

All three climb back in, resuming the same seating arrangement. Rachael sighs, turns toward the passenger window, and focuses her stare on a far mountain. Tucker angrily spins the steering wheel and hits the gas, throwing up a whirlwind of dirt and grass.

April looks left, then right. "It's awful frosty in here. I don't know what's going on between you two, but now's not the time."

Tucker lines the truck up on the bison trail down to the river. "You've got that right, April." Tucker drops the shifter into low gear. "Everyone, hold on. If we stop, we're stuck." Tucker feeds more gas to the engine as they bounce down the bank and splash through the water. The truck is on the verge of stalling as they hit the opposite riverbank. Tucker mashes the gas and grunts as he works to maintain a firm grasp on the wheel. The path up is a meandering mess, and he spins the wheel, trying to stay in the ruts, as mud roostertails from all four wheels. The tires begin to spin and Tucker floors the gas. "Don't know if we're going to make it," he shouts over the screaming engine. But the tires find purchase and the old pickup rockets up the bank.

After dodging around another collection of deadfall trees, Tucker aims for a point west of Bunsen Peak.

They travel in silence for the next mile before picking up a dry wash that leads them to Glenn Creek. Tucker pulls the truck to a stop to search for another crossing. Before stepping out of the cab, he unclips the sat phone from his belt and hands it across to Rachael. "See if you can contact Eric to see what the latest is."

Rachael snatches the phone from his hand. "You're the boss."

Tucker sighs, lowers his head, and pushes out of the cab. Once Tucker is out of earshot April says, "What's up with you two?"

Rachael punches in a phone number. "Not a damn thing." She puts the phone to her ear and stares off in the distance as the phone rings. The call is answered on the fourth ring. She asks to speak with Dr. Eric Snider and is put on hold. "And that's the problem," she mutters as she waits.

"What's the problem?" April asks.

"Never— Hi, Eric, what's the latest?" She drums her fingers on the passenger door as she listens. But then she sits up straight in her seat. "Oh shit. Did you say two feet?" She listens for another moment, then says, "I'll call you back in a minute." She tosses the phone onto the dash and jumps from the truck, shouting for Tucker. "We need to move. An area just east of Norris is uplifted two feet."

Tucker races back to the truck and scoots behind the wheel. "Time frame?"

"Over the last three hours. And they registered a quake in the high fives only minutes ago."

Tucker drops the truck into gear and grabs for the radio handset. "Please get Eric back on the phone. We need minute-by-minute reports."

Rachael dials as all thoughts about the situation between her and Tucker fade into the background.

Tucker triggers the radio. "Tucker Mayfield for Walt Stringer."

After a delay of a couple of moments he hears, "Go, Tucker."

"Walt, find them and then get the hell out of the area as quickly as you can. We're running out of time."

CHAPTER 35

Eldon Harjo tries to signal the crew about the sirens, but he's ignored as they continue to make the final connections. Time is money, and the crew is hell-bent on fracking. A dozen switches are flipped and the high-pressure pumps roar to life. Eldon squishes a pair of foam earplugs and inserts them in his ears as he threads his way through the trucks, trailers, and multitude of containers all jammed tight as teeth around the wellhead. The expanding foam lessens the roar, but the vibrations from the massive machinery tremor up his legs. Eldon climbs up into the cab of his truck and cranks up the window.

What the oil company geologists don't know is that the morning's seismic activity has drastically altered the landscape two miles beneath the ground.

After shaking out a cigarette and lighting up, Eldon clicks on the dusty AM/FM radio. The local station isn't playing Merle Haggard or Johnny Paycheck. Instead Eldon catches the last bits of a verbal announcement. He twirls the dial and is surprised when he hears no music whatsoever. He dials to the other local station and catches more of the announcement: ". . . Park is being evacuated. Please follow park ranger directions for a safe and orderly evacuation process."

Eldon lowers the volume and digs his cell phone out of his pocket to discover six missed calls from home. With a trembling finger he punches a speed dial button and waits for the call to connect. The phone rings eight times before he hangs up. He punches another speed dial, his wife's cell phone.

Across the drilling pad, a worker gets the thumbs-up and begins to crank open one of the valves at the wellhead. At pressures beyond 10,000 PSI, the fracking fluid is injected down the borehole. The liquid, searching for the path of least resistance, blows through the now-fractured well casing. The jet of water and chemicals slams into a recently developed fault, launching a wave of seismic tremors toward Yellowstone. Then, in its relentless pursuit, the fracking fluid turns back toward the surface, blasting through the drill pad at an old surface fault covered over during recent dirt work to level the site. Those standing near are sliced in half as the water shoots skyward.

The cell phone slips from Eldon Harjo's hand when he catches sight of the horror unfolding before him. A scramble of people race to turn off the pumps as the jet of water grows in circumference, tossing rocks and debris like the shrapnel from an exploding bomb. Eldon struggles with the decision of what to do. He reaches for the door handle just as the plume of water dies and falls back to earth. He exhales with relief. But his relief is short-lived when the natural gas that had accumulated within the two miles of pipe breaks through the surface and ignites. The explosion overturns trucks, and the ball of fire incinerates everything in its path. Parked on the other side of the drilling pad, Eldon rams his truck in gear and tries to steer around the truck in front of him.

As the seismic waves slam into Yellowstone, and just as Eldon thinks he's in the clear, the fire ignites a diesel tanker parked along the road. As the fire burns through the cab of his truck, Eldon's mind flashes on Quincy's prophecy—*It's only a matter of time, Chief, until something up here . . .*

CHAPTER 36

Yellowstone park headquarters

Superintendent Barlow slams the phone down in disgust. Even with pressure from the governor of Wyoming, the bus companies continue to refuse his pleas for help, citing concern for their employees and possible legal implications. He pushes to his feet and racks his head back and forth to relieve the pain flaring in his neck. After several pops, he strides over to the map pinned to the wall. "There has to be some way to speed the evacuation process," he mutters as he concentrates on the limited number of escape routes. After studying the map for a few moments, he returns to his desk and picks up the handheld radio, only to find the battery dead. He curses, places the radio into a charger, and puts on his hat before exiting the office.

Several employees shout questions his way, but he waves them away as he strides down the hall, taking the stairs two at a time to the ground floor. He pushes through the back door of the building and hurries across the street to the communications building. Inside, he goes straight to the radio base station and picks up the microphone. With over two million acres of parkland, radio base stations and frequency repeaters are scattered throughout the park, allowing nearly 100 percent radio coverage.

He triggers the transmit button. "Attention, all park rangers and other park personnel. Please switch all radios to the tactical channel." He pauses for a couple of moments to allow everyone time to switch radio channels. "I don't have time to know who's on the radio and who's not, but we will use this channel going forward. I want all snow plows, dozers, and any other heavy equipment we have moving within the next five minutes. Any vehicles blocking access are to be pushed off the roadways, no questions asked. We don't have time to worry about personal property. For those people who don't have access to transportation, put them in a vehicle. Only those vehicles that are fully loaded will be allowed to proceed. We have no other options. Do your best to steer most of the traffic north or west. East and south will bear the brunt of the ash due to prevailing winds." Barlow pauses to catch his breath. "I can't predict when or if the caldera will erupt, but I'm asking for your help. I know you have concerns about your own well-being or that of family members, but the backbone of the National Park Service is built on our service to others. Godspeed." Barlow replaces the microphone and slowly turns for the door when he's halted by another voice over the radio.

"Superintendent Barlow, this is Air Ranger Susan Maxwell. I'm doing an overflight of the park and traffic is backed up in every direction. I'll be here to direct crews to critical locations."

Barlow picks up the handset. "Thank you. All crews—Ranger Maxwell is in charge of road clearance. Please follow her directions. Susan, I'd also request that you keep us informed of anything unusual you see from the air."

"Roger, sir. I'll keep you posted."

Barlow picks up an extra radio and makes his way outside, where he takes a moment to let the cool breeze drift across his face. After a brief moment of respite, he pulls out his cell phone and punches one of the speed dials.

"Hi, Dad," the voice says on the other end.

"Andy, I need you to grab Michelle and get out of Jackson."

"I'm just about to take a group down the river, Dad." Andy pauses. "Besides, Michelle and I are on the outs." Andy Barlow, a recent college graduate, is spending his last free summer guiding along the Snake River.

"I don't care what you're doing right now, Andy. I'm telling you to leave town. And if you ever want to see Michelle again, you'll take her with you."

"What the hell is going on?"

"We're evacuating the park. We think the caldera could be on the verge of eruption."

"What . . . how . . . could that be possible?"

"We knew it could be a possibility, son. Why now, I don't know.

"What about you and Mom?"

"When the time comes we'll scoot toward the northwest. But Jackson Hole could be in the direct path of a pyroclastic flow. It won't be long before the governor orders an evacuation for most of western Wyoming, but you need to get started out of town now. Once the evacuation order hits, there'll be chaos, just like what's happening up here."

"How far do we need to go, Dad?"

"Go until you can't go anymore. Get to the southern part of Nevada before you even think about stopping. I want you to call your mother on your way out of town. Will you do that for me?"

"How am I supposed to get in touch with you, after . . ."

"We'll figure it out, son. Electricity and communications will be spotty, but if you can get to your uncle Dave's place in Phoenix we'll have a starting point."

"Okay. I need to get Michelle moving. I love you, Dad."

Ralph smiles, thinking briefly about the fragility of young love. "I love you, too, son. Give Michelle a hug for me." He disconnects the call and stuffs the phone back in his pocket.

As he recrosses the street, he spots a mud-splattered pickup turning off Washtub Row. Hoping it's Tucker, he waits for the vehicle to arrive.

Chapter 37

After searching the area around the Old Faithful Inn for Tucker's family and not finding them, Walt Stringer hops on his four-wheeler. As he fires up the engine, heads turn. Several people begin moving his way. Walt gooses the throttle and steers around the people trying to flag him down. When he reaches the relative safety of the loop trail he cranks the throttle wide open, letting the cool rush of air rising off the Firehole River soothe his blistered face. He follows the trail until it dead-ends at the Morning Glory Pool, then diverts over to a fire road and follows that all the way to Biscuit Basin before turning into a well-concealed maintenance barn. He kills the four-wheeler and climbs down as one of the snowplows starts up, belching a stream of black smoke.

Walt climbs up on the plow's steps to talk to the driver. "What's going on?"

The driver takes one look at Walt and rears back. "What the hell happened to you?"

"Let's just say it's been a bad morning," Walt answers. "What's with all the heavy equipment?"

"The boss ordered us out to clear the roads. We're supposed to push any stalled or wrecked vehicles off the road." The man shrugs. "I'm sure the tourists are going to be thrilled to see their new travel trailers crumpled like a beer can."

"All that stuff's replaceable. But I'll grant you that some of those people will be downright pissed. Probably best if you don't even get out of the cab."

"I'm not planning on it. You heard any more about the volcano?"

Walt shakes his head. "Nothing recent. How bad are the roads?"

"Bad. Traffic's at a standstill."

Walt slaps the door. "I'll let you get to it, then." Walt steps down, hesitates, then climbs back up. "Hey, I'm looking for one family in particular." Walt describes the Mayfield family and provides a description of their vehicle. "Give me a shout on the radio if you run across them."

"Ten-four," the driver says.

Walt steps down and the driver eases off the clutch, creeping the old plow forward. Before he's gone too far, the driver shouts out the window, "Don't know if you heard, but all the radios are switched to the tactical channel."

Walt gives a thumbs-up and walks over to his pick-up parked in the dusty lot. He fiddles with the radio buttons on top of the device, then puts it to his lips. "Walt Stringer to Tucker Mayfield."

After a delay he hears, "Go, Walt."

"What's your twenty, Tucker?"

"Just pulled into park headquarters. Any luck?"

"Negative. But it's going to be like finding a needle in a needle stack."

"I know, Walt. But I know they're headed north. Let me try their cell phones again. I'll give you a shout over the radio if I get through."

"Roger that." Walt opens the door to the cab of the truck and clicks on the ignition to check the fuel level. The needle shows less than a quarter of a tank. He curses as he twists the key off and returns to the barn in search of fuel. The radio sounds. "Walt?"

"Go, Tucker."

"I got through to my sister-in-law for a quick second before losing the connection. The only thing I could make out was Madison Campground. I don't know if they just passed it or are coming up on it. It's a starting point."

"I can get in the neighborhood by crossing over to the west side where Madison River crosses under the highway. I'll find them, Tucker."

Before Tucker can reply, a panicked voice fills the airwaves. "Break—Break—Break. This is Air Ranger Susan Maxwell, airborne over Yellowstone Lake . . . Oh God . . . something . . . something strange is going on. There's like a tidal wave . . . Oh no . . . the area west of the lake is underwater."

Walt grabs two gas containers and races for his truck.

"It's washing the cars off of the roadway . . . my God, those poor people . . . Grant Village is completely engulfed . . . there are travel trailers bobbing around like corks. Vehicles are being washed off the road as far north as Little Thumb Creek. The water level is . . . rising quickly as it strikes the upward slope on the west side of the road. Anyone on the highway between Grant Village and Bluff Point to the north is . . . Oh God, I see people in the water . . . we need the lake patrol with their boats . . . there are entire families down there . . ."

Walt starts his truck, but before putting it in gear, changes his mind. He hurries back to the shed and grabs two metal loading ramps, which he uses to load the ATV into the bed of his truck. He hurries back to the cab and slams the truck into gear. He mashes the gas pedal, sending a cyclone of gravel and grit skyward as Ranger Maxwell continues her macabre play-by-play over the radio.

". . . the entire western perimeter of West Thumb is now inundated with water. Where's the lake patrol boats? We have survivors . . . I repeat . . . we have survivors. They won't survive long in the cold water. Damn it, please hurry. Those people are dying!"

A new voice sounds, distorted by wind noise. "This is lake patrol. We're on the way. We've launched every boat we have."

"Lake patrol—move your asses. I can see at least two dozen people in the water. Location is near the Occasional Geyser area, just east of Duck Lake and . . ."

Walt turns off the fire road and heads north, bouncing over earthen berms one moment and plunging down gullies the next, as he follows a power company cut through the forest. Once back on relatively level ground, he feeds more gas to the big V-8 as a deepening sense of dread races down his spine.

Camp 86—near Chattanooga, Tennessee

Interview: Larry from Littleton, CO—auto mechanic

"It was a sight you wouldn't believe unless you saw it with your own eyes. We'd spent the morning fly-fishing the backcountry along the Snake River and were trying to get back to our campsite up at Grant Village. Didn't have a clue anything was going on until we tried to get back on the highway. Traffic headed south was at a standstill and was taking up most of the road. We eked our way north, and as we came around a bend, the road just disappeared into the water. And I'm not talking a small puddle. There was water everywhere, and we hadn't even made the turn-off to the campsite. There were a bunch of cars bobbing in the water and there's no telling how many had already sunk. People were splashing around in that ice-cold water and we tried to help out, but there was a strong current and there wasn't much we could do. We turned the car around and got in line."

CHAPTER 38

White House Cabinet Room

Claire Espinoza glances down when she hears a vibration emanating from the leather tote at her feet. Not sure of the proper protocol when in the presence of the President of the Untied States, she slowly slips her hand down, retrieves her phone, and places it in her lap. She follows along with the conversations at the table before surreptitiously stealing a glance at the lighted screen. Claire is surprised to see a text message from Emily West urging her to check her e-mail.

With her laptop already open before her, Claire clicks on the mail icon and begins to search through the dozens of new e-mails for face creams and low mortgage rates before finding two marked *urgent*. She clicks on the first, a message from the U.S. Geological Survey's office in Menlo Park, California. Her eyes widen with surprise at the contents. "Jeremy," she says, interrupting the teleconference with Jeremy Lyndsey, "this is Claire. Are you in contact with your colleagues down the hall at the California Volcano Observatory?" She glances up to see a look of dismay on the President's face.

Lyndsey answers via speakerphone. "No. I've been a little preoccupied. Why?"

"A significant earthquake swarm is occurring just south of the Long Valley Caldera. It appears the"—she clicks on the other urgent message as she continues— "the earthquakes are increasing . . . Oh shit—" She glances up and gives the President an embarrassed smile. "The same thing's happening along the Cascades in Oregon and Washington."

President Drummond reaches her limit. "Dr. Espinoza, would you like to fill in the rest of us about what's going on?"

Without thinking, Claire holds up her hand in a stopping motion as she opens and quickly scans the e-mail from Emily West. A red-faced, burly man enters the room and makes a hurried approach to his assigned chair as secretary of agriculture.

"Glad you could join us, Henry," President Drummond says.

He shrugs and mouths a *sorry*.

"Dr. Espinoza, you do realize there is a room full of people waiting to hear an explanation, myself included."

Claire closes the lid of the laptop. "I'm sorry, Madam President. In addition to those e-mails, I received an e-mail from a colleague who's following the seismicity at Yellowstone—"

"I don't need an inventory of your e-mails, Dr. Espinoza. What I need are answers," the President snaps.

Flustered, Claire stops and starts. "Yes . . . well . . ."

She inhales a deep breath and releases it. "Basically, in a nutshell, the events happening now in Yellowstone are triggering events elsewhere. There are some scientists who believe that a massive eruption of the caldera could produce seismic waves strong enough to trigger volcanic eruptions in California, Oregon, and Washington."

"My God, you're talking about wiping out a majority of our nation's agricultural production," the new arrival, Ag Secretary Henry Edmonds, says.

President Drummond waves a hand in the air. "Henry, welcome to the latest round in the game of what-ifs. We don't have a clue if any of these volcanoes are going to erupt. But my main focus is on Yellowstone. Doesn't it have the capacity to produce the most damage?"

"Yes and no, Madam President," Claire says. "The last eruption of California's Long Valley Caldera ejected some 144 cubic miles of material, making it third or fourth among the largest eruptions on earth. The largest Yellowstone eruption spewed some 585 cubic miles of material. To put that in perspective, Madam President, that much ash would bury the entire state of Texas about ten feet deep."

The room falls silent as the President begins to tap her pen on the table. Dr. Espinoza breaks the silence. "The Long Valley Caldera is just one of about forty-four volcanoes, sixteen of which are considered high threat potential for erupt—"

"Thank you, Dr. Espinoza. All I'm hearing are suppositions. I need to know whether the damn volcano is going to erupt." President Drummond stands from her chair. "But if Yellowstone is truly as large as you suggest, then I need a plan of action and I need it now. Get busy, people." President Drummond turns and exits the room, followed closely by Ethan Granger.

He catches up to her and says, "Madam President, your presence is requested in the Situation Room."

She never breaks stride. "Christ, why did I ever run for this office, Ethan? I've got the Russians meddling in Ukraine, North Korea test-firing missiles like they're bottle rockets, and Iraq is being overrun by a group of nasty terrorists." She stops and turns to her aide. "And now I'm faced with possibly the worst natural disaster in our country's history?"

CHAPTER 39

Tucker slots the pickup into the first available spot near the Center for Resources building and jumps from the cab. Superintendent Barlow hurries across the road to meet up with them as Tucker strides into the building. Rachael and April scramble to catch up.

Barlow removes his hat and wipes his brow. "What's happening with the lake, Tucker?"

"I need to see the GPS feeds and satellite data to know for sure, but I believe the lake bottom is rising. Could be a buildup of carbon dioxide or magma rising."

Barlow replaces his hat. "But the inflated plain is all the way on the east side of the lake."

"The one we know about," Rachael says, catching up and joining the conversation. "The lake bottom is littered with thermal vents and fissures. Not much of a stretch to think there is further ground deformation at other areas of the lake floor."

Tucker leads them down the hall to the Spatial Analysis Center. "The lake tilts toward the west, and that section of shoreline is at a lower elevation than anywhere else around the lake. If there was a sudden upward movement along the lake bottom, the tidal wave would naturally flow in that direction."

Rachael steps around the group and hurries over to the computer array, where she logs on and begins pulling up data. "All instruments at Grant Village are offline. The last data we received indicated ground deformation at minus eleven inches."

Tucker rests his hip on one of the desks. "Check the readings at Mary Bay and the Promontory." As Rachael clicks through pages, Tucker makes a radio call to Air Ranger Maxwell, asking her to do a flyover of the eastern side of the lake.

April steps up and peers over Rachael's shoulder. "What's the data from the eastern side of the lake going to tell you?"

"Hopefully, a reason for the sudden shift at the lake," Tucker says.

Rachael pulls up the data from the tiltmeter, seismometer, and the GPS unit located at the Promontory, on the southeast arm of the lake. When the data pops onto the screen, she rocks backward against the chair, stunned. "There's nothing significant on any of the instruments." She glances up at Tucker. "How could that be?"

"That's exactly what I was afraid of." Tucker pushes off the desk and begins to pace. "Now, pull up the Mary Bay data."

Rachael's fingers fly across the keyboard, and she's stunned again by the results. "The tiltmeter maxed out at 10,000 microradians."

"What's a micro-whatever?" Barlow asks.

"Just a unit of measure we use," Tucker answers. "Rachael, what's the data from the GPS unit?"

Rachael clicks on a window to bring the data full screen. "Upward deformation of fifteen inches."

"What does all this mean?" Barlow asks.

Tucker walks over to a park map tacked to the wall. This one is different from the map in Ralph's office—on this map the outline of the massive caldera is clearly marked, highlighting a vast portion of land smack in the middle of the park. He places a finger on Yellowstone Lake and traces a line. "The rim of the caldera runs south of West Thumb, but cuts across the eastern basin of the lake between Mary Bay and the Promontory." Tucker turns away from the map. "If the rim of the caldera is being forced up, the source can be traced to only one thing."

"Which is?" Barlow asks.

"Magma movement."

Chapter 40

Doctor Eric Snider hurries into the seismology lab as another round of seismic activity rocks Yellowstone. "Where did this latest round of activity originate?"

"The seismometers on the eastern side of the park triggered first," someone answers.

Professor Snider groans and strides across the room, coming to a halt near Emily West's desk. "Drilling activity?"

Emily rakes her fingers through her dark hair. "Most likely."

"Can't we get them to stop drilling for at least a couple of days?"

"I don't think it's going to make much of a difference now."

Snider pulls out a vacant chair and takes a seat. "Why?"

Emily types for a moment on her keyboard, and another data feed pops onto the screen. "GPS numbers from Mary Bay."

"Jeez, what's that doing to the lake? If it's a foot at that location, there's no telling what the uplift is along the lake bottom. What about the north side?"

Before Emily can answer, someone shouts, "Professor Snider, a call on line two."

"Take a message," he shouts in reply.

"It's Josh, sir. He sounds upset."

Dr. Snider blows out a breath and snatches up the handset. "What is it, Josh?"

"Dr. Snider, I . . ." Josh sobs. "It's . . . I'm driving . . ." Another sob is followed by a sniffling inhalation of air.

"Josh, take a deep breath and tell me what's going on."

"Ooo—oookay, sir." After pausing a moment to regain his composure, Josh continues. "They won't let me enter the park. They told me the road ahead is underwater . . . and I . . . I was talking to someone else, and they said . . . they said Grant Village is gone. Completely submerged. That's where my . . . where my family . . . was staying."

Eric Snider puts a palm on the mouthpiece. "Emily, start pulling up all the data we have from the Yellowstone Lake area." He removes his hand and summons up his most soothing voice. "Josh, you need to turn around and head back this way. The park is under an evacuation order."

"I heard the sirens, but I can't leave. My family's up there somewhere."

"Josh, listen to me. Your family could already be out of the park and— Hello? Josh, you there? Josh?" Snider waits for a reply. "Josh?" Dead air. He reluctantly hangs up the phone.

"What do we have for data?"

"Ground deformation all around the lake. Uplift on the east side with substantial deflation on the west side."

"Hence, the westward water movement. Think we can get NASA to start shooting some InSAR images of the caldera?" InSAR is a satellite-based radar system designed to accurately measure ground deformation.

"I don't know if there's time. It will take a couple of satellite passes to complete the image. Could take a couple of days."

A loud, urgent pinging sounds from the computer monitor on Emily's desk.

Snider startles. "What the hell's that?"

Emily's finger is a blur as she clicks through pages of data. "I have an alert program installed on my computer."

"An alert for what?"

Emily stops clicking and sags against her chair. "For that," she says, pointing at the screen.

Eric stares at the data. "Which station?"

"The seismometer at Norris."

"Unbelievable. How big?"

"Well over a magnitude six." She stares at the screen and says, "The largest to hit the park in decades."

Camp 29—Hattiesburg, Mississippi

Interview: Thomas from Twin Falls, ID—funeral director

"June is typically a slow month for my business. People are always dying to get in, but ... well ... probably not the best topic to discuss in our present state. The wife and I loaded up the three kids for a week of fun at the park. We were staying up at Mammoth Hot Springs, but drove down to Norris for the day. It was a beautiful day and the area was full of visitors. They have these elevated wooden walkways that wind through the various geysers. I'd heard people talking about the earthquakes around the Old Faithful area, but I didn't pay much attention to it because the park has earthquakes all the time. We might have felt some small tremors at Norris but nothing major. We were a third of the way out on this walkway when a very large quake struck. People started screaming and grabbing each other to keep from falling. The motion was violent and portions of the walkway collapsed. Terror. It was pure terror. We had to work our way through the brush and boulders, and several older couples were really struggling. We helped as best we could, but there comes a moment when family comes first. Know what I mean?"

CHAPTER 41

Somewhere along Grand Loop Road, Yellowstone National Park

Now past the Madison Campground area, Walt Stringer takes advantage of every upward elevation change to jump from his pickup and scan the adjacent road for the Mayfield family. This is his fifth such stop and still no luck. He retrieves one of the gasoline containers from the bed of the truck and dumps the contents into the tank. His radio rests on the dash, playing one horror story after another as the park visitors scramble to leave Yellowstone.

Walt takes a moment to unzip and relieve the pressure on his bladder before climbing back in the cab. His body is stiff and sore from the pounding drive. But that pain is nothing compared to how his face feels. The blisters are growing larger, and the pain is like someone holding a blowtorch a few inches away from his face. He takes a moment to hunt down the bottle of painkillers and finds them on the floorboard. After popping two into his mouth, he dry swallows them before dropping the truck into gear. He weaves his way down the hill, dodging in and out of the trees and around boulders. At the bottom he skirts a little farther west and begins the ascent up another hill, cursing when he gets to the top, because only small portions of the roadway are visible through the gaps in the trees. "This is taking too long," he mutters, climbing from the truck again.

Holding the binoculars away from his tender face, Walt scans the three or four vehicles that are visible and sees no sign of a 2005 red Suburban. "Screw it," he mumbles as he retrieves his radio from the pickup and locks the doors. He aligns the ramps and backs the four-wheeler out of the bed. Unscrewing the gas cap, he discovers the tank is nearly empty. After refilling the tank with the last of the gas, Walt fires up the engine and takes off toward the west, hoping to find a clearing along the Grand Loop Road.

Traveling as fast as the terrain allows, he weaves among the trees, branches tugging at his clothing. A pine bough slaps him in the face, bringing tears to his eyes. He doesn't slow as he gently wipes a free hand across his blistered face, checking his palm for blood. No blood, but the pain is intense. He breaks into the clear near a bend in the Gibbon River and drives along the bank, searching for shallower water.

"Did you feel that?" Jessica asks, turning to her husband. He's sitting in the passenger seat of their going-nowhere vehicle as stopped traffic stretches beyond the horizon. The two-laner is now one-wayer with outbound traffic filling both sides of the road.

"I felt it. Think it's larger than any of the others?"

Jess glances toward the backseat before answering.

Both Maddie and Mason are busy playing games on their iPads. "Yes, much larger. We need to find another way out of here."

Matt waves toward the rock-strewn hills lining both sides of the road. "Where are we going to go?"

"I don't know, Matt. But we haven't moved more than half a mile in the last forty-five minutes." Jess pulls a park map from the center console and spreads it across the steering wheel. "What's the last landmark you remember seeing?"

"A turnout for Gibbon Falls."

Traffic inches ahead and Jess releases the brake to coast forward, then returns to the map. With a blue-lacquered fingernail, she traces their route. "We're about halfway between Madison and Norris." She glances up at her husband. "With a long way still left to go. If that last earthquake is any indication, we may be on borrowed time."

"What are we supposed to do? Start hiking?"

"Not with your injured leg. You can barely walk as it is." Jess studies the map some more. "Up ahead, the Gibbon River crosses back under the road. If we can find somewhere to steer off the road, we can scoot northwest around Norris."

"There's nowhere to scoot to, Jess. Even if we could find a place, we won't get far. You'd need four-wheel drive to even attempt it. And we don't have four-wheel drive."

Jess scowls. "I'm well aware we don't have four-wheel drive. But we're going to have to try—"

"Mommy, what are you and Daddy arguing about?" Maddie asks.

Jess turns to give her daughter a smile. "We're not

arguing, sweetheart. We're just trying to find the quickest way to Uncle Tucker's office."

"Good, because I don't think this way is working very well."

"I think you're right, honey."

"Is Uncle Tucker still going to show us the bears?"

Matt swivels in his seat. "And the lions and tigers, oh my."

"Daddy, you're silly. There aren't any lions and tigers here."

"Are too. Maybe not tigers, but there are lions. They're really cougars but most people call them mountain lions. The ones here at Yellowstone are some of the biggest cats in North—"

"Give it a rest, Matt," Jess snaps.

"Mom, Dad—there's a man on a four-wheeler headed straight for our car," Mason says.

Walt spots the red Suburban and guns the four-wheeler up next to the SUV. Walt climbs off as car doors begin opening up and down the road. He hurries to the passenger window. "Tucker sent me. We don't have time for introductions, but grab any water you have and come with me. And make it quick."

"What about our Suburban?" Matt asks.

"Leave it." Walt glances in both directions as people begin hurrying toward them. "As a matter of fact, leave everything. Get out right now and get on the four-wheeler."

The Mayfield family begins scrambling from their car. "Where do you want us?" Matt asks as he hobbles around the side of the vehicle.

People are coming from all directions and they're just feet away from Walt's position. "Just get on the damn thing." Walt draws his weapon, and the crowd halts.

"You can't shoot all of us," one man says at the front of the pack.

With his gun swinging in an arc among the crowd, Walt throws his leg over the seat. "No, but I can shoot you."

The Mayfields squeeze onto the ATV, with the kids on the seat behind Walt, and Matt and Jess clinging to the rear rack extending over the back fenders.

"I don't want to shoot anyone, but I will if you interfere with our leaving."

The man takes a couple of steps forward and is now within six feet of the ATV. "My family's here, too. You going to ride off and leave all of us here to die?"

Walt takes a moment to make sure the radio is secure and then switches the pistol to his left hand. "No one's dying." Walt avoids the word *yet*. "If the traffic doesn't clear soon, put the sun in front of you and start hiking. The West Entrance to the park is about sixteen miles due west."

Walt sees the man tense up to make a move and guns the throttle just as the man lunges, leaving him nothing but the ground to halt his progress. Other people begin to run toward them. "Hold on tight," Walt shouts as he quickly reholsters his pistol before steering the four-wheeler down a steep embankment.

The added weight makes steering the ATV unwieldy, but Walt keeps the throttle down as he weaves through the trees, only slowing when they reach the river a couple of hundred yards away. Following his tracks, he finds the crossing and drives down the bank. The cold water shoots out in sheets, drenching everyone aboard. Walt struggles to keep a grip on the now-slippery handlebars. He misses his mark on the other side and hits a washed-out area that nearly jettisons everyone off the ATV. Somehow, they all hang on, and he races up the opposite bank. He glances back to make sure there are no pursuers and then slows to a more moderate pace.

They reach the truck minutes later and everyone climbs off. Walt kills the engine and unfastens the radio, pushing the transmit button. "Walt to Tucker." There is no immediate response. He tries again. "Walt Stringer for Tucker Mayfield."

The radio squawks. "This is Tucker, Walt. You find them?"

"Ten-four. I've got 'em."

"What's your twenty?"

"We're probably six or seven miles southwest of Norris."

There's a long pause on the other end. Walt checks to make sure the radio is still on. Finally he hears, "Walt, switch over to channel two."

Walt clicks over to channel two.

"Can you talk?" Tucker asks.

Walt glances around. Jessica is tending to Matt's leg while the children look on. He meanders away from the group.

"Can now. What's up?"

"You need to get away from Norris as quickly as possible. The ground deformation numbers are off the chart and the latest earthquake registered over six with an epicenter just south of the Norris area."

"How much time do we have?" Walt asks.

"I don't know, Walt. It'll take you the better part of two hours to make your way up here to Mammoth."

"I'll load them up and start hauling ass. About all we can do."

"Keep your radio close and I'll keep you updated."

"Will do."

"Walt . . ." Tucker's voice fades away.

Walt clicks the transmit button. "Yeah, Tucker?"

"Hurry, Walt. Please hurry."

CHAPTER 42

President Drummond walks quickly into the Situation Room with Ethan Granger right on her heels. The military personnel present have shed their jackets and loosened their ties. The chairman of the Joint Chiefs shoots to his feet when he spots the President entering the room. The others begin to rise, but President Drummond waves them down. "Keep your seats. We don't have time for all of that foolishness." Before taking her seat she turns to her aide. "Ethan, see if we can get Dr. Lyndsey on videoconference."

Ethan nods and heads for the control room, home to all the technology used in the Situation Room.

President Drummond pulls out a chair and sits. "I assumed you summoned me because you've come up with a plan?"

Secretary of Defense Lauren Petit clears her throat before speaking. "Yes and no, Madam President. I've requested that all military aircraft, stationed in any areas west of Missouri and north of Oklahoma, relocate to bases on both coasts. In addition, all military bases within that—"

President Drummond holds up her hand. "Lauren, I was just informed that an eruption at Yellowstone might trigger other eruptions in California, Oregon, and Washington."

The color drains from Lauren's face. "If that's the case we're in serious trouble. There's no way the bases outside the danger zone will be able to handle the aircraft and personnel from some of the largest military bases we have. We're talking about evacuating over fifty military installations."

With two fingers on either side of her head, President Drummond massages her temples. "How long does it take to evacuate a base?"

General Jose Cardenas, chairman of the Joint Chiefs, answers. "We can move the aircraft fairly quickly, but moving the personnel is another matter entirely. It will take days, possibly weeks, to sort out the situation."

President Drummond stops massaging and leans back in her chair. "Reposition the aircraft but keep personnel in place in areas outside the danger zone of Yellowstone. I'm not sure I put much stock in their theory about other eruptions. But the Yellowstone threat is real."

Ethan returns and sits next to the President. He leans over to whisper in her ear. "Dr. Lyndsey should be on-screen momentarily."

The President nods, then turns to the others at the table. "I've asked the scientist-in-charge of the Yellow-stone Volcano Observatory to join us on videoconference. But before we bring him in, I want to hear your plan for the nukes."

The military personnel look at one another, waiting for someone to start.

"Well?" the President asks.

General Truelove speaks from the video screen at the front of the room. "Madam President, I'll answer since I'm the commanding officer of the Global Strike Command. Basically we have two options. We can install larger air scrubbers to filter the ash and have crews shelter in place, or evacuate the silos and pray our enemies don't find out."

President Drummond starts in on her temples again. "How long would it take to install the new air scrubbers?"

General Truelove hesitates before answering. "We've hit a small snag, ma'am. But we're working with NASA to get our hands on the equipment. Once we locate them we'll have to fly them up and retrofit them into the missile command silos. We estimate the task could take up to a month to complete."

"So what you're really saying, General, is we should start praying."

General Truelove hangs his head. "Yes, ma'am."

President Drummond turns to General Cardenas. "How many missile subs do we have available?"

"We have fourteen boomers, ma'am. But only ten are in service."

"What's the deal with the other—never mind, I'm not going there. With what launch capabilities?"

"Each is capable of launching twenty-four Trident II D5 nuclear missiles."

The President takes a moment to do the math in her

head. "So we have the ability to target over two hundred forty nuclear missiles at any point on the globe?"

"If we put all operational missile subs on station, yes."

"General Cardenas, put all subs on station and evacuate any silos within five hundred miles of Yellowstone. This decision doesn't leave the room. Is that clear?"

Nods from all those present.

"Let's move on. Can we get Dr. Lyndsey on the screen?"

The face of Dr. Jeremy Lyndsey fills one half of the large screen. His face is pinched with worry and beads of perspiration are evident on his forehead.

"Dr. Lyndsey, nice to finally see you," the President says.

"Wish I could say the same, ma'am, but I don't have a monitor."

"Since you're flying blind, I'll tell you we are joined by various military personnel along with the secretary of defense. An eruption could have far-reaching effects on our military capabilities. But before we get to Yellowstone, tell me your thoughts about the theory of an eruption triggering activity elsewhere."

"First, ma'am, I need to report that Yellowstone was just rocked by a 6.2 magnitude earthquake. The second strongest ever recorded at the park."

"Strong enough to trigger an eruption?" the President asks.

"Maybe. As I've stated before, volcanology is an inexact science, ma'am. We can't tell you exactly when an eruption will occur, but we can predict the possibilities for an eruption."

President Drummond sighs. "And Yellowstone is primed?"

"I'd say the fuse has already been lit, ma'am. As for your first question, yes, seismic activity in one area can trigger activity in other areas. At the time of the last Yellowstone earthquake, the intensity of earthquake swarms occurring in California and the Cascades also increased. Whether they increase enough to trigger eruptions is unknown at this point. Either way, an eruption of the Yellowstone Caldera would dwarf any other eruption by a factor measured in the thousands. To put it bluntly, Madam President, with the exception of the Long Valley Caldera in Northern California, all the other eruptions would be a puff of smoke compared to an eruption at Yellowstone."

Jaws drop on a few of the people gathered around the table. General Cardenas leans forward in his chair. "Anything we can do militarily, Dr. Lyndsey?"

"No, sir. The only thing we can do is get the hell out of the way. That being said, the aftereffects will demand military intervention. I'd suggest you put the National Guard on standby."

General Cardenas jots down a note and then says, "How widespread are the effects going to be?"

"Global, sir. I've had this conversation with President Drummond so I'll give you the condensed version. Ash and sulfur dioxide will explode into the stratosphere. Once that sulfur dioxide is aerosolized it will create a veil, diminishing the sun's intensity. Global temperatures could drop as much as ten degrees Fahrenheit."

President Drummond rubs the back of her neck.

"You mentioned the ten-degree number earlier. That doesn't sound like a drastic temperature difference."

"It's not if you look at it from the perspective of daily temperature changes. But the impact from an overall temperature decrease of ten degrees will be devastating. We'd be looking at freezes in the tropics and frost or freezes in June or July, eliminating growing seasons all across the planet. With no crop production for one to two years, or longer in some cases, the possible human death toll could approach a billion or more."

CHAPTER 43

The radio on the other side of the Spatial Analysis Center sounds. "Tucker Mayfield, Air Ranger Susan Maxwell. Over."

Tucker hurries across the room and picks up the base station microphone. "Go, Susan."

"Sir, I'm flying over the eastern side of the lake. I don't see any obvious signs of ground deformation."

"Ten-four. It could very well be under the surface of the lake. Has the water flow stabilized?"

"Hard to tell, sir. Grant Village and the road are still underwater."

"Are the lake patrol boats on scene?"

"That's affirmative, sir. I'm too far away to see exactly what's happening, but they are in the area. I'm going to return to road duty. It's one hell of a mess out here, sir."

"Susan, before you return to the roads, I'd like you to overfly the area around Norris, specifically the Back Basin area. A ranger reported a recently opened surface fault near Steamboat Geyser."

"Large enough to be seen from the air?"

"Unknown. But a significant quake just struck the area."

"Roger, I'm headed that direction. I should be over the area shortly and will report back."

"Thank you, Susan. Be safe up there." Tucker places the radio on the desk and returns to the computer. "We can't do anything about the lake, but we need to find out what the hell is happening at Norris."

Barlow paces back and forth behind Tucker and Rachael as they sit, working the computers. Being way out of her element, April grabs an old magazine and tucks herself into a corner on the other side of the room.

"Rachael, can you check the temps at Steamboat and Opalescent Pool?" Tucker asks.

"I've already checked the temps for the Gray Lakes area and it's running about ten degrees hotter than normal," Rachael says as she clicks from one screen to another. "Uh-oh. Steamboat is up nearly forty degrees and the Vixen soil temp is up—no, that can't be right."

"What?" Tucker and Ralph say at the same time.

"I don't know if there's been a malfunction or what, but the soil temp is approaching 120 degrees Farenheit."

"What's normal?" Ralph asks.

Tucker pedals his chair over to Rachael's computer. "This time of the year, the soil temps should be in the sixty-degree range. Rach, will you pull up the temp readings for Constant Geyser?"

Rachael clicks to another screen and her eyes widen in surprise. "The temps are normal."

"That's what I was afraid of."

"Why?" Ralph asks.

"Constant Geyser lies outside the caldera boundary. The rim brushes up against the Norris area, including Steamboat and the soil temp station."

Ralph leans in to look at the monitor. "Meaning what, exactly?"

Tucker pedals back over to his computer. "Again, I believe the magma is moving closer to the surface. That's the only explanation for that big of an increase in temperatures." Tucker pulls up the webicorder display from the Norris seismometer and compares it with other instruments around the area. "Where we're seeing the increase in temps is exactly where the epicenter of the last earthquake was."

"And that last quake registered shallow at about a mile and a half," Rachael says.

Ralph sags into a vacant chair. "So you think an eruption will happen at Norris? I thought we were more concerned with the Old Faithful area?"

Tucker leans back in his chair. "As I've reiterated numerous times, we could see an eruption anywhere within the caldera. It might be several smaller eruptions around the caldera before the grand finale."

"What type of time frame are you thinking?" Ralph asks.

"Unknown," Tucker answers. "It could be hours between eruptions, maybe as much as a day or two." Tucker throws his hands up in the air. "We just don't know. Hell, I could be wrong and the whole damn thing erupts simultaneously. But I do believe some type of eruption is inevitable at this point."

"I concur," Rachael says, "but I don't think there's any way we get away with one or two small eruptions. There's too much caldera instability."

"Well, I can't disagree with either of you, but I hope like hell Rachael's wrong about the big one," Barlow says as he pushes out of his chair. "I need to check on evacuation progress. Keep me posted." Barlow grabs his handheld radio and exits the room.

"Rachael, will you collate all the deformation—"

"Air Ranger Susan Maxwell for Tucker Mayfield. Over." Her voice over the radio is laced with tenseness.

Tucker hurries over to the radio. "Go, Susan."

"Sir, I've found your surface fault just south of the Steamboat Geyser. The news is not good, sir."

"How so, Susan?"

"It's venting steam and heavy clouds of white smoke."

Tucker turns toward Rachael. "What do you think?"

"Could be just a hydrothermal explosion. Or it could be the beginnings of a vent opening."

"What does your gut tell you?"

"With the temperature increases and ground deformation? I'd vote for a vent."

Tucker winces before keying the microphone. "Susan, can you continue circling the area for a few more minutes?"

"Ten-four. I'll keep a visual on it."

"Thanks. And Susan, maintain a safe distance from that area."

"What's a safe distance, sir?"

Tucker looks to Rachael for an answer.

She shrugs. "I wouldn't want to be within fifty

miles of the place. She might have more maneuverability if she flies at a higher altitude."

Tucker keys the radio. "Susan, ascend to your flight ceiling and keep the area in sight. How are the roads in that area?"

"Will do. Traffic is at a standstill for as far north as I can see."

CHAPTER 44

The backwoods of Yellowstone National Park

With the four Mayfields and Walt riding in a single-cab pickup, elbow space is at a premium. There are groans and grunts as the pickup bounces across the rough terrain. Matt, hugging the outer door, cries out every time his injured leg slams against the vinyl seat.

"How far are we from Mammoth?" Jessica shouts above the wind noise shooting through the open windows.

"As the crow flies—less than twenty miles," Walt answers. "But I'm guessing a little more than thirty on our current route."

"How long?" Matt asks, his face a sheen of perspiration.

"At this rate, maybe an hour and a half, if we're lucky. But we've got some rugged terrain in front of us. Could take as long as a couple of hours."

"Do we have that long?" Jess asks.

Walt shrugs and taps the brakes as he slows the truck

near a small creek. "Keep an eye out for a place to cross." He turns the truck to the right, now driving perpendicular to the small stream. He pulls the truck to a halt near a game trail leading down to the water and steps out for a closer look. The area at the bottom is muddy, dotted with deep imprints from either elk or bison. Walt scans the bank for another crossing area in the distance, but sees nothing. He returns to the truck and squeezes back aboard. "The crossing's muddy, but it's our only option." He turns the pickup in a wide circle and lines up on the trail. "Everybody, hold on."

After dropping the gearshift into low, Walt gooses the gas and the truck rockets down the bank. The front tires splash into the mud and the truck sinks several inches, halting all forward momentum. Walt floors the accelerator, cursing the truck to move. Large gouts of mud spin skyward as Walt labors to free the pickup. He jams the gearshift into reverse and tries to back out, but the back tires spin in place. Shifting from reverse to drive over and over again, he tries to rock the truck from the quagmire, but succeeds only in burying the pickup to the fender wells. Dejected, he slams the transmission into park.

Jess gives him a stern look. "Now what? We can't walk to Mammoth."

Walt turns toward her. "I'm aware of that. Just give me a minute to think."

"Mason and I can get out and push," Matt says.

"I can, too," Maddie adds.

Walt opens the door. "I don't think a dozen men could push us out of this mess. There's a place up ahead where the road crews store salt for the winter. I'll walk up and get one of the loaders."

"We're going with you," Jess says.

"You'll just slow me down. Can't be more than a mile over to the place. I'll be up there and back before you know it."

"Walt, we're going with you." Jess enunciates each word, making her stance clear.

"Suit yourself." He steps from the truck and sinks up to his knees in the mud. He mutters a few curse words, some aimed at Tucker, as he struggles to pull a leg free. With effort, he extricates himself from the deepest mud. "Hand me one of the kids. I'll carry them over to the other side."

Maddie scrambles across the seat and climbs into Walt's outstretched arms. He slogs across the creek and returns to retrieve Mason. "Jess, can you help get Matt across? Probably need to keep his injured leg out of the mud as much as you can."

"We'll make it. Wouldn't want to slow you down."

Walt turns around and asks Mason to ride piggyback. Mason climbs aboard and wraps his arms around Walt's neck. They wade through the mud and Walt lowers him to the ground next to his sister. He turns around in time to see Jessica face-plant into the sludge. The children start laughing, and Walt gnaws on his bottom lip as he wades through the muck to help her up. When he gets her back on her feet, the only things visible are the whites of her eyes. Walt leads her over to a deeper pool of water to wash off before returning for Matt.

Once all of the Mayfields are ashore, Walt leads them up and out of the ravine with one of Matt's arms draped across his broad shoulders. Jess's face is somewhat clean, but mud clings to her hair and clothes.

"You should have just jumped into the water," Walt says.

"Easy for you to say. That pool of water was burning hot."

Walt comes to a halt and turns toward Jess. "The water wasn't cold?"

"I don't know what your definition of *cold* is, but that pool of water was scalding hot."

Walt starts walking as fast as he can while half dragging Matt. "We need to move quickly. Hustle up."

"Why? What's up?"

"That creek is spring fed out of a spot just east of Norris. It's usually so cold it'll numb your fingers."

"Oh shit," Jess mutters quietly, trying to keep the children from overhearing.

"That and more," Walt says.

"What difference does it make if the water's hot or cold?" Matt asks.

"Where are we?" Jess asks Matt.

"Yellowstone?" He takes a moment to ponder his response. "Oh shit."

"Exactly," Jess says. "We need to haul ass and we need to do it quickly."

Camp 11—Bossier City, Louisiana

Interview: Patty from Pinedale, WY—hairstylist

"The kids were out of school for the summer and driving me up a wall. I have two boys, ten and twelve. Always wanting to do something, you know what I mean? Their dad, my ex, works in the oil fields. The boys still haven't heard from him, so we don't know if he got out in time. It won't be the end of the world for me, but I hate it for the boys. But back to my story. I took two days off from work and took the boys camping. They'd been pestering me about seeing the buffalo up at Yellowstone, so that's where we ended up.

"We'd just gotten the tent put up when the earthquakes started. I don't mind a little moving and shaking if I'm on a dance floor, but I didn't much care for the ground moving under my feet. Told the boys to take down the tent, and they did after some screaming and hollering. Don't get me started on the trip out of the park. We made it back home and put the tent up in the backyard. I'll be damned if we weren't ordered to evacuate from there. But I guess we're camping now, huh?"

CHAPTER 45

Affordable Air Flight 2136, cruising at 31,000 feet

Captain Neil Lockhart glances out the front windscreen of the 737-400. "Looks like clear sailing to me."

Co-captain Victoria Delgado glances at the map display. "We're still a ways from Yellowstone."

"Yeah, but if anything was going on we'd see it from here. Especially if it's as large as you claim."

"It's not what I claim. It's what the scientists can prove. Want me to plot a course to divert around the area?"

"I don't see any reason for it," Lockhart replies. "Besides, as I said earlier, I can't take another late arrival on my record."

Delgado turns toward Lockhart. "Why the hell do you care about arrival times? This time next year, you'll be at your favorite fishing hole with a twelve-pack of Bud iced down in your favorite cooler."

"I don't like to fish, but I do like me some Budweiser. No, I'm worried because I wouldn't put it past the bastards to put me out to pasture early. Corporate would cream their pants if they could cut me loose without paying any retirement benefits."

"That's what I like about you, Neil, always trying to find the positive in any situation."

Lockhart laughs, his belly jiggling against the taught fabric of his shirt. "Hey, somebody has to tell it like it is. Would you switch the radio over to Salt Lake Center?"

Delgado reaches down to the console between the seats and dials the radio knob to the appropriate frequency. "Good to go."

Lockhart triggers the transmit button. "Salt Lake Center, Affordable Air 2136."

After a brief delay a female voice answers. "Go, 2136."

"Yellowstone volcano status?"

"Threat level remains orange, 2136."

"Roger, Salt Lake Center. Requesting 38-zero."

"2136, climb to 38-zero and maintain."

"2136 climbing to 38-zero. Good day."

"Good day, sir. Notify if you observe any anomalies."

"Roger, Salt Lake Center. You'll be the first to know."

Delgado turns her head and smiles. "If you're not worried, why are we ascending to 38,000?"

"A little more wiggle room—just in case."

"Seven thousand feet is not going to buy us much if the Yellowstone blows."

"How far out are we now?"

Delgado glances at the flight computer. "Less than sixty. Still not too late to divert."

"Nah. We're good to go. Though it would be a hell of a sight to see from up here."

"No, thank you," Delgado says. "I don't want anything else to do with volcanic ash. Our squadron hit some ash over Iceland when we were on military maneuvers. Seized up my engine and I had to dive down for a restart. Scared the hell out of me. It scoured the canopy so bad you couldn't see out. I'll pass on tangling with any more volcanoes."

"Didn't ground control alert you to possible ash clouds?"

"Yeah, after the fact. Apparently one of their smaller volcanoes just decided to randomly spew out some ash. That's the thing about volcanoes—they're totally unpredictable."

CHAPTER 46

White House Cabinet Room

President Saundra Drummond shuffles back into the Cabinet Room, her shoulders slumped. Those present stand at her entrance but she waves them down as she pulls out her chair and sits. She turns her focus to Henry Edmonds, secretary of agriculture.

"Henry, how much grain do we have in storage?"

"I don't know the number off the top of my head, ma'am. But not as much as in past years. The continuing drought has significantly reduced yields. Most of the grain is stored on private farms or farmers' cooperatives with the overall capacity somewhere in the neighborhood of thirteen billion bushels. I'd guesstimate we have maybe eight billion bushels in storage, and that includes corn, wheat, and soybeans, but mostly wheat and corn. Soybeans are more difficult to store because of their moisture content."

President Drummond begins massaging her temples. "How long would that last us?"

"Not long, and probably a third of that is feeder corn that's used in the livestock industry."

"That feeder corn may be going to human consumption," the President says. "And most of these grains are stored where the ash fallout is predicted to be heaviest?"

Edmonds takes a sip of coffee and rattles the saucer when replacing his cup. "Unfortunately, yes. But grain loss is not our only problem. The beef, hog, and poultry industries might very well be decimated. Some of the largest feeder cattle operations in the world are in the Midwest. Same for the hog and poultry industries. If the Yellowstone volcano erupts, we could be in for a long slog, Madam President."

"That's an understatement, Henry."

The Cabinet Room remains eerily silent for a brief moment. Dr. Claire Espinoza takes advantage of the lull. "Madam President, there are many hurdles we'll face, but two of the most important will be water and electricity."

President Drummond swivels her chair around. "How so, Claire?"

"As you know, most municipalities rely on water reservoirs, or lakes, to use another term, to store their potable water. Volcanic ash, especially in the amounts we're talking about, can change the water chemistry. The ash can leach some pretty nasty chemicals into the water supply, and ash can remain suspended in water for long periods of time, causing high levels of turbidity. This turbidity causes a marked decrease in disinfection rates, which leads, in turn, to a substantial increase of harmful bacterial levels. But that may all be moot, because the ash could clog every pump and valve in the water supply system. Potable water will only be attainable from underground sources for a period of weeks or months, which leads to the second significant problem."

President Drummond moves the massage from her temples to the back of her neck. "Power?"

"Yes, ma'am. Volcanic ash is highly conductive, especially when wet. We could be looking at sustained power outages across a large portion of the country."

"For how long?" the President asks.

"Weeks, almost certainly. Months or years in the hardest-hit areas."

"Anything we can do to mitigate the damage?" President Drummond asks as she swivels her gaze around the table. "Anyone?" A lot of eyes are staring at the table. "We're here to solve the hard problems, people. I want a plan on my desk no later than tomorrow morning on how we're going to deal with the water and power issues. What else?"

"Madam President, if I may," the director of the Federal Aviation Administration says with his hand in the air.

"More good news, Nolan?"

Nolan Kinney, a short man who's carrying a few extra pounds after retiring from the cockpit, cringes at her statement. "Unfortunately, yes, Madam President. If the eruption is as large as predicted, air travel anywhere in North America will be extremely limited, if at all. As a matter of fact, any type of travel would be severely hampered."

President Drummond picks up a pen from the table. "What about planes in the air, if, or when, the volcano erupts?"

"Depends on location. Any flights within two or three hundred miles of the eruption could face catastrophic engine damage."

"Should we issue a grounding order, now?"

"How certain are we of an eruption?" Kinney asks.

"That's the million-dollar question, Nolan. Claire, would you call Dr. Lyndsey on the speaker system?"

Claire nods and pulls Lyndsey's cell number up on her contacts list. As she's scrolling to his office number, her phone rings. She glances at the display and answers. "Jeremy, I was in the process of calling you."

"Claire, it's happening."

"Hold on, Jeremy. I need to put you on the speaker system." She glances around the table. "Anyone have an aux cord?"

"Forget the cord, Claire, just put him on your phone speaker," the President snaps.

She does. "Jeremy, you're on speaker."

"Is the President there, Claire?"

"I'm here, Dr. Lyndsey," the President shouts across the table. "What's happening?"

"We have a possible vent opening just southeast of the Norris area, ma'am. Right now it appears to be only smoke and steam."

"How do you know this one is volcano related and not another hydrothermal explosion?" the President asks.

"This particular opening is beyond any of the park's known hydrology features. We believe the smoke and steam are the result of an upward intrusion of magma. Ground temperatures in Norris are increasing significantly, providing further evidence of rising magma."

"To be clear, Dr. Lyndsey, you and your team believe what?"

"We believe an eruption could occur at any moment, ma'am."

President Drummond looks over to the FAA director. "I want all airspace within three hundred miles of Yellowstone cleared immediately."

CHAPTER 47

The backwoods of Yellowstone National Park

What should have been a ten-minute walk is now approaching forty minutes as Walt helps Matt across the treacherous terrain. Dead trees lay scattered all across the ground, their spiny limbs lying in wait as trip hazards. Everyone in the hiking party is covered with dirt and pine needles after several tumbles. As they break through a clearing near the salt storage area, Walt is praying that all the heavy equipment is not out on the roads.

After they work their way around the piles of salt and sand, Walt's prayers are partially answered when he discovers one old loader remaining. That's the good news. The bad news is that all of the glass is shot out and the left rear tire is flatter than a roadkill squirrel. Walt sighs as he pulls a ring of keys from his pocket and opens the side door to the barn. "Can't buy a damn break," he mutters before turning back to the May-fields. "You guys look around for things we might need. Chains, pry bars, and even water jugs if you can find any. I'm going to see if the loader will start, then air up that tire. But we need to be quick about it."

Walt walks over to a pegboard next to a small office to search for keys. Finding none, he conducts a quick search through the office and comes up empty again. Another string of curse words escapes his mouth as he exits the office and grabs a pair of wire cutters before heading out to the loader. With tires large enough to have their own zip code, the Caterpillar 980 is a beast of a machine. It stands over twelve feet tall, weighs nearly thirty-three tons, and the bucket mounted on the front is large enough to hold the family car. The loader was new back in the late '80s, but the Wyoming winters have exacted their revenge. The once bright yellow paint has faded to the color of watered-down mustard and the dash is riddled with cracks. But Walt pays no mind to any of this as he climbs up into the cab and ducks his head under the dash. He traces the wires leading to the ignition and cuts them. After stripping away the insulation, he pauses to run through a list of positive thoughts before touching the wires together.

"Tucker for Walt Stringer," the radio on his belt blurts, causing the wires to slip from his hand.

Walt fumbles the radio free. "Go, Tucker."

"What's your twenty?"

"At the salt depot just east of Norris."

"Damn it Walt, you should have been clear of that area a long time ago."

"The pickup . . . we've had some issues, Tucker. But we're working through them."

"Walt, you need to move your ass. There may be a vent opening near Norris."

"How large?"

"Size is irrelevant. It's only a matter of time until the vent—"

The radio goes dead in Walt's hand. He slams it against his leg, then shakes it, hoping to get a little more juice out of the battery. No luck. He tosses the dead radio onto the dash and retrieves the fallen wires. He forgoes any more positive thinking and touches the wires together. The big diesel engine groans and turns over, but doesn't start. He switches on the choke and tries again. After a few sluggish seconds, the engine fires to life, belching a cloud of black smoke into the clear mountain air. He allows the engine to warm up for a couple of minutes before pulling the loader over to the barn. He climbs down from the cab and shouts toward the Mayfields. "Toss everything into the bucket. We need to move."

Walt hurries across the barn, scoops up the air hose, and races back to the loader.

"Why are we suddenly in such a big hurry?" Jess shouts over the engine noise.

"Talked to Tucker. We're running out of time. Put the kids in the cab and see if you can find some rope. You and Matt will have to tie yourselves onto the steps." Walt squats down and begins filling the tire.

Jess steps over and squats down next to him. "What's happened, Walt?"

"There might be a vent opening over at the Norris basin. That's all I know. Find some rope and get the kids situated so we can get the hell out of here."

"We're not going to make it to Mammoth."

"I don't know if we will or won't, but we don't have

time to mess with the pickup. We'll drive the loader and plow our own damn road if we have to."

Jess jumps to her feet and starts shouting directions. As the kids scramble up to the cab, she grabs a length of rope from a hook on the barn wall and helps Matt up to the landing at the top of the stairs. She wraps the rope around both of them and ties it off on the handrail. "How's the leg?"

"Hurts like hell and might be getting infected. But that's the least of our problems at the moment. What did Tucker say?"

She brushes a stray strand of red hair from his face. "A small vent may be opening."

Matt takes his wife's hand. "We going to make it, Jess?"

She leans in and brushes her lips against his. "Bet your ass, we are."

Matt shakes his head and smiles before giving his wife's hand a squeeze.

Once Walt decides there's enough air in the tire, he tosses the air hose aside and climbs up into the cab. "Everyone, hold on," he shouts before jamming the beast into gear and steering away from the barn.

Camp 241—Fayetteville, North Carolina

Interview: Stella from Scottsbluff, NE—camp counselor

"My husband and I ran a small summer church camp for the teenagers back home. Gave us a chance to interact with our two girls among their peers. An eye-opening experience, I'm here to tell you. We decided to take the group on a one week hiking and camping trip up to Yellowstone. There were ten of us on the trip. The other parents pitched in to help rent one of those big passenger vans so we wouldn't have to take more than one car. Now that I think about it, I hope they bought the insurance. But I guess that's beside the point now. Our last day was when everything started happening. We were already headed home when the rangers turned us around and told us to go out the west exit. I'm a Christian and all, but I did have a few choice words for the man. Anyway, we inched along in the traffic, and on the other side of the Norris area we heard a loud explosion."

CHAPTER 48

Yellowstone Center for Resources

"Walt, are you there?" Tucker pauses for a response, the radio gripped tightly in his hand. "Walt Stringer, this is Tucker Mayfield. Do you copy?" No response. Tucker places the radio back on the desk and turns away from the computer array at the Spatial Analysis Center.

Rachael pauses her data crunching and glances over her shoulder. "Probably a dead battery. Walt's been on that thing all morning. Why don't you see if Sally can do a flyover of the area?"

"Good idea." Tucker makes the radio call and walks over to April, who's on the other side of the room, flicking her finger across the screen of her iPhone. "April, do you have somewhere you can stay?"

April looks up from her phone. "Not really. Just my room down at Grant Village, which I guess is now underwater."

"Where's home when you're not working here?" Tucker asks.

"I gave up my apartment at the end of the semester

when I came out here. I was planning on heading home to my parents in Georgia until I found a real job. Why?"

"If the caldera erupts, we're all going to be looking for a place to live. If you can make it to the airport in Bozeman before an eruption, you just might make it home. Otherwise, an eruption will ground air traffic over most of the country for a significant length of time."

April stands in one fluid, feline movement. "How significant?"

"Weeks, certainly. Maybe months. Georgia would be a pretty good place to be in the aftermath."

Rachael gasps and swivels her chair around. "You're not going to make it to Bozeman, April. Tucker, we now have indications of a harmonic tremor at Norris."

Tucker hurries over to the computer and quickly scans the data on the screen. "Damn. Can you pull up the GPS data?"

Rachael manipulates the mouse and pulls up the data feed. "Uplift of over sixteen inches and—"

"Dr. Mayfield, Air Ranger Sally Maxwell. Over."

Tucker picks up the radio. "Go, Sally."

"I don't know if it's your family or not, but there's a group of people on one of the loaders. Best I can tell, there's three in the cab and two more riding on the outside stairs."

"Is one of them a woman?"

"Possibly, sir. I buzzed them but I couldn't tell much."

"Are they headed toward Mammoth?"

"Negative, Dr. Mayfield. They're heading in an east-northeasterly direction."

Tucker mutters a few curse words before responding. "How much room do you need to land that thing?"

"Sir, I was a bush pilot in Alaska. I can put her down on a damn Band-Aid if I need to."

"Think you could scoop them up and head this way?"

"Roger, sir . . . oh shit . . . there's debris in the air, I think—"

Tucker mashes the transmit button. "Sally?" Nothing. "Sally, can you read me?" He pauses to listen. "Come in, Air Ranger Maxwell."

Dead air.

Tucker hurls the radio at the wall.

CHAPTER 49

Rachael leans back in her chair, crosses her arms, and stares at the display. "How come we're not seeing evidence of a harmonic tremor on other nearby instruments?"

April wheels her chair closer. "What is this tremor thing?"

Rachael gives April an annoyed look as Tucker answers. "A harmonic tremor is a continuous, low-grade disturbance that signals magma movement through a narrow opening. It's frequently a precursor to an impending volcanic eruption."

Rachael tries to tune out their conversation, but can't. "Maybe it's water jetting through the hydrothermal system."

Tucker turns back to Rachael and points to the computer screen. "That's a borehole seismometer buried about a thousand feet deep. That's below most of the hydrothermal activity. I believe it's magma related, and we could be looking at the first eruption site."

April scoots her chair closer, her knee making contact with Tucker's. "First eruption? How many are there going to be?"

"The caldera is huge. It's large enough to fit the city of Los Angeles into the basin of the volcano. An eruption could occur at a single vent before spreading into a caldera-wide event. But no one really knows what will happen once the cork pops."

Rachael uncrosses her arms and leans forward. "It's all a little more complicated than the hospitality business, April."

April glares at Rachael. "Thanks. That's very helpful. Thank you for enlightening me."

Rachael scowls and turns back to her screen as Tucker stands to gain some distance from the two women.

"What about the anomalies we're seeing at Old Faithful?" Rachael asks.

"We could have two vents opening. If that's the case you can Katy bar the door, because all bets are off."

Superintendent Barlow barges into the room. "Why are some people so damn dense? Trying to evacuate the park is like herding cats. I swear, some people don't have a lick of—"

"Ralph, we've lost contact with Sally," Tucker says in a soft voice. "She was flying around the Norris area and her last words were something about debris in the air."

Barlow walks unsteadily to a chair and sits. His voice is barely above a whisper when he speaks. "There are still thousands of people out there . . . I just . . ." He rakes a hand across his face. "I just don't know what else to do."

Tucker squats down next to him. "My family's out there, too, Ralph, and I don't have a clue where they are. Maybe we should warn park personnel about what's happening at Norris."

Barlow shakes off his melancholy and angrily pushes to his feet. "Warn them about what? That they're about to be incinerated?" He waves a hand in the air. "Hey, people, bend over and kiss your ass good-bye." He turns away to stare at the wall.

"If they can get deep underground, they might survive the pyroclastic flows."

Barlow whirls around. "Underground where? Half the fucking park is sitting on top of the volcano."

Tucker shrugs. "I don't know, Ralph. There are no good answers. You need to think about rounding up the staff here at Mammoth and pushing further north."

"I'm not going anywhere. This park is my responsibility."

Tucker steps up close and lowers his voice. "There won't be a park anymore, Ralph. The pyroclastic flows could reach a hundred miles in every direction. And what that doesn't get the wildfires certainly will."

Barlow stomps his foot down. "I'm staying."

"What about your wife?"

"I'll send her north with you."

"And you really believe she'll leave without you? Bullshit." Tucker softens his tone. "This is not a captain-going-down-with-the-ship moment, Ralph. We have no control over what might happen. All we can do is try to survive."

Barlow walks over to a window and stares into the distance. "We should've started evacuating the park when the earthquake swarms started happening."

Across the room, Rachael stands from her chair and approaches Barlow. "We've had a dozen earthquake swarms over the years, Ralph. We can't evacuate the park every time there's instability. This just happens to be the one time—"

"All rangers," the radio on Ralph's belt squawks. "This is Ranger Teague up by Nez Perce Creek and Loop Road. I just heard an ungodly explosion down south. Can anyone see what's happening?"

Tucker hurries over to the map to pinpoint the ranger's location. "Please don't tell me we might have two vents opening. Did he say north or south of his position?"

Ralph turns from the window. "Don't bother, Tucker. The closest thing south of there is Old Faithful."

Camp 46—Columbus, Georgia

Interview: Tamara from Woodward, OK— petroleum engineer

"We've been to Yellowstone a couple of times. Usually we'll camp for three or four days and then move into the Old Faithful Inn for the last couple of days. I merely tolerate the outdoors and have a max limit of about three days. You asked if I was angry. Yes, I am. They should have begun the evacuation much sooner. Surely they had to have had a plan? I'm an engineer and we plan for everything. I put what happened on the National Park Service. There's just no excuse for the way things turned out."

CHAPTER 50

Ten miles from the northern border of Yellowstone National Park, Captain Neil Lockhart disengages the autopilot.

"I thought you weren't worried," Co-captain Victoria Delgado says.

"I'm not. But I want to be able to maneuver if we have to." He glances down at the radar display. "Looks like clear sailing to me." Flying at 450 knots with a fairly strong tailwind, the aircraft is cruising along at a ground speed of 520 miles per hour, quickly eating up the miles.

Lockhart squirms in his seat. "We'll be across the park and gone in about six minutes. How much can happen during that short time frame?"

"Six minutes can seem like an eternity in certain situations."

"Barely a pimple on a gnat's ass. Why don't you radio for an update on the volcano status?"

"Why don't we just skirt around the area? It'll only

add about ten minutes to the flight time. Hell, we can make that up with the tailwind."

"Too late. We just passed over Highway 191. We're over the park right now."

Delgado sighs. "Then why did you want a status update?"

"Trying to keep you occupied."

Delgado mutters a few curses as she leans forward in her chair, peering out the front windscreen.

Lockhart chuckles. "T minus five minutes and counting."

Delgado turns and scowls. "You can be such an ass sometimes, Neil." She glances back forward and her blood runs cold. "Hard right turn," she shouts.

"What is it?" Lockhart shouts as he whips the yoke over. The fuselage rotates sideways twenty-five degrees as any unsecured items slam against the far cockpit wall.

"Ash and debris. Turn the goddamn plane, Neil."

"I'm turning. How far out?"

"Too close." She reaches over and slams the throttles forward. "Try to gain some altitude." Delgado grabs the wheel on her side and pulls it toward her chest.

"You're going to stall us," Lockhart shouts. "Ease off."

Delgado eases off the wheel. "Steepen your bank." She glances at the altimeter before turning her gaze back to the front window. "We're not going to clear it."

A buzzer sounds as a red light flashes on the console. "Flameout on engine two. Level off and descend.

Maybe we can get it restarted." Delgado silences the alarm with a punch of a button.

Lockhart eases the wheel back to center and pushes the yoke forward as a bead of sweat pops on his forehead. "Descending." Debris begins pelting the windscreen as the jet picks up speed. "If one of those rocks pierces the fuselage, we're toast."

The radio squawks over their headphones. "AA 2136, Salt Lake Center. The FAA just issued an order to clear all airspace within three hundred miles of Yellowstone. Turn left to a heading of one-one-zero and ascend to 38,000."

Lockhart triggers the radio. "Too damn late. Ash is already in the air."

"Delivering fuel to engine two." Delgado watches the pressure gauge as the fuel floods into the combustion chamber. She flips the switch to trigger the starter, and her hopes diminish. "Negative on restart."

"Let's try a windmilling relight," Lockhart says through clenched teeth as he wrestles with the wounded plane.

"Salt Lake Center. Please repeat, AA 2136. Is ash currently present?"

"We need to bleed off some speed," Delgado says. "Need to be between 300 and 330 knots."

"How the hell am I going to bleed speed and descend at the same time?" Lockhart glances at the instrument panel, willing the plane to slow. "Let's try flaps at ten degrees." His legs are pistoning up and down as he works the rudder.

Delgado brings the flap lever to ten degrees. "We're really in stall territory now. Keep an eye on the attitude indicator." She triggers the radio button. "Salt Lake

Center, this is Affordable Air Flight 2136. Yes, ash is present and we are experiencing flight difficulties."

"What's your status, 2136?"

"We've had engine flameout due to volcanic ash. Attempting to do a windmilling relight and need to descend below 28,000."

"Roger, 2136. You are clear to descend."

"Ten-four, descending."

"Please confirm upon engine restart, 2136. Prayers your way."

"I don't think prayers are going to be enough, Salt Lake Center, but I'll keep you updated." Delgado glances down at the instrument cluster and winces. "More bad news. The temp on engine one is climbing." She leans forward and eases back on the throttle for engine one. "We're about to be in a world of hurt."

Lockhart grimaces. "We already are. Where are we on altitude?"

"Just broke through 28,000. Slow her down about 10 knots and we'll try for a relight on engine two."

"Might want to start looking for a place to put down. Maybe we could make Jackson, if we're lucky."

"Let's worry about the restart before contemplating putting her down." She reaches over and feeds more fuel into engine two. "I have zero pressure on engine two. I think it's seized up." She immediately kills the flow of fuel to the engine and starts thumbing through the atlas she keeps handy in one of the side pockets of the cockpit. "Come to a heading of one-nine-three. That should put us on a path to Jackson."

Another shrill buzzer sounds, and both pilots sag in their seats when they discover the source. "Flameout on engine one," Delgado shouts above the noise.

Captain Neil Lockhart triggers the radio button. "Mayday, Mayday, Mayday . . . this is Affordable Air Flight 2136."

"More debris," Delgado shouts as the erupted material tears through the thin aluminum skin of the aircraft. The mortally wounded plane spirals toward the ground.

CHAPTER 51

Old Faithful Inn

Sylvia Fallingwater, the manager of the Old Faithful Inn, is tidying up behind the front counter while awaiting the return of her husband, who had been dispatched to clear the roads. With April and the other staff gone and the doors locked, the place is eerily silent. After graduating with a degree in hospitality from the University of Nevada, Las Vegas, Sylvia dreamt of managing one of the glamorous, over-the-top resorts that line the Vegas strip. But reality set in after apprenticing for two years at Caesars Palace, where the grimy underbelly of the City of Sin had exposed her to the worst of humanity. The well-heeled clientele treated her like the lowest form of human life, and she had to pick up the pieces after a number of raucous bachelor and bachelorette parties, in fits of extravagant exuberance, destroyed entire suites. A summer internship at Yellowstone opened a window onto a different world, and she's been employed here for several years.

Sylvia logs off the computer and shuts it down.

After grabbing her purse from her office, she walks around the lobby, making sure the doors are all secure before taking a seat in one of the leather club chairs. The dust storm created by the fireplace collapse coats every stationary surface of the magnificent lobby. She picks up a well-used issue of *Park Life* and wipes the cover clean before riffling through the pages.

Exhausted from the morning's activities, she tosses the magazine onto a table and digs her phone out. She's surprised to see a text message from her husband, an elder on the Wind River Indian Reservation. Sylvia had instantly fallen in love with Sam Fallingwater, a three-quarter Shoshone Indian whose sole purpose in life is to break the cycle of poverty and alcoholism that runs rampant on the rez. She keys in her passcode and brings up his text message: *Bring pickup. Working around west entrance. Follow fire trails as much as possible. We'll leave from here.*

She thumbs a quick *okay* and pushes to her feet. Married for only three years, Sylvia and Sam haven't yet started a family, though both want children. After grabbing the keys from her purse, she lets herself out the employee entrance and relocks the door. The hinges on the door of the Fallingwaters' eight-year-old Chevy Silverado squeal as she climbs into the cab. She wonders if she should return home to retrieve a few of their belongings, but makes the decision not to. After firing up the engine, she backs out of the space and heads for the exit. A few patrons are still milling around the parking lot waiting for rides. She spots a young couple buried under large backpacks and eases up to them. "I'm going as far as the West Entrance if you want a ride."

The young man speaks. "We were hoping to head south. We left our car down there a week ago and hiked through the Tetons up to Yellowstone."

"South is a no-go. A good portion of the road is still underwater. C'mon, climb in. You can always circle back to pick up your car later."

After a few moments of indecision, the couple eases their backpacks into the bed of the truck and climb aboard. The young woman's long blond hair is tucked into a ponytail and there's a splash of bright red freckles across her narrow nose. "You really think the volcano is going to blow?" she asks.

"Don't know. That's not my bailiwick, but something strange is happening." Sylvia drives the old pickup behind the inn, bouncing over the curb and picking up the loop trail that runs alongside the Firehole River. Old Faithful lies dormant, for the moment, but what was once a small opening in the earth is now a crater that spans forty of fifty yards across. Sylvia glances in that direction, then back to the trail as she tries to maneuver around some of the wreckage from the helicopter. The fire is out but a putrid stench still hangs in the air. She wonders if anyone is coming to retrieve the bodies, a thought she tries to push from her mind. "Where're you guys from?"

"We're from Omaha," the young woman says. "I'm Autumn, by the way, and this is my boyfriend, Jackson. We decided to spend a couple of weeks backpacking through the Tetons and Yellowstone before grad school starts."

"I'm Sylvia. Congrats on the college graduations, but I don't think traipsing through the woods carrying a heavy backpack is my idea of a perfect retreat."

The young couple laughs, and Jackson reaches over to take his girlfriend's hand. "Autumn worked hard to convince me. I wanted to head for the beach, where we could just chill." Jackson leans in and kisses Autumn on the cheek. "I hate to admit it, but she was right. The scenery around here is spectacular, and there's something sexy about sleeping in a tent in the middle of the wild."

Sylvia laughs. "I think you're right about that. My husband and I try to spend a weekend a month camping here in the park. Must be some sort of primal instinct or something. I'm not sure I would have used the word *sexy* to describe camping out, but it does kind of feel that way, now that you mention it."

Autumn giggles before turning serious. "I guess our timing could have been better. Have they ever evacuated the park before?"

Sylvia cranks down the side window. "Not that I know of. Or if they have, it was a long time ago. I don't think they even knew there was a volcano here until the early 1970s. If you ask me, this is a whole lot of to-do about nothing. We have earthquakes all the time, but I'll grant you, the ones we had this morning were some of the strongest ones I've felt."

They banter back and forth as they continue on, but as they near the Giant Geyser area, a sudden whipsaw of the ground sends the truck off the trail. Before the three can register their surprise, a rupture in the earth opens and a plume of molten rock and ash shoots skyward as a pyroclastic flow washes over the truck, incinerating the three people inside. Within seconds, the 1,500-degree heat wave of hot ash and gases melts the

pickup and ignites the surrounding forests as the conflagration of certain death rushes outward at hurricane
speeds.

Camp 180—Clarksville, Tennessee

Interview: Olivia from Omaha, NE—homemaker

"We're still holding out hope. I mean, it's possible
she could be at another camp or something. We know
Autumn and Jackson were going to Yellowstone, but
that doesn't mean . . . that they're . . . gone. I told her
to get a summer job to help pay for some of the college
expenses, but John, that's my husband, said 'Oh, let
them have a little fun. They've got the rest of their
lives to work.' It's his fault they went. If she'd have
listened to me . . . it's the not knowing that's eating us
alive. No one has any information. We can't find out a
damn thing. But we wouldn't be in this position if John
hadn't . . . Oh God, I just want to strangle him."

CHAPTER 52

Jackson, Wyoming

"C'mon, Michelle, we should have been on the road an hour ago," Andy Barlow says while perched on the bed of her one-bedroom apartment they had once shared. Andy had moved out two weeks ago after a heated argument about something neither could remember. A good amount of alcohol had precipitated the argument, but after a couple of days of no returned texts, Andy arrived at her doorstep with a dozen roses and a blubbery apology. The makeup sex healed most of the wounds.

Michelle Marchetti peeks around the closet door. "I don't know what to pack. How long do you think we'll be gone?" Tall and lean, with the olive skin, dark hair, and the almond-shaped, dark eyes of her ancestors, Michelle also inherited the famous Italian temper. With a hawkish-looking nose perched above her large, full lips, her face is classic Italian—à la Sophia Loren.

"I don't know. Just grab enough clothes for a few days." A tall, broad-shouldered young man with long, dirty blond hair, Andy has well-defined shoulders from his work on the river. He hasn't broken the news to Michelle that they might never return. "Grab all your jewelry, too, but be quick about it. We're running out of time."

Michelle sticks her head beyond the door again. "I don't know what the rush is. The damn volcano hasn't erupted in forever. Can't I spend a few extra minutes to gather my stuff?"

"Not according to my dad. He thinks the thing could blow any minute."

"Whatever. Where are we going, again?"

Andy sighs. "Down to Arizona, if we can make it." Andy stands from the bed and begins to pace around the small room.

"So I need mostly warm-weather stuff?"

"Listen, Michelle. I don't care what you pack, but you need to pack whatever it is right now."

"Don't use that tone of voice with me, Andy. I'll send you right back to John's place."

Andy's cell phone trills and he fumbles it from his pocket to find a text from his father: *Vent open at Old Faithful. Could be the start of catastrophic eruption. Hope you're well on your way to Arizona. Talk soon.*

Andy types out a quick reply—*headed that way*—before ramming the phone back into his pocket. He strides into the closet, grabs the clothing from Michelle's hands, and stuffs it into a suitcase. "We're leaving right damn now."

"I don't have everything I need."

"You're not going to need anything except what you'll wear at your funeral if we don't get the hell out of here. My dad just texted to say a vent is opening right now at Old Faithful."

Michelle relents and follows Andy to the front door. "Wait, I need to find my sunglasses."

"Forget the fucking sunglasses. There'll be enough ash in the air to blot out the sun."

They hustle to the old Honda Accord and climb in. Andy fires the engine and they screech out of the parking lot. He sails up the on-ramp to Highway 26 and heads south, gunning the four-cylinder engine to the redline. But just as quickly, he stomps on the brakes, sending white tire smoke boiling from beneath the car as he tries to avoid a collision with the stopped traffic ahead of them. The car comes to rest mere inches from the back bumper of a black SUV. Andy sucks in a deep breath. As the adrenaline begins to subside, he turns toward Michelle and says, "We could be in some serious trouble."

CHAPTER 53

Yellowstone Center for Resources

Rachael gasps. "Tucker, the borehole seismometer at Norris is indicating a substantial quake."

Tucker steps closer to the monitor. "How large?"

"Larger than anything we've seen up to now." She glances up at Tucker. "Think that vent's now open?"

"There's no way to know unless we get a report from one of the rangers. But I sure as hell hope not."

"If we're going to head north, now might be a good time," Rachael says. "At least get as far as Bozeman."

Tucker ignores her comment. After a moment of contemplation, he walks over and picks up the replacement radio. "Tucker Mayfield to Walt Stringer." No response. "Tucker to Walt. Over."

Rachael stands and walks over to Tucker, putting a hand on his arm. "I doubt he's had an opportunity to recharge the battery."

Tucker pulls away from her touch and tries the radio one more time with the same result. He digs the satellite phone from his pocket and discovers *that* battery's dead. "I'm going to run up to my office and get a phone charger."

Rachael returns to her computer. "What about Bozeman? Want me to roust Ralph and his wife?"

Tucker stops. "Yes. You guys need to be on the road as quickly as possible."

"What about you?" Rachael asks.

Tucker doesn't respond as he pushes through the door. He takes the stairs two at a time and enters his office. After snagging another freshly charged radio and the phone charger, he hurries back to the analysis center.

"What did you mean, 'you guys'?" Rachael asks, standing from her chair.

"Did you talk to Ralph?"

"I did. Now, quit ignoring my question."

Tucker reaches behind a table to plug in the phone charger. "Is he packed up and ready to go?"

Rachael plants her hands on her hips. "Damn it, Tucker, tell me what's going on."

Tucker sighs. "I can't leave with my family out there. I need to find them."

Rachael steps over, invading Tucker's personal space. "The rest of the caldera could blow any moment. Walt is a wily old man. He'll figure out something."

"Walt can't protect them from a pyroclastic flow."

"They can survive if they get belowground, but you've got zero chance of surviving out in the open."

"Maybe I can find them before the larger eruption happens."

"Bullshit. You don't even know where to start looking."

April decides it's time for a bathroom break and escapes out the door.

Tucker angers as he points toward the window. "That's my brother out there. The only one I'll ever have. And the only niece and nephew I have."

"And don't forget Jessica."

"Fuck you, Rachael." Tucker whirls away and stalks to the other side of the room.

Rachael allows them both a moment to cool off before following. "That was a low blow, Tucker. I'm sorry. If you're going to look for them, so am I."

"No, you're not."

Rachael steps in and pokes him in the chest. "Watch me."

Tucker takes a step back. "You don't have any skin in the game."

Rachael steps forward, erasing the distance. "I don't care if I don't have any *skin* in the game, or whatever the fuck that means."

They separate when April returns to the room.

The two radios sound in unison. "To anyone still on the radio . . . I'm near the West Entrance and just heard a massive explosion. A huge column of ash is visible to the northeast. Could be the Norris area. It's far larger than what happened at Old Faithful."

The radio goes silent for a moment, leaving Tucker and Rachael hanging.

The man's voice returns, more full of astonishment than alarm. "I bet the ash is already forty thousand feet in the air."

Tucker picks up one of the radios and triggers the transmit button. "You need to move west as quickly as you can. You don't have much time."

"Time for what?" the voice asks.

"Stop talking and start moving! A pyroclastic flow

is going to incinerate the ground you're standing on in about ten minutes. Move."

Panic fills the man's voice. "The only vehicle I have is one of the park's loaders."

Tucker races over to the map on the wall. "Rachael, sound the sirens again. The town of West Yellowstone has about twenty minutes of existence left on this planet. April, get on the phone to Superintendent Barlow. Tell him to alert the governors of Montana, Wyoming, and Idaho. We are out of time."

Tucker studies the map as a hot coal simmers in his gut. There is nowhere for the man to go. Tucker slowly places the radio to his lips. "Your only chance for survival is the Madison River, just north of your position."

The man answers, his breathing labored. "Do I just stay in the water?"

"That's the only choice you have." With a very slim chance of survival, the man could well die of hypothermia.

Rachael stands from her chair. "April, tell Ralph that you guys need to be on the road."

Tucker places the radio on the table. "You're going, too, Rachael. I'll hold down the fort."

"There won't be any fort left to hold down," Rachael snaps. "And I think I'm quite capable of making my own decisions."

April hangs up the phone and gathers up her things. "I'll have Ralph give you a call when we get to Bozeman."

"Thanks, April. We'll see you guys up that way in a day or two."

April steps over and gives Tucker a hug and a lingering kiss on the lips before exiting the room.

Rachael watches her depart. "I guess I don't merit a hug, much less a kiss."

"Please, Rachael, go with them."

"No, I think I'll hang out here for a while."

Tucker kicks one of the table legs. "I swear, you're borderline crazy."

Rachael smiles. "Takes one to know one."

Tucker scowls as he picks up the sat phone to call Jeremy Lyndsey.

CHAPTER 54

White House Cabinet Room

President Drummond ducks into her private rest-room, not only to answer nature's call, but also for a moment of silence. After finishing, she washes her hands and winces when she looks in the mirror. The suitcases under her eyes are far too large and droopy to be called *bags*, and her normally bright blue eyes are as red as a Radio Flyer wagon. She retrieves her tooth-brush from the medicine cabinet, hoping to reclaim some semblance of that minty-fresh feel. After replacing her toothbrush, she pushes through the door to be greeted by Ethan Granger.

"Ma'am, they're ready for you in the Cabinet Room." Although he's logged even more sleepless hours than the President, Ethan is still dressed in full wardrobe. His tie is cinched tight and the pocket square is perfectly aligned, nestled neatly in the front pocket of his suit coat.

"You can shed the jacket, Ethan," she says as she brushes past.

"Never. I always dress to impress."

President Drummond pauses. "I don't think anyone in that room cares whether you're wearing your suit coat or not."

"Oh, but I'll care, ma'am."

She gives him a tired smile before proceeding into the room. The crowd is growing with the recent additions of a few members of the military brass. Assistant secretaries of the interior, Claire Espinoza and Hayden Fulton, are pecking away at laptops, and the secretary of agriculture is on the phone. The head of the Federal Aviation Administration is huddled in the corner with several staffers. President Drummond pulls out her chair and drops into her seat. "Nolan, how bad is it?"

The FAA administrator stands and straightens his tie before approaching the table. "There was a slight delay in getting the warning out. We're talking about a delay of no more than a few minutes, but the results of that delay are devastating. We have three confirmed crashes, all related to volcanic ash. An Affordable Air Boeing 737-400, traveling from Seattle to Kansas City, crashed inside Yellowstone Park with a hundred forty-two souls on board. The second aircraft was a Canadian Air Embraer E-190, en route from Denver to Vancouver that went down just south of Bozeman, Montana, with ninety-seven passengers and five crew members aboard. The third was a Skyway Airbus A320, bound for Winnipeg out of Los Angeles, which crashed east of Billings, Montana. That aircraft was carrying a hundred fifty-six passengers and crew. There are apparently no survivors, but we won't know more until the NTSB crews arrive on the scenes of all three accidents."

President Drummond finishes scribbling on a pad and looks up. "That's four hundred lives that would have been saved if we had grounded planes earlier. Please tell me nothing is flying now."

"All domestic air travel is grounded, ma'am. There are a few international flights departing out of Los Angeles and New York."

The President leans forward in her chair. "That stops now. I'll not have another plane crash under my watch."

"But, Madam President—"

President Drummond holds up her hand. "Until we can get this all sorted out, there will be no aircraft departing or landing anywhere in the United States. End of story."

Kinney leans forward and places his palms on the table. "The airlines are going to raise hell."

"Tough titty. I've made my stance perfectly clear. And tell the National Transportation Safety Board to hold off sending crews. I don't want to be responsible for further unnecessary deaths."

Kinney nods and slinks away as President Drummond turns to Granger. "Do we have Dr. Lyndsey on teleconference?"

"Yes, we do." Ethan leans forward and punches a button on the speakerphone array.

"Dr. Lyndsey, are you with us?" the President asks.

"I'm here, ma'am." His weary voice echoes across the room.

"What do we know, Doc?"

"I've lost contact with the chief scientist at Yellowstone, and most of the equipment in the southern portions of the park are offline. The latest satellite imagery shows just the one vent around the Old Faithful area."

President Drummond drums her fingers on the table. "The governor of Wyoming has issued an evacuation

order for the western half of the state. Do we need to
widen the evacuation to other areas?"

"Everything within a radius of one hundred miles
needs immediate evacuation. Beyond that, we might
need to think of a relocation rather than an evacuation."

"Why do you say that, Dr. Lyndsey?" the President
asks.

"Some portions of the country might well be uninhabitable for several years. With ongoing power outages and all the other lingering issues with volcanic
ash, the situation will be untenable."

The shrill ringing of a cell phone blasts through the
speakers. "Madam President, may I take this call?"

"If it's important, yes."

"It is, ma'am. Hello, Tucker . . ."

The President tunes out Lyndsey for the moment
and turns her focus to Henry Edmonds, secretary of
agriculture. "Henry, anything we can do to prepare?"

"Some of the cattle operators are shipping herds
down to an area we've made available near Big Bend
National Park, between El Paso and Del Rio, Texas.
But with the ongoing drought, the area can only support two to three cattle per acre. They're struggling to
round up enough hay. We started shipping grain, via
train car, from some of the storage facilities in the
Midwest, but it's a time-consuming proce—"

"Madam President?" Lyndsey's urgent voice booms
through the array of speakers.

"Go ahead, Dr. Lyndsey," President Drummond
says.

"That phone call was from Dr. Tucker Mayfield at
Yellowstone. We've had a major eruption at the Norris

area of the park. Norris lies along the northern rim of the caldera, a good distance from the first eruption. He and I believe an eruption of the entire caldera could occur at any time."

President Drummond massages both temples. "How soon?"

"Could be minutes or hours, maybe as much as a day or two. But this eruption is much larger than the first, and an updated satellite image shows ash already ascending into the stratosphere."

"Will this really be the largest eruption since man's existence, Dr. Lyndsey? Or has the severity been overstated?"

"To answer your questions—yes and no. The effects haven't been overstated, ma'am. This will be a globally changing event and, unfortunately for the United States, we'll bear the brunt of it."

CHAPTER 55

Near the east entrance of Yellowstone Park,
outskirts of Cody, Wyoming

Josh Tolbert climbs down from the cab of the borrowed pickup and sneaks around the back to take a piss. After being told about the closure of the South Entrance, the most likely route his parents would have taken, Josh worked his way around to the east side of the park. He had to drive a big loop to get here—southeast to Riverton, then north on 120 to Cody, nearly two hundred miles out of the way. He found out the hard way that roads are sparse in this part of the country.

He rezips his shorts and returns to the pickup. He's been sitting beside Highway 14 for the past few hours, hoping for any sight of his family. So far, no luck. A steady stream of traffic has trickled past but no cherry red Ford F-250 pulling a bright aluminum, completely restored Airstream trailer. The only time he's vacated his post was to make a food run into Cody. Besides food, he stocked an ice chest with bottled water and Red Bull and added one of those $5.99 cell phone chargers that are ubiquitous at most roadside convenience stores. The Red Bull and water are responsible for his frequent trips to the rear of the truck.

He thumbs his glasses farther up his nose and reaches for his cell phone sitting in one of the cup holders. He checks again for messages and, finding none, starts dialing—Mom, then Dad, with the same results: no answer. He tries his sister, the one person who normally answers her cell come hell or high water, and hears, "I'm sorry but the cellular customer you are—"

Josh punches the end button and drops the phone back into the cup holder. He squirms in the driver's seat, trying to get comfortable, then turns the radio on and finds only static. He drums his fingers on the steering wheel for a few moments before he starts squirming again. He exhales a loud sigh and reaches for another energy drink. After shaking off the residual water, he pops the top.

The can slips from his grasp when a loud explosion shatters the air and the ground beneath the pickup convulses. "What the hell was that?" Josh says out loud as he grabs for the spilled container before the sticky liquid can ooze into Professor Snider's leather seats. The sirens in Cody start winding up. Josh tosses the can out the window and uses his palm to splash the liquid out of the seat.

The sat phone trills. He dries his hand on his shorts and picks up the phone.

"Josh, are you there?"

"I'm here, Professor Snider. I just heard a loud explosion."

"That's why I'm calling. Where are you at the moment?"

"Just a little ways west of Cody on Highway 14."

"Hold on, let me pull up a map."

Josh hears the click of the keyboard. "What's happening, Professor?"

"Okay I've got it. Josh, there's been a major eruption around the Norris area . . . Hold on, I need to check the distances." There is more typing and clicking. "Oh shit, you're too close. Josh, I need you to get in the truck and start driving."

"I'm not safe here?"

"No. There will be other, larger eruptions, and the pyroclastic flows could stretch for many miles in every direction."

Josh fires up the pickup. "Which way do I need to go?"

"You can only go east from there, Josh. Head for Sheridan, then circle back north toward Billings, Montana."

"But that's the completely opposite way I need to go to get home."

"Don't worry about getting home right now, Josh. You need to get out of the danger zone first."

"But I still haven't found my family."

"Listen carefully, Josh. There's no telling where your parents are. They could've gone west or north out of the park. You need to concentrate on yourself for the moment. Can you do that?"

"Yeah. How long do I have?"

"At your location, maybe fifteen minutes. But that's only a guesstimate. You should be clear once you're on the other side of Cody, but you need to be moving now."

Josh lowers the shifter into drive and mashes the gas pedal. Traffic is a tad lighter and he shoots through a gap and out onto the highway. "I don't know how much battery I have left on this phone."

"Just keep driving. Call me when you're safe. Might need to find a landline phone, though. A satellite connection will be dicey with all the ash."

"Okay. I'm on the highway now. Thanks, Professor, for the warning."

"You're welcome. I'm looking forward to reading your thesis. Be safe, Josh."

"I will, sir. Talk to you soon." Josh ends the call and tosses the phone onto the passenger seat. He places both hands on the wheel as he pushes the pickup up to seventy, passing the slower cars on the straightaways. Flying around a curve he has to swerve into the other lane to avoid colliding with a slow-moving tanker truck. He jerks the truck back into his lane, narrowly avoiding a head-on collision with another oil field semi. As he ascends the next hill, he checks the rearview. Nothing yet. Cresting the ridge, he sees a convoy of tanker trucks in front of him, with no hopes for passing. He curses, slows, and checks the mirror again.

The convoy is poking along at about 35 miles an hour. Ten minutes later and about two miles from Cody, Josh spots the first sign of trouble. The sky behind him is dark and angry, with glowing embers shooting out like tracer bullets. Best he can tell, it's still about seven or eight miles behind him. Josh lays on the horn and starts flashing his headlights, but the convoy only slows, as the first truck turtles a left turn onto a narrow dirt road. The six trucks crawl forward, their left-turn signals flashing, as they wait for the first driver to complete his turn. Josh slows enough to engage the four-wheel drive before steering off the road, now straddling the narrow shoulder and the sloped embankment on the right side of the road.

Tires squeal as the westbound traffic tries to stop when they catch a glimpse of what lies before them. Two large semitrucks jackknife, their trailers skidding across the asphalt, trailing thick clouds of white smoke. Another pickup sees the slowdown too late and steers up the steep side of a hill. The truck comes to a stop, teeters for a moment, then starts flipping down the hill. Josh looks away from the melee and feeds the engine more gas. He swerves around the back side of a guardrail and bounces over a rock outcropping, his jaws snapping together, catching a portion of his tongue. He cries out in agony.

Josh clears the line of trucks and shoots back up onto the roadway, flooring the gas. He glances in the mirror to see a large power flash and an eruption of sparks. When he turns his eyes forward he sees all the lighted signs in town wink out. Tapping the brakes, he slows for a series of long, swooping curves before the road widens into a four-laner at the edge of town. Josh hits the main drag going sixty-five. Zipping past a Pizza Hut, a Days Inn, two tanning salons, and a half a dozen churches, he hits the first stoplight. He slows enough to check opposing traffic before blowing through the intersection.

He glances in the rearview again and discovers a wall of smoke and fire eating its way toward town. The highway takes a dado to the left, but Josh shoots down a residential street, hoping no one steps out in front of him. Now racing down Stampede Avenue, he passes a cop. As expected, the cop lights his overheads and whips onto the road behind him. Josh stomps on the gas pedal. He spots a sign for Highway 20 and makes the turn, the truck careening up on two wheels. The police car looms large in his mirror when he hits the bridge over Beck Lake. Josh feeds the big V-8 more gas. On the other side of Cody, Josh opens the truck up all the way. He glances in the side-view mirror to see the cop car make a sliding U-turn to go back the other way. He exhales a sigh of relief.

He's flying down the highway when a dash light flickers and a chime sounds. He glances at the display to discover the gas gauge hovering just above empty. He eases up on the pedal and casts another furtive glance at the mirror. The wall of smoke seems to have slowed and now lingers over the heart of downtown Cody. Josh slows a little more, hoping to stretch the remaining gas. As he passes the one of the last feeder roads into town, he spots a KOA campground in the distance, a large SHELL sign silhouetted against the smoky sky.

Josh steers the truck up to a pump and jumps from the cab. He leans over and vomits, a mixture of Red Bull and water gushing from his nostrils. He wipes the snot from his nose and begins filling the truck with gas. Behind him, the wall of flames stretches across the width of the horizon. Josh turns away from the horrific sight and vomits again. When the tank is full, he replaces the handle and climbs up into the cab. As tears stream down his cheeks, his brain clicks through a bevy of scenarios. *Getting back to Salt Lake City will be an impossibility. What to do?* Josh heaves out a heavy sigh. *Where's my family?* Josh wipes away the tears and drops the truck into gear. The only place he can think to go is home. He steers the truck out onto the highway and feeds the big engine more gas.

CHAPTER 56

Though technically located in Montana, the town of West Yellowstone sits four miles from Wyoming and eight miles from Idaho. As the gateway city to the western entrance of the nation's oldest national park, the annual population of 1,200 swells during the summer months. Tourists flock to the hotels, restaurants, and western wear stores that line the main drag of the 360-acre town.

Richard Altmiller slots the family minivan into a parking spot in front of one such western outfitter. On their way back to Los Angeles, their two teenage girls are hoping to score some cowboy boots to spring on their friends back home.

Kelley Altmiller, the matriarch of the family, removes her sunglasses. Still struggling to lose the baby weight from eleven years ago, there's a stubborn heaviness that clings to her hips. "Richard, are you sure we have time for this? Maybe we should stop somewhere else."

He arches his back against the seat. "I think we're

fine, and frankly, I could use some walking-around time. In addition to the sunburn, my back is stiff as a board." The Altmillers have spent most of the day on the Madison River where Richard was attempting to teach the girls how to fly fish. That lasted all of about 15 minutes, the girls quickly losing interest.

"I know, but maybe we should drive on to Idaho Falls or somewhere else. I'd feel more comfortable if we could put some more distance between us and that damn volcano."

Lacy, at thirteen, the older of the two girls, leans forward, wedging between the two captain's chairs that make up the cockpit area of the van. She sweeps the dark hair from her eyes. "C'mon, Mom, it won't take long. I know exactly what I'm looking for. I Googled it."

"Yeah, and I know which ones I want. They're red with light blue straps," Lori, their eleven-year-old, says.

Kelley swivels in her seat to look back at her daughters. "What makes you think this store will have them? I've done plenty of shopping with you two. You'll want to try on a dozen pairs before deciding."

Richard reaches over to put a hand on his wife's leg. "Honey, we're still on vacation. Besides, I might find a pair for myself."

Kelley turns to her husband, laughing. "You in cowboy boots? You live in flip-flops. It's a struggle for you to put on real shoes to go to work."

Richard swings open the driver's door. "Maybe I'll find a cowboy hat, then. Keep the sun off my balding pate. C'mon, babe, let them pick out some cowboy boots."

Kelley relents, and the Altmiller family spills out of the van. She takes one long lingering look down the street toward Yellowstone before following her family into the store.

Fifteen minutes later, Lacy is trying on her sixth pair of boots and Lori is carrying her eighth pair over to an old wooden chair at one end of the rows of boots. Richard walks by modeling another cowboy hat to the delight of his daughters. With a dozen racks of boots lining one side of the store, Kelley cruises the aisles, trying to tamp down her sudden urge for a pair. She picks up a pair of bronze lizard boots and flips one over to look at the price tag. She gasps and delicately places it back on the shelf. Farther down the aisle a red pair catches her eye. She flips it over and is glad to see the price is less than $200. After double-checking the size, she lugs them over to a chair and plops down.

Richard walks by modeling a Hoss Cartwright hat, with about two feet of empty space between the top of his head and the top of the hat. She chuckles as she toes off her tennis shoes. But the chuckles die in her throat when the echoing of sirens pierces the inner sanctum of the store. She lurches out of the chair and runs barefooted toward the large windows. She looks up and down the street and sees nothing amiss. She strides over to the sales counter where a teenage girl is texting on her cell phone. "What're the sirens for?"

The girl glances up from the screen. "Don't know. First time I heard them was this morning. I'm just working here for the summer."

"You mean when they ordered the evacuation of the park?"

"Yeah, I guess. I think they're for tornado warnings,

but I didn't think we were going to get any bad weather today."

Kelley turns away, her heart hammering in her chest. She spots Richard trying on a straw hat and hurries over. "Do you not hear the sirens?"

"I hear them. Maybe they're just reaffirming the evacuation." He rakes a finger across the rim of the hat. "What do you think?"

"I think we need to get the hell out of here. Why would they blow the sirens again if the evacuation is already under way?"

Richard thinks about her question for a moment, then whips the hat from his head. "You're right. Let's round up the girls."

They hurry toward the back of the store, where they find both girls posing in front of the mirror, shiny new cowboy boots on their feet.

Kelley latches a hand on each daughter's arm. "We're leaving."

"But I just found the perfect pair of boots," Lori whines.

"We need to leave now, girls. I promise I'll buy you some on the Internet."

"They all fit different, Mom," Lacy says. "These fit perfectly."

"Okay, just take the damn things off." Both girls work on prying the boots from their feet as Kelley turns to her husband. "Grab the damn boots and pay while I load up the girls."

Richard scoops up the boots, once free of his daughters' feet, and begins sorting through the boxes scattered across the floor.

"Mom, I need my real shoes," Lori says.

Kelley lowers her voice. "Find your shoes right this damn minute."

The girls scurry up and down the aisles searching for the shoes they arrived in.

Kelley whirls on her husband. "Fuck the boxes, Richard. Just go pay."

"But I don't know how much they are."

"Maybe Einstein behind the counter will know the price."

The girls return, carrying their sneakers. Kelley pushes them toward the car as another round of the sirens begins. Kelley stops, whips out her wallet, and digs out a wad of hundred-dollar bills. "Give me the goddamn boots, Richard. Go start the car." She snatches the boots from his grasp and hurries to the counter, where she plops down four of the bills. "That's for two pair of girl's boots. Keep the change." She spins away and hurries for the exit. When she steps outside she glances toward Yellowstone and sees a row of dark clouds boiling toward them. She flings open the door, tosses the boots into the backseat, and piles in. "Go, Richard. Something's headed this way."

He squeals the tires reversing out of the parking spot and rams the transmission into drive. He mashes the gas, but they hit a red light at the next intersection.

"Run it," Kelley shouts as she leans forward to peer out the side-view mirror.

"Traffic's coming," Richard says.

She glances up at the intersection. "You can beat it. Punch the damn accelerator."

He floors the accelerator and the minivan jumps into the intersection. The girls scream as a pickup clips their back bumper. Richard hits the brakes.

"Don't stop. Drive!" Kelley screams.

Richard glances in the rearview to see if the truck is turning to come after them. The truck is slowing, but what he sees beyond the truck sends fear racing along his spine. He floors the gas and barely misses a car trying to back out of a parking space. He lays on the horn as the minivan shoots by.

"Faster, Richard," Kelley shouts.

"I'm trying."

In the backseat the two girls turn to look out the back window. They shriek in terror and begin begging their father to speed up. Richard blows through the next light and sees open road ahead of them. He floors the gas but the small V-6 is straining in the altitude. Another glance at the mirror, and a pit the size of Yellowstone canyon forms in his stomach. Half the town is now ablaze.

Kelley turns to her husband. "We're not going—"

The pyroclastic flow, traveling at over 100 miles an hour, envelops the minivan. The seething mass of superheated gas and ash begins melting the tires as the van lurches off the road. After a few brief seconds of coughing and choking, the sounds end as the Altmiller family is incinerated. The last items to ignite are the new cowboy boots that lay scattered across the backseat.

CHAPTER 57

West of Cody, Wyoming

Kenny Huff, owner-operator of Huff Wireline Services, climbs from the cab of his brand-new unit and turns to one of his workers. "Go around and make sure all cell phones are switched off. I don't want the damn perf gun to blow while I'm loading it."

The worker scurries away, and Kenny opens the back bay of the truck and begins assembling the perforating gun. This afternoon he's using a two-inch hollow carrier gun with six deep penetrating charges per foot. Working with a six-foot section of pipe he begins loading the thirty-six shaped charges, carefully removing them from their egg-shaped carton and inserting them into the holes of the gun. He's placing the detonator cord in the last charge when he hears the faint echo of sirens.

He wipes his hands on his grease-stained coveralls and sweeps his gaze around the drilling pad. "What now?" he shouts.

Hank Caldwell, the oil company geologist, slips out from behind the truck where he had sought cover. When you've seen a perf gun explode and rip through the man loading it, you quickly learn to find a safe place to hide. With a velocity of 25,000 to 30,000 feet per second, to better punch through the casing and into the rock formations, a human body offers little resistance. "I think they're still trying to evacuate Yellowstone. I think they had a small eruption earlier."

"Are we safe here?"

"We are as long as the whole thing doesn't blow. Believe me, you'll know when that happens. Gun ready to shoot? J.J.'s about to have a cow to get these wells producing. Hell, you'd think the man was down to his last dime, the way he acts sometimes. But hey, he pays better than anyone else."

"Gun's ready as soon as we get her fed into the well." Huff bends over and delicately feeds the gun into the riser pipe that will connect to the wellhead. "What do you think old J.J.'s worth now?"

Hank kicks at a dirt clod. "Several billion dollars. Not sure of the exact figure, but I figure any man's got more than one billion is one rich son of a bitch."

"If I had several billion dollars, you'd find my ass down in the Caribbean with my own damn island. Nothing but margaritas, blue skies, and pretty women." Kenny finishes his task and walks around the pad making sure all of his workers are in place. One mans the crane, another handles the wire, and the third member of the crew climbs into a lift unit to connect the perf gun to the blowout preventer at the top of the Christmas tree.

They're fifteen minutes into the operation when a dark cloud appears on the horizon. But with everyone focused on their area of responsibility and the mind-numbing roar of the diesel engines, the approaching pyroclastic flow goes unnoticed. Kenny rotates his hand in the air to signal the crane operator to begin lifting. All eyes are on the perf gun as it slowly rises in the air, all hoping it doesn't slam into the wellhead and detonate. With most of Huff's more experienced workers leaving to take more lucrative jobs in North Dakota, this is the crane operators second month on the job.

The crane man pauses the lift to dry his hands on his coveralls. He works his head back and forth to relieve the tension and, when he rocks back to the right, he spots the seething cloud of ash, now only a half a mile away. He turns to warn the others, and his forearm slams into one of the levers. The sudden movement causes the pipe to lurch, and it slams into the stacked collection of valves, knocking the blowout preventer from the stem. With five thousand pounds of flowing pressure, the mixture of oil and gas shoots high into the air.

Before the whole series of events can register in Kenny's mind, the wave of scorching ash and debris races across the drilling pad, igniting the oil and gas in a fiery explosion that launches his new wireline truck thirty feet into the air. None are alive to witness the truck's fall back to earth.

Camp 6—Panama City, Florida

Interview: Rhonda from Red Lodge, MT—grocery store manager

"My husband has worked in the oil fields all his damn life. And there are plenty of others down here who have done the same. But boy, if anybody brings up the subject, we get more dirty looks than one of them homosexuals kissing his lover on Main Street. Some of these crazy-ass people have a wild hair up their ass that drilling had something to do with what happened. That's bullshit, that's what it is. They don't give a damn that my husband busted his ass so they could drive out to the mall or sit in their warm houses. And on top of the disrespect, I haven't heard from my husband since the whole mess started. He got him a brand-new truck and started his own business. Things were starting to look up, you know what I mean? Now this. Can I give you my information in case you come across my husband somewhere? His name's Kenny and our last name is Huff. He was working down around Cody that morning."

CHAPTER 58

South of Jackson, Wyoming

The town of Jackson, Wyoming, is nestled within the Jackson Hole area, a long narrow valley, or "hole" in the Teton Range. With a little more than 9,500 residents, Jackson is a frequent winter playground for skiers and snowboarders looking for the thrill of steep terrain and abundant snow. But in the middle of June, most of the town is occupied by a transient population headed for Yellowstone National Park, Grand Teton National Park, or a half a dozen national forests that line the slopes of the Teton Range. Now the residents and tourists are running for their lives as the ash paints a hazy smudge on the horizon.

Andy Barlow steps over to the cabin window and lifts the curtain to see heavy ash falling from the sky. The ash, a mixture of rock and glass particles, infiltrated the air intake of his Accord, killing the engine only ten miles south of town. But he and Michelle weren't the only ones left stranded. The highway is littered with dead automobiles, a mixture of RVs, eighteen-wheelers, pickups, and motorcycles—an entire smorgasbord of vehicle types. After a grueling two-hour hike, they arrive at a cabin owned by one of Andy's friends.

Michelle Marchetti steps out of the bathroom with a towel swirled around her head. She's outfitted in a lacy black thong and a matching black spaghetti-strap bra.

Andy ogles the outfit before saying, "We need to get going, babe."

"Yeah, where are we going?" She cocks her hip out. "If you haven't noticed we no longer have a car."

"I don't know how yet, but we can't stay here."

"I thought one of your buddies owned this cabin?"

"I mean, we can't stay in Jackson, Michelle."

Michelle sits on the edge of the bed and unfurls the towel, running her fingers through her hair. "There's no hair dryer."

"The lack of a hair dryer is way, way down the list of our problems at the moment." Andy drops the curtain and walks over to the bed. "Which part of *volcano eruption* do you not understand?"

She scowls. "Don't start on me, Andy. I mean it."

He kneels before her and places his hands on her smooth, muscled thighs, which are honed twice a week by a trainer at the local gym. "The town of Jackson will cease to exist if a larger eruption happens at Yellowstone."

"All I've seen is a bunch of ash. I think we should hitch a ride back to my apartment."

Andy sighs and stands. "A ride with who? If you haven't noticed, most of the cars are dead."

"Andy, I told you not to start." She stands from the bed and brushes past him on the way back to the bathroom. "We'll walk, then."

Andy throws his hands up in the air. "You want to walk back to a certain death?"

She glances back over her shoulder. "I think you're being a little melodramatic, Andy."

Andy's cell phone chimes. He walks over to the bedside table and groans when he sees a message from his father: *Where r u?*

Andy thumbs out a response: *Where are you?*

His father's reply: *Bozeman. Now where are you?*

Andy sighs as he types: *Just south of Jackson.*

He waits for his father's scolding reply, but instead the phone rings. Andy answers.

"Andy, why the hell are you still in Jackson? I told you to get the hell out of town."

"Well, Dad, it's a long—"

"Listen to me, son. A major eruption just occurred around the Norris area. You need to get in that car of yours and start driving. And I do mean now."

"Dad, my car died. I think it inhaled too much ash."

A long, pained sigh hisses across the connection. "Andy, this is only a precursor event. But it could be strong enough to hit Jackson with a pyroclastic flow. If not this one, then most certainly the next eruption will. I don't care how you do it, but you need to get as far south as you can. Move, son. Call me when you're in the clear."

Andy begins to gather up Michelle's clothes with the phone pinched between his shoulder and ear. "I'll call as soon as I can."

"Your mother and I love you, Andy. Please don't fuck around with this."

The call clicks off and Andy pockets his phone. He

steps into the bathroom and lays Michelle's clothes on the vanity. "Get dressed, Michelle. We're leaving."

"Where are we going?"

"South. And we're going now!"

"Don't yell at me, Andy."

Andy grabs her by the wrist. "I don't know what it takes to get through to you, but if we stay here, we die. You have a choice—come with me now or get left behind."

"Fine." She begins to pull on her jeans and top. "How are we going? We going to spread our wings and fly?"

Andy pushes through the cabin door and stands on the porch for a moment, his mind spinning fast enough to make him dizzy. "How?" he mumbles as he searches for an escape route, his head swiveling one direction, then the other. The sky to the north is dark, ominous. A wash of dread rushes down his spine as his eyes drift toward the river. He stares at the rushing water for a moment before turning and hurrying back into the cabin. He grabs Michelle by the hand. "We're leaving."

"I don't know where my shoes are."

Andy tamps down the urge to strangle her and flips up the comforter, finding her shoes. He scoops them up and heads for the door. "Let's go."

Michelle follows him outside. "Where are we going?"

He thrusts the shoes into her hands. "Head down to the river. I'm right behind you."

"We can't swim our way out of here. That water's freezing cold."

He grabs her by the shoulders. "Just trust me, okay? Wait for me down at the water."

She nods and tiptoes through the high grass toward

the river. Andy hustles around the side of the cabin, quickly unlashes a two-person kayak, and grabs a couple of double paddles. After tossing the paddles into the kayak, he drags it down to the river, where he eases it out into the cold, clear water. He holds out a hand to help Michelle aboard.

"We're going to float the river?"

"Only option we have." Andy gives the kayak a shove and scampers aboard. He grabs a paddle and backstrokes far enough into the river to catch the current. The kayak picks up speed. The Snake River runs almost parallel to the road, and they shoot through the bridge under the highway. Andy looks back to see a group of people watching their retreat from the bridge. Andy shouts out, "Start moving. Head south as quickly as you can."

An older couple waves and laughs, and Andy shakes his head. "I warned them."

Michelle hunkers down in her seat, trailing a hand through the water. "I still think you're overreacting." She sits up and turns around. "I left my cell phone back there."

"It's a goner now."

"My whole life is on that phone. We have to go back."

Using the paddle like a rudder, Andy steers the kayak over to the far bank. "Hop out."

"I can't get out here. Take us back up to the road and I'll run back to the cabin."

Andy hands her a paddle. "Start paddling." He ships his oar and leans back in his seat as Michelle flounders around, windmilling the paddle and barely skimming the surface.

Michelle screams and whirls to face him. "Are you going to help?"

He crosses his arms. "Nope. Paddling upstream is nearly impossible, huh?"

She screeches and stands, swinging the paddle toward his head. He ducks, and the paddle flies out of her hands, sailing into the river. She screams again and balls her hands into fists. Andy swallows a chuckle as he steers the kayak over to retrieve the paddle. Michelle spins away, loses her balance, and tumbles head over ass into the water. He offers his hand and Michelle slaps it away. She flounders around and finally crawls back aboard, flopping over the front of the kayak like a landed fish. Andy watches as she repositions her butt into her seat, never uttering a word.

They float along in peaceful silence, the rocky cliffs lining both sides of the river creating a cocoon for the swift-moving water. Five miles downstream, the river makes a big sweeping turn back under the highway, their first glance of open sky since shoving off. Andy's mouth flops open when he looks back to the north. The hills are dancing with fire. A roar like a thousand freight trains drowns out all other noises, and a dark, angry cloud of debris hovers on the horizon. Rocks and other debris splash into the water around them like rifle fire, some rattling off the plastic hull of the kayak. Andy scoops up the second oar and hands it to Michelle. "Paddle toward the far side," he shouts over the roar.

She pinwheels both ends of the paddle through the water as Andy takes huge, lunging stabs, pulling with all his might. The kayak shoots down the river as a torrent of debris continues to pelt them. A jagged piece of something lands on Andy's leg, scorching the fabric of his jeans. He grabs it and hurls it into the river, his fingers stinging from the burn. Michelle drops her paddle as she struggles to pull the hot ash from her hair. Andy snags the paddle and uses the broad end to splash water onto her head before steering the kayak toward the cover of an overhanging group of pine trees.

The deluge continues as larger rocks hit the water, shooting up great gouts of water—a hiss of steam with each splash. Andy snags one of the branches, bringing the kayak to a halt. "Are you okay?" he shouts above the noise.

Michelle turns and he sees a small rivulet of blood running down her cheek. "Do I look okay to you?"

"We can't stay here." He hands her the paddle. "Use one end to shield your head."

She braces one end against the kayak, holding the other end over her head.

Andy glances back over his shoulder. The fire is closer. He turns back to Michelle. "Hold on tight. Rapids ahead."

She wails as he lets go of the branch. With rapids ahead, the current is swifter, and Andy tries to keep the kayak under the overhanging branches for as long as possible. Two hundred yards later, the overhead canopy disappears and the rain of hot rocks and ash bombards them again. He steers the kayak toward the middle of the stream, lining up for the pass through the rapids. Having worked the last two summers guiding along the river, Andy has made this trip a hundred times. But never while being deluged by a hellish monsoon of burning debris.

He steals another glance behind him. The wall of

flames is licking at the edges of the last bend they'd passed. Andy gulps in a lungful of air as he turns to focus on his task. The first portion of the rapids consists of a group of larger boulders lined up in the middle of the stream. He steers toward the far bank as the nose of the kayak dips into the water. Michelle, catching sight of the danger ahead, screams.

Andy carves a sharp left turn, shifts his paddle to the other side, and cuts a hard right, shooting the gap between two boulders. The boat goes airborne, and he braces his body for impact. "Hold on!"

Michelle's arms are tight, her tendons and muscles pushing against the surface of her skin as she maintains a death grip on the sides of the kayak. Ahead, two large boulders lie diagonally across the stream with only a small window of daylight between them. Using the paddle, Andy rudders the rear end around and points the nose toward the gap. Water swirls in a whirlpool, pulling the front of the boat out of line, but Andy switches hands and plunges his paddle deep into the water. The left edge of the kayak scrapes against the rock as they shoot through.

There's no time to rejoice, because the worst of the rapids is just ahead.

Maneuvering first one way then the other, Andy cuts back and forth through a shallow section of gravel, trying to straighten the kayak out for the six-foot plunge ahead. "Hold on tight," he shouts. "Falls ahead. Be underwater."

She gives an imperceptible nod as he pulls his paddle from the water at the last moment. The kayak falls through the air, plunging beneath the icy water, Andy and Michelle hanging on for dear life. The boat surfaces, but it's sluggish from taking on water. He steers around another rock, but the response times are slow and the kayak slams broadside into a massive boulder. They bounce off and go careening down the stream, pinballing among the boulders until Andy can regain control. After one final turn, they clear the last grouping of rocks, and the kayak slows. He steers toward the far bank, nosing the kayak up on a sandbar. They climb out on shaky legs.

"I think we're out of the worst of it," Michelle says, looking back upriver. Small splashes ripple across the water but there is no longer a constant deluge.

"I don't want to stand around to find out. Let's empty the water and get back on the river."

Michelle helps him flip the boat, then turns to give Andy a hug. She nuzzles his neck. "Thank you."

Andy stifles the *I told you so* and tilts his head down to give her a kiss. "You're welcome."

They climb back aboard the kayak and Andy steers them toward the center of the current as a thick layer of smoke settles over the water.

CHAPTER 59

Outskirts of Bozeman, Montana

Ralph Barlow nurses the Park Service truck into the hotel parking lot. Stop number ten on their search for a place to bed down. Sputtering and shaking, the pickup may be traveling its last mile after sucking up too much ash. With two vents at the caldera now open, an enormous amount of ash is in the air, causing trouble for motorists all over northeastern Wyoming. Ralph had stopped to shake out the air filter three or four times to little effect. He pushes open the driver's door while his wife, June, and April exit on the other side. Ralph could go the rest of his life without hearing either one talk again about finding a "May" to join their little group.

Ralph is beyond grumpy. He'd called all of his hotel contacts to find everyone overbooked. With all flights canceled and better than half the cars dead from ash exposure, finding a place to hole up in Bozeman is becoming a nearly impossible task. Hence their stop at Happy Acres Motel, a place that looks as if it hadn't been tickled by a paintbrush since Reagan left office.

A smattering of weeds sprouts through the gravel parking lot, and the pool had been turned into a flower garden, minus the flowers. Cigarette butts litter the cracked sidewalk, and empty pint bottles glint in the sunlight.

Ralph pushes through the door. Stale sweat, decades of cigarette smoke, and the rank odor of cat piss are the first things to greet him. An old television is blaring a daytime talk show behind the counter, and a big, fat cat is perched on a broken-down recliner in the lobby. Ralph takes a step back toward the door, but stops. They're out of options. He steps up to the counter and rings the bell with the snap of his index finger.

A rotund woman, dressed in a tattered housecoat, pushes through a set of curtains staked over a doorway. "Need a room, sweetie?"

"Need two rooms if you have them."

"I can do you one, honey, the last of the bunch."

Ralph is doing his best to breathe through his mouth. "How much?"

"Two hundred a night is the going rate."

"Dollars?" Ralph asks, a look of astonishment on his face. "That's highway robbery."

The woman's smile turns to a frown. "Take it or leave it, sweetie pie. Makes me no never mind."

Ralph hesitates for a moment, then begins digging out his wallet. "Credit cards all right?"

"There's a ten-percent surcharge if you use a credit card. Most of my customers pay with cash money."

Ralph mutters a few curse words as he hands over his card.

"How many nights you wantin' it for, sweetie?"

"Let's do two for now."

The woman extends an oversized paw and snatches

his card. "I won't be able to guarantee you a room if you change your mind."

"Just two nights."

"There aren't any other rooms within fifty miles of this place."

"I realize that, ma'am, but I'm not sure we'll be staying in Bozeman longer than that," he says while thinking a pyroclastic flow would be the best thing to ever happen to this place.

"Suit yourself." The woman gives him a frown as she turns and disappears behind the curtain.

Ralph steps over to pet the cat and gets a hiss for his efforts. He turns back to the counter when the woman waddles back in.

"Sign here and put your tag number on the bottom of the slip."

Ralph scrawls his name on the line and scribbles down a group of random numbers for the tag.

She places a key attached to a horseshoe on the counter. "A lost key will set you back about fifty bucks."

Ralph picks up the horseshoe and dangles the key. "Be kind of hard to lose, wouldn't it?"

"You'd be surprised," the woman says. "You work for the Park Service?"

"Huh?"

"I saw the pickup. You didn't steal it, did you?"

"Of course not." Ralph turns to make his escape.

"Hell of a thing happening down there. What with that volcano and all."

Ralph pauses at the door and turns. "Yep, sure is. You have an ice machine?"

"Had. Went out last summer."

Ralph pushes through the door and takes several deep breaths of fresh air.

"You get two rooms?" June calls from the pickup.

He dangles the key. "One. If you can call it that."

April and June clasp hands as they stroll across the parking lot. Ralph hands them the key. "I'm going to take a look at the pickup. See if I can get her running better."

"Why, Ralph? We have a place to stay."

"The room was only available for two nights. We need to push on further north and we can't do that unless the truck is running."

June gives him a scowl. "Okay, Ralph. You don't have to bite my head off."

"I'm sorry, sweet . . . June. Been a long day. April, use the phone to make some calls if you need to. I'm not sure how much longer we'll have phone service."

"I've already talked to my parents. There's no way for me to get home. So I guess you and June are stuck with me."

Ralph's gut twists. "Hey, no problem. You guys check out the room and see if there's someplace we can go for dinner."

June and April scoot off as he pops the hood. An older-model truck, thanks to budget constraints, the engine relies on a carburetor to deliver fuel to the cylinders. The fuel is mixed with outside air and is forced down through the four barrels to create an air-fuel mixture. Ralph unscrews the lid and carefully removes the air filter, hoping to spill as little ash as possible into the carb. As he suspected, the filter is clogged. He tosses it onto the gravel, sending up a plume of ash. He bends over and hits the filter against the ground, but the ash is so fine it clings to the paper element. Ralph stands, looking around for a gas station to buy a replacement, when his cell phone rings. He glances at the caller ID, groans, and puts the phone to his ear. "Tell me you have good news, Jeremy."

"I wish I did, Ralph. But I don't. The eruption occurring near the Norris area appears to be growing in scope."

"Is this the big one?"

"No, but with two vents open, it's only a matter of time before we have a caldera-wide eruption."

"How soon?"

"Unknown, Ralph. Could be an hour or as long as a couple of days."

"Are we safe here in Bozeman?"

"I don't have a good answer for you."

"Well, let me put it to you this way, Jeremy: If you were standing where I am, would you stay?"

"No, Ralph, I don't think I would."

DAY 2

CHAPTER 60

Yellowstone park headquarters

Tucker takes a sip of water from one of the water bottles they'd jimmied from the vending machine at the Center for Resources. "Any candles left?"

"Last one," Rachael says, pointing toward the candle tucked into a corner of the cellar. This one is mulberry scented, and the sweet aroma is cloying in such a confined space.

They had searched for shelter all around the headquarters area before stumbling upon an old root cellar beneath the field officers' quarters building, part of the old Fort Yellowstone. They lugged a piece of sheet steel over from the maintenance shop to cover the wooden doors. There's enough of a draft to allow them to breathe, but the accommodations are miserable. Usually cool underground, the cellar is now a hotbox created by the fires raging overhead. Tucker is down to his boxers, and Rachael is wearing a sports bra and boy-short panties. They've had ample opportunities to ogle each other.

Tucker leans back against the earthen wall. "Tell me about your family."

Rachael rolls over to her side, seeking coolness from the dirt floor. "You mean the biracial part?"

"If that's what you want to talk about, sure."

"That's the part you want to hear about, isn't it?"

"Rachael, quit being so defensive about your heritage. It's like you have a chip the size of Mount Washburn on your shoulder."

Rachael sighs and traces a finger through an area of loosened soil. "It's difficult growing up with a black mother and a white father. We couldn't go out as a family without people staring at us. And in a small town, you see the same people over and over again. You'd think they would have grown accustomed to the oddity of it. And some of them did, but a larger portion continued to treat us as some type of rare anomaly. I couldn't wait to get out of that town."

"I grew up in a small town with what you'd call"— Tucker makes air quotes with his fingers—"a normal family. You have any siblings?"

"A younger sister who's a senior at the University of Texas."

"Is she majoring in one of the geology fields?"

"Nope. International business. Wants to travel the world." She glances up at Tucker. "Matt your only sibling?"

"Yep. Two rowdy boys, and we did our share of hell-raising. I'm sure some of the older people in town were glad to see us go off to college."

Rachael chuckles. "Probably boring there now, with the two Mayfield boys long gone."

"I'm sure there have been many who came along to

take our place. Wasn't much to do after school or work, other than drive around looking for something to do. Most of the time it ended in some type of mischief."

The conversation fades for a few moments until Rachael says, "Tell me about your father. I remember what you told me while we were driving to Mammoth."

"About him being a racist?"

Rachael nods in the dim light.

Tucker blows out a heavy breath. "He is a product of his history, although that's no excuse for his bigotry. We had a hardware store in town. That's where I worked when I wasn't in school. When I was smaller, I didn't think much of it. But as I grew older, I cringed every time someone other than a white person came into the store. Every Indian, or, I guess, Native American, that came in he called *Chief*. 'Hey, Chief, whatcha need?' Didn't matter if it was man or woman, young or old, if you were Native American your name was Chief." Tucker digs a small hole in the dirt with the heel of his boot.

"There weren't very many black people in town. But there were a few who would come in looking for some piece of hardware. He refused to wait on them. 'I ain't here to serve no niggers,' he'd mutter as he pushed me or my brother out from behind the counter. I don't know what happened the days we weren't there. He probably told them to get the hell out." Tucker glances up at Rachael. "I made a promise to myself during one of those instances that, for the rest of my life, I will treat everyone as an equal. Man, woman, black, white, or brown, everyone's equal in my eyes. I've lived by that mantra since the age of eleven."

"Where's your father now?"

"In a nursing home. He has advanced Alzheimer's. Doesn't know who he is most of the time, but he hasn't forgotten his bigotry. A few of the nurses at the home are African American, and he won't let any of them care for him. Or they refuse to—I don't know which is true." Tucker digs the hole a little deeper with the heel of his boot. "At home he had moments of levity, but I just don't understand how he could be so coldhearted to others."

Rachael scoots up to a sitting position. "I think you hit the nail on the head. He's a product of history. A lot of people from that generation cursed the blacks all through the civil rights era and rooted for the South in their fight against integration. It was a difficult time for the entire country. I just hope we can put the whole race issue behind us as the older generation fades away. What about your mother? Was she cut from the same cloth?"

"God, no, she was an angel. Never had a bad word to say about anyone. She died when I was a junior in high school. Cancer. After that my dad got drunker and meaner. I could never figure out what she saw in him."

The conversation hits another lull and they fall into a silence, the faint hiss of the burning candle the only noise. After a lengthy few moments, Rachael says, "Tell me about you and Jessica."

"I'm sorry, Rachael, but that subject's off-limits."

The silence returns, this time for a longer stretch. Tucker pushes to his feet and walks over to the metal cover, where he tests the temperature with the back of his hand.

"Still hot?" Rachael asks.

"Yeah, but not nearly as hot as it has been. We might be able to push it out of the way in a little while."

He turns and Rachael pats the earth next to her. "I won't bite, and I promise no more annoying questions."

Tucker sniffs his armpit. "I don't smell very pleasant."

"I'm no bouquet of roses, either."

Tucker kneels and plops his butt down next to Rachael, leaning his back against the dirt wall. "I need to be out there looking for Matt, Jess, and the kids."

Rachael reaches across and threads her fingers through his. "Tucker, you need to get your mind around the possibility that—"

"They're out there, Rachael. Alive."

"I hope you're right, but you need to consider the alternative."

"Walt knows this park better than anyone on staff. He could have found a place for them to ride out the worst of it."

"You don't think we've seen the last of the eruptions, do you?"

"Not by a long shot. That's why it's imperative to find them as quickly as possible."

"But if there's another eruption while we're searching we'll be exposed."

"There is no *we*, Rachael. My family, my risk."

"Four eyes are better than two. And I've been to every nook and cranny within the park while working on my hydrology study."

"I'm not going to ask you to risk your life on my behalf."

Rachael gives his hand a squeeze. "You don't need to ask. I'm all in."

Tucker shakes his head. "Too risky for you."

"It's a risk I'm willing to assume." Rachael leans forward and brushes her lips across his. "It's about time you let someone into your world, Tucker."

Tucker squeezes her hand. "I *could* use your help. I'm not as familiar as I should be with the eastern portions of the park. Most of my activity has been centered around the caldera."

Rachael leans in and gives Tucker a firmer, longer kiss. "All you had to do was ask." She pulls away. "We need to make a mental checklist of what we need. We'll want to take food and water for sure, and we need some way to deal with the ash. I wonder if there are any respirators anywhere around here?"

Tucker pulls his hand free and places it on her cheek. He leans in and kisses her. "Thank you."

Rachael lies back, pulling Tucker on top of her. "I have a better way for you to display your thanks."

CHAPTER 61

J. John Jackson pushes out of the Escalade and arches his back. After driving straight through from Woodward, Oklahoma, he's haggard from nearly twenty hours behind the wheel. But time is money, and there's no time to waste. He reaches back into the car to retrieve his black cowboy hat and places it on his head. The hat, 100 percent pure beaver and custom made out of a shop in Santa Fe, New Mexico, cost J. John, or J.J., as most of his hands call him, a cool $5,000. But when you're worth billions, $5,000 is pocket change.

J.J. slams the door and saunters toward one of the airport's private aircraft operators. Everything about J.J. is large. His broad torso is stacked onto a pair of long legs and he's heavily muscled from five decades of working oil fields all over the world. Ash swirls up with each step of his long stride as he approaches the door and pushes through. Inside he finds a long counter littered with flying magazines and a tall, skinny man outfitted in greasy coveralls, the name *Joey* stitched

over the right breast pocket. "I need to rent me a helicopter."

"I'm sorry, sir, but all of our aircraft are grounded."

"Unground them. I've got to have me a helicopter."

"Sir, the federal government has ordered all aircraft
grounded."

J.J. leans over and places his forearms on the counter.
"I don't give a damn what the federal government ordered. I've got a half a billion dollars in abandoned
drilling rigs up at the Bighorn Basin. And I need to get
a look at 'em."

"I'm sorry, sir. Even if I could help you, we don't
have a pilot."

"Now listen to me, son. I want one of those whirlybirds and a pilot to go with it. Now you get your ass
over to the phone and get ahold of that boss of yours."

The man's face turns red, and J.J. can tell he's
thinking about a response, but instead the man shrugs
and turns for the phone. You don't play poker for a
bunch of money and not learn how to read a man. J.J.
stands to his full height of six-four and leans against
the counter, wiping the ash from the top of boots behind each calf. The crocodile boots, also custom made
from an outfit in Fort Worth, set J.J. back about seven
grand. He stares at the man on the phone and plops a
toothpick into the side of his mouth.

After a couple of minutes of hushed conversation,
the man approaches, the phone extended like he's
holding an angry rattler. J.J. snatches up the handset.
"Who's this?"

"This is George Kingwell, owner and operator of
Flight Time. Who are you?"

"I'm a man with a fat wallet, George, and I'm goin' to use it to rent one of your helicopters."

"Even if I could rent you a chopper, there's not a pilot anywhere who'd risk losing his license by disobeying a national grounding order."

"I'll pay one of these flyboys here at your base to take me up."

"There aren't any pilots at Warren that I know about. It's a missile base."

"It said 'Air Force' on the sign comin' into town. *Air Force* means flyin', don't it? You can bet your ass someone out there can fly one of your choppers."

"Whether there are pilots out there or not is a moot point. I can't rent you a helicopter."

"Then I'll buy one off of you. How much?"

"They're not for sale. I have two and they're worth in excess of a million dollars each."

"Sold."

Kingwell sighs on the other end of the line. "You can't buy one if they're not for sale."

"George, everything's for sale. And I do mean everything. Two million, cash, for one of your whirlybirds."

"You walk around with two million dollars in cash, Mr. Jackson?"

"Course not. But I can damn sure have it wired to your account lickety-split. Do we have a deal?"

"You'd be wasting your money, Mr. Johnson. The FAA is not going to let you fly."

"I don't give a rat's ass about the FAA, George. I own about half of Congress and if I want to fly my own goddamn helicopter, I will."

"You're serious about the two million dollars?"

"As a heart attack. Now get your ass in here and start the paperwork. I'm goin' to have your man Joey find me a pilot." He hands the handset back across the desk.

Joey smirks as he hangs up the phone. "Mr. Jackson, you've got more money than sense. You could have bought one of those helicopters for less than seven hundred grand."

"You know what, Joey? When I get those wells pumpin' up there in the Powder River I'll be able to buy me a two-million-dollar helicopter about every hour. Sometimes you have to overspend to make a man feel better. Now, see about gettin' me a pilot."

"No one's going to fly with all the ash."

"Can you fly one of those choppers, Joey?"

"I can, but I'm not licensed."

"Whether you have a license or not don't matter one shit to me. Can you fly one or not?"

Joey nods. "But it'd be a suicide mission. Once that ash gets into the engine, you'll drop like a rock."

J.J. leans across the counter. "How much?"

"How much what?"

"To fly me up there to my rigs."

"What does it matter? I can't spend it if I'm dead."

J.J. leans back. "Not a risk taker, Joey?"

"Not when the risk is a virtual certainty."

J.J. slaps the counter. "Call around. Somebody'll fly me up there if I offer them about fifty grand. Hell, there'll be people out there beggin' to let them fly for that kind of money. Make some calls, you'll see."

Joey gulps. "You'd have to find a place to refuel. The helicopter only has a range of about three hundred miles."

"All that'll be up to the pilot. But maybe we won't have to worry about refueling if the fucker's goin' to crash anyway."

"Why is it so important to go see your drilling equipment?"

"Because, Joey, I've got 'em insured for close to a billion dollars. If they're fucked up I need to get busy buyin' some more. And dealin' with those cocksuckin' insurance adjusters takes forever. Time is money, Joey." J.J. turns away from the counter. "I'm gonna find a bar to get me a cold beer. Call me when the boss man comes in." He turns and flicks a business card onto the counter.

"One hundred thousand dollars. Paid in advance," Joey says.

"For what?"

"To fly you up there."

J.J. steps back to the counter and extends his hand. "You got yourself a deal there, pard."

Joey hesitates for a moment, then shakes on the deal.

"Thought a dead man couldn't spend no money?" J.J. asks.

"It's for my wife. She wants reconstructive surgery after surviving breast cancer."

J.J. thumps his knuckle on the counter, then removes the toothpick from his mouth. "Tell you what, Joey, you fly me up there and back and I'll give you a hundred grand, plus pay for her surgery. That sound like a good deal?"

"As long as you pay the cost of surgery in advance, too."

"How much?"

"A full reconstruction is about sixty grand."

J.J. smiles. "I can do that. That way she'll have enough to get the surgery and still have a little walkin'-around money in case we buy the farm."

Joey dry swallows and nods.

"You worried about dyin', Joey?"

"Yeah, aren't most people?"

J.J. laughs. "Fuck, Joey, life's too short to worry about dyin' all the time."

"Well, I don't really want to die. I'm going to see if there's a way to filter the ash out the air intake. Only chance we'll have."

"Do what you gotta do, Joey. Hey, you gotta last name?"

"Yeah, Jimmerson."

"Well, if that ain't the shits. Two J.J.'s, huh. Can't go wrong with that." He raps a knuckle on the counter again. "I've got me a hankerin' for a cold beer. My cell number's on the card. Give me a shout when the boss rolls in."

CHAPTER 62

The Oval Office

In the quiet of her office President Drummond massages her temples while looking over the latest ash fall estimates. The Cabinet Room is now a war room and the body odor is rank enough to be nauseating. She tosses the papers onto the desk and turns to Granger. "Ethan, have the service open the doors to the Rose Garden. We need to air that room out."

"Too big of a security risk, ma'am. Might have another crazy climb the fence welding a knife."

"The main security risk is I might pass out if I have to spend any more time in there. Open the damn doors."

Ethan stands. "Yes, ma'am."

"And offer them the showers in the basement. No, belay that. Insist on the showers. And see if we can wrestle up some new clothing."

Ethan waves a hand in the air as he retreats. "I'm on it."

Someone knocks on the side door to the study. "Come," the President shouts.

The door swings open.

"Well, if it's not the First Husband come to visit."

Sean Drummond shoots his wife the finger as he walks across the office, taking a seat next to the desk. "You know how much I hate that fucking title?"

President Drummond laughs. "I know, but jeez, it sure gets you riled up."

"The press needs to come up with something else. First Husband is such a pussified title."

The President reaches out to take her husband's hand. "First Lover?"

He opens her hand and strokes her palm with his thumb. "Too personal. I prefer Mr. President."

"I believe that's my title."

"No, you're Madam President. Nothing wrong with *mister* for me."

The two laugh. "So what brings you to the Oval, Mr. President?"

Sean Drummond is a tall, well-groomed man, who wears the same size suit coat he wore his senior year of college, size 44 extra long. He releases his wife's hand and leans back in the chair, crossing one leg over the other while running a hand through his mane of silver hair. An attorney by trade, he gave up practicing when he and his wife moved into 1600 Pennsylvania Avenue.

"How bad is it going to get?"

"It's already bad. We're in disastrous territory at the moment."

"How so?"

"Well, let's see." She holds up her hand and begins counting off fingers. "Two towns have been wiped off the map. Half of the Midwest is already without power, and no one has a clue when the power might be restored. Ash is already playing havoc and the larger eruption hasn't even happened yet . . . Want me to continue?"

"No, I think I get the gist of it. Let me guess. You're being blamed for it?"

President Drummond fakes being surprised. "How did you know? The spin doctors on Fox News are all over my ass for not having the country prepared."

"Hell, you can't prepare for a natural disaster on this scale."

"Tell me something I don't know." The President leans forward in her chair, propping her elbows on her desk. "I'm worried about what's yet to come, Sean."

"The larger eruption?"

"That's one part of it, but we're already in deep shit. We could be facing famine on a global scale." She traces the wood grain of the desk with a fingernail bitten to the quick. "Some estimates suggest as many as a billion deaths worldwide."

Sean Drummond reaches for his wife's hand again. "We can't control what might happen. All we can do is worry about the here and now. You're only one woman, Saundra."

"No, Sean, I'm the President of the United States. And that comes with a mountain of responsibilities. Solving the nation's problems is in my job description."

"Congress is supposed to play an equal role."

"The Senate could spend a month arguing over where to set the thermostat and still not come up with an acceptable answer. And the House would do the same, except take longer doing it. Congress is dysfunctional, Sean."

"You can't solve the world's problems by yourself."

"No, but I'm expected to lead the charge. And I will. I just wish I knew which direction to go."

"I'm here as a resource."

She covers his hands with hers. "I know you are, sweetie. You're one of the smartest people I've ever met, but I don't want to overburden you with my job. I'm the one who got us in this mess."

"No, Saundra, the decision was mutual. I'm here, but I'm not going to step on your toes."

Ethan enters the office. "I'm sorry, I didn't know you were in here, sir."

"It's okay, Ethan, I'm leaving." Sean stands and leans over to kiss his wife. "I'm here if you need me."

"Thank you. Now scoot. You taking command of the kitchen to make dinner?"

"I am. I discovered an old Julia Child cookbook in the library. Be ready for the finest of French cuisine."

President Drummond blows her husband a kiss. "Pick a nice wine from the cellar to pair with it."

"Already done." He waves toward Ethan. "You're invited to join us if you wish."

"Thank you, sir, but I think your wife gets her fill of me during working hours."

Sean slips through the door and closes it behind him as the President turns to Ethan. "Where are we on evacuations?"

"The governors of Wyoming, Montana, and Colorado

have issued evacuation orders for their entire states. Other governors in the nearby states are keeping a close eye on the situation."

President Drummond pushes out of her chair and walks over to the window. "Where in the world are we going to put all these people, Ethan?"

"Schools, churches, or any vacant buildings for now. The Red Cross and other charities are mobilizing. But I'm afraid the situation could become untenable."

"Temporary housing moves to the top of the to-do list. I want a plan and I want it yesterday."

Ethan leans against the desk and sighs. "The team is already hard at work on viable options."

"Good. Is there any good news?"

"Other than the fact that the rest of the volcano hasn't yet erupted, no."

The telephone trills and Ethan leans over to punch the speaker button.

The President's secretary says, "Ma'am, Secretary Edmonds is on line two."

"Thank you, Helen," the President says. "Put it on speaker, Ethan."

Ethan punches off and hits line two.

"What's the latest, Henry?" President Drummond asks as she walks back to her desk and sags into her chair.

"The ash is already having a major impact."

The President leans forward. "How so?"

"Well, ma'am, only about a third of the winter wheat has been harvested due to recent rainfall. Most of the remaining crops in the upper Midwest are now buried by the ash. The same goes for the spring wheat, soybeans, and about every other agricultural crop in the Midwest. The death toll for livestock is already on the uptick and the worst hasn't even hit yet."

President Drummond twists her wedding band around her finger. "Any chance we can import some grain?"

"Not likely. China produces about eighteen percent of the world's wheat, but they still need imports to satisfy their growing population. Canada's in the same boat we're in. Unfortunately, ma'am, the U.S. is the largest exporter of wheat in the world, and those countries we export to are also going to be in a world of hurt."

"My main focus is this country, Henry. There have to be other viable alternatives."

"If there are, I'm not seeing them, ma'am. The entire Ag Department is searching for possible solutions, but we can't squeeze blood out of a turnip, ma'am."

President Drummond thumbs a tight spot on her neck. "Can we import livestock, Henry?"

"We can, ma'am, but we'd have to cut through about a mile of red tape."

"I'm your cutter, Henry. Tell me what I need to do."

"I'll have staff put together a plan."

"Do it quickly, Henry."

"I'm on it, Madam President. I'll have something by the end of the day."

President Drummond reaches over and disconnects the call. "What are the death toll estimates so far, Ethan?"

"I don't have the latest numbers, ma'am, but it's north of ten thousand. And those are only taking into account the plane crashes and those deaths around the Yellowstone National Park area. I expect the numbers to grow significantly as the situation worsens."

President Drummond stands and begins to pace. "I know we've started evacuations but there has to be more we can do."

"I think we're doing everything we can humanly do, Madam President."

She stops and turns to her aide and confidant. "It's not going to be enough, is it?"

CHAPTER 63

The corner of S. Parker Road and S. Peoria Street,
Denver, Colorado

Abhay Kapoor, a second-generation Indian-American, stands behind the locked door of the family-owned grocery store, watching the foot traffic along Parker Road through the ash-filtered sunlight. His parents had fled the growing unrest between India and Pakistan, choosing to leave the random gunfire of Punjab for the safety of Denver, Colorado. The transition was difficult, but with other family members close by, the Kapoor family settled in and his father used their life savings to purchase the small grocery store.

Abhay turns from the glass and meanders down the aisles, taking a mental inventory of remaining stock. The count doesn't take long. With no power, he hustled to move most of the frozen and refrigerated stock, and had a run on most of the canned goods. All the bottled drinks were hot sellers, and Abhay had quickly squirreled away several cases of water for family use. About the only things left in the store are greeting cards, automotive accessories, and assorted overripe fruit. At least that's all that's left for sale. Abhay also stashed a pallet of canned goods in the small locked office at the rear of the store.

With the store abutting a residential area, most of the patrons are local, many of them Indian immigrants much like his family. But over the last day or so, a steady stream of unfamiliar faces has invaded the neighborhood. Robbed last night, the Quick Cash store across the street stands abandoned, the glass shattered and the front door ripped from its hinges. Luckily the owner escaped, suffering only a moderate concussion. National Guard troops have filtered into the area, but their focus appears to be evacuation.

Abhay wrings his hands and returns to the front of the store, astounded at how quickly events have spiraled out of control. His father refused to leave the store abandoned, so Abhay is standing guard. But at five feet six, and 150 pounds, Abhay is not exactly an imposing presence. Across the street he spots a group of four or five individuals, all carrying baseball bats. Teenagers, by the look of them. His body gives an involuntary shudder and he steps back into the shadows. With his gaze focused on the group of boys, Abhay doesn't see the brick that comes crashing through the window. He screams as a group of three older men follow the brick through. One puts a knife to Abhay's throat as the other two fan out through the store.

"Money and food. Where is it?"

"We . . . we . . . have neither."

The man, with greasy long hair and a teardrop tattoo near his left eye, leans his head down, now nose to nose with Abhay. "Bullshit. You fuckers come to town, take our jobs, and then hoard your money like pack rats. I want it."

Abhay swallows, his mouth as dry as cotton. He fumbles his wallet from the back pocket and tries to hand it across to the man. "This is all the money I have. And . . . and as you can clearly see"—he pauses to lick his lips—"we have little food remaining."

The man slices across Abhay's cheek with the knife. He swallows the scream as the hot poker of pain registers in his brain.

"I guess I'm not seeing clearly. Where's the safe?"

Abhay puts a hand to his face to stanch the flow of blood. His jaw clenched in pain, he mutters, "Back office. Empty."

With a flick of his wrist, the man opens a gash on Abhay's other cheek. This time he screams. His knees sag with the pain, but the thug grabs him by the shirt collar and drags him toward the back of the store, Abhay's feet cutting a groove through the blood splattering onto the floor. The man kicks in the door to the office.

"Well, looky here." He pulls Abhay upright. "Thought you didn't have any food?" He draws back a foot and kicks Abhay in the crotch.

Abhay moans and sags against the man's hold as hot bile shoots up the back of his throat.

"Lied about the food and you're lying about the money. Where's the safe?"

Abhay manages to mumble out "closet."

The man drags him toward the closet and swings open the door. He releases Abhay, allowing him to sink to the floor. "Open it."

Abhay uses a bloody hand to protect his crotch. "Safe . . . empty."

The man rears back and sends a heavy boot into Abhay's midsection. "I'm supposed to trust you after lyin' about the food? Open the fuckin' safe."

Abhay crawls toward the safe, leaving bloody smears across the linoleum. He shakily pecks out the four-digit combination as the other two men enter. The man levers open the safe and screams as he begins stomping on Abhay's arm. "You little cocksucker. Where's the money?"

Abhay manages a small shake of his head. "There is no—"

The words die in his throat as the other two men begin kicking and stomping him. Worked into a fury, the men don't stop until long after the light dies in Abhay's eyes.

Camp 53—Augusta, Georgia

Interview: Alyssa from Aurora, CO—high school student

"I'm disappointed to be away from my friends, but being down here is better than those last couple of days at home. It was scary. Aurora is really part of Denver, and when the power went out, it was like someone loosened the hounds of hell. All the stores were looted. People carrying these crazy-big televisions and there wasn't any power to watch them. Just crazy stuff like that. My parents wouldn't let me go outside after that first day, not that I wanted to go out anyway. I would sit on the back porch and, at night, it was freaky dark. Couldn't see the hand in front of my face. Oh, and it wasn't just dark, you could hear gunfire all across the city. Sounded like one of those war zones you see on CNN. You know, those reporters with the helmet and the bulletproof vests with a scene of destruction in the background? Anyway, I do feel safe down here, though they are pretty strict. *Zero tolerance*, they call it. Several people have been hauled away, and no one really knows where they took them. Scary, now that I think about it."

CHAPTER 64

Yellowstone park headquarters

Tucker pulls on his pants and stoops to tie his boots. "You ready to go out there?"

Rachel pulls her T-shirt over her head. "I'm ready for air. It's stifling down here."

Tucker rips his undershirt in half and hands Rachel a portion. "This'll help until we can find some respirators or masks."

Rachael ties the rag over her nose and mouth. "I feel like a masked bandit."

Tucker struggles to slide his Park Service shirt over his sweaty arms. "Let's hope there's something left to steal." After covering his own nose and mouth, he carries a bucket over to the sealed entrance. "Better stand back. No telling what could fall through." He steps on the bucket and levers his shoulder against the steel plating. With a grunt, he inches the makeshift door open. Ash pours into the opening, obscuring his vision. The bucket wobbles under the weight, but with one more shove he opens the plate wide enough for them to make their escape.

Rachael steps over to climb up.

Tucker holds up a hand. "Let me go first."

"Southern chivalry is dead, Tucker." She latches on to the edge of the metal plate and pulls herself topside. "Oh my God," she shouts.

Tucker scrambles out behind her and stops in his tracks. The only things left standing are a few scattered stone fireplaces. Flames flare at the remaining hot spots, and heavy smoke hangs in the still breeze.

"I feel as if I just landed on the moon," Rachael says in amazement.

"Any hope for masks or respirators is out the window," Tucker says.

Rachael points toward the distance. "So is our transportation."

Tucker squints, trying to peer through the smoke. His stomach plummets when he spots a smoldering chunk of scorched metal where the pickup had been parked.

"Is all of this volcanic ash?" Rachael asks.

Tucker bends down and scoops up a handful, letting it slide through his fingers. "A mixture of fire ash and volcanic ash, but mostly volcanic." He takes her by the elbow and steers her toward the faint outlines of the road. Ash swirls with each step and the smoke stings their eyes.

"You still have the sat phone?" Rachael asks.

"Battery's dead. I was hoping to recharge it."

"Yeah, well, that's out the window, too. How are we getting out of here?"

"I haven't thought that far ahead. I wasn't expecting the fires to have incinerated everything in sight." They trudge forward, both rubbing their eyes. A breeze stirs out of the south, whirling the smoke into wispy contrails. "Let's head east."

"We can't walk all the way to where your family might be. We're on borrowed time as it is."

"No, but we can walk that way. Maybe we'll get lucky and stumble across some type of vehicle in the staff housing area."

They walk east. If the smoke isn't bad enough, the heat from the remaining hot spots radiates like a furnace.

"We're going to need water, and lots of it," Rachael says.

"And something to carry the water in. Keep your eyes peeled for any type of container."

"My eyes are stinging so bad I can't see much of anything."

"Mine, too. You're the water expert. Any natural springs in this area, other than the geysers?"

"There's a little spring-fed creek off the southern loop of Lower Mammoth Road."

"I guess we have a destination."

They leave the remnants of Officers' Row and walk onto Grand Loop Road. One wall of the old stone chapel stands erect against the horizon, the stone cross at the precipice standing guard over the ruins.

"Want to look in there? There might be a chalice or two."

"We'd waste half a day digging through all that rubble. Need to keep pushing forward."

They walk around a wide turn and start the long descent into the valley. The once-lush sage hills continue to smolder, and the only breaks in the blackened earth are the granite boulders that have surfaced after centuries of erosion. Rachael grabs for Tucker's arm as she leans forward, racked by coughing. Once finished, he helps her to a standing position and tucks the edges of the rag down into her shirt.

"You"—she coughs again—"trying to feel me up?"

"Yeah, was it good for you? Try to keep that rag tucked in. The volcanic ash is extremely fine. It can sneak in through the tiniest of crevices. Ten times worse than beach sand."

Rachael nods and Tucker turns to continue their journey. A little farther down the road he leads them off the highway, taking a shortcut to Lower Mammoth Road. The ash is much heavier where it collected on the undulating terrain, and they plunge ahead as if trudging down a snow-covered mountain. Once they reach the smoother surface of the road, the walking grows easier. The lower Mammoth region, which once hosted a row of small homes for park staff, now more closely resembles the old photos of war-torn London. Mostly stick built out of two-by-fours and sided by wood siding, the homes lie in mounded heaps of ash. Charred autos are parked in driveways to nowhere.

They walk along the neighborhood streets where they and their friends lived, their sorrow weighing on every footstep. "Good thing they evacuated when they did," Rachael says.

"Still, a lot of memorable items are lost forever."

"They're just things, Tucker. It's the human lives that are irreplaceable. Anything at your house we could use to carry water?"

"Don't know. I lived in pretty sparse accommodations." Tucker snaps his fingers. "Wait. I did have a couple of old metal canteens."

"There you go. Just what we're looking for. And I'm not really surprised about your scanty living quarters. Did you even have a picture on the wall?"

Tucker looks away. "No. But I did have some maps on the wall."

"'Bout what I figured."

Tucker leads them through the side yards of crumbled houses and pulls up short when he sees the pile of rubble that was once his home. Borrowed, but still home for seven years. "That's going to be like looking for a needle in a haystack. Anything over at your place?"

"My roommate and I drank out of plastic cups from random bars. No chance of finding anything over there. Do you remember where in the house those canteens were located?"

"I do. The spare bedroom." They step across the ash-covered lawn and Tucker points to a spot on the far side of the debris. "It was over in that corner."

"That'll give us a starting point."

"Okay, but we can't afford to spend a lot of time looking for them."

"I think I could've done without that reminder. We're not going anywhere without water. We need those canteens."

They sidestep around the larger rubble and start digging through the wreckage. Within minutes they're covered in soot that runs in rivulets down their faces as the sweat leaches from their bodies. Tucker finds a couple of fishing reels, minus the fiberglass poles, and tosses them aside in hopes of retrieving them later. Rachael backhands the sweat from her eyes, leaving a dark smear across her milk chocolate cheeks. She pauses in her search.

"Which side of the room would they have been on?"

Tucker thinks for a moment, replaying a movie in his mind. "One of them was on top of a bookshelf against the outer wall."

Rachael high-steps over the wreckage and begins digging in an area near the foundation. She pulls something from the ruins and screams. She holds the canteen aloft as if hoisting the Super Bowl trophy. One down, one to go.

"Where would the other one have been?" Rachael asks.

"That's what I'm trying to figure out. Might have been in the closet." He climbs over the remains of a sofa. "Which would have been right around here." He pulls away a stacked of charred wood, and Rachael comes over to help. They dig and pry but after a few minutes, Tucker stands and stretches his back. "Maybe we should go with the bird in hand and move on down the road."

"We could probably share one canteen, but your family is going to be thirsty." Tucker agrees and they renew the search with vigor. Ten minutes later, he pulls the second canteen from beneath a pile of smoldering books. "Lead us to water, oh messiah."

After climbing out of the detritus of a past life, Rachael leads them to the spring-fed creek the next road over. "We've solved one problem, but a bigger one looms. How are we going to get out of here?"

Tucker raises a finger in the air. "I think I might have just the ticket."

CHAPTER 65

University Seismic Observation Lab

Eric Snider glances out of his window, where it appears to be snowing in June as the ash rains down on Salt Lake City. He stands and exits his office, striding down the hall to the lab area. The room is fully staffed, and people are working around the clock as the crisis at Yellowstone continues. Most of the geology instructors are apprehensive, yet also somewhat excited to bear witness to possibly the largest volcanic eruption in the history of mankind.

Snider approaches Emily West and takes a seat in a vacant chair. "Have you seen any recent InSAR data for Yellowstone?" InSAR is the acronym for Interferometric Synthetic Aperture Radar, a satellite-based system used to measure ground deformation.

West twirls a finger around a strand of her hair as she uses the other hand to steer the computer mouse. She scrolls through a series of bookmarks and clicks on a page. "Latest data package is two months old."

"I asked for a new data study yesterday."

"Could be they're having trouble with orbital repeat

times or, more likely, atmospheric problems with all the ash."

"With half the instruments offline, we don't have a clue what's happening at the caldera."

"We're still getting intermittent data from the borehole seismometer at Lake Yellowstone." West pulls up the webicorder display for seismometer B208. A normal seismogram is a continuous series of multicolor lines in fifteen-minute increments. The webicorder display for B208 is littered with gaps, some as much as two hours in duration.

Snider points at the screen. "We could have an eight magnitude earthquake and that instrument wouldn't help a damn bit. Do we have *any* active seismographic data from within the caldera?"

West shakes her head. "Just the spastic borehole. Tiltmeters are offline and the GPS units aren't sending data. They might be functioning but the ash is obscuring all transmissions. We do have recent satellite imagery but most of the park is obscured."

Snider picks up a paper clip and begins to straighten it. "I've been on the phone for what seems like thirty days. What's the latest seismic activity out west?"

"Continuing earthquake swarms. There was a fairly large spike with the last eruption at the park."

"Strong enough to trigger an eruption?"

West shrugs. "Who knows? But a caldera-wide eruption might well tip the scales." She turns away from the monitor. "Do they really matter, Eric? Yellowstone's the headliner. All those others are just background noise."

"It's not background noise if one of those volcanoes is in your backyard. Seattle is sandwiched between

Glacier Peak and Mount Rainier. They're both listed as a very high threat for eruption. You can bet those people will worry if one of those erupts."

"I didn't say that to be insensitive, Eric. Hell, I spent some of my formative years in Seattle. Yes, there will be devastating regional effects if any of the Cascade or California volcanoes erupt. But Yellowstone will be a global event. We can't become distracted by what might happen elsewhere. The greatest show on earth is happening right under our noses."

"You're passionate about the subject."

West blushes. "I'm fascinated and horrified at the same time. We spend all our lives studying and analyzing data about what might occur. Now we're living it."

Snider works on putting the paper clip back into its original form. "And many are dying or will die."

"Yes, that's the horrifying part. But we have no physical control of the caldera. It's Mother Nature in her most violent state."

"And that doesn't scare the shit out of you?"

"Yes, that scares me. But you have to admit—"

A pinging alarm sounds from her monitor. She turns back to her computer, quickly scrolling through data.

"Is that one of the alarms you programmed?"

West nods as she continues to click through screens. She stops and points to the webicorder display for Soda Butte, in the far northeastern part of the park.

Snider leans in. "Jeez. How big?"

"I haven't seen a live seismogram of this magnitude since this all started. I would think somewhere in the low sevens."

"That's many miles away from the caldera. Could it be fault activity?"

"There aren't many faults in that portion of the park. My vote is magma movement. And a whole bunch of it."

Snider picks up the phone and punches in a number, tapping a foot as he waits for the call to be answered. After four rings it does. "Jeremy, you see the data from Soda Butte?"

"I'm looking at it right now. That's a major earthquake."

"What do you think?"

"I think we may have underestimated the amount of eruptible material within the caldera."

"Why? Do you think this earthquake is the result of a rapid infusion of magma?" Snider asks.

"I don't think there's any way we'll ever know for sure. I wish we had a working seismometer within the caldera so that we could pinpoint the epicenter. But with the lack of active fault zones in that area, and the fact that we haven't had another eruption, it leads me to believe the chamber could be receiving a large intrusion."

"How much magma do you think is now present?"

"I don't think we have enough data to even hazard a guess, Eric. We may never truly know how much magma is in the chamber. There's just no way to quantify it. Hell, it wasn't until a couple of years ago that we figured out the magma chamber was twice as large as we originally thought. But without any working instruments and their data, we're shooting in the dark."

"Screw the data. What's your gut telling you?"

Lyndsey sighs. "I don't know. Maybe as much as 400 cubic miles of eruptible material."

"Jesus, Jeremy, that's nearly twice the size we've predicted."

"You asked for my gut estimate. Either way, it's going to be one hell of a big bang."

CHAPTER 66

Yellowstone park headquarters

Rachael grabs on to Tucker to steady herself. "You feel that?"

"Hell yes, I felt that. Strongest one yet."

The large earthquake hastens their pace. They top a low rise and pause to catch their breath. "There it is," Tucker says pointing forward. "It" is an old stone barn with a metal roof slapped haphazardly across the top. "C'mon, let's move."

They hurry down the incline, kicking great gouts of ash into the wind. The large metal door squeals when Tucker heaves it open. The scent of used motor oil, diesel, and fifty years of sunbaked upholstery overwhelms them. Inside the barn rests a vehicle with a frog-looking snout and a long, rounded body, painted a deep yellow. Rubber tracks are looped around the four back wheels and skis are mounted where the front tires should have been.

"We're going to drive the old snow coach?" Rachael asks as she rakes her hand across the hood, disturbing the accumulated ash and dust. "Does it even run?"

"It did this winter and has for sixty-some years. Let's just hope the battery has some juice."

"Won't the ash foul the engine?"

"Look around for some old rags. The engine takes in air through those grilles at the back. If we can cover them with some oil-soaked rags or some other type of filtration material it might get us where we're going. It's not like we have any other options. We walk or we take Old Yeller, here."

Rachael rummages around the barn while Tucker works on starting the ancient vehicle. He climbs in and spends a brief moment familiarizing himself with the cockpit area and, with only two gauges and a couple of toggle switches, it doesn't take long. He presses down on the clutch and moves the column-mounted shifter up and down, trying to get a feel for the gear pattern. He finds a small round knob labeled CHOKE and pulls it out before turning the key. The gauges activate, but the key will turn no farther. While he's glad to see the old girl with some juice, he has no clue on how to trigger the starter. He leans out through the open door. "Rachael, any ideas on how to start this thing?"

She walks over, an oil-stained blanket trailing behind her, and peers into the cab. "The starter's on the floor, right next to the gas pedal."

Tucker glances up. "How do you know that?"

"My grandpa had a couple of old trucks on the farm. When I was little, I'd drive him around the pasture while he threw hay out to the cows."

"How about you drive, then. I haven't driven a stick shift in about twenty years."

"See if it'll start before we have any discussions about who's driving."

"Cross your fingers," Tucker says as he double-checks the choke and puts his foot to the starter. After several sluggish turns, the engine fires to life. "Guess you're driving. Find something to cover the intakes?"

Rachael holds up the raggedy blanket. "Covered with cat hair. No telling how many litters called this blanket home."

Tucker climbs out, takes the blanket from her, and carries it over to an old workbench that's listing on one end. After ripping the blanket into strips, he drizzles some used motor oil over the fabric. "Rach, see if you can find some string or wire. We need some way to affix these to the intakes."

She returns with a ball of coiled-up baling wire, and he hands her a rag to attach. Once both complete their tasks, Rachael slides behind the wheel. "Find any extra fuel?"

"Found two five-gallon containers and stashed them in the back. The tank is full but I have no idea how far all that will get us."

Rachael works the shifter and eases out on the clutch. The snow coach lurches forward and dies. She glances over at Tucker. "Been a while for me, too." After restarting, she eases the beast out of the barn. "Think the skis will work on the ash?"

"Should. I guess we're about to find out."

She gooses the gas pedal and steers them out toward the road. "Where exactly are we going?"

"Let's start with Mount Washburn. Used to be some old mine shafts up that way, and I'm betting Walt knows about them. That's about the only place they could have gone and survived the last pyroclastic flow."

CHAPTER 67

Jeremy Lyndsey hangs up the phone and runs his fingers through the wispy tendrils at the top of his skull. After a brief moment of contemplation, he lifts the handset again and punches in the phone number scrawled across a note stuck haphazardly to his computer monitor.

The call is answered on the second ring. "Mr. Granger, this is Jeremy Lyndsey."

"I know, Doc. I've got you programmed into my cell. More bad news?" Ethan Grangers asks.

"Potentially. Is the President available to take my call?"

"She's in a meeting at the moment, Doc, but I'll pass on your message."

Lyndsey bristles at the man's seeming lack of concern. "The message is this: Yellowstone was struck by a 7.4 magnitude earthquake only moments ago. This is the largest earthquake ever recorded on park grounds. And by a very wide margin. After conferring with my colleagues, we believe the earthquake was caused by a massive intrusion of magma into the main chamber."

"Meaning the larger eruption could occur at any time, Dr. Lyndsey?"

"Yes, but we now believe the eruption could be far larger than anyone predicted."

Silence fills the line for a moment. "Mr. Granger, are you still there?"

"I'm still here, Doc. How large are we talking about?"

"The original estimate was the caldera contained about 250 cubic miles of ejectable material. But the mantle plume that feeds the caldera runs nearly four hundred miles deep and stretches over a hundred fifty miles west toward Idaho. In other words, Mr. Granger, the caldera is fed by an almost limitless supply of magma. The key factor, which we have no way to determine, is how much of that magma is melt. But to answer your original question, Mr. Granger, the caldera could produce upwards of 400 cubic miles of ejectable material."

"Meaning what?"

"Meaning, Mr. Granger, this could be one of the largest volcanic eruptions in the history of the planet. Life-altering large."

"But according to what you previously said, Doc, we were already facing changes on a global scale."

"Yes, but previous ash fall estimates put most of the ash over the Midwest. Now we could be looking at substantial ash fall from California to Louisiana. And when I say *substantial*, I mean several inches or more.

The Midwest will be absolutely buried, maybe to the point where the area remains uninhabitable for decades or even centuries. The original estimate spared most of Texas and her large agricultural industry, but, depending on wind patterns, most of the state could receive several inches of ash. To be blunt, Mr. Granger, a larger eruption could tip the scales of our country's ability to survive. Unfortunately, the bad news doesn't end—"

"But Doc, you just stated that no one knows for sure how much melted magma is involved. Are we back to conjecture and theory?"

"You can classify it any way you want, Mr. Granger, but we strongly believe the magma intrusion is real. The large quake also jumped the needles out west. Are you familiar with the volcanoes along Northern California and up through the Cascade Range?"

"I know a couple of them are a very high threat for eruption."

"More than a couple, Mr. Granger. There are nine volcanoes that could erupt at any moment. If the instability in the region leads to more eruptions, you can write off well over half the United States. And, unless you're going to live on reserves of tobacco and cotton, most of this country's fertile fields will be sterilized for generations."

"What are we supposed to do, Doc? We can't alter Mother Nature."

Lyndsey sighs. "I don't know, Mr. Granger. I guess your job is to save as many people as possible. And, sir, in case you're wondering, we're already on borrowed time."

Camp 17—Biloxi, Mississippi

Interview: George from Greybull, WY—retired geologist

"Hell of a thing, huh? I spent a lot of time studying Yellowstone. We didn't fully understand the complexity of the park. Hell, we didn't even know there was a volcano there until the 70's. Hard to believe, I know. And only a couple of years ago, we discovered how large the magma chamber was. We had an idea, but it was twice the size we thought it would be. And there's a continuous stream of magma that feeds into the system. All of that pristine landscape setting atop one of the largest volcanoes on Earth. Never in a million years did I believe I would be alive to witness an eruption."

CHAPTER 68

As Tucker and Rachael travel west on the Grand Loop Road, the ash continues to plummet from the slate-colored sky. The ash is deep enough to completely conceal the guardrails, and the few lodgepole pine trees to survive the fire are sagging under the weight of the heavy ash.

For an old gal, the yellow snow coach motors at a good clip, and Rachael feeds the engine a little more gas. The speedometer is broken, but Tucker estimates their speed to be in the neighborhood of 40 miles per hour and, other than having to steer around fallen trees, they're making good progress. But that all changes when they reach the next summit of the undulating road. Rachael gasps and slows the snow coach to a stop. Partially melted cars stand all in a line as far as the eye can see, many of them still smoldering. Dozens of large RVs are included in the ruins, their roofs collapsed and the walls blown out by the force of the wind accompanying the pyroclastic flow.

Rachael turns to Tucker, her face a mask of horror. "Were there people in all those vehicles?"

Tucker releases a heavy breath. "Most likely. Some might have tried to escape on foot, but they didn't stand a chance."

"Should we look for survivors?"

Tucker places a hand on her arm. "There are no survivors, Rachael. The cloud of ash and rocks was probably close to a thousand degrees when it swept through here. I won't go into the gory details about what happens to a human body in those kinds of temps, but the only saving grace is that no one suffered. Death would have been instantaneous."

Tears begin rolling down Rachael's cheeks, cutting imperfect trails through the dust and ash clinging to her face. "That's hundreds . . . maybe thousands of people."

"Rachael, look at me."

She turns and he gently thumbs away a tear. "We can't do anything to help those people. But my family might still be alive. We need to push on."

Rachael nods and eases out on the clutch.

"We need to get off this road. There could be miles of vehicles ahead of us. Are there any fire roads around this area?"

Rachael steers around the cars while wiping the tears from her cheeks with her free hand. "An old trail connects to the road at the Roosevelt Cabins." She rubs a knuckle across her nose. "It runs parallel to the road, but dead-ends at Tower Creek." Rachael slows the snow coach to a crawl while they contemplate their next move.

"I bet the main road clears up that far south. Do you know how to find the trail?"

Rachael nods as she takes a final swipe to clear the last of the tears. "I used it while shuttling between Tower Creek and Lost Creek for my hydrology study."

Tucker digs through the side pocket of the door looking for a park map. He finds one and unfurls it on his lap. "Tower Creek runs basically southwest"—he traces the creek with his finger—"and merges into Carnelian Creek just north of the Mount Washburn area. I say we shoot for the trail."

"I agree. Anything's better than driving past all this destruction. Those poor people . . ."

"Rachael, we can't do anything for those other people. We need to work on finding Walt and my family so we can get the hell out of here before the rest of the caldera erupts. How far to the Roosevelt Cabins area?"

"Maybe half a mile. Want me to pull off the road?"

"No, let's see if we can ease our way to the turnoff first. This whole area is lousy with tree stumps. We'd risk ripping the front end off of this thing. Just take her slow and easy."

Rachael struggles with the gearshift, curses, and finally shifts into first. She slowly weaves the snow coach around and through the wreckage. Nearing their turnoff, they pass what used to be a gas station, the lot jammed with the scorched husks of automobiles. Neither offers a comment as they continue on. The landscape transitions from the rolling hills of charred timber to a wide-open valley, cut through by the Yellowstone River. Once covered with sagebrush and wildflowers, the valley now appears cold and foreboding—a gray desert, seemingly absent of life.

Rachael makes the turnoff at Tower Junction and heads for the area where the cabins once stood. The trees around the campground are bunched tight together, with some hints of green still visible from a few lucky survivors.

"Can you find the trail in all this ash?" Tucker asks.

"I think so. I used the last cabin on the left as a trail marker. I guess I'll target that smoldering pile of debris on the far left." She aims for a cut through the seared trees and slows the snow coach, swiveling her head from left to right. She extends a finger. "I think the trail is right through that clearing."

"You're the driver."

Rachael scowls at his remark as she steers for the gap, giving the snow coach a little more gas. After several stops and starts and one back track, they break into the clear. After motoring all the way to Tower Creek, they stop to clean the makeshift filters before getting back on the road. Several incinerated cars litter the road, but the numbers are significantly lower than what they encountered near the northeast exit road. They travel along a series of long, sweeping curves through the foothills of the Washburn Range, with Tucker white-knuckling the armrest because of the sheer drop-off on his side of the road.

"The turnoff for Mount Washburn is just up ahead. It'll take us to the summit."

"Take it. I'd much rather climb down the mountain than try to climb up."

Rachael takes the turnoff, and the road leading to the summit feels like traveling up a corkscrew, complete with hairpin turns. The skis on the front of the vehicle scrabble for traction, and she's forced to slow down as she cranks the wheel one way then the other.

"I think my arms might fall off." She swipes a bead of perspiration from her forehead.

"Want me to drive for a while?"

"No, I just wish this thing had power steering. I think we're almost there, anyway. Which side of the mountain?"

"I think the one Walt showed me a long time ago was on the west side."

"So you don't know which side?"

"No, no, I remember. We were up there late in the day and I remember watching the sunset."

As they near the summit, they're rewarded with a 360-degree panoramic view of the park. In the distance, barely visible through the ash and smoky haze, the volcano continues to spew great columns of ash that stretch upward until they disappear from sight.

"My God, would you look at that," Tucker says with wonderment in his voice. "And that's just a fraction of what she can erupt."

"I damn sure don't want to be anywhere in the neighborhood when the rest of it blows."

Rachael and Tucker are so preoccupied by the volcano that they don't see the five people standing on the edge of the parking lot, waving like mad.

CHAPTER 69

Near Happy Acres Motel, Bozeman, Montana

The mechanic hands the pickup keys over to Ralph Barlow. "Rebuilt the carburetor, put in a new air filter, and fashioned a prefilter up under the grille. There's a case of spare filters in the backseat, but I can't make no guarantees if you're going to be driving through this ash."

"I don't expect any guarantees, but thanks for fixing me up."

"Sorry it took so long. Been a while since I had to rebuild a carburetor."

"How much do I owe you?"

"I figure about two hundred with the extra filters."

Ralph counts out the cash and passes it over. "How often should I change the filters?"

"When she starts to feel sluggish, slap a new one in. I can't tell you how long that'll be. I guess it depends on how much more ash we get."

"I appreciate what you did for me, Rusty, so I'll let you in on a little secret. Take your family and go as far north as you can, as quick as you can. This is just the tip of the iceberg."

"You a volcano expert?"

"Yeah, I guess you could call me an expert. Don't wonder if you're making the right decision. Just pack up and go."

"You're kinda scaring me, Mr. Barlow."

"A little fear is not such a bad thing if it's an impetus for action, Rusty. I know what's likely to happen and, to tell the truth, it scares the hell out of me." Ralph pats him on the shoulder. "Travel safely, Rusty." He exits the garage and climbs into the cab of his pickup and eases down the road.

Ralph pulls into the motel parking lot and picks up June and April, who are standing out front. They toss the suitcases onto the backseat and climb in.

June rakes her fingers through her hair. "If I live the rest of my life without seeing another cockroach, I'll be the happiest woman on earth. I can't shake the feeling that something's crawling across my scalp."

April begins searching her own scalp with the tips of her fingers. "I didn't think Montana had cockroaches."

Ralph eases out on the roadway. "I think their habitat must be limited to the Happy Acres Motel. I don't recall ever seeing another roach while living in Wyoming, either."

April finishes with her hair and takes a peek down her shirt. "Lucky us. We stumbled across the only surviving cockroach colony in a two-state area."

June gives a little shudder. "Happiness is Happy Acres in the rearview mirror. We should have asked for a refund for the second night we paid for, but, truthfully, I'm just glad to be out of there. Where are we headed, Ralph?"

"We're going to stop in on Virgil Winkler. He's now a district ranger up at the Helena National Forest."

June gives her husband a surprised look. "I love Virgy, but shouldn't we put a little more distance between us and the volcano?"

Ralph ignores her question as he veers around a stalled car.

"Ralph, why are we going to Virgil's?"

"To get some ideas where we might go."

June turns to look out the window, but quickly turns back. "Bullshit. You've been all over this country up here. You probably know this place better than anyone around. Now, what's really going on?"

Ralph turns to look out the side window, his mind clicking through a litany of excuses. He turns back to look at his wife. "I might know the area around here, but Virgil's spent a lot of time up around Calgary. We'd be safe up there."

The answer seems to placate her, for now. April and June chatter away while Ralph focuses on keeping the truck on the road. The volcanic ash is nearly as slippery as three inches of snowfall. Traveling at reduced speeds, Ralph makes the right turn onto 287 after nearly an hour of driving.

The sky overhead is hazy with ash, but nothing like it was in Bozeman. With a prevailing northwesterly wind, a majority of the early ash drifted east and south over Wyoming and Colorado. Ralph cracks the window to let in some fresh air. A farmer is baling hay in a large pasture along the east side of the road, and the fragrant aroma of fresh-cut grass fills the cab. Ralph inhales several deep breaths, his first breaths of truly fresh air in a while. He cranks the window all the way down, creating a vortex of accumulated ash within the cab.

"June, roll your window down. See if we can clear some of this ash out."

She smiles and cranks down the window. They ride along, the wind blowing through their hair.

April fiddles with the AM radio, standard issue under the government's purchase agreement, trying to pick up a station. All she finds is static. She gives up and leans back against the seat. Ralph glances over to see her eyes closed, her long hair swirling behind her, the blond strands highlighted by the midday sun.

After crossing over the Missouri River, they roll into Townsend, Montana, a one-red-light town, complete with a farmer's co-op and an Ace Hardware. The downtown area is one-building deep and runs for two blocks, with about a third of the buildings boarded up or posted with FOR LEASE signs. The next street over is home to the post office and the local high school, with room for what looks like about forty students.

Ralph pauses at the flashing red light and makes a right turn onto Highway 12. The small town quickly fades away, and he travels a little farther before turning off on Diamond Gulch Road.

June leans forward to better see around April. "Ralph, I've been trying to call Andy all day. Have you talked to him?"

Ralph winces at his son's name. "Yeah, I talked to him. He and Michelle are out of Jackson and headed south." Ralph had been sick with worry until Andy called from a pay phone to say all was well.

"You could have told me."

"I'm sorry, honey. I guess I didn't think about it."
Ralph turns into the driveway of a small ranch-style
home, fronted by a large flower bed filled with pink
bitterroot, the state flower of Montana. The front door
opens and Virgil comes out to greet them. In his late
thirties, Virgil Winkler is a big man, standing six-four
and weighing north of 250 pounds. His smile is as
broad as his shoulders. With a big, brushy mustache
and longer-than-regulation hair, he looks exactly like
the mountain man he is. Twice divorced, Virgil has
been unlucky at love.

June climbs out of the truck and rushes in for a hug.

"How's my Junie Bug?" he asks.

"Good, Virgy. So good to see you." She steps back
and introduces April.

He buries her in a hug. "Welcome to Big Sky Country, ma'am."

Ralph walks around the front of the truck for his
own hug. Virgil started in the National Park Service
while Ralph was working his way up through the ranks.
Ralph invited Virgil along as they moved between national parks, and Virgil became like a second son to
Ralph and June Barlow.

Virgil steps back. "Ladies, the bathroom's clean if
you need it."

They rush toward the house as Virgil turns to his
mentor. "She know what you have planned?"

"Not yet. I was hoping your presence would be a
mitigating factor."

"Ralph, she's going to be mad as a hornet. And I
can't say I'd blame her."

"Virg, I left two people behind who I care for very much. I have to go back."

"Where are they?"

"My best guess is somewhere around Mount Washburn. That's the only place Tucker's family could have been and survived the last eruption."

"Let me go with you."

"I need you to look after June and April. Things are going to get tough around here. I'd like for you to take them to your cabin outside of Calgary."

"Things really going to get that bad?"

"Worse than you can imagine if the entire caldera erupts. About half of the country will be uninhabitable, and the other half will face starvation. I'm not sure even Calgary is far enough away, but it's the only option I could come up with."

"Okay, Ralph, I'll look after Junie Bug and that pretty lil gal. You'll meet up with us in Calgary?"

"Absolutely."

Virgil claps his friend on the shoulder. "Okay. I've got a couple of cold beers for when the fireworks start."

Ralph follows Virgil into the house, his feet growing heavier with each step.

CHAPTER 70

Summit of Mount Washburn, Yellowstone National Park

After a round of tearful greetings, Rachael tries to herd everyone into the snow coach. Maddie, Mason, Matt, and Jess are covered with grime, and Walt's face is just beginning to scab over. Jess takes Tucker by the elbow and leads him away from the group.

"I think Matt's leg might be infected. Anywhere we can get some antibiotics?"

"No. One of the ranger stations would have been an option, but they're all gone. How bad is it?"

"It's red and swollen. Maybe it'll help if we stop along the way for him to soak his leg in one of the streams."

"We can try, Jess, but we're running out of time. The entire caldera could erupt at any moment."

"All we can do is try." Jess steps up and wraps Tucker in a hug. "Thanks for finding us."

Rachael, watching over the top of the snow coach, shouts, "Let's go, people. Time's a-wasting."

Jess breaks the embrace and climbs into the back as Tucker grabs one of the gas cans to pour into the coach's tank.

Rachael gives Tucker an annoyed look when he climbs in. "Did you use both containers?"

"Just one. Should be good to go."

He spreads the map out on his lap. "Fastest way out of here is to head for the northeast exit." He glances up at Rachael. "We're going to need to navigate along the entrance road to get out of here."

Rachael takes a deep breath. "Gotta do what we have to do." She presses the starter, puts the snow coach into gear, and turns a big circle around the parking lot.

"Uncle Tucker, what is this thing?" Maddie asks from the backseat.

Tucker pats the dash. "This is our escape vehicle. Now, hold on, Rachael drives a little crazy."

"Only because your uncle doesn't know how to drive a stick shift," Rachael says as she lines up on the road and feeds the engine more gas. "Here we go."

Those in the back pass the canteens around like sharing the finest champagne. Tucker hands out snacks they had raided from the vending machines. They devour the food as Rachael navigates down the mountain, picking up the road back north. It's not long before Walt and the Mayfields conk out, the jostling of the snow coach rocking them into a deep sleep. So far, Walt has told Tucker little of their ordeal, other than to say it had been a close call. They had burrowed deep into the abandoned mine shaft, drinking water that dripped through the roof of the mine. Walt had fashioned some torches out of sticks and rags, otherwise they would have spent the time in absolute darkness. Tucker shudders at the thought. The root cellar had been bad enough.

The snow coach engine sputters and surges and Rachael finesses the gas pedal to keep it going.

"Pull over. Let's check the filters."

Rachael eases off the gas and the yellow beast coasts to a stop. "Why now? We didn't have any problems on the way here."

"We're carrying more weight, and I bet the tracks are kicking up a lot more ash." Tucker climbs out of the cab and sets to work shaking out the makeshift filters.

Rachael climbs out to confer. "Maybe we should consider heading back toward Mammoth and pick up the road north to Bozeman."

Tucker glances up from his task. "Will you grab the spare rags? This one has a large hole in it. Could have sucked some ash into the engine."

Rachael retrieves the strips of blanket and hands them over. "What do you think of my suggestion?"

"Are you concerned with driving past all the carnage?"

Rachael looks away, nibbling her bottom lip.

"If we turn west the chances of surviving a larger eruption are almost nil. If we head northeast our chances improve considerably. And we don't know if this engine issue is going to worsen. I think if we make it to Red Lodge we might be clear of the pyroclastic flow." Tucker fits the filter against the grille and stands up.

Rachael steps closer and rests her head on his shoulder. "Will you drive?"

"Of course. Now, help me with the other side so we can get back on the road."

After finishing the other side, Tucker takes the wheel. He hits the starter with his foot and the engine cranks but refuses to start. He pulls out the choke and pats the steering wheel. "C'mon, baby, you can't let us down now." The starter cranks for fifteen seconds before the engine sputters to life. He high fives Rachael as a cloud of black smoke billows from the tailpipe. "Back in business." Tucker eases off the clutch, and the snow coach stutters forward, starts to take off, then dies.

"Maybe I should drive," Rachael says.

"It's not me. The thing just died."

"It died because you let the clutch out too fast."

Tucker turns for an angry response but bites his tongue. "Maybe so." He triggers the starter and the engine fires up.

"Nice and slow, Tuck. She's finicky."

Tucker slowly releases the clutch and the snow coach lurches forward, pauses, and lurches again before finally moving ahead. Maddie leans over the front seat. "She was right, Uncle Tucker, you suck at driving."

Tucker ruffles her hair. "Do not. They still asleep?"

"Yeah, but I don't know how after that. When are we going to be home?"

How do you tell a nine-year-old that she may never make it home or that her home may no longer exist? "It'll be a while yet, Maddie. You thirsty?"

"No, but I really need to pee."

Rachael turns and brushes the hair from Maddie's face. "Can you hold it for a little while, sweetheart?"

"Maybe. Are you Uncle Tucker's girlfriend?"

"I'm . . . well . . ."

Tucker glances over his shoulder. "It's complicated, Maddie."

"You need a girlfriend, Uncle Tucker." Maddie scoots away from the front seat.

Rachael reaches over to take Tucker's hand. "I think you should take your niece's advice."

"Right now I'm worried about keeping us alive."

Rachael yanks her hand back as if stung by a bee.

Tucker glances her way. "Can we sort all this out later?"

"You didn't have any trouble sorting it out in the cellar."

Tucker turns back to the front and parks both hands on the wheel. They ride in silence as the ash continues to fall. Rocky cliffs hug the left side of the road, soaring skyward at nearly a ninety-degree angle. The guardrails on the right side are buried under the ash as the ground slopes steeply downward toward the Yellowstone River. Tucker white-knuckles the wheel, steering through the narrow cut that was once a road. Singed lodgepole pines stand sentinel, refusing, for now, to give up their hold on the rocky soil.

A low, loud rumble rolls across the landscape, vibrating the wheel in Tucker's hands. He glances at Rachael. She felt it, too.

"We need a shortcut. Any shallow areas where we could cross the river?"

Rachael stares out the side window.

"Rachael—any shallow areas? I really need your help here."

Rachael answers in a flat voice. "No. Our only hope is to stick to the roads."

Tucker sighs, grabs the map, and glances between the road and the map, trying to find a shortcut. Rachael yanks the map from his hands. "I told you, there are no shallow crossings, plus, like you said, there are thousands of tree stumps scattered all across the landscape. Our only option is the road."

Tucker lowers his voice. "You felt the rumble. It could be a third vent opening. We're out of time."

"Uncle Tucker, I really need to pee," Maddie says from the backseat.

Tucker gently taps the brakes and brings the snow coach to a stop. The others stir awake. "Okay, guys, last bathroom break for a while. I put some rags back there somewhere. You need to cover your nose and mouth before going outside."

They all tie rags around their faces and climb out to do their business. Tucker reaches over to take Rachael's now-limp hand. "I like you, Rachael"—she tries to pull her hand away, but he grasps it tighter—"hell, I probably even love you. But I haven't been in a relationship for a very long time. Can we please sort this out at another time?"

She turns to face him. "There may not be another time, Tucker. And you're not the only one who hasn't had a relationship in forever, but . . . but I don't want to die without having made a lasting connection with another human being. Preferably with you."

"We're not going to die."

"I'd say the odds for our survival are less than fifty-fifty." Rachael pushes open the passenger door and steps outside.

Tucker exhales a long breath before putting the coach into neutral and applying the emergency brake. He steps out to relieve himself, his mind tumbling through an obstacle course of emotions—from fear to confusion, then back to fear before coming to rest against the lip of a dark hole—a hollowness at his core. He quickly zips up and slogs around to the front of the coach. He catches Rachael before she can climb in and pulls her to him and buries his face in her curly hair. He whispers, "I love you, Rachael, and probably have for a long time without admitting it to myself. I don't know what lies ahead, but I want us to face it together." He tilts her head back and gently puts his lips to hers.

"I thought she wasn't your girlfriend, Uncle Tucker," Maddie says, her hands on her hips.

"I lied, Maddie. Let's roll." Rachael reclaims the passenger seat while he helps his brother into the back. "How's the leg?"

"Hurts like hell, but I think it's the least of our worries." Matt lowers his voice to a whisper. "You've got yourself one hot girlfriend. You tell her about our old man?"

"I told her. Hopefully she'll never have the unfortunate experience of meeting him."

Tucker returns to the driver's seat. Once everyone is situated, he eases out on the clutch without stalling. He gives Rachael a smile and she rolls her eyes. With everyone awake, the coach is pleasantly noisy. A few miles down the road the conversations come to a screeching halt when another rumble sounds and the coach lurches violently. There's a deafening crack, and a portion of the roadway splits apart, tumbling down the steep hillside. Tucker floors the gas, hugging the cliff side of the road. He glances in the rearview mirror to see a massive rock slide burying a portion of road just behind them. "Help me watch for rock slides," he shouts as he keeps the accelerator to the floor. More pavement crumbles away, taking a section of guardrail with it. A large boulder slams the road ahead, momentum sending it tumbling down the valley.

After two miles of harrowing travel, they break out into the valley. No rocky cliffs and no deep drop-offs, just rolling hills dotted with clumps of blackened trees. Tucker tries to turn on the entrance road, but has to veer out over the once-grassy terrain. He bumps over something solid and smashes his head against the roof.

"Take it slow, Tucker," Rachael says.

"I don't think we have time to slow down."

"It's either slow or not at all. Another rock like that and we're stranded."

"Uncle Tucker, what happened to all these cars?" Mason asks.

Tucker glances at Rachael before answering and receives a shrug. "Fires swept through the park while all of you were in the mine."

Don't ask, don't ask, Tucker thinks.

"Were there people in them?" Mason asks.

He asked. Lie or don't lie? Tucker goes for the middle ground. "Maybe in some of them."

"Gross. What happened to them?"

Leave it to the twelve-year-old boy to ask for the gory details.

Tucker glances at the mirror. "Matt, help me out here." Tucker turns his focus back to the road. With another blockage ahead, he's forced off the road. Driving slowly, he looks for unusual bumps in the ash and does his best to steer around them, jostling the passengers from one side of the coach to the other. Up and down, left and right, he struggles to navigate the terrain. As they near the Lamar River, he's forced to bring the snow coach to a halt. "The bridge is blocked. Walt, anywhere to cross the river?"

"Don't know for sure." He pushes open the back door. "But I'll find us a place. How much water you think she'll clear?"

Tucker steps out to take a look at the undercarriage. "I don't know, Walt. I'd say no more than a couple of feet, to be safe."

"I know it narrows down a few hundred yards to the east. Sit tight." Walt walks off, kicking up clouds of ash.

Sitting at idle, the engine dies. "Rach, let's clean the filters while Walt looks for a crossing. Kids, now's the time if you need to go again. And Mason, stay away from those cars on the road."

Rachael slides out of the vehicle, and she and Tucker begin cleaning the filters as Mason and Maddie make for the river. "Any springs around here?" Tucker asks.

"Not that I can recall."

"Is the water in the river safe to drink?"

"On a normal day, maybe. But with all this ash—no chance. There's a natural spring that feeds McBride Lake but that's a couple of miles north of here."

"Any chance we can get there in Old Yeller?"

"I doubt it. It's nearly impossible to walk, much less drive, unless you come in on the north side."

Tucker and Rachael finish with the filters and reattach them. Jess and Matt slip out to stretch. Walt comes walking back. "I found a crossing but it's a little deep. Maybe closer to three feet or so."

Tucker looks over the exterior of the snow coach, trying to judge where three feet of water might hit. "Might work. Best shot we'll have." He shouts for Mason and Maddie and they wade back from the river, the ash nearly up to their thighs. Everyone piles back into the coach and Tucker slides behind the wheel. He nudges the starter and the engine cranks for three seconds before a loud grinding noise shrieks through the cabin and the motor grinds to a halt. He waits a few seconds and tries again. Nothing. He curses and stomps on the starter. A faint clicking sound is the only response.

He rests his forehead on the wheel. "Matt, can you walk?"

"I'll give it my best shot."

"Kids, grab the canteens." He turns to Rachael. "Can you get us to McBride Lake?"

"It'll be much easier if we skirt along the edges of Slough Creek."

"Is that in the direction we need to go?"

"Yes."

Tucker swivels in his seat. "I guess we're hoofing it. Best I can tell, the Montana state line is about five miles north. But even that won't be safe. We need to go well beyond that if we're going to survive a caldera-wide eruption. Matt—Walt and I will switch off helping you."

They exit the snow coach and Walt takes a moment to survey the sky. "I don't know, Tucker. Might be best to bed down here for the night. Light's almost gone and I don't think we want to be wandering around in the dark."

They spend several moments discussing their options, but the discussion is interrupted when another explosion echoes across the park.

"Is that the caldera?" Walt asks.

Tucker shakes his head. "Another vent. When the caldera blows, we'll all know it."

"Where do you think that eruption is?" Walt asks.

Tucker and Walt look back toward the south. "My guess is it happened down by the lake. It didn't sound very large, but it could generate another pyroclastic flow. We'll need to keep a close eye on the horizon."

"And what the hell are we supposed to do if we see one?" Walt asks.

Tucker scans the area. "The best option would be to get in the river and hunker down under the bridge. But I don't think we have anything to worry about."

Walt turns to face Tucker. "You mean, other than the whole damn thing blowing sky-high?"

"Well, there is that."

Camp 28—Meridian, Mississippi

Interview: Karl from Kansas City, MO—stock analyst

"We were probably one of the last cars through the Northeast Entrance. Even with the windows up you could hear the approaching conflagration. Sounded like a freight train. Traffic was moving maybe five miles an hour, but steady, when I glanced in the rearview and just about crapped my pants. Those poor people. They didn't stand a chance. There was a bunch of people who got out of their cars and started running, trying to get away. They just disappeared. It was a hurricane of fire destroying everything in its path. And God, the heat. Like standing in front of a blast furnace. It was touch and go on whether we'd make it or not. We made it to Red Lodge and I climbed out of the car. All the paint was blistered, like someone had run a torch across it. I have nightmares now. Those people running . . ."

CHAPTER 71

The Oval Office

Ethan Granger taps on the door of the Oval Office and waits for a reply. Upon reply, he takes a deep breath and pushes through the door. President Drummond is sitting behind her desk, the phone next to her ear. Ethan walks across the carpet and sags into one of the chairs flanking her desk.

The President is angry. "Listen to me, sir. I'm the President of the United States. Now get off your ass and make it happen." President Drummond slams down the phone.

"Who was that?" Ethan asks.

"The asshole senator from Texas. Remind me to campaign against his ass when he's up for reelection."

"What's his problem?"

"Henry signed a contract for a hundred thousand head of cattle out of Mexico. The senator refuses to fund the agreement. Say's it'll kill the cattle industry in his state."

"Did you tell him there most likely won't be a cattle industry?"

"He's not convinced the volcano eruption will be as devastating as we're making it out to be. And, yes, he's one of those assholes who doesn't believe in climate change." President Drummond sighs. "What do you have?"

"The governor of Colorado is requesting permission for the use of deadly force by National Guard troops to curtail the looting in Denver."

President Drummond stands and begins to pace. "Why are we worried about looters if we're evacuating everyone?"

"The evacuation in Denver is off the rails because the National Guard is trying to deal with the looters. But it's not just looters. There's been a significant increase in violence throughout the city."

The President's pace quickens. "Is there a precedent for the use of deadly force?"

"I don't think the National Guard has fired on American citizens since Kent State. There were rumors during the aftermath of Hurricane Katrina, but I don't think those were ever confirmed."

The President pauses her pacing. "We're not shooting American citizens on my watch."

"Is your stance going to be the same six months down the road?"

"You mean when the shit really hits the fan?" President Drummond resumes her pacing. "I believe it will be. However, I do want the murderers caught and prosecuted to the full extent of the law. The National Guard is authorized to apprehend any citizens culpable of murder or other serious crimes. But I won't allow the guard to turn their weapons on Americans."

Ethan watches the President pace for a few more moments, then says, "Maybe you should reconsider."

President Drummond walks back to her desk, hovering over her chief of staff. "No, Ethan, I won't reconsider. Where's this coming from? You're about as far left as a man can go and still be in our solar system. You want to just herd the people up and start shooting? There's a thing called due process, Ethan. One of the benchmarks this country was founded on."

Ethan looks up at his boss. "I understand due process, ma'am, but if we don't get a handle on the violence now we may never stop it. Especially when the situation worsens. Safety of her citizens is also one of our country's benchmarks. I just don't want my country turned into an outlaw society like some dystopian novel."

President Drummond steps over to her chair and sits. She begins massaging her temples with her thumbs. "Why does this job have to be so fucking hard?"

Ethan doesn't answer. Eventually, the President stops the massage and drops her hands to her lap. "I can't do it, Ethan. Joseph Stalin, Saddam Hussein, and a host of other two-bit dictators have murdered their own people. But this is the United States of America, the beacon of freedom and home to civil liberties. I will not be responsible for murdering her citizens. No matter what the future holds for us."

Ethan stands. "I'll pass on your decision."

He turns for the door but is halted when President Drummond asks, "Am I wrong, Ethan?"

He turns and walks back to the desk. "My brain tells me you're exactly right, ma'am, but my gut clenches when I think of the potential violence ahead of us. I'm a lover not a fighter, ma'am, but we all may be fighters by the time this is over."

"If we are, we'll fight as a united country, Ethan. Together we can overcome any obstacle."

"I certainly hope you're right, ma'am. The alternative is a return to the feudal system where everyone takes what they want, no matter the consequences."

"Ethan, I swear to you as President that I'll not let that happen. We'll survive this disaster, and the next one, and the one after that, growing stronger as we overcome each adversity. This is the strongest nation on earth, not because we have bigger guns or a bigger purse. We're strong because we are bound together by a single ideal—freedom."

"I agree with everything you say, ma'am, with one exception. Freedom's not going to put food on the table. Hungry people do desperate things."

DAY 3

CHAPTER 72

The Winkler home, Townsend, Montana

Ralph Barlow rolls out of bed before daybreak. He fumbles around for his clothes and tiptoes out of the guest bedroom, softly closing the door behind him. He makes his way through the house, his hand extended in front of him to keep from bumping into something. The aroma of brewing coffee draws him into the kitchen, where he finds Virgil sitting at the table.

"Morning, Ralph."

"Hey, Virg. You always get up this early?"

"Only when my friend is planning on sneaking out of the house without saying good-bye. Junie Bug any better?"

"Cried most of the night. Finally fell asleep around two."

"Can't say I blame her. You're putting yourself in a precarious position by heading back toward Yellowstone."

"You know Tucker and you've met Rachael. They're worth my effort."

"Not to rain on your parade, but how do you know they're still alive?"

"They're both resourceful, and Tucker knows more about volcanoes than just about anyone I've ever met. If anybody's alive it will be those two."

"Okay, say they're alive. How are you going to find them?"

"I'm going to track them if the ash hasn't covered their tracks."

"Are you a good tracker, kemosabe?"

"Funny. Can't be much different than tracking game through the snow."

"Okay, the sixty-four-thousand-dollar question. What are you going to do if the rest of the volcano blows?"

"That one I don't have an answer for. Pray, I guess."

"A prayer and two dollars might get you a cup of coffee."

"Not feeling very spiritual, Virg?"

"Only when I'm in the woods. And it has nothing to do with all those fancy church buildings. You have a rifle?"

"I do if I borrow one of yours."

"Gun safe's in the same place, and I unlocked it. You can have the pick of the litter."

"I'll grab one on the way to the truck. When are you thinking of heading up to Calgary?"

"Probably the next day or two. Think that's soon enough?"

"I sure as hell hope so since I'm going to be prowling around down there."

Virgil pushes out of his chair and grabs a bag that sags in his massive hand. "I put plenty of food in here."

Ralph takes the bag. "Jeez, I'm not moving down there, Virgil."

"I expect they'll all be hungry when you find them."

"Good point." Ralph stops at the gun safe and grabs a rifle and a handgun. Virgil scoops up a couple of boxes of ammo for each and follows Ralph out to the truck, where Ralph stows everything in the backseat. "Andy made it out of Jackson, but he hasn't answered any of his cell calls. I told him to head for June's brother's house in Arizona, but I'm not sure they'll be able to make it that far." Ralph eases the back door closed. "If Andy gets in touch with his mother, you okay with him heading up to Calgary if they can make their way up here?"

"Hey, the more the merrier. I'll tell her."

Ralph sticks out his hand but Virgil sidesteps it and wraps him in a bear hug. "I put a big ice chest full of drinks in the bed of the truck. I even included a case of my precious Bud Light." Virgil steps back. "You take care of yourself, Ralph."

"I will, and thanks for looking after the girls."

"You'd do the same for me. Anyone staked a claim on April?"

Ralph chuckles. "Don't know. That's something you're going to need to ask."

"I might work my way around to it."

"Wouldn't wait too long. I'd hate for her to get away." Ralph climbs in, fires up the pickup, and backs out of the drive. The ash fall seems heavier as it reflects off the headlights. He makes a mental note to call Jeremy for an update around daybreak.

An hour and a half later, Ralph makes the turn into Mammoth as the sun breaks on the horizon. What he sees takes his breath away. Mammoth Hot Springs is gone. He passes slowly through the area, his jaw sagging open at the desolation. Other than a few chimneys, the only thing left standing is the front facade of the old chapel. He stops on the outskirts to scout for sign and powers up the satellite phone. He meanders around the area while the phone searches for a signal. What he sees in the ash makes absolutely no sense. No tire tracks heading toward Mount Washburn. But there are faint ski marks in the ash along with some disappearing track imprints. While his mind sorts out what his eyes see, he checks the phone screen. He's not really surprised to find no service, but that doesn't lessen his dismay. He powers off the phone and tucks it into his pocket.

Ralph walks a little farther down the road and squats down for a closer inspection. "What the hell is that?" he mutters. He stands up and heads back to the truck, studying the surroundings again. "Think this through, Ralph," he castigates himself. After changing out air filters, he climbs back into the truck and leans back against the seat, letting his mind drift. He begins muttering again. "Most likely the fire burned all the vehicles. If that's the case, what are the tracks?"

After several moments of thought, he sits upright, smiling. "Clever, Tucker, really clever," he mutters as he fires up the truck and eases down the road.

Camp 27—Meridian, Mississippi

Interview: Greg from Greeley, CO—retired electrical engineer

"No, we weren't at Yellowstone. We just happened to be lucky enough to live downwind from the damn thing. But yeah, I think *unprepared* is a good word. I worked for a power company before I retired and I can tell you we were, and still are, woefully unprepared for events such as this. I told them for years the grid was fragile. And I wasn't the only one telling them that. There's not enough redundancy and damn sure not enough replaceable equipment available. Add all that together with the hodgepodge network of grids across the country and you're asking for trouble. I wouldn't be surprised if the Midwest is without power for decades. And now all those people are jammed into this part of the country, where the power grid was already struggling to meet demand. It doesn't bode well for the future, young lady. Your generation may be forced to relinquish all of your electrical gadgets just to have enough electricity to survive."

CHAPTER 73

Near the Lamar River and Northeast Entrance Road,
Yellowstone National Park

With very little usable wood remaining to burn, the group stirs awake, shivering. Even though it's summer, the nighttime temps at Yellowstone often drop into the low thirties. Rachael, Matt, Jess, and the kids had slept in the snow coach while Walt and Tucker, with rags tied around their faces, braved the elements and snuggled together under three light jackets. Walt and Tucker rotated watch, keeping an eye on the distant horizon for pyroclastic flows. But there were none, suggesting the third eruption had been a fairly small event.

Everyone piles out of the coach, and Rachael begins rubbing her arms, trying to generate a little heat. The ash fall is heavier with three vents now open, and it rains down like heavy snowfall. The scent of sulfur is heavy on the morning breeze. People scatter in opposite directions to take care of their morning business, rags wrapped around their faces, like a gang of outlaws.

Tucker sorts through the remaining snacks. The pickings are slim—several bags of chips and a half-dozen candy bars. Tucker rips open a bag of Funyuns and grabs a handful before handing the bag to Rachael. She turns up her nose and continues rubbing her arms.

Tucker gobbles one of the crunchy rings. "Canteens are empty. We need water. Are you sure there are no natural springs close around here?"

"Not that I'm aware of. But I guess we could look around a bit."

Walt grabs his pistol from the front hatch of the snow coach. "I'm going to look for some game. Doubt there's much but I might scare up a deer along the creek."

Tucker glances around at the scarred landscape. "Want us to find wood for a fire?"

"Not worth the effort, yet. Let's see if I can find anything first." Walt surveys the ash-filled sky. "I won't be gone long. It's probably best not to hang around here too much longer." Walt pulls his T-shirt up over his lower face and plunges through the ash, hugging the riverbank in search of prey.

Tucker leans down, scoops up a handful of ash, and rubs it through his fingers. "The ash particles are larger. Maybe three or four millimeters in size, and there's a lot of glass."

Rachael steps over and runs a finger through the ash in his palm. "Meaning what?"

Tucker drops the ash, the lighter fragments floating away on the wind. "Meaning we're too damn close." He wipes his palm against his pant leg as he focuses on the sky. "We need to blow off looking for water and game and get the hell out of here."

"We need water. And the only spring I know about is at the lake."

"I don't think there's time to hike all the way to the lake. We need to take the path of least resistance to put some distance behind us."

Rachael winces as she glances toward the wreckage scattered haphazardly across the tarmac. "The road?"

"It's our only option at this point. For water we'll have to make do with one of these smaller creeks."

"We're tempting dysentery fate."

Matt comes limping back from the river with Jess tucked under his arm for support.

Tucker nods toward his brother. "There's no way Matt's going to hike up and down a bunch of hills. I'll settle for dysentery if it means staying alive." He shouts toward Walt and waves him back.

"Uncle Tucker, I'm hungry," Maddie says, her voice muffled by the makeshift mask.

"We've got candy bars or chips, baby girl."

"Ugh! Again?"

Mason grabs a Snickers bar and carefully folds back the wrapper. "I haven't had this much candy since Halloween."

Maddie picks a bag of pretzels and stomps away. Tucker grabs the canteens and Rachael follows him down to a small creek. But all they find after digging through the ash is a small trickle of water filled with sediment.

Rachael scoops up a handful and sniffs it. "I think we're better off with the river. At least that's been filtered through some gravel."

They leave the creek and trudge down to the river, where they find standing pools of water unfit to drink.

They backtrack, cross the road, and find a rippled section of river flowing over a gravel bed.

Rachael repeats her sniff test. "I think this is the best we're going to find."

Tucker squats down and lifts a palmful of water to his lips. "It tastes okay." They fill the canteens and return to the snow coach. Tucker passes the water around and everyone takes a long drink.

Walt arrives, huffing from exertion. "This ash is ten times harder to walk through than snow."

Tucker hands him a canteen. "It's much denser and heavier than snow. I was hoping it would pack down some, but it is what it is. Let's roll."

Tucker returns to the river to refill the canteens and catches up to the group as they lumber forward through the ash, a winding road of death and destruction spread before them as far as the eye can see.

CHAPTER 74

Cheyenne Regional Airport

J. John Jackson steps out of the Escalade and affixes the cowboy hat on his now-pulsing head. He had knocked back too much bourbon at the hotel bar after signing the paperwork and wiring $2 million to Flight Time Flight Services. However, this is not the first time J.J. has ever had a hangover. Not by a long shot. He reaches back into the SUV, grabs a big bottle of water, and guzzles the contents. J.J. thinks briefly of a cold beer in a hair-of-the-dog attempt to ease the throbbing in his brain, but talks himself out of it. Too much to do today.

He pushes through the door of Flight Time and takes a moment to wipe the ash from his boots. The counter is unoccupied, so J.J. steps over to a door marked EMPLOYEES ONLY and walks through. Inside is a large hangar space where two helicopters, each a mirror image of the other, are parked. J.J. wonders which one of them belongs to him. One has the upper cowling pulled away from the rotor section of the aircraft. A wrench hits the floor, followed by a string of curse words. J.J. heads that way, walking around the front of the closest bird to see Joey standing on a ladder. "Joey, I thought we were flyin' today?"

"We'll be ready to go in a few, Mr. Jackson. Just need to finish installing this filter. Take a look at your new helicopter while I finish up. She's a 1991 Bell 206L-3 Longranger, powered by an Allison—"

J.J. holds up a hand. "Joey, I wouldn't know the difference between a 206-whatever and another fuckin' helicopter. All I give a damn about is whether she can fly."

"She'll fly, Mr. Jackson. I found the filtration kits we bought several years ago during a particularly bad fire season. I'm putting one in and stowing the other one, in case we need to change them out."

J.J. pushes his hat back and massages his forehead. "Sounds good, Joey. If you'll wrestle up your account numbers, I'll get somebody to wire your money."

Joey reattaches the cowling and fastens it in place before climbing down the ladder. He digs out his wallet, pulls out a blank check, and hands it across, a large grease thumbprint stuck dead center. "I'll wash up and pull her out of the hangar. Should be ready to go whenever you're ready."

"Joey, you seem pretty fuckin' happy to be takin' your last flight."

"We caught two breaks I wasn't expecting, Mr. Jackson—the filters and a northerly breeze. That'll hopefully push the ash farther south."

"So I reckon I don't need to cancel my proctologist's appointment next week?"

Joey cackles. "I hope you make that appointment, Mr. Jackson."

"Joey, the name's J.J. We don't need none of that *mister* bullshit." He removes a cell phone from his pocket. "Soon as I finish getting your money sent, I'll be ready to go. You find a place to get some more gas?"

"We'll top off at Riverton going and coming. I also have a refuel spot up at Red Lodge if we need it."

"Sounds like you're the man with the plan, Joey." J.J. pushes a speed dial button on his phone and meanders around the hangar. The call is answered on the second ring. "Bud, you got a pencil handy?"

"I do, boss. Whatcha need?"

"I need you to wire some more cash." J.J. reads off the account numbers and waits for Bud to read them back.

"How much do I need to wire?" Bud asks.

"A hundred and sixty grand. But I want another hundred grand ready to go if I live to call you later in the day."

"Damn, J.J., you're spendin' money faster than shit through a goose. What's this about you livin' through the day? Somethin' you need to tell me about what you're up to?"

"Just goin' for a little whirlybird ride, Bud. Catch you later." J.J. disconnects the call and slides the phone back into his pocket.

Joey, back from washing up, slides a small dolly beneath the helicopter and jacks it up, much like a pallet jack would work. Once the skids clear the ground, he hooks the dolly to a golf cart and wheels the chopper outside, parking it on the tarmac. He lowers the helicopter and returns the dolly and golf cart to the hangar. "I think we're ready to go, Mr. . . . J.J."

J.J.'s stomach is suddenly queasy, and not from last night's bourbon. "You sure you can fly this thing?"

"Like I told you, I'm not licensed, but I can fly her. Thought you weren't worried about dying?"

J.J. dry swallows. "I'm not. I just get a little torqued up, bein' in the air and all."

"You'll do fine. Climb into that left cockpit seat. View's better up front."

J.J. opens the door and climbs in. His hat hits the ceiling, pushing it down around his ears. He takes it off and tosses it into the back as Joey climbs in.

Joey hands across a headset. "Put your seat belt on and plug that in. That way we'll be able to talk to one another."

J.J. claps the headset over his ears as Joey clicks a slew of switches before firing up the chopper.

After a few moments of idling, J.J. shouts out a question. "Aren't we takin' off?"

Joey reaches over, plugs in J.J.'s headset, and demonstrates how to trigger the microphone.

J.J. depresses the button. "How come we're not movin'?"

"Need to wait for the pressures and temps to come up. Just sit back and relax, J.J. We'll be in the air shortly."

J.J. scowls as the engine revs and the rotor picks up speed. Joey slowly lifts the collective, and the helicopter lifts off the ground. He eases the cyclic forward and works the pedals to adjust for the crosswind. The helicopter moves forward, and Joey increases the RPMs, lifting the helicopter higher in the sky.

After an hour and a half of relatively easy flying, the ash grows heavier as they approach Riverton. With no planes in the air, Joey doesn't bother with a radio call. He guides the chopper close to the refueling station and touches down, the rotor wash sending up plumes of ash. J.J. climbs from the cockpit to stretch his legs while Joey refuels.

"J.J., walk over to the hangar and see if a ladder's handy. I'd like to check the filters before we take off again."

J.J. nods and walks toward the hangar, sending up large sprays of ash with each step of his long stride. He finds a ladder and lugs it back to the helicopter. Joey finishes the refueling and climbs up to check the filters.

"Filters are pretty nasty. These things picked up a ton of ash as we were landing. Something we need to keep an eye on."

"Want to change out the filters?" J.J. asks.

"No, we only have the one extra set with a long way to go. If you'll hand me my tool kit in the back, I'll take these out and shake off as much ash as I can."

"Maybe someone here has extra filters," J.J. says hopefully.

Joey shakes his head. "I called around last night. There's not another set of filters within a three-state area. Most sane people just park their helicopters if flight conditions are terrible."

"You callin' us crazy?"

Joey scans the horizon. "Yeah. We're crazy. And the conditions are going to get worse. We're still over two hundred miles from the volcano." Joey climbs down and smacks the filters against the tarmac.

"How close is too close?" J.J. asks, arching his bushy eyebrows.

Joey looks up from his task. "Where exactly are these oil rigs of yours?"

J.J. scrapes the heel of his boot through the ash. "They run from Thermopolis to Cody and on up toward the Crow Reservation."

Joey stands up. "You are crazy. Cody's about forty miles from the park. When you said Wind River Basin, I just assumed you were talking about much farther east, out toward the Bighorn National Forest."

"Is Cody in the fuckin' Wind River Basin or not?"

"Yes, on the fringes. But I didn't think anyone was drilling around there."

"There is now—me." He claps Joey on the shoulder. "Let's get this fucker in the air. We're burnin' daylight."

They take to the air again and spend the next two hours surveying the oil fields. As they approach one of the wells near Cody, they discover a huge ball of flame shooting from the wellhead. The charred remains of an overturned wireline truck lie about forty feet away.

Joey triggers his mic. "What happened?"

"Looks like we had a well blowout. That bitch'll burn until I can get someone in here to cap it. That's a shitload of money being pissed away."

"Did the people escape?"

"Don't know. I sure as hell hope so. Had one of my best geologists sittin' on that well."

CHAPTER 75

Along Grand Loop Road, Yellowstone National Park

Ralph Barlow eases the pickup to a stop at the junction of Grand Loop Road and the Northeast Entrance Road. He climbs from the cab and grabs a cold beer before wrapping a red paisley handkerchief around the lower portion of his face. Ralph slips the beer under the mask and takes a long draw of the the ice-cold beer. "That's about the best beer I've ever tasted," he mumbles before draining the rest of the can and tossing it into the truck bed.

After a loud burp, Ralph begins reading the tracks. Two sets of tracks run along the road toward Mount Washburn, but the most concerning issue is that the tracks are now nearly obscured by the falling ash. A sudden surge of adrenaline floods his system as he walks a circle around the intersection. From the tracks it appears the snow coach has been to Mount Washburn and already returned. The fact that the coach had cut deeper ruts on the return trip suggests Tucker and Rachael had found Tucker's family or were hauling a very large moose. Ralph votes family and blows out a sigh of relief as he hustles back to the pickup.

His sense of relief fades when he hits the snarl of charred automobiles. His anger quickly turns to deep remorse when he realizes the vehicles once contained people. The weight of the tragedy descends, driving him deeper into his seat as tears work their way down the creases and valleys of his weathered face.

After another mile the remorse transitions back to anger. He berates himself for not doing more. His mind runs through a list of things he could have done better. The fact that they didn't evacuate earlier is the one element that drills into his brain. He worries that thought over for the next few miles, trying to come up with a realistic answer for not doing so. In the end, no one, not the so-called experts or the scientists in charge of all the instruments, thought an eruption of the caldera likely. The fact that the volcano hadn't erupted in over 640,000 years had skewed everyone's perception. With odds of a million to one against an eruption, the caldera is winning the bet. The answer provides little solace to those who had died a horrible death. Ralph wipes his eyes and tries to flip his mind back to task.

As he approaches the blocked bridge, he spots the snow coach parked off the side of the road. He gooses the gas to close the distance, hoping to see friendly faces. But nothing stirs but the ash when he brakes to a stop. Ralph jumps from the cab and strides over to the coach to find it empty. He hurries to read the quickly diminishing footprints. There are dozens of prints in a variety of sizes, and all radiate away from the vehicle in a willy-nilly mishmash of compacted ash. Ralph walks a wide circle around the coach. Footprints lead to the river and back, and a heavy-footed set of prints follows the bank of the river toward the south, but none of the prints indicates a definitive direction.

Ralph hustles back to the road and finds two sets of just-visible footprints leading down to the other side of the river. "Surely they wouldn't split up," he mumbles as he continues to search. He stops searching, takes a breath, and spends a moment refocusing. He studies the landscape, deciding the road is the only route that makes sense. But where are the footprints? A north breeze is blowing, whipping the ash around the ground. A sudden thought pops into his mind. There is no ash on the hoods or tops of the burned vehicles. He rolls that thought around for a moment or two, then weaves his way through the tangle of cars. Ralph releases the held breath when, on the other side of the bridge, he spots an assortment of prints that leads away into the distance.

After walking both sides of the bridge in search of a crossing, Ralph hurries back to the truck. He switches out air filters and hops into the cab. The truck is equipped with a brush guard mounted to the front bumper, and Ralph noses into one of the wrecks to push it out of the way. He shoots down the bank on the north side of the bridge and splashes across the shallower section of the river, using the brush guard to create a new opening on the other side. Once back on the road, he picks up speed.

Two miles farther on, he spots several figures through the haze. He blasts the horn and hits the gas, pulling up next to the group. With their faces covered and their heads coated with ash, it's hard to tell if Tucker and

Rachael are in the group. He throws the truck in park and jumps from the cab, wading around the front of the truck. Three of the group break from the pack and turn toward him. For a moment Ralph wonders if he has made a terrible mistake. But his fear dissipates when they pull the masks from their faces and swamp Ralph in a group hug.

"Ralph, what the hell are you doing out here?" Walt asks.

"I was told someone was hiking through my park without a permit."

The four chuckle, something none of them has done over the past three days. "We'll get to all that, but for now, let's load up and get the hell out of here." Ralph turns to Tucker. "How long before the caldera blows?"

"Not long. Sooner rather than later, for sure."

Ralph waves the rest of the group forward. "There's drinks in the back of the truck and food on the back-seat." He turns back to Tucker and lowers his voice. "I do have one piece of distressing news."

"More distressing than being thirty miles away from an erupting supervolcano?"

"Yes. Jeremy thinks there might be twice the amount of eruptible material than first thought."

Tucker's eyes widen. "Based on what?"

"He believes the last large earthquake was caused by a massive intrusion of magma."

"Damn. If that's the case, this country may never re-cover." Tucker pauses and glances out over the land-scape. "There's not a damn thing we can do about it. Let's get the hell out of here."

Rachael climbs in the backseat with Matt, Jess, and the kids. Ralph, Walt, and Tucker take the front seat with Walt riding bitch. The number of seared automobiles increases exponentially the closer they get to the park exit. Hemmed in by trees on one side and the Soda Butte Creek on the other, the traveling slows to a crawl as Ralph tries to work the pickup around and through the blocked roadway. Eventually the creek circles back under the road and Ralph steers toward the shoulder.

The last portion of the park road is a steady uphill climb that stretches for several miles. Midway through the climb, the truck begins to sputter and surge as if the transmission is slipping. Ralph eases off the gas and nurses the truck onward. Most everyone gives a little cheer when they pass over the Montana state line, and another when they drive past what remains of the park entrance. Tucker is not one of those cheering, knowing they still have a long way to go before they're safe.

The Beartooth Highway runs along the state border before taking a long winding dip back into Wyoming. Going downhill the pickup does fine but any hint of an incline and the truck begins to lurch and quaver like a frightened animal. Ralph pulls over to change the air filter.

While Ralph grabs a filter from the back, Walt pops the hood and starts cursing. "The top half of the damn filter housing is gone."

Ralph steps around the front of the truck. "We're down to the last—" He stops when he sees the expression on Walt's face. "What's wrong?"

"I think the last of the new filters is the least of our worries."

Ralph scans the engine. "Where's the top to the housing?"

Walt wipes a hand across his face. "Gone."

"What do you mean, *gone*? You didn't take it off?"

"No."

They search the engine compartment for the missing cover but come up empty.

Walt looks over at Ralph. "Did you tighten the wing nut the last time you changed the filter?"

Ralph bristles. "Of course I tightened the fucking wing nut. Do you think—"

Tucker steps between the two men. "None of that matters. What matters is how much ash has been sucked into the engine. Think we can make it to Red Lodge?"

Walt throws his hands up. "Who knows?"

Ralph looks like he wants to start something that he won't be able to finish, being about fifty pounds and six inches shorter than Walt Stringer. Tucker decides to head them off at the pass. "If you two want to fight like a couple of fucking first graders, you'll need to do it later. Right now we need to—"

Tucker's words are cut off by a massive explosion that violently shakes the earth beneath their feet. While that explosion is still registering on their brains, another series of ear-numbing explosions erupts like a string of dynamite. But instead of fizzling out at the end, the explosions intensify. It feels as if all the air has been sucked out of the atmosphere before the blast wave hammers them like a punch to the gut. Once he regains his balance, Tucker slams the hood and glances toward the sky to see a mushroom cloud, easily thirty miles in circumference, rocketing upward and already penetrating the stratosphere. The three men pile into the pickup, and Ralph stomps the gas. The pickup lurches, stalls, stutters before finally accelerating.

Rachael leans forward, propping her elbows on the front seat. "How long?"

Tucker glances at Ralph. "How fast are we going?"

"Forty, right now."

"How far do you think we are from the north rim of the caldera?"

Walt swivels his head back and forth with each exchange.

"From the north rim? Maybe thirty miles."

"Are we traveling north?"

"Still east. The road turns back north about five miles ahead."

Walt finally speaks. "How long till what?"

Rachael puts a hand on his shoulder. "Until we're incinerated by a pyroclastic flow."

Tucker digs a pencil and a piece of paper from the glove box. He scribbles some numbers, tallies the results, then scribbles another set of numbers. When he's finished he drops his hands to his lap and leans his head against the headrest.

Rachael kneads his neck. "What did you come up with?"

"It's all relative to the speed of the flow, but judging from the size of the explosions, they'll be in excess of a hundred miles per hour. If we can maintain the same rate of speed once we turn back north—"

Another explosion sounds, this one much closer. The pickup shudders as if shot and begins to slow.

Tucker turns to Walt. "Any old mines around here?"

Walt shakes his head as the truck coasts to a stop.

CHAPTER 76

The White House

Knowing that the President is in the Oval by herself, Ethan Granger taps on the door and pushes through, striding over to the television. President Drummond glances up. "What is it, Ethan?"

"May I turn on the television?"

"Of course. Another suicide bombing in Iraq?" She stands from her chair and moves around the desk.

He clicks on the television and scans through the inputs. "A little closer to home. I asked the Sit Room to patch the military satellite feed up here." He finds the right one and punches the button. A dark, grainy image dotted with flashes of fire and lightning fills the screen.

President Drummond walks closer. "Is that Yellowstone?"

"Yes, ma'am. The entire caldera erupted minutes ago."

"My God. I didn't really fathom the size when they described the dimensions of the volcano. It's enormous." She puts a hand on Ethan's arm. "Is this satellite zoomed in over the park?"

Ethan steps over to the screen and begins using his finger as a pointer. "No, ma'am, the picture encompasses nearly three states. The entire state of Wyoming is obscured by the ash, but you can distinguish the edges of northern Montana and the far western edge of Idaho."

President Drummond sags onto one of the yellow sofas. She spends a moment massaging her temples before pushing out of the sofa and striding toward her desk as she ticks off a to-do list. "We need the National Guard to begin the immediate evacuation of all states west of the Mississippi. FEMA and the Red Cross need to be mobilizing now. Homeland Security needs to be alerted and . . ." She stops and hangs her head for a moment. When she turns back to her chief of staff there are tears in her eyes. "Where in God's name are we going to put all these people, Ethan?"

Ethan walks over to put a hand on her shoulder. "We'll have to establish temporary camps in the more temperate climates, such as Alabama, Georgia, Mississippi, and Florida."

President Drummond spins away, her cheeks pinking with anger. "This is the United States, Ethan, not some third world country. We do not put people in *camps*."

"Madam President, these are all issues we need to work out."

She waves toward the television. "We don't have time to form a committee or wade through a whole gaggle of bureaucratic bullshit. This is happening now and we need to be moving. How many people are still in the Cabinet Room?"

"Quite a few. Several have rotated in and out."

President Drummond begins to pace, her heels clicking against the hardwood with every determined step. "I want the heads of every conceivable agency in that room within the hour."

"Which ones, ma'am?"

"Every damn one, Ethan, from Agriculture to Treasury. And no one's leaving until we have a definitive plan to save what's left of this country."

Ethan hurries toward the door. "I'll have my staff start making calls."

President Drummond paces for a few more moments, but finds herself drawn back to the screen. She stares at the eruption for several minutes before sagging onto the sofa, burying her face in her hands.

CHAPTER 77

Red Lodge Airport, Red Lodge, Montana

J.J. and Joey are lifting off from the Red Lodge Airport when the world to the west explodes. With a delay of several seconds, the shock wave slams into the chopper, and Joey fights for control. He increases the throttle and pulls on the collective, trying to gain altitude. The chopper yaws one way, and he overcorrects, swinging the tail boom in the opposite direction. They're on the verge of losing their grip on the air before Joey gets the aircraft back under control. J.J. swallows the bile that has collected at the back of his throat. Both gulp for air as the chopper stabilizes.

Joey triggers his mic, and when he speaks his voice sounds three octaves higher. "Just about lost her. I don't think there's any going back to Cheyenne."

"Take a deep breath, Joey. You're not goin' to do me a damn bit of good if you stroke out on me."

Joey nods and inhales a few deep breaths.

Once he's calmed, J.J. triggers his microphone. "Do we return to Red Lodge?"

Joey glances toward the colossal column of ash,

then turns his gaze toward the ground, where a vast cloud of debris is racing outward, tearing across the landscape at incredible speeds. "I don't think Red Lodge is safe." He points out the window. "Looks like a tidal wave of fire. To tell the truth, J.J., I don't know what the hell to do, but we've got about ten minutes to figure it out. No way can those filters handle all that ash."

J.J. is watching the advancing wave of certain death when something out of the corner of his eye grabs his attention. "Joey, there's a pickup right there to the west. Fly over it."

"Are you crazy? That's the exact opposite way we need to be going."

"I think that's one of my company trucks. And look, it still has paint on it, which means it hasn't been there long. If that's my fuckin' geologist, I want him."

Joey shakes his head like a dog with a snake. "Did you not hear what I just said?"

"We're wastin' time talkin' about it. Won't take us but an extra minute or two to find out."

Joey continues to shake his head as he pushes the cyclic forward. The helicopter chews through the air and they arrive over the truck a minute later. Eight people are frantically waving their hands in the air.

"Not my geologist, but there's a whole pack of people down there. Let's get 'em."

"If we set the chopper down, we're dead. And I don't even know if we can carry that much weight."

"So you want to turn tail and leave all those people down there to die?"

Joey slams his palm on his thigh and screams a long string of curse words as a stream of sweat runs down his face.

J.J. points to a nearby ridge. "Go set her down on the ridge. Shouldn't be as much ash up there."

"There's no place to land up there."

"Then go hover over the fucker. Let 'em climb up to us. You can get her that close to the ground, can't you?"

"You're about the craziest mother-humping son of a bitch I've ever met," Joey shouts as he steers toward the ridge, where he puts the chopper in a hover.

It doesn't take long for those on the ground to figure it out. They hurry toward the ridge, with one injured man braced between two other men. As the others begin scrambling up the slope, a shower of rocks shoots down the slope, further slowing those with the injured man. J.J. unstraps and belly flops over the bulkhead behind them. He pushes open the back door, and a whirlwind of ash and debris nearly blinds him. He wipes his eyes and forces them open. Tears are streaming down his cheeks when he glances outside. The angry wave of fire and rock is moving like a freight train going downhill.

The first of the climbers reaches the skid of the helicopter, and J.J. pulls a young boy aboard. One of the females hands up a smaller girl, and J.J. scoops her up and she scrambles over close to the boy. J.J. glances up at the churning wall of hell and winces. He pulls one woman aboard and then the other. Looking down, he sees the men only about halfway up the slope. He crawls over to the seat and slips on a headset. "Four down, three to go. Hold your position, Joey."

"We're all going to be dead in about three minutes."

"Just hold your goddamn horses. I'll get 'em in here."

J.J. tosses off the headset and returns to the door. The three men are closer but still some distance away. No way they're going to make it. J.J., relatively quick for a big man, jumps from the chopper and races downhill. With a lifetime spent working in the oil fields he's still strong as an ox, even in his sixth decade. He reaches the men, grabs the injured one, and throws him over his shoulder. "Move your ass," he shouts, urging the men forward. Rocks and debris pepper them like angry bees.

The roar from the approaching mass is now louder than the blades cutting through the air overhead.

J.J. clenches his jaw and digs deep. His legs are burning and his high-dollar cowboy boots are slipping and sliding. He glances up to see the first man lunge aboard. The second appears to be waiting to help him. J.J. waves a hand and shouts, "Get in!" The man climbs in and four steps later J.J. reaches the chopper. Hands reach for the injured man as J.J. pushes aboard. He slams the door and pounds the bulkhead between the rear and the cockpit. The helicopter inches higher.

He snags a headset and puts it on. "Go, go, go!"

"Too heavy," Joey groans. The helicopter rises about six feet and stops.

J.J. triggers his mic. "Goose the damn thing, Joey."

Joey's voice is strained. "Burn the engine . . ."

"Fuck the engine. Give her everything she's got."

The RPMs increase as the chopper inches higher. Then, as if unshackled from earthly bounds, the chopper shoots fifty feet into the air. Joey banks hard right and aims the nose north. J.J. wiggles back over the bulkhead and resumes his position in the copilot's seat.

Everyone exhales a deep sigh of relief, thankful to

have escaped with their lives. Two miles north of Red Lodge, cruising at an altitude of a thousand feet, the console lights up like a Christmas parade. A buzzer sounds, followed by the wail of an alarm. J.J.'s sphincter clenches tight as Joey begins punching buttons and toggling switches.

"What the hell's that?"

"Turbine flameout."

"What the hell is a turbine flameout?"

"The engine's gone."

"Well, shit. After all that and we're goin' to die anyway?"

Joey continues with the switches before calmly latching on to the cyclic and collective. "I'm not going to let you die, J.J. I'd hate for you to miss your appointment with the proctologist."

"We don't have an engine and we're about a thousand feet in the air. You going to sprout some damn wings?"

"I'm going to do an autorotation. Does the ground look clear below us?"

J.J. cranes his neck to look out the window. "There's a stand of trees to your left."

Joey nudges the right pedal forward, walking the helicopter a little right. Even with the engine dead the blades continue to chop the air, as the ground grows closer. Joey shouts over his shoulder, "Brace for impact." His feet continue to work the pedals. "Might want to hold on, J.J. We're way heavy and I've only done this once before."

J.J. reaches for the upper handle. "Now you tell me."

About fifty feet from the surface, Joey lifts the nose slightly with the cyclic and lifts slowly on the collective, flaring the blades. The helicopter hits the ground with a jarring thud and settles down. Joey's hands begin to shake uncontrollably when he removes them from the controls.

J.J. reaches over to steady them with one of his big paws. "You did good, Joey. You can fly my damn chopper anytime you want." He releases his grip and kicks open the door. "Are we far enough away?" he asks the group spilling out the back.

"We should be safe from the pyroclastic flows, but this ash is falling at a rate of about a foot an hour. That and the wildfires are going to be our biggest concern. I'd feel more comfortable if we could find someplace belowground." The man steps forward and extends his hand. "Thanks for saving our asses, J.J."

J.J., still holding the man's hand, rears back in surprise, then leans forward for a closer inspection before swiveling over to look at the injured man. He begins to laugh. "Well, I'll be damned if it's not the fuckin' Mayfield boys." He releases Tucker's hand and turns to look at one of the women and points a finger. "And you're Jimmy Hightower's baby girl. Jessica, isn't it?"

Jess nods and steps over, wrapping her arms around J.J.

J.J. nods toward the remaining group. "Them your two kids? The ones that go to school with my grandbaby?"

Jess steps back. "Yes. Mason and Madison. Kids, this is Hannah's grandfather."

Joey walks around the front of the chopper and the crowd breaks into spontaneous applause. He blushes and offers a small wave.

Rachael sidles up next to Tucker. "Did I just cross over to the twilight zone?"

J.J. belts out a big laugh. "Not quite the twilight zone, young lady. But if I knew we was having a fuck"—he glances at the kids—"having a town reunion, I'd have invited the high school band."

Rachael places both hands on her hips. "Will somebody please tell me what the hell is going on?"

Tucker walks over and drapes an arm across her shoulders. "Matt, Jessica, and I grew up in the small town of Woodward, out in western Oklahoma. The town is also home to Jimmy John Jackson, legendary wildcatter, who also happens to be one of the richest men in the world. J.J., this is my girlfriend, Rachael. Those two men over there are Park Ranger Walt Stringer, and Ralph Barlow, superintendent of Yellowstone National Park."

"Sorry about your place, Ralph. Nice to meet you, Walt. Well, gang, I'd like to hang around here and chat all fu . . . damn day, but we'd probably be better off gettin' the hell out of here. Anyplace I can buy us a couple of cars?"

Walt and Ralph move closer. "We wouldn't get three miles even if we had a car," Walt says. "But I've got a . . . *buddy*'s the wrong word . . . an acquaintance who's one of those prepper guys. Built and buried this ginormous bunker, stocked it with food and everything. About a month after he finished, his wife up and left him, taking the two girls with her. Couldn't take the cold, I guess. That, or she got tired of living with her crazy-ass husband. He lives about two miles up the road."

"Is he one of those shoot-on-sight type of guys?" Tucker asks.

"Now that you mention it, it might be better if I

went in alone once we get up there. See if I can broker a deal."

J.J. rubs his chin. "Tell him I'll buy the place and sign it back over to him free and clear. If you need a pot sweetener, tell him I'll buy the whole damn section and sign it over to him. If that doesn't work, I'll knock the fucker in the head."

Rachael gasps.

"Just kiddin', darlin'." He looks around to see where the children are before lowering his voice. "Whatever I need to do to make the deal happen I will. Shit, tell him he can get come this chopper if he wants it. Ought to be worth close to five hundred grand if he parts it out."

"Okay, we have a plan," Tucker says, "but we need to really protect our noses and mouths if we're going to be walking around in all this ash. Once a fair amount of ash gets into your lungs you're a goner. And it's a miserable death."

"I'll take care of that," Joey says. He pulls out a knife as he walks back toward the chopper. With several quick slashes he cuts the fabric upholstery from the back three seats and hands out pieces to everyone.

Tucker and Walt buddy up on either side of Matt while Mason and Maddie latch on to Jess's hands. Rachael falls in, and the group begins trudging down the road, J.J. and Joey bringing up the rear.

Joey leans toward J.J. "Jimmy John, huh? You start all those sandwich shops?"

J.J. scowls. "Do I look like a fuckin' sandwich guy to you, Joey?"

CHAPTER 78

The White House

President Saundra Drummond shuffles into the room, looking as if she hasn't slept in days, which happens to be the case. The Cabinet Room is jammed and there's a spillover of people lining the halls and filling other nearby offices. The doors to the Rose Garden are open and a nice morning breeze flutters the reams of paper consuming nearly every inch of the long, oval table. The President pulls out her chair and drops into it as a staffer places a cup of coffee in front of her. She takes a small sip. "Where are we, people?"

Like a professor asking for a detailed explanation from a new class of freshmen, hands are glued to laps and eyes remain downcast. "Please, not everyone at once," the President says. "Okay, let's start with Homeland Security. Molly, what's the latest?"

Molly Brewster, director of Homeland Security, is a still-honed former collegiate volleyball player with well-defined arms and shoulders layered on her six-foot frame. At forty-seven, Molly's most attractive feature, other than her chiseled body, are her almond-shaped eyes, colored an arresting shade of agate green. She tucks a strand of short blond hair behind her ear and leans back in her chair. "It's a mess, ma'am. The number of people left homeless continues to increase, and it seems each one is willing to fight for their space. We've had multiple shootings at abandoned airports, vacant factories, and shopping malls. Basically, any place capable of holding numerous people is a hotbed for violence. We simply don't have the manpower. It's like we've stepped into a time machine and ended up in the Old West. Unfortunately, guns are too prevalent in our society. Most everyone has one and, in this desperate situation, most are willing to use them."

"What about the National Guard?" the President asks.

"They're focusing most of their efforts on rescue and recovery at the moment. But even with the guard working in a law enforcement capacity, we still don't have the manpower."

President Drummond sighs. "Okay, what do we need to do?"

Brewster leans forward and shuffles a stack of papers, delaying. "We'd like a declaration of martial law, Madam President. That would allow us the use of active-duty military."

"We're not there yet, Molly. I will not declare martial law just days into this event. We'll just have to do the best we can for now."

"But ma'am, if we don't get a handle—"

"Martial law is off the table," President Drummond interrupts, punching the table with a finger for emphasis. "This country hasn't declared martial law since the Civil War, and I'll be damned if I do it now. This is a natural disaster not some attempt to overthrow the government. Our focus needs to be on assistance, not persecution."

A few of those present nod in agreement, but just as many remain stoic as President Drummond glances around the table. "We'll get to the power situation, but first, Claire, what's the status of the volcanoes out West?"

Claire Espinoza looks up from the laptop. "Contact with staff out West is intermittent, but the latest data I received showed increased levels of seismic activity. Some of that might be a bleed over from the ongoing eruption at Yellowstone. But so far, so good, ma'am, in relation to the other volcanoes. There is one more piece of troubling news: Most of California and Oregon have received nearly two feet of ash, with the fertile central valley region of central California receiving nearly twice that much. It could be years before crops can be replanted in that portion of the state."

"Do we have any indications how long the Yellowstone volcano will continue erupting?"

"Best estimates are weeks to months."

President Drummond turns to the director of the Federal Aviation Administration, Nolan Kinney. "I assume no air travel until the eruption dies down?"

"That's correct, ma'am. Even then, air travel will be severely limited by the amount of ash already in the atmosphere."

The President swivels back to Claire Espinoza. "Claire, how long before this ash dissipates from overhead?"

"There are no definitive answers, ma'am. Research targeting that precise question has been ongoing for several years with no consensus. Guesstimates are anywhere from one to three years once the eruption ceases, but we've never witnessed an eruption on this scale. Basically, ma'am, there's a lot we don't know about the behaviors of ash in the atmosphere. But, keep in mind it's not only ash we're concerned about. There are now enormous amounts of sulfur dioxide and other gases spreading across the globe."

President Drummond drums her fingers on the table. "And these gases will be responsible for lowering global temperatures?"

"Yes, ma'am."

The President stops drumming and leans back in her chair. "Let's turn our focus to matters we *can* control. Where are we in establishing temporary housing?"

The administrator of the Federal Emergency Management Agency (FEMA), Brian Norvell, thick glasses perched on his nose, begins shuffling paper. A bald man with a protruding belly, he clears his throat before speaking. "We're still in the process of establishing shelters throughout the eastern portions of the nation. Right now we are using schools, churches, and vacant office spaces to house some of the refugees, but the situation is quickly deteriorating. With the lack of potable water and sewage treatment, health complications are expected to soar. We estimate the number of people left homeless by this disaster could approach one hundred million, nearly a third of our entire population. During our original planning, we didn't factor in California and Oregon, thinking the prevailing winds would spread the ash in a more easterly direction. Apparently, the norms don't apply for an eruption of this size. There are pockets that are habitable, but they are isolated in the extreme southern portions of California."

Norvell pauses for a drink of water. "We've declared a national emergency, allowing us access to other modes of transportation, mainly shipping, which we're using to evacuate portions of the West Coast. As a matter of fact, shipping is our only mode of transportation for any area west of the Mississippi. There is some travel in the east-central portions of the country, say, from Ohio and south from there and—"

"Mr. Norvell, I'm more interested in how we're going to house these people. How they get here isn't my top priority at the moment," President Drummond says.

"Yes, ma'am. We're proposing a large number of refugee camps be erected in the more temperate regions of the South."

"They will not be called refugees, Mr. Norvell. We are not some third world country."

"Yes, ma'am, but despite the nomenclature, we'll need upward of five hundred camps with projected capacities of ten thousand inhabitants each. Even then, we'll have space for only half the refug . . . survivors. There will be, of course, some attrition, but that's our starting point."

"When you say *attrition*, you mean *deaths*. Is that correct, Mr. Norvell?"

"Yes, Madam President. Housed in close quarters, any spread of disease will be rapid. Factoring in food shortages and other unforeseeable events, we could see the death toll climb into the millions."

The statement elicits a number of gasps. After a moment of silence, President Drummond takes a deep breath. "Why haven't we already started construction of these camps?"

"We have some legal hurdles to overcome. If we don't have access to the numerous military bases scattered across the Southeast, we'll have to appropriate land via the use of eminent domain."

President Drummond leans forward in her seat. "Who denied your request for use of military installations?"

Norvell is taken aback by her question. "We made a request to the military and were rebuffed. They insist all bases are secure facilities, essential to the defense of the country."

"We'll see about that, Mr. Norvell." President Drummond leans over to whisper in Ethan's ear. "I want the Joint Chiefs in the Situation Room within the hour."

"Yes, ma'am," Ethan says, pushing out of his chair.

She reaches out to grab his elbow. "I want Homeland Security and the NSA included."

"I'm on it, ma'am." Ethan crosses over to Molly Brewster and whispers the command before exiting the room.

President Drummond returns to Norvell. "I'll work on freeing up some space for you, Mr. Norvell. But I want these camps erected yesterday. Is that clear?"

"Yes, ma'am. We're ready to go the moment we have a place to put them."

"Now a brief update on the power grids."

"Frankly, ma'am, the electrical grid is the least of our problems. The eastern seaboard continues to experience rolling blackouts. Power in the Southeast is intermittent. Everything west of Saint Louis is dead and may well remain that way for several years. Wet ash has destroyed most of the electrical transformers, and the power utilities have very few spare parts. What spares they do have will be transported east. No sense restoring the power grid in portions of the country that may not be habitable for years, if ever."

"Let's hope that's not the case, Mr. Norvell. I want daily updates on the construction progress."

"Yes, ma'am."

President Drummond unwraps three antacids beneath the table and slips them into her mouth. "Henry, where are we on food supplies?"

"I hope you like fish, ma'am. For anything else the outlook is extremely dismal. We barely have enough grain to last us a month and the livestock death toll is beyond all expectations. We have about a half-million head of cattle corralled in south Texas, and that includes the livestock we purchased from Mexico. There are still some hog and chicken operators in the Southeast, but that's a small fraction of what we'll need."

"Have you tried to purchase grain?"

"We've offered up to fifty times the market rate but have had no takers. We might eventually have some grain trickle in but it won't amount to much."

President Drummond plants her forearms on the table. "We've fought wars for our allies, sent food all over the world, and, in our time of need, nothing?"

Edmonds tosses his pen on the table and leans back in his chair. "I think, ma'am, before this is all over, we're all going to be in the same boat. And that boat will be taking on water with nary a coffee can among us to bail it out."

Camp 53—Forest Park, Georgia

Interview: Owen from Omaha, NE—farmer

"Been farming my whole life. Don't know anything else. Suffered through the droughts, the hailstorms, and every other thing Mother Nature could throw at us. Never thought a volcano a thousand miles away would be the thing to do us in. Now they're telling me my place might not grow crops for twenty years or more. *Give me a tractor and a plow and I'll have that ash turned over in no time,* I told them. But it's never as simple as it seems, is it? The ash sterilizes the dirt. Kills all the microbes and stuff that make the crops grow. I remember my Daddy and Momma talking about the old Depression days. I guess we're about to have our own stories to tell. Or at least you will."

CHAPTER 79

The White House

President Drummond retreats to her office before heading downstairs to the Situation Room. She shuffles across the floor and sags into her chair, ignoring the stack of phone messages as she swivels around to stare out the window. It's a beautiful summer day and the roses are in bloom, providing pops of red along the perimeter of the South Lawn. She rises from her chair and walks over. A groundskeeper is cutting the grass, his riding mover crossing back and forth in a meticulous perpendicular pattern. A cardinal alights on a nearby branch, his urgent call silenced by the bulletproof glass. His scarlet breast feathers glisten in the sunlight, but he doesn't stay long, flitting away to attend to other matters. President Drummond turns away from the windows and walks over to the bookshelf where family photos display happier times. The intercom buzzes and she walks over to answer.

"Ma'am, they're all assembled in the Sit Room."

"Thank you, Ethan. I'll be down in a moment." She

hovers over her desk a few more moments before exiting the office.

As she enters the Situation Room, all rise. Usually she waves them down, but today she lets them stand until taking her seat. Once the men have retaken their seats, she turns to Lauren Petit, secretary of defense. "Lauren, how much federal land is in use by domestic military bases?"

"I don't know the exact figure, Madam President, but it's somewhere in the neighborhood of twenty million acres."

"And of those twenty million acres, how many are along the East Coast and further down south?"

"It would be a guess on my part, ma'am, but I'd estimate close to half."

"Ten million acres?"

"Probably in the neighborhood, ma'am. May I ask why all these questions about military acreage?"

"I'm glad you asked, Lauren. General Cardenas, did you deny FEMA's request to access this land?"

"I did after consulting with the other commanders. These are restricted military bases, essential to the defense of our nation."

"Lauren, were you aware of this request?"

"Only now, ma'am."

"General, I'm ordering all unoccupied lands be made available for survivor housing."

General Cardenas straightens his jacket before answering. "Madam President, most of the undeveloped land is used for training readiness, and the bases themselves contain all manner of weapon systems, ordnance, and aircraft. Allowing the general public access to these areas would severely hamper our ability to respond to potential conflicts around the world. We're already hamstrung by the temporary loss of two legs of our nuclear arsenal triad: the bombers can't fly and our ICBMs are buried under mountains of ash. But allowing public access to our military facilities could well be the fatal blow. We are a sitting duck, ma'am, extremely vulnerable to an attack by any of our many enemies. We have no air cover, the satellite systems are erratic, and we're ripe for the picking."

"Gentlemen, there is a crisis here at home, and it has nothing to do with war. Lauren, military training is now reserved for bases outside the United States. General, secure your weapons, secure your facilities, establish a secure perimeter, do whatever you need to do, but I'm allowing FEMA access to build the camps."

General Cardenas shoots to his feet. "You can't do that, ma'am. I won't allow it."

The SECDEF shoots to her feet. "General, stand down."

The President ignores Petit as she stands slowly from her chair. "You won't allow it? General, the last time I looked at the Constitution, I believe it stated that the President of the United States is the commander in chief." She steps closer to the general. "Have they made amendments since I last read it?"

"General, for the last time, stand down," the SECDEF says in a low, urgent tone.

"It's all right, Lauren. I'd like to hear his answer."

"No, ma'am, but I will not stand by while you castrate our military. I, too, have friends on the Hill."

Petit sags back into her seat.

"Good, you can use those friends to help you look for a new job. General Jose Cardenas, you are hereby relieved of command. Please exit the premises."

General Cardenas pivots on his heel and marches out of the room. The rest of the military leaders are leaning forward in their chairs. "Who's up next in the batter's box? Or would you all prefer to follow General Cardenas out the door?"

The secretary of defense works her way around the table. "As vice chairman, I believe Admiral Nichols would be next in line."

The President turns to the man dressed in white, four bright brass stars attached to the epaulets of his uniform. "Admiral, you can work with me or you can follow the general out the door."

Admiral Nichols stands to attention and salutes. "I prefer to work with you, ma'am. We have enough sea power to wreak havoc on most anyone in the world, so I'm not concerned with allowing access to the uninhabited portions of our military bases. I'd only ask you to allow us a day to sort things out."

President Drummond turns to Petit. "Any portions you can release today? We've got nearly a hundred million Americans who are displaced."

"Let me confer with the admiral. I will get back to you in an hour. Is that acceptable?"

"That'll work, Lauren." The President turns and extends her hand to Admiral Nichols, who grasps hers with both of his. "Thanks for answering the call, Admiral. We've got quite a shitstorm ahead of us."

"It won't be my first rodeo, ma'am. I'll serve in whatever capacity you choose."

President Drummond nods and takes Petit by the elbow, steering her out the door. "So I've made an enemy for life, it appears."

"Jose is a little high-strung. But he's a hell of an officer, and I hate to see him go."

"Put him somewhere back in the army, Lauren. Let him serve out his time."

"You don't want him fired?"

"If I fired everyone who disagreed with me, I'd be working by myself. He's relieved from the Joint Chiefs, but not the army. Just give me a heads-up if he starts plotting a friendly fire incident involving me."

Lauren chuckles before turning serious. "Anything I can do to help, Saundra?"

"You could assign some of those military personnel to help assemble the camps."

"Done. We've gotten pretty good at setting up tent cities. I'll have someone from the military liaise with Brian Norvell. Might take a day or two to get everything ironed out, but once they start, they move quickly."

"Thank you, Lauren."

"How are the food supplies, ma'am?"

"Your grandparents ever talk about the soup lines during the Great Depression?"

"Some, why?"

"Because, if we're lucky, you'll be telling your grandchildren a similar story."

DAY 10

CHAPTER 80

Tucker pulls on his mask and pushes open the door to the underground bunker for another look around. The ash is still falling, adding to the nearly nine feet they have already received. They had been taking turns shoveling away the ash blocking the door, creating a mound nearly twenty feet tall next to the walkway. What Walt called a *ginormous bunker* turns small when you insert eleven people inside. The owner, Jerry Cavanaugh, is now the proud owner of an entire section of ash-covered land with an additional guarantee of $1 million in cash when J.J. makes his way to a telephone. The money did wonders in softening his stance about no visitors. But seven days confined underground is seven long, miserable days. Although all have taken trips outdoors, the ash is too heavy to spend much time outside. Most haven't stayed beyond the time it takes to take care of the necessary bodily functions. Tucker is the only one to spend considerable time outdoors, and he glances once more at the sky, humbled by Mother Nature's fury. The cloud over the main eruption now stretches across the horizons, and though it's midmorning, it feels more like dusk.

The door creaks open and his brother, Matt, steps out. Cavanaugh, a pack rat of the highest order, has stocked enough food to last a year, a water tank that holds a thousand gallons, and all manner of might-need items, including antibiotics. Matt's leg is nearly healed.

"What's the plan, Tuck?"

"I don't know. But we can't stay here much longer. Might be on the verge of overstaying our welcome."

"I agree with you. Although Jerry saved our lives, there's something not quite right with him. And the way he looks at Rachael and Jessica is downright creepy."

"There's no doubt he has a screw or two loose, but he won't try anything while we're around."

"Just the same, I'd like to get the hell out of here. And if I have to hear another of J.J.'s oil stories, I might go insane."

"He's lived a large life, hasn't he? I swear the guy looks just the same as he did thirty years ago."

"I guess once you're past your thirties, the physical changes become more subtle. But you're right—other than a few more wrinkles and that mane of silver hair, he looks remarkably well considering he's probably closer to seventy than sixty."

Tucker turns serious. "There's no way for you to make your way back to Oklahoma. You know that, right?"

"I do, Tucker. We'll have to wait for conditions to improve."

"Matt, I hate to tell you this, but they may not. Just clearing the ash will be a monumental task. Throw in rebuilding the power grids and it could be a decade or more before life returns to anything resembling normal. Out here, they may never recover."

"What are we going to do?"

"I guess we're all going to head north up into Canada. Ralph knows a place up around Calgary. Maybe we can work our way over to Alaska."

"Great, another state where they have more volcanoes than you can shake a stick at. I'll stick to Canada. I've had my fill of volcanoes. I assume Rachael is going with us."

"I hope so. But that'll be her decision."

"No, Tucker, it'll have to be a decision you both make. You're a pair now. You've lived so long by yourself, you need to change your whole philosophy. She's terrific and if you let her go, you're a damn fool."

Tucker traces his boot heel through the ash. "Any more advice, Dr. Phil?"

"Make fun if you want, but she's about the best damn thing that ever happened to you."

Tucker abruptly changes the subject. "You think Jerry has any snowshoes?"

"Why? Are we walking out of here?"

"About the only option we have. The ash should thin out the farther north we travel, but it'll be a chore getting there."

"Maybe Jerry has one of those things you arrived on the mountain in. Or maybe he knows someone who has one."

"Another snow coach, huh? I doubt it. Those things are few and far between, but you may have given me an idea."

"What?"

"Don't know yet. I need to think about it. I'm going to take a walk down the road. Want to come?"

"Hell no. My leg is just now getting to where I can walk on it. Don't stray too far."

Tucker is gasping for breath only twenty yards down the road. He retraces his steps back to the bunker. "Walking is out of the question," he mutters as he takes a seat on a mound of ash. Having spent most of his time within the park, he's not familiar with this area of Montana. He lumbers to his feet and opens the door, asking Walt to step outside.

Walt pushes through the door. His face is scabbed over and, other than looking like the Creature from the Black Lagoon, he's healing. "Don't tell me. You've got another harebrained idea."

"Kind of, but it's not well formed yet. Are there any ski areas around this part of the country?"

"One that I know about. Red Lodge Mountain is just down the road."

"Is it a commercial ski area? A place where they groom the slopes?"

"Sure. It's pretty busy in the wintertime. I think they have multiple ski runs. Why?"

"Think we can hike down that way?"

"Not without something to walk on."

"I'm hoping Jerry has some snowshoes."

"Could be. He's got about two of everything else. To tell you the truth, if I have to hear any more of his moose-hunting stories, I'm liable to put a bullet in his head or mine. It's also rank as hell in there, so I'm open to damn near anything at this point."

"I'll ask him." Tucker enters the bunker and spots Jerry toward the back. A short, thin man, Jerry has the rugged face of an outdoorsman, at least the parts of his face you can see. Most of it is covered by a long, shaggy salt-and-pepper beard that hasn't been trimmed in at least a couple of decades. The same applies to his hair, and it hangs limply, a greasy, stringy mess. He's braiding a piece of leather, his hands seemingly always in motion. Tucker weaves through the cramped space. "Jerry, you have any snowshoes?"

Jerry's hands continue to work. "I have two pair in the barn. You planning on a walk?"

"Something like that. You mind if I borrow them?"

"Suit yourself. Should be hanging right near the door, if I remember correctly."

"Thanks, Jerry. And thanks for everything else you've done for us."

He shrugs. "Hey, I made out like a bandit." Jerry puts a piece of leather into his mouth to soften it as Tucker turns away. Before returning outside he stops next to Rachael to tell her his plans. When he's finished he gives her a quick kiss on the lips and slips outside. "Jerry says there are two sets of snowshoes in his barn."

"Of course there are. I told you the man has two of everything. No sense in both of us hiking up there. I'll go get the shoes."

"I can go."

"Naw, I need to stretch my legs a bit." Walt sets off,

plowing through the ash like a bull in the snow. He returns a half hour later, his shirt soaked through and his breathing labored. One set of snowshoes is tied onto his boots and he hands the other pair to Tucker. "They work pretty damn good. I still sink up to my ankles but it's a hell of a lot better than trying to wade through this stuff. I didn't know if I was going to make it to the barn without my old ticker exploding in my chest. I've walked through my share of deep snow, but this ash is like walking with cement shoes."

"We have zero chance of making it out of here if we can't find some form of transportation." Tucker ties the webbed shoes onto his boots and tests them out. "Much better. You ready for a hike?"

Walt and Tucker make the town of Red Lodge after an hour of hiking. The place is buried in ash with only the occasional roof peak or chimney showing through. Some of the upper floors of the two-story buildings are visible, but the light poles lining the main drag look more like path lighting, their plastic lenses only a few feet above the ash. The lights are the only proof that a road once existed here. The men trudge through town and cross under the now-dead electrical lines, turning east toward the Red Lodge Resort.

Some of the taller pine trees push up through the ash, looking like recently planted shrubs on the surface of the moon. As Walt and Tucker approach the mountain, the going gets tougher as they ascend the steep incline. They pass a canteen back and forth, trying to stay hydrated. The ash drifts into their shoes and creeps down their backs, abrading their skin. Their shirts sag under the weight of wet ash as it soaks up the perspiration as soon as it forms. Four hours after beginning, they arrive at the remains of the resort.

The upper windows of the two-story log structure are at eye level, and Tucker peers into the dusty interior. A large dining room table is set for a meal service that won't be served for a very long time. Groupings of tall-backed leather chairs are arranged just so, scattered across the lobby to facilitate friendly gatherings. Tucker turns away with dismay.

They strip off their shirts and shake them out, laying them on the remnants of a pine tree to dry. Both strip off their shoes and shake out their socks. Their feet are red and raw, covered with bloody blisters. "If we have to walk back, I might just stay here," Walt says, gently massaging his feet.

Tucker trickles some water across his feet to rinse the blood. "I hear you. That was way worse than when we were hiking the road after the snow coach died. Of course the ash was only a few inches deep at the time. Let's just hope the maintenance barn is close."

After resting for a few minutes, they regretfully pull on their socks and lace up their boots, reattaching the snowshoes. Shirtless, they scout around for the maintenance facility. Around the back of the lodge they hit pay dirt when they discover a large, partially opened door. They climb through and drop to their feet. Walt clicks on a flashlight, and the beam reflects off the windshields of three massive snow machines. "Hot damn," Tucker shouts, his voice echoing around the cavernous space. "We're in business now."

The machines are outfitted with tracks about four feet wide and twelve feet long, with large plow blades attached to the front. Two are single cabs and the third is a double, stenciled with MOUNTAIN RESCUE along the side.

"How are we going to get them out of here?" Walt asks.

"We're going to use one to open the door and push through the ash. We'll work it hard and if we tear it up in the process, so be it. But we need to devise some type of filtration system for the engines before we go anywhere. And we need fuel and lots of it."

"I bet there's a big diesel tank around here some-where. Might be buried, but we can dig out a path to it."

They rummage through the barn and find a dozen five-gallon diesel containers, and Walt scores big when he discovers two boxes of home air conditioner filters, obviously for use up at the lodge. They spend the next hour building a patchwork system to hold the filters before beginning the tedious process of digging out. The snowcat Tucker chooses is beat to hell by the time he finishes, but he's cleared a path out of the barn and dug out around a thousand-gallon diesel tank up on legs about eight feet in the air. Another good find, because now they don't need to worry about powering a pump. After topping off the tanks on the remaining two snowcats, they begin filling the containers.

Normally one of the longer days of the year, dark-ness arrives quicker with the slate-colored sky of ash. The temperature plummets and they quickly don their still-damp shirts. "I wish we had more gas cans," Walt says, screwing the lid on the last jug.

"I think this will get us where we need to go. Hope-fully, the farther north we go the less ash there will be.

We should be able to commandeer a couple of real vehicles."

Walt takes the single cab and the lead as they fire up the engines and click on the lights. They move out like rovers traversing the Martian landscape—the only things missing are the space suits and bubble helmets.

DAY 146

CHAPTER 81

The White House

After one final glance at the mirror, President Saundra Drummond exits the restroom and takes her husband's hand as they walk down the corridor. A staffer hands her a stack of papers, and she gives Sean a peck on the cheek before pushing through the door to the White House's media room. Once standing room only on such occasions, tonight only a handful of are present—what's left of the nation's media.

President Drummond steps up to the lectern. "I'll begin this evening with a few preliminaries. We continue to search for available food options. We have a standing offer for any available grain, and we've contracted with the Brazilian government for 100,000 head of cattle. We are now in the process of shipping those cattle here. That's one bit of good news. I'm also happy to report that most of the electrical grids east of the Mississippi River are now functional with only sporadic blackouts. Power officials say the occasional blackouts might be with us for a while due to the large number of people inhabiting the area. The grids are extremely stressed but some power is much better than none. I'll now take a few questions." President Drummond points to a man on the front row. "John?"

"Thank you Madam President. Can you give us the latest estimates on the death toll?"

President Drummond bows her head for a moment. When she lifts back up, tears are pooling in her eyes. "Over 30 million Americans have perished, John. The outlook remains bleak, with future deaths expected to rise as the famine worsens."

"One follow up, ma'am?"

The president nods.

"How many deaths are related to the H1N1 flu that spread through the survivor camps?"

"I don't have the exact number, but I know those deaths were numerous." President Drummond points to a woman in the second row.

The woman stands and straightens her skirt before saying, "President Drummond, why weren't evacuations started earlier?"

The president's face flashes red with anger. "I've addressed that issue numerous times and I'm not going to rehash that now. We did all we could humanly do." She turns to another woman on the first row.

"Madam President, is there a timeline to reestablish air service?"

"The airlines are hoping the atmospheric ash will subside, but, from what I understand, there are no real timelines. The railroads are working to reopen traffic to portions of the West Coast that remain habitable. Unfortunately, they have a big hill to climb with the large swath of destruction between here and there." She nods to a man on her left.

"Thank you, ma'am. How long until the financial systems are all up and running?"

"A few banks are operating now, especially in the larger cities. The fed is working around the clock to open more. I received word last week that the stock markets in New York are hoping to be up and running by year's end. We're making daily improvements, but still have a long ways to go in certain areas. We're recovering from the largest natural disaster in the history of humanity." The president nods to a man on her right.

"Madame President, what's the current status of the volcano?"

"I'm glad you asked, Bob. Joining us on a conference call is Dr. Jeremy Lyndsey, the Chief Scientist at the Yellowstone Volcano Observatory." The president punches a button. "Dr. Lyndsey are you there?"

"I am, ma'am."

"What's the current status of the volcano?"

"The volcano is still erupting, but the amount of material being erupted has declined significantly. It is now mainly a hydrothermal event, with significant amounts of steam still being produced."

"Will it ever stop?"

"Some day, but the worst is over as far as the eruption is concerned. We now have the larger global issues to deal with."

"What are some of those issues, Dr. Lyndsey?" the president asks.

"The major issue is the enormous amounts of sulfur dioxide now present in the atmosphere, not just here in the states, but all across the world. Think of it as a thin blanket draped over the entire globe. We estimate only seventy percent of the sun's energy is penetrating that veil, or blanket, so to speak."

"And this causes the drop in temperatures as we've already witnessed?"

"Yes, ma'am. That's exactly the cause. The growing season for most of the planet will be eliminated for the next year or two."

"When can we look forward to conditions improving, Dr. Lyndsey?"

"Well, ma'am, I hate to be the bearer of bad news, but things will get much, much worse before we see any improvement. We don't know for sure how long the ash and sulfur will remain in the atmosphere. Years certainly, and maybe longer."

"A grim prognosis, Dr. Lyndsey. Thank you for joining us, " the president says before punching the off button. She glances up at the audience of journalists. "We still have a long way to go, but we will get there. That I can promise. Thank you."

CHAPTER 82

The muted morning sun is leaking through the window of their one-bedroom flat when Abby Stoneshire leans over to nibble her fiancé's ear. She nibbles and kisses until he stirs awake. "I had the most wonderful dream last night."

Roger stuffs a pillow behind his head and rubs his eyes. "Wild, passionate sex involving handcuffs and blindfolds?"

"No, I dreamt of a warm, steamy loaf of French bread fresh out of the oven. I think my mouth began to water in my sleep."

He pounds a palm on the bed. "Do not talk about bread. You know how much I love bread."

"God, I could smell it, too. That warm, yeasty aroma that has just the right amount of pungency." Abby rolls up on her elbows. "Remember going to Benny's Bakery every Sunday morning?"

"Abby, if you don't shut up I'm going to put a pillow over your face."

"Oh, that'd be great. 'Local resident killed after

sharing bread dream with fiancé.' I can see the head-
lines now." Abby pushes off the bed and wriggles into
her jeans.

"Where are you going?"

"I told Mum I'd spell her at the food queue. Today's
their day for weekly rations and she's been there since
midnight. I bet she's on the verge of wetting her knick-
ers by now." She pulls on a sweatshirt and puts her
dark hair up in a ponytail.

"God, Abby, I wish you hadn't mentioned bread.
That's all I can bloody think about."

Abby belly flops onto the bed. "At least we don't
have it as bad as the Yanks. Ashley was telling me they
barely have any food. They're offering other countries
these exorbitant sums just to purchase food. I think our
government is in the process of sending food over,
what with all they've done for our country in our times
of need."

"Why? We barely have enough for ourselves."

"It's the compassionate thing to do, Roger."

"Screw compassion. I just want a loaf of bread.
God, my mouth is watering, all thanks to you."

Abby crawls over to kiss him. "Think about wild,
passionate sex. I may be up for blindfolds, but the
handcuffs are a deal killer."

Roger reaches out to grab her ass, but she slithers
away, laughing. "Hopefully, her queue will move as
fast as ours does. But with all those old biddies, I could
be a while. I'm hoping to be back in three or four
hours."

"I'll have the blindfold ready."

Abby smiles as she slips on a coat and takes the
stairs down to ground level. People are out and about

on the street, but their faces remind Abby of the pictures of Londoners during the war. The weather is cold and damp but she tries to shake off the melancholy mood, whistling a U2 tune as she strides down the street. After twelve blocks she cuts over four streets, and the whistle dies on her lips when she sees the queue nearly fifteen blocks long and her mother waving frantically only one block ahead. All thoughts of blindfolds are whisked from her mind.

CHAPTER 83

Quetzaltenango, Guatemala

Thirteen-year-old Estuardo Carillo is trying to eke out the last few minutes of sleep before a long workday ahead. The oldest of five children, Estuardo's parents require him to work to help provide for the family. Living in a two-room hut with dirt floors, the family's needs are minimal—food, sometimes medicine, and an occasional article of clothing that will be passed down until threadbare. With the parents already gone for work, his younger brother races into the hut and tries to shake Estuardo awake.

Estuardo pushes him away, but the younger brother is relentless.

"Come see, Esty. You have to come see."

Estuardo pulls the blanket over his head, only to have it ripped away moments later.

"Esty, get up. You have to see."

Estuardo mutters a string of Guatemalan curse words he's not supposed to know and rises from bed. He suddenly feels cold, a very uncommon feeling for this part of the world. He slips on his shorts and follows his brother outside. He stops and stares up at the sky in amazement as big, fat snowflakes drift down from the heavens. They don't stay long on the warm ground, and for two boys who've never seen snow, they're bewildered by this sudden appearance. Estuardo holds out his hand and several flakes hit his palm, melting on impact but leaving faint traces of moisture behind.

"What is it, Esty?"

Estuardo shrugs and sticks out his tongue, hoping to land one of the fat flakes. Darting one way, then the other, the boys are giggling as they race to see who can capture the most. Both are shivering, but the game is afoot and neither is worried about being cold. But just as suddenly as it started the flakes stop falling, leaving the boys to wonder if they had imagined the entire episode. But no, the cold is real, as is the moisture Estuardo felt in the palm of his hand. He leads his brother back into the hut and throws a blanket around them.

"What was that, Esty?"

Estuardo slips from the blanket and digs through a small stack of magazines the missionaries had left on their last trip. He finds the one he wants and carries it back to his brother. He can't read the letters on the cover, so he doesn't know he's holding a copy of *ESPN The Magazine*. He quickly thumbs through the pages, stopping on an image he's already seen a hundred times. An alien-looking creature is moving down a white mountain with something attached to his feet. Estuardo points to the picture: "Snow."

CHAPTER 84

The White House

The Cabinet Room is back to its usual state—empty. Most everyone left a week after the last major eruption. There is a small team of advisors camped out in the Roosevelt Room, but their numbers pale in comparison to the former crowd of occupants. Dressed casually in navy slacks and a maroon sweater, President Drummond passes by the room on her way to the Oval. Her steps are slower, as if the weight of the nation's problems are resting on her shoulders. She offers a tepid good morning to her secretary before slipping into the office. Before she can make it to her desk, Ethan Granger taps on the door and enters.

"Ma'am, I wanted to update you on our farmer's initiative."

"Let me guess. More bad news?" The President turns and walks to her desk, sagging into her chair.

Ethan walks over and sits in one of the chairs flanking the desk. "Unfortunately, yes. All of those crops we paid the farmers to plant were wiped out by a hard freeze overnight. It'll be spring before we can try again, and even then the predicted outcomes are dismal. It may be two to three years before we have viable crop outputs from states such as Alabama, Mississippi, and Georgia. It could be decades before we see any production from our biggest crop-producing states."

"Is there nothing we can do?"

"Some scientists suggest building greenhouses on a massive scale, but even then we couldn't produce enough grain to make much of a difference. Besides, the costs far exceed any expected output."

"The Ag Department making any inroads?"

"They have a standing order for any surplus crops from around the world, the price to be negotiated. So far there have been no takers, and no one realistically believes the order will ever be filled. The State Department is also working every available angle. Everyone's running scared."

"Can't we trade oil for food? We've fought wars for the damn stuff. Surely China needs oil."

"The Chinese government would love nothing better than to corner the oil market at our expense, but they have too many mouths to feed. They've halted all building projects and instituted very strict travel policies, to tamp down the demand for oil. The entire country is locked up tighter than a drum."

President Drummond massages her temples. "It wouldn't surprise me if they tried to start a war, just to take advantage of our situation."

"I don't think anyone has the stomach for war. They harvested crops this year, but next year will be a different story. For everyone."

The President sighs and leans back in her chair. "God help us all. Aren't you going to say *I told you so*?"

"Concerning what, ma'am?"

"My declaration of martial law."

"There were no other options. It was either martial law or total loss of control. I know you're catching hell for the decision, but it had to be done."

President Drummond stands from her chair and walks over to the window. "The attorney general is already inundated with lawsuits that will take years to wade through. And members of my own party are voicing extreme displeasure with my decision."

"The declaration of martial law will trump most, if not all, of those lawsuits. If we hadn't activated the military and streamlined the judicial system, this country would have collapsed. As for our fellow party members—fuck them. It's easy to judge from afar, but to sit in your chair and make extremely difficult decisions for the greater good of the nation takes real courage, ma'am."

The President turns from the window. "Well, the decision's been made and I'll live with the consequences. Where are we in camp construction?"

"I think the latest tally is around two hundred and fifty. And construction has tapered off. The outbreak of the flu was devastating. Some are leery of the camps."

"Where are those people living?"

"Wherever they can find a place to bed down. Even with the overcrowding issues, violence is down. It seems as if there's some implicit agreement that we're all in this together. Or it could simply be that people are too hungry to fight."

The President turns to face her aide. "I think hunger's a part of it, Ethan, but not the driving force. This country has the innate ability to bond together during times of crisis. Time and again we have united for a common cause. Social, racial, and socioeconomic barriers fall by the wayside, exposing us for who we really are—a kind, caring society with a natural tendency to help our fellow man. It's the American way, Ethan, this intertwining of cultures and beliefs that have the ability to solidify into one voice in the face of calamity. We're down, but we're damn sure not out. We will overcome."

CHAPTER 85

Survivor Camp 136, Fort Polk, Louisiana

In the heart of the Kisatchie National Forest, where the army owns 100,000 acres and the U.S. Forest Service owns another 98,000 acres, is Fort Polk, home to survivor camps 136 and 137. The temperatures at Fort Polk range between fifty-five and eighty-seven degrees year round, with humidity levels between comfortable and dripping wet. Today is pleasant and the humidity is being held at bay by a ridge of high pressure over southern Louisiana.

Working on her master's thesis on the complications of human displacement, Casey Cartwright closes her notebook and shakes hands with the interviewee. This is Casey's fourteenth camp over the last thirty days. She stands from her chair, puts a fist against her lower back, and arches backward, trying to free the stiffened muscles. At twenty-four, Casey still has a runner's body—light and lean, with an oval face and deep-set hazel-colored eyes. Today her long, dark hair is covered by a baseball cap, with a ponytail that snakes through the back, drifting across her shoulders with every turn of her head.

"How many more?" Dylan Hellfort, her on-again, off-again boyfriend, asks. This month they're on, and he comes when he wants a break from studying. But he doesn't necessarily like it. Too much misery, he says.

"I have one more person, but you don't need to hang around here."

"Where am I going to go? Hang out by the latrine?" Dylan is working on his MBA, but job prospects are expected to be slim and none. He's grown out his dark hair and let his beard go as a form of protest. Tall and stocky, he likes to think of himself as Casey's protector.

Casey is set up beneath an ancient oak tree, its gracefully arching limbs draped with moss. She's hoping the serene setting will help the interviewees open up about their experiences. Around them, neatly ordered tents, aligned precisely to army standards, stretch as far as the eye can see. The olive and khaki fabric blends well with the forested environment and is interrupted only by the gravel paths that cut through the camp like city streets.

"You could go for a walk," Casey says.

"I'll hang here. I'd feel like a Peeping Tom walking past all those families."

"This is their home, Dylan. It's not any different than walking through a neighborhood."

"Yeah, it is. The tents are only about two feet apart, and the only thing between me and being inside is a thin piece of cloth. It just makes me uncomfortable. Like I'm invading their space."

"If we didn't live in Mississippi, we'd be in a place just like this."

"Chalk one up for the home state," Dylan says

The next interviewee arrives, shakes hands, and takes a seat, while Dylan slinks away.

"How many of the camps have you been to?" he asks.

"Fourteen, so far. Not sure how much longer I can do this. What about you?" Casey asks.

"This is number 43 for me. I'm trying to compile as many eyewitness reports as I can."

"Thanks for taking some time to meet with me, Dr. Snider. How bad were things in Salt Lake City?"

"You're welcome and Salt Lake City is a ghost town. We lost power on the second day after the larger eruption. That was the start of the mass exodus. I was lucky to get out. I know there were many who didn't," Eric Snider says.

Casey glances down at her notes, then swallows and glances up. "You played a role with Yellowstone Volcano Observatory, correct?"

"I'm still in that role. My work, now, will hopefully provide further information. We'll be studying this eruption for the next several hundred years."

"Why did your group not order an evacuation sooner?"

Snider stares off into the distance. After a few moments, he turns back to Casey. "That's a question that haunts all of us: myself, Jeremy Lyndsey and Tucker Mayfield. Unfortunately, there's no right answer. I guess we couldn't wrap our heads around the possibility for an eruption. Hell, it's been 640,000 years since the last one." Snider returns his gaze to some faraway object. "Things snowballed quickly. The time frame between the first seismic swarm and the first eruption was measured in hours." He pauses and looks down at his hands fisted in his lap. Slowly, he unfurls his fingers. "We issued the evacuation order the moment we felt the situation escalating. There just wasn't enough time."

Casey gives him a moment then says, "What have you learned from the eyewitness accounts?"

"Some are too horrific to repeat. There are some heart-warming stories but they pale in comparison. To tell you the truth, the last couple of months have been especially difficult for me. I go to bed with what-ifs buzzing my brain and they linger there all the next day." Snider releases a long sigh. "Hopefully, the reports will allow us to firm up the time line before that last eruption. I do have one heartwarming story. I ran into a former student of mine, a fellow named Josh Tolbert. His family was camping at Yellowstone when it all started. They all made it home alive. Did lose a fairly new pickup in the process, though."

Casey waves a hand in a long arc. "How long do you believe these people will be housed in camps?"

Snider sighs, again. "Years. A great swath of the United States may not be habitable for generations. "

Casey leans back in her chair, surprised. "Really, that long?"

"Yes, really."

"Will they be able to survive in these camps for that long?"

"What choice do they have? Humans haven't experienced a natural disaster on this scale. And the results will linger for years. The only thing we can do is push on."

"Are there other volcanoes that are a threat for eruption?"

"With 1,500 volcanoes scattered across the planet, yes. There are still numerous volcanoes along the Cascades in northern California, Oregon and Washington. But none are as large as the one at Yellowstone. At least of the ones we know about. There could be larger volcanoes along the ocean floor that haven't been discovered. I don't know enough about underwater volcanoes to hazard a guess about their destructive capabilities, but I would assume there would be substantial tidal waves."

Casey tucks a stray strand of hair behind her ear. "I tremble at the thought. I've had enough of volcanoes to last a lifetime."

"You and me both. Mother Nature can be a bitch when she wants to be."

CHAPTER 86

Outskirts of Calgary, Alberta, Canada

Virgil gently pulls his arm from beneath April and climbs out of bed. He pulls on his jeans and an old T-shirt and slips out of the bedroom, tiptoeing down the hall. He turns into the kitchen to find Andy Barlow putting on a pot of coffee. "Why are you up so early?"

"Couldn't sleep. Michelle and I spent most of yesterday trying to pinpoint where to move." Michelle and Andy arrived a week after the last eruption after renting a car and driving along the West Coast to Calgary.

"You and your parents can stay here as long as you want." Virgil's rustic cabin was designed to sleep three and is now host to six.

"What about the Canadian government's mandate asking all foreigners to leave?"

"Screw the government. Hell, they don't know you're here. And I'm sure as hell not going to tell them. It pisses me off to no end."

"How long have you had dual citizenship?" Andy asks.

"Since I was born. My mom is Canadian."

Ralph Barlow shuffles into the kitchen, wiping the sleep from his eyes, and takes a seat next to Virgil at the table. Andy grabs another mug from the shelf and fills all three when the coffee finishes. He carries them to the table and sits.

"Walt out hunting?" Ralph asks

"He left out well before daybreak. Hopefully we'll be feasting this evening."

Andy picks up his cup and blows the steam away. "Dad, Michelle and I are thinking of moving on,"

"Where are you going to go?" Ralph takes a sip of coffee.

"She wants to go somewhere along the East Coast. She thinks it's too cold up here."

Virgil chuckles and Ralph rolls his eyes. "I hate to tell you this, son, but I don't think she's going to be happy no matter where you go."

"You may be right. Still, I wouldn't mind heading out that way."

"You two getting hitched?" Virgil asks.

"Maybe," Andy says before taking a sip of coffee. "She runs hot and cold on the issue."

Ralph arches his brow but remains silent.

"What about you and April?" Andy asks.

"Don't know. I've done the marriage thing a time or two. Nothing wrong with the way things are now, if you ask me."

Michelle saunters into the kitchen and the conversation dries up. "Andy, I thought you were bringing me a cup of coffee."

"You're here now. Might as well pour your own," Andy says.

Virgil and Ralph share a look as Michelle puts her hands on her hips, in full retort mode.

"Pour yourself a cup and join us," Virgil says, easing the sudden tension present in the room.

Michelle gives Andy a withering look before turning to pour her own coffee. She ignores the group as she hastily exits.

"She's a firecracker," Virgil says.

Ralph studies the wood grain of the rustic tabletop.

"That might be an understatement," Andy says. He smiles. "Her temper is part of her attraction, I think." Andy stands. "I better go make nice. We'll talk later, Dad, when Mom gets up and around."

Once Andy is out of earshot, Ralph says, "I don't think firecracker would be the word I'd use to describe Michelle."

Virgil laughs. "Ah hell, Ralph, nothing wrong with a little spiciness. She'll come around. Besides, I'm not sure you have much say in the matter."

Ralph smiles. "You're right, Virgi. Better him than me, that's for damn sure."

"It takes all types to make a world," Virgil says. "You and Junie Bug going to stay with me and April for a while? I think Walt's planning to move on in the next week or so."

"I guess until they run us out of the country or the park service finds me a job."

"What're the odds of that happening?"

"Slim to none would be my guess. So I guess you're stuck with us for a while."

"The more the merrier, I always say. Think Yellowstone will ever be like it was?"

"In a couple of million years she'll be good as new."

CHAPTER 87

Nestled in the foothills of the Canadian Rockies and overlooking the blue-green waters of Barrier Lake, J.J.'s new vacation home is tucked neatly into the landscape. Purchased for $3 million, the home is spacious, with a gourmet kitchen and five luxurious bedrooms. Stunning views of the lake and Mount Baldy are visible through the numerous floor-to-ceiling windows. J.J. hangs up the phone. "My company plane will be here later this afternoon."

"Is it safe to fly?" Tucker asks.

"Guess so or the damn thing wouldn't be coming. He's flying out from my offices in Houston. Says he's going to fly way out west and come in from the north, or something like that. I don't really care how he gets here. I just want his ass here. I've got business to attend to."

"You've been working the phones since we got here."

"Not the same. Cat's away, mice will play and all that bullshit."

Tucker laughs as J.J. dials another number. Tucker pours a cup of coffee and carries it out to the back deck, where Matt is leaning against the rail. "So it's settled? You, Jess, and the kids going to Houston?"

"Yeah. J.J.'s offered us both terrific jobs. Jess can do her geology thing and I'll work the business side. Plus, we'll be able to transfer back to Oklahoma if that option becomes available."

"I wouldn't count on that happening anytime soon."

"We could make a home in Houston. There are worse places to live. And Maddie and Mason need to be in school." Matt takes a sip of coffee. "Why don't you and Rachael come with us?"

"I think we'd both last about fifteen minutes in the big city." The two brothers lean against the rail, looking out over the landscape.

"So, you're going to Alaska?" Matt asks.

"Don't have much choice with the Canadian government asking all foreigners to leave."

"That's a shitty thing for them to do."

"Not when you stop to think about it. This is their country and they're struggling to feed what they have."

"Still, it's not right. Why don't you head south, back to the States?"

"Our only option would be out east, and that's wall-to-wall people. Alaska sounds just fine to me."

"What's Ralph going to do?"

"Stay with Virgil until they work out a new Park Service position for him."

"When's that going to happen?"

"Who knows? Probably not going to happen for a long while. Don't think anyone's in the mood, or can even travel to the remaining national parks."

"Is the Canadian government going to allow them to stay?" Matt asks.

"Apparently Virgil has dual citizenship, and he and April are talking about getting hitched. No need to tell the authorities about a few extra houseguests. I think Walt's going to hang out with Virgil for as long as he can, too. I don't know if he has plans to return to the Park Service or not."

"We owe Walt our lives."

"Walt will never acknowledge that fact. Just the type of guy he is. Think Joey is back with his wife?" Tucker asks.

"He's a pretty determined fellow. Probably so, but I don't know where they'd be. Cheyenne is probably a wasteland."

"The whole state of Wyoming is a wasteland. J.J. gave Joey a standing job offer. Thinks he wants another helicopter. I wouldn't be surprised if Joey shows up in Houston."

Tucker glances out in the distance and spots Rachael and Jessica walking hand in hand along the lake's shore.

"Think you and Tucker will get married?" Jess asks

"We've talked a little bit about it. No firm plans, though."

"I'll get his brother to put a little pressure on him." The two women share a laugh. "Would you get married in Alaska?"

"Probably Houston, so we could all be together. Maybe we could get J.J. to send his plane up to get us."

"He'd do it in a heartbeat. I wouldn't be surprised if

he insisted on paying for the wedding, too. There's a big teddy bear under that gruff exterior. He's loved back home because of his generosity. He makes a boatload of money but he's quick to share with those less fortunate. And his wife, Beverly, is a gem. A farm girl from town who doesn't have a pretentious bone in her body."

"I'm glad you brought up home." Rachael pauses while her brain runs through a list of suitable questions. "I don't want to be nosy, and I don't want to pry, but there's a tenseness in Tucker when he's around you."

Jessica walks away, leaving Rachael to wonder if it's all in her head. But Jess takes a seat on a large boulder and waves her over. "What happened was a long time ago." Tears spring to her eyes. "God, I went about it all the wrong ways." She wipes the tears away but she's fighting a losing battle. "We grew up together. Matt was already in college when Tucker and I started dating. We were quite the item in high school. Young and in love." She sighs and stares out over the water. "We went to college together and dated the first two years. We had all these plans. We were both going to be geologists and travel the world finding the next big thing. But I realized somewhere in that second year that wasn't going to be the life for me. I wanted a home, kids, a stable job. Our relationship started to sour when we both realized we had completely different outlooks on what we wanted life to be." Jess wipes her eyes and stands up, meandering farther down the shore. Rachael follows.

"We eventually broke up, and I transferred to the other state school. We still felt something for each other and I couldn't bear to see the hurt on his face. We both graduated, and I went home to work in the oil fields while Tucker went off chasing volcanoes."

"And *you* married his brother," Rachael says with a little too much heat.

Jess grabs Rachael's hand and holds it like it's a lifeline. "It wasn't like that at all. I knew Matt, but I didn't really know him. Know what I mean?"

Rachael nods, not speaking for fear of interrupting the story.

"Matt's a lot like Tucker. The same values. The same determination. I guess what attracted me to Tucker also attracted me to Matt. Tucker had been out of my life for four years before Matt and I went on our first date. We dated two years before getting married."

"And what did Tucker have to say about all of this?"

"Nothing. He came to the wedding. Had a good time. And over the years we've spent a lot of time together as a family. He's a wonderful uncle to the kids. They think the world of him."

"Did you and Tucker ever sit down and have a frank discussion about what happened?"

"Not really. As time stretched on we both kind of brushed it aside."

"How did Matt feel about all of this?"

"It was hard, at first. Tucker and Matt were . . . are close. They didn't have the best childhood. Did Tucker tell you about his dad?"

"He told me. Is he as bad as Tucker portrays him to be?"

"He wasn't while the boy's mother was alive. After that he went off the deep end. But to answer your question, yes, he's a bigoted, opinionated, rude man. He's incoherent most of the time now, but that mean streak still exists."

"I hope I never have to meet him," Rachael says.

"Count yourself lucky if you don't."

"So, back to you and Matt?"

Jess dries the last of her tears. "We both struggled with the Tucker situation. Even after we were married. But life goes on. Do you know what I mean?"

"I do." They turn back toward the house, hands still clasped together. "Will you do me one favor before leaving?" Rachael asks.

"Of course. What?"

"Have that discussion with Tucker."

The two women climb up the stairs of the back deck, and Rachael slips inside to pour a cup of coffee for them. She returns to the deck and hands a steaming mug to Jessica, who takes a few tentative sips before placing the cup on the rail. She steps over to Tucker and takes his hand. "Can we talk before Matt and I leave?"

Tucker's eyebrows arch with surprise. "Yeah, I guess."

Rachael and Tucker disappear down the steps and Rachael steps over to stand next to Matt.

"What's that about?"

"I thought maybe they should clear the air."

"I think you're a wise woman, Rachael. Want to help me finish packing up the kids?"

"Absolutely. I'm going to miss those two."

Matt and Rachael return inside and start filling suit-cases. There's not much to pack other than a few clothes. Matt makes the decision that the heavy winter coats will serve no purpose in Houston, so he hangs them up in the closet for J.J.'s grandkids in case they get the opportunity to come up here. Once the packing is done, Matt wheels the cases over to the front door and Rachael dives between Maddie and Mason on the couch. She drapes her arms around both.

"You two get to go back to school."

"Don't remind me," Mason says.

A long while later, Tucker and Jessica return, their eyes red. Both faces are still damp, but there's easiness between them that didn't exist before.

J.J. barrels out of his office. "Van's here to pick us up." He tosses the keys to the new Range Rover Tucker's way. "A little going-away present. Sure you two don't want to come? I could always use a couple more geologists."

"Houston's not my type of place," Tucker says. The entire group descends the front steps to the waiting van. After a round of tearful hugs and good-byes, the departing group piles into the van. Tucker and Rachael watch as it disappears down the road. As they turn back for the house, Tucker wraps an arm around Rachael. "Alaska, here we come. Ready for more volcanoes?"

"Not really, but I guess it's what we do."

ACKNOWLEDGMENTS

Thanks go first to you, the reader. Without you, books wouldn't exist. I'm eternally grateful for Gary Goldstein, my editor at Kensington. Gary, you're a rock star! Many thanks to the other hardworking people at Kensington: Elizabeth May, Morgan Elwell, Lauren Jernigan, Kimberly Richardson, Vida Engstrand, Alexandra Nicolajsen, Randie Lipkin, Arthur Maisel, and Lou Malcangi. Please know your work is greatly appreciated.

Thanks to my agent, Jim Donovan. When Jim isn't wearing his agenting hat, he's busy working on his own material. Check out some of Jim's terrific nonfiction work.

A special thanks to my brother, Daniel Washburn, and his wife, Nancy. Thanks also to Justin Washburn, Jared Champlin, and Andrea Chandler and her husband, Deke. You are my favorite niece and nephews.

Thanks, Kelsey, and husband, Andrew Snider, Nickolas, and Karley for supporting your old man as he chases his dream.

Finally, to the love of my life, Tonya: thank you for being you.